Heading

Home

Copyright© Lisa Henry 2022

Copyright© C400-Recordings

All Rights Reserved

All scenarios in this book are fictitious. Any resemblance to any persons, living or dead is purely coincidental.

No parts of this book are to be reproduced with prior permission from the copyright owner and writer, except for brief quotation use in book reviews.

Editor: Lisa Henry

Cover Designer: Lisa Henry

Printed by Amazon Great Britain

All mistakes are my own.

To Jill

I hope you enjoy Aquila's story!

Lisa Henry
x

Acknowledgements

As always to my husband, without your support, I wouldn't have even started writing. Thank you.

To my children, you are all part of my books, from your suggestions to your encouragement. It is immense.

To the bestest friend a girl could have. Michelle you are amazing and strong. Never change.

To the endless authors and supporters of my Twitter page, you are all blessings in disguise, Thank you all.

To me beta readers, you know who you are, thank you for your insights and your advice and encouragement. It kept me going.

Prologue

The city of Astrodia exploded with joy at the news of a Princess having been born to Queen Quintara and King Elio. Her name was Aquilia.

King Elio's brother heard the news and sent his congratulations. He was secretly overjoyed with the news, and not because he was now an uncle. King Elio's brother, Altair, was happy because he knew that only a male child could take over the reign should anything happen to Elio. Not that Altair wished harm on him, or did he?

Altair had his own son, Janus, who he had hoped would someday become King, but these hopes were dashed the day Altair gave up his line within the succession to marry Lyra. She was from a rival family who would have done anything to take over Astrodia. Altair had found her one day, sitting at the fountain, which provided water for the city, with a bottle of cyanide. He had then banished her and her family to the outer wastelands of Saturn never to return under any circumstances. He kept Janus with him and brought him up alone. Janus had never asked about his mum, he was only six months old at the time she was banished so he barely remembers her.

Altair and Quintara never really hit it off. She was originally the Queen of Enceladus and she met Elio there at the Annual Banquet of The Solar Eclipse just over ten years ago. They grew fond of each other so quickly and so deeply that there was a big wedding only six months after they met. They had tried for so long to bring a child into their family but they hadn't been lucky until that fateful day three years ago.

Quintara had started to feel unwell. Elio was worried beyond belief, he worried that living in an unstable atmosphere would make Quintara ill. He had summoned the Galactic Medic at once. She was prompt and polite. After checking on Quintara, she beckoned Elio into the room where she announced that he would soon become a father. Elio was overjoyed. Something they had prayed to the Elders for had been finally granted. He thanked them with overwhelming emotion, tears rolling, unapologetically, down his cyan toned face. He turned to look at his wife, her normally pale complexion glowing purple. The Galactic Medic explained this was to show she was with child and that child was a girl.

Altair continually reminded Elio that only a son could continue the reign of Astrodia and Saturn, but Elio wasn't listening. He was too happy about the impending arrival of his baby to worry about that now, besides; he had many, many years left to worry about that. As King, he could always change the rules, but he would think about that later too. Now was the time to prepare for the arrival of his Princess.

As Quintara came closer to the birth of their child, she became more aware of Altair's hostility towards her. She would try to avoid him as best she could, leaving her husband to attend Royal engagements alone and spending her time crocheting blankets and socks. Elio never questioned his wife; he believed she had her own reasons. He accepted gifts from the people of Astrodia, vast arrays of teddies, blankets and handed down toys, all of which weren't needed but were gratefully received. The people of Astrodia loved Elio and Quintara, and they wished them every happiness.

Chapter 1

Elio was watching as his three-year-old daughter, Aquilia, played on the grass with their two jaglions, Paxy and Plexys. She giggled as they both nuzzled her.

"They adore her, don't they, my darling?" Elio cooed to Quintara.

"They certainly do," she replied smiling.

Aquilia rolled onto her belly and pretended to swim along the grass; all the while Paxy and Plexys guarded the little Princess, watching the surrounding area with their sharp, citrine coloured eyes, their fur alternating from jet-black to sandy with every movement. Almost like clockwork, every two minutes, they would swap places, glancing towards the baby girl and back to their patrol.

A low growl caught the attention of King Elio. He glanced from the balcony in the direction of the noise to see Plexys and Paxy on guard at the steps to the garden and Janus attempting to calm them down, his hands outstretched and open, his voice low and calm.

"Down!" boomed King Elio, "down. Calm."

Both jaglions settled instantly, resuming their positions next to the Princess.

"Janus! How lovely to see you! What brings you here so early?" King Elio exclaimed, bringing him in for a brief hug.

"Hello Uncle! Father wanted me to offer my assistance for tonight's banquet for the Princess's birthday party," he replied with a bright smile.

"That's very kind of you Janus. We could use some extra hands, if you really don't mind?" Elio said.

"Thank you Janus. You're very kind to offer," Quintara said from behind the curtain. She felt this rather strange considering she and Altair had not really been close, but she would let her thoughts slide for now, there was plenty of time to work out Altair's plan after the party.

While Elio and Janus set about blowing up balloons and hanging birthday bunting, Quintara gathered a young

Aquilia up into her arms and set about dressing the young Princess for her party, choosing the perfect glittery tiara that brought attention to her gold embroidered gown, handmade especially for the Princess's party. Quintara selected the most dazzling, sparkly shoes and a small diamante necklace to finish off the outfit.

"Mummy, why do I have to wear this thing?" Aquilia asked, pointing at the tiara atop her head.

"You are the Princess, my darling. It is expected of you, just as I wear mine and Daddy wears his crown," Quintara replied.

Aquilia was yet to understand where she stood in the world and just how important she really was.

"Is Aunt Quintara happy here Uncle Elio?" Janus asked.

"I believe so young Janus, why do you ask? Elio responded.

"It's just; I've noticed her looking towards Enceladus recently. I was becoming worried that she wasn't happy here on Saturn," he replied looking down towards his feet.

"A lot happened up there, maybe she misses it, maybe having Aquilia has brought back some memories, I'm sure she will be just fine," Elio replied, scratching his silver hair.

Elio, darling," Quintara beckoned from the balcony, breaking Elio's thoughts, "please look at our Princess."

"On my way my sweet," he called back.

He made his way up the winding staircase that was the centrepiece of their Palace, with its crystal banisters and marble steps. Upon reaching the top, he gasps in awe at the sight before him; his little Aquilia is all her Royal glory, standing gracefully next to her Mother, who looked equally as beautiful. The sight brought a tear to his eye. Never, in his wildest dreams, did he think he would have such a beautiful family. Now his dream was complete.

Chapter 2

The banquet was progressing well, the whole kingdom had been invited to celebrate the Princess's birthday, and she was 'their' Princess after all. Elio and Quintara surveyed their people as they enjoyed the masses of food on offer to them, danced to every piece of music played and listened as speeches were made to honour Aquilia.

"So much fuss for such a young girl," Altair sneered through gritted teeth.

"I'm not sure father. She is the Princess after all," Janus replied to his father's jeering.

"Oh stop it!" Altair demanded. "You never had any of that growing up and you turned out just fine. It's all material things."

Janus remembered how he was given mediocre gifts growing up, things that would help him through life. He had received a mass amount of books and pens, craft items, discovery books, academic books. These things never interested him. He had wanted toys and games but his father had forbidden them. He had said he needed to 'be prepared' for the future. Janus had no idea what he meant but over the past few years, Janus had begun to wonder where his mother was. He had felt a pang of jealousy whenever he had seen Aquilia with her mother, but whenever he had asked Altair about her, the subject was changed in an instant. This had perked his interest.

Janus watched with a smile as Elio spun Aquilia around like a spinning top, round son many times, she toppled over and just sat on the floor giggling. Altair snorted beside him.

"That's no way for a Princess to act! She should be acting with dignity and grace!"

"She's three Dad, not thirteen. She probably doesn't even understand what she is supposed to be doing yet," Janus said.

"That's because her MOTHER hasn't taught her well enough! It may be like that on Enceladus, but not here on Saturn!" Altair boomed. "It's unacceptable."

Janus watched his father walk away from the crowd and off into the night. He worried about his Dad. He was never satisfied with anything Elio had done as King; he always said he could have done better. Janus never understood why his father wasn't King, he was older than Elio, and that normally meant he would have succeeded before Elio, but he didn't. He made a mental note to ask his Dad about it one day.

Trumpets blew and everyone fell silent.

"We would like to thank you all for the gifts and well wishes you have all bestowed upon our beloved Princess Aquilia," King Elio began, "it has been our greatest pleasure to include everyone on the celebrations."

Princess Aquilia squealed when she saw the four-tier, turquoise, pink and purple cake, covered with rainbow sprinkles and topped with a neon pink rabbit.

"We would especially like to thank the anonymous donation of the cake, it really is tremendous! Queen Quintara announced.

Aquilia jumped around the cake, her eyes so big they rivalled some of the plates on the tables. The whole kingdom sang Happy Birthday to the Princess.

Outside, Altair could hear the celebrations continue and he cursed himself for passing up the throne, cursed himself for falling for Lyra's charms. He knew she was off limits but her aqua eyes had been so hard to ignore, her magenta hair just flowed down her back, and the way she walked past him that night had enchanted him beyond anybodies help. Upon telling his family that he had fallen in love, he had been informed of who she really was, and that if he really wanted to be with her, he would have to relinquish his succession in line to the throne, which he happily did.

On the day of their wedding, she was proudly conveying her bump, glowing a slight shade of blue, which seriously clashed with her normal rose complexion. His family had agreed to accept her into their family, but had warned her that only she would be welcome. She seemed happy with the arrangement. She gave birth to a healthy baby boy, ten fingers, and eleven toes, a normal Saturnite. His hair as white as Tethys and his eyes as green as emeralds, he smiled a toothless smile and Altair's heart burst with pride. He convinced himself that he had made the right choice when it came to being King, who needed that when he had this amazing being in his arms, someone he had created. He hadn't told Lyra about the deal he had made with his parents, so when they were killed during an attack from Neptune, Lyra assumed that Altair was now Kind and demanded to be addressed as Queen Lyra. She began to make a list of things she would change, including bringing her family to live in the Palace.

Altair had been worried about this day, but he took it upon himself to inform his wife that he would never be King and tell her the reason why.

"WHAT do you mean?" Lyra had shouted.

"It was a choice I had to make, marry you, or be King. I chose you. Are you not happy?" Altair had asked.

Lyra had wept and wept. "I thought I would become Queen, that I could correct everything wrong with this world. Fix everything your family broke!" She had screamed, her eyes now a brazen purple. Gone were the aqua eyes that had once enticed him, replaced by a horror filled purple. Her once rose coloured complexion now a constant changing red and orange colour, her hair now a mass of blue flames. She ran from the Palace, towards the centre of town, towards the fountain that would normally be filled with the children of Astrodia. Altair had followed her. He arrived just in time to hear her plans.

"If I can't be Queen, then no-one in Astrodia will live any longer," she said almost singing the words.

She then pulled a bottle from her pocket, Altair could read the label, 'CYANIDE-TOXIC', he jumped forward and grabbed the bottle before she could uncork it.

"What are you doing?" He had demanded.

She refused to answer; she just turned her back on him.

"You are to leave immediately, take your family and leave, you are granted asylum in the outer wastelands. If you leave now, I won't tell anyone what I stopped you doing," Altair had said, "Janus stays with me."

She spun on her heels and stared at him, now back to her usual appearance.

"But..." She began.

"No! Go now," he boomed. With that, he turned back to the Palace.

Lyra was never seen again, at least not to his knowledge. He knew she was still alive; he had spies on the edge of the wastelands watching her family, they couldn't be trusted not to try to snatch Janus.

Elio dragged Altair from his memories.

"Are you alright brother? I saw you leave," Elio enquired.

"Ah! I'm just a little emotional, that's all. Aquilia is growing up so fast," Altair replied. "It will soon be time for her to undertake Royal duties!"

"Indeed! Quintara wants to prepare her for school first. She must be educated if she is ever to become Queen of Astrodia," Elio responded.

"But she can't! She's female! Females never succeed to the throne! It should be passed to the next male in line," Altair said, sounding appalled.

"There are no other males in line Altair, you know that. No, the rules will have to be altered. I shall get to it next week," Elio replied.

"There's Janus!" Altair screamed.

"Altair, we BOTH know Janus cannot succeed to the throne and we BOTH know why," Elio said with a solemn smile. "I'm sorry."

He didn't understand why Altair had chosen Lyra over the many others available to him, but that was who he chose and the choice he made. He wondered where Lyra had gone and how she could have just left poor Janus.

Chapter 3

It had been a week since Aquilia's birthday and King Elio had set about changing the Kingdoms rules. Reading the list, he noted each change he wanted to make and what they would become.

First up was 'ONLY MALE HEIR'. This had been instilled by his great-great-great granddad. Luckily, for his family, there had been no end of male heirs born. He changed this to 'FIRST BORN CHILD OF CURRENT REIGNING MONARCH BECOMES HEIR'. Signing the declaration, Elio smiled.

Next up were the days of market trading, currently only listed to be held on a Saturday morning, Elio decided it was time for it to run any day the stallholders decided to open, he also appointed authority over to Julius, the oldest market trader. He signed the deeds with a smile. He wondered why he hadn't thought to do all this sooner. Just then, a slight tickle caught his throat, he coughed which seemed to clear it away. 'Strange' he thought, 'I've never felt that before.' Brushing it off, he continued down the list, diverting decision making between different people, lowering costs where he could and raising them where he had no choice to but only where it wouldn't affect his poorer subjects.

Watching his brother change the rules hurt Altair's heart. Those rules had been in place for as long as their family had governed Astrodia. To watch his brother destroy everything his family had built up made him angry. Altair arranged to meet up with his long time friend, Layson. He was always there for him and Altair needed someone to talk to now.

They met up for coffee and Layson knew something was wrong instantly.

"What is it old friend?" He asked.

"Elio is changing the kingdoms rules, changing the heir rules. What am I to do?" Altair replied.

"I'm unsure how to reply Altair. Isn't Elio the King? Is he not allowed to change the rules?" Layson said a confused look passing across his green face.

"Of course he is! Of course he can! But he is only doing it so Aquilia can, one day, become Queen," Altair said, rage eating away at him like a virus.

"Altair, you are my oldest, dearest friend. What can I do to aid you through this?" Layson asked.

"I'm not sure yet, I'm still trying to think of something, but stay alert," he replied.

They discussed Layson's family, how his son was finding school, how his wife was getting on in her new job. They spoke about how Janus still hadn't decided what to do after school. Altair wanted him to attend the Higher School of Arts, which he would study Ancient Arts of Saturn. They spoke for a while longer before parting ways.

"Janus? Janus where are you boy?" Altair shouted when he returned home.

"I'm here father, whatever is the matter?" Janus replied, emerging from the kitchen.

"Ah there you are. Have you thought anymore about your studies?" Altair asked.

Janus shrugged, "I've thought a bit about college and of your suggestions to study Art. I think I may just sign up, see if I enjoy it. If not I can always quit, right?" he responded.

"Of course, my boy. Of course! We shall inform the college right away!" Altair declared with passion.

"Ah Altair, there you are!" Elio exclaimed.

"Indeed I am brother, what seems to be so urgent?" Altair replied, forcing a smile to cross his lips.

"I wanted to; personally, inform you that I have placed you in charge of our military. You have an unlimited budget, so to speak," Elio announced.

Altair's expression changed to a state of shock. His father had specifically stated that, if he gave up his succession, then he would have no active role within the family duties. 'Why would Elio change this?' he thought.

"Why Elio, I'm honoured that you would allow me this, may I ask why?" Altair's voice shaking slightly.

"I feel you would be best suited to lead us, should we ever have to go into battle again," Elio stated.

"Well, I'll start right away. I'll recruit new soldiers, draw up plans for new vehicles, everything we could possible need to protect our planet," Altair said, ticking things off with his fingers.

"That's sorted!" Elio said, turning to leave. "One other thing, Altair."

"Certainly," he replied.

"Try to bring Janus in too?" Elio asked.

"I'll try my very best," he replied.

Altair got to work immediately. He requests the Kingdoms registry of residents between the ages of fifteen and forty, this gave him a wide range of choices. He wanted healthy men and women, ready to protect the planet at any costs. He will need to interview potential candidates. Would they be prepared to leave their families if a war were to begin? It was a lot to ask of some but some would protect their homes with their lives.

"Quintara darling?" Elio asked as he arrived back at the Palace.

"I'm here dear," she replied, placing her book carefully on the table next to her and quietly stepping over Aquilia as she practised her handwriting on the floor.

"I've finished the rule changes, our daughter will be able to become Queen if anything were to happen to us," Elio announced with a smile.

"Oh Elio, you know you didn't have to do that," Quintara said, half frowning half-smiling.

"I know, but we don't know if we will be blessed with another child. I want my legacy to continue and I know that will if Aquilia is Queen," he replied, taking her hand and spinning her around.

She laughed and laughed as he smiled at her. He loved to hear her laugh, loved to watch her purple eyes twinkle when the chandelier lights hit them. They stopped spinning when a streak of red and silver darted across the room past them.

"Janus!" Aquilia screeched. "Why you here?"

"Aquilia, you gave me away," he laughed, stooped down and gave her nose a nudge with his own.

"Uncle Elio, Aunt Quintara, father told me what you did. I'm thankful. Truly." He said as he bowed his head towards them.

"That's quite alright Janus. Has he spoken to you with regards to joining up too?" Elio asked.

"He has uncle and I have agreed. I will protect and serve until my dying day," Janus said as he held his hand to head in a salute.

"Now now Janus, there's no need for that," Quintara giggled. "Tell me, how are you getting on with your studies?"

"I've decided to study Art, specifically Saturn Ancient Arts," Janus replied politely.

"That's fantastic news Janus, I'm sure you will excel in all your studies," Quintara said with a smile.

"Thank you Aunt Quintara," he replied. "Do you mind if I stick around for a while? Maybe help Aquilia with her writing?"

"It would certainly help me out, thank you," Quintara said.

"Yay, come Janus," Aquilia squealed, dragging him away from her parents.

He went with Aquilia and they sat at a makeshift table whilst she showed him what she could write so far. Quintara could hear them laughing and it warmed her heart. From behind her, she could hear Elio coughing.

"What is it Elio?" She asked, concern flooding her voice.

"I'm not sure dear. Maybe send for the doctor, I don't feel myself all of a sudden," he replied, his cyan skin changing to black and then back again.

Quintara rushed off to find the doctor. Janus worried about why Quintara was in such a rush, peeked through the door in time to see his uncle's skin change again, this time from cyan to pink, then green and back to cyan, he was in shock, he couldn't move.

"Dear Janus, please step in," Elio motioned as he caught him looking.

Janus entered the room and sat with his uncle.

"What's wrong Uncle?" He asked sounding worried,

"Of that I am unsure, but you must promise me something," Elio gasped, struggling to hold a sentence.

"Of course, you are my King after all," he replied.

"If something happens to me, promise me that you will look after my girls?" Elio finished with a sigh.

"Yes sir, absolutely," Janus replied. "Uncle? Uncle?"

Elio's skin had changed to black and that is how it remained. His eyes slowly closing as Quintara rushed back with the doctor.

"Elio, my darling?" Quintara said, rubbing his cheeks. "I brought the doctor."

"I'm afraid he has departed my Queen," the doctor said with sympathy.

"Shall I announce a time of mourning?" Janus hesitated to ask.

Quintara nodded as she held her husband close and cried deep red tears.

Janus announced that there was to be a month of mourning for King Elio and that his funeral was to be attended by all. Altair was against the idea.

"I think Quintara poisoned him," he told Layson. "It's such a coincidence how he died just after changing the rules to accommodate her child!"

"Aquilia is Elio's child too Altair, maybe he wanted a good life for her," Layson replied.

Altair scoffed, "I will find out what happened, and she will pay!"

Chapter 4 – Two Years Later

"But Mummy, I don't want to go to school today. It's Daddy's memorial. I want to be there! I wasn't allowed to go to his funeral because I was too little. I'm bigger now, please Mummy!" Aquilia begged while her Mother pulled her hair up into a high bun, fitted with a sparkling hair tie.

"I know, you're such a big girl now, Daddy would be very proud of you," Quintara said while thinking. 'Maybe it would be a good idea, a way for her to say goodbye at least,' she thought. "Alright. You can have today off, but you are straight back tomorrow. Go and find one of your dresses that Daddy liked. You can change into that."

"Thank you Mummy. I'll wear the blue glittery one. Daddy loved that one," Aquilia said as she hugged her Mother hard.

Quintara returned to her room to prepare for Elio's memorial. The Kingdom had held a month long mourning for the King. His funeral had been a grand event, the whole Kingdom had pulled together, even Altair had been there for her, which seemed odd in a way, but Quintara had put it to one side. She hoped to have put the past behind them. She places the crown on top of her head, fixing it in place; she then looked at herself in the mirror. She hadn't been looking after herself well since Elio died. She had made sure Aquilia had everything she needed, all the love and care she desired but Quintara had cared very little about herself.

"Mummy" Aquilia asked from the doorway. "Is my tiara straight?"

Quintara turned to see her daughter fiddling with her tiara and smiled, "I don't think you could make it any straighter if you tried my sweet."

Quintara took Aquilia's hand, leading her to the front of the Palace. Janus, Altair, and the whole Kingdom were there to greet them.

"Do you think it is wise to bring the Princess?" Altair asked.

"She wants to say goodbye. I think it's time, don't you?" She whispered, not wanting to upset Aquilia.

"As you wish, but I strongly advise against it," he responded.

Quintara turned her head away and proceeded to address her Kingdom.

"My people. I have been absent from your eyes for too long. It is time to put myself forward and continue the work my husband, King Elio, started," she said looking amongst the crowd below.

"Mummy, can I say something?" Aquilia asked.

"I don't think that is wise," Altair said sternly.

Quintara looked hard at him. She bent down so she was face to face with Aquilia. "Do you think you are ready?"

"Yes Mummy, may I?" Aquilia asked politely.

Quintara gestured to the on looking crowd. Aquilia took a breath, stepped up onto the stool placed in front of her and looked out on the Kingdom. She smiled at the sight of everyone.

"I am Princess Aquilia of Astrodia," she started.

Everyone began to applaud her. Altair rolled his eyes, 'if this were Janus he would do a better job,' he thought.

"I stand here to say thank you. You are all very kind and all the flowers you have sent are very pretty," she continues, briefly smiling at her Mother. "We are all very grateful."

The crowd erupted in cheers and whistles. Aquilia stepped down, proud of herself for her first public speech.

Altair had left Quintara's side just as Aquilia had started to speak. He was appalled that she had been allowed to address everyone like that. When he and Elio were that age, they were taught to stay quiet and smile. He searched the crowd for Layson, knowing he would be there somewhere. He looked over masses or purple, green and orange haired Saturnites, finally spotting his aqua haired friend next to a tree.

"Layson," Altair shouted. "Layson!"

"Altair, wait there, I'm coming," Layson replied, making his way through the crowd, pushing past a magenta haired woman with aqua eyes, "sorry miss."

She waited as he met up with Altair, followed as they entered an alleyway next to the Palace. She kept her distance, searched her pocket for her LifeLens, and filmed the exchange. She knew that anyone meeting up with Altair in such a shady place couldn't be a good thing.

The LifeLens could record perfect 8k video and record audio at 24bit from a distance of up to 75 feet. She watched as Altair and Layson spoke, she could only pick up a few words but at the mention of The Queen and The Princess she took more interest. She allowed it to record until their meeting ended and they parted ways. Upon watching it back and hearing the full conversation, she knew she had the right instinct to record it.

"She has to go," Altair said. "She will ruin everything my family built up."

"Are you sure Altair? I've never questioned you before, but, well now?" Layson asked.

"I'm positive, they both have to go. I cannot and will not be ruled by two women!" Altair demanded.

"How would you like it achieved?" Layson asked.

"Not sure yet. I will be in touch," Altair responded before heading back into the Palace.

After watching the video back, the woman decided that Quintara needed to see it in order to protect herself and her child, something she hadn't been able to do herself. She returned to her rented space, transferred the clip to a flash drive and ordered a special hamper be delivered to the Palace for the Queen and The Princess. She would insist the envelope, which contained the drive, be delivered with the hamper. She signed the card:

Queen Quintara and Princess Aquilia.

Please accept my gift. I send best wishes and deepest condolences.

This you need to see.

Signed

E.L

She hoped it would be enough to save them both from whatever Altair had planned.

"Delivery Madam."

Quintara's butler broke her train of thought. She was so proud of Aquilia today. It was a shame Altair had missed it, but as Head of Military, he had to keep his wits about him. How else would he protect Saturn from another invasion?

"Thank you. Please place it on the table," Quintara replied.

He gave a curt nod and placed the basket on the tabletop. Aquilia quickly ran to it, poking her head right inside and taking a deep breath.

"Smells like cookies and chocolate Mummy," she said with a wide toothed smile.

Quintara laughed and picked up the enveloped. She studied the handwriting, it wasn't one she recognised. She pulled the note from inside and read the message, all the while fiddling with the flash drive. She was confused, 'who would send her a flash drive with no information about what was on it?' she thought. She took her own LifeLens and inserted the drive. She then watched in horror as the afternoons events unfolded before her. The hopes she had had for a peaceful reign had come crashing down, and her hopes for a truce with Altair, torn to shreds. She had to act fact to protect Aquilia. No matter what.

Chapter 5

"But I don't want to go away without you Mummy," Aquilia cried, stomping her tiny foot on the ground. It didn't make a sound but she tried again anyway.

"It's not up for discussion young lady!" Quintara said sternly. "Now, put this on." Quintara handed her a silver helmet, made to fit her perfectly. She snapped Aquilia's belt shut and closed the hatch. She nodded towards the controllers.

WOOSH!

Up Aquilia lifted inside a capsule just big enough for one. Quintara let a single tear fall from her eye before opening her Bilaphone.

"She is on her way. Maybe fifteen minutes or so. Keep her safe. I'll stay in touch," she said, then closed her phone. 'It's for the best' she told herself. She turned and walked back to the Palace.

Altair watched as the pod shot into the sky.

"I wonder who is off on a journey now." He questioned aloud. "Janus!"

"Yes Father," Janus replied. "What is it?"

"I put you in charge of all flights departing and arriving, did I not?" He asked.

"Yes sir, you did," Janus replied.

"So who has just taken off?" Altair demanded.

"Wait...Someone took off without my permission?" Janus asked looking out of the window and the trail that had been left behind just moments ago.

Altair looked angry. He turned back towards the window and watched the trail fade away.

"You better find out who it was son," he boomed.

"Yes sir. Right away," Janus said as he turned and ran from the room.

Janus practically ran the whole way to the command centre. He slowed down by the fountain and watched the children splashing around. He smiled as he was about to start running again, he turned and almost collided with an aqua-eyed woman.

"Pardon me Miss, are you alright?" He asked politely.

"Absolutely fine, thank you," she replied, turning to enter the shop quickly.

Janus tilted his head in a quick bow and began on his way again, but the encounter with the aqua-eyed woman stuck in his mind. He almost forgot what he went out for.

"There was an unscheduled departure this morning, who was it and where did it go?" Janus demanded as soon as he entered the room.

"Direct orders from Queen Quintara, sir. The Elders of Enceladus had summoned Princess Aquilia. Queen Quintara said she was to leave immediately," the youngest of the crew replied.

"I should have been informed to clear her to leave, but if the Queen insisted, who are we to refuse. Has she landed safely? He asked.

"She is about five minutes out, and cleared to land," the crewmember replied.

"Keep me informed of her return," Janus said as he made his way to the exit.

He called Altair to inform him of his findings.

"I think Aquilia is a little young to be travelling alone, don't you think?" He asked his son.

"If Quintara is happy with it, who are we to question it Dad? Janus asked. "She will land in five minutes. I will make contact with their control centre and check she lands safe," he replied and hung up.

'Something seems odd' Altair thought to himself, 'I mentioned to Layson that I wanted them gone only last night. I think I need to talk to my friend.'

Queen Quintara paced her bedroom frantically thinking of a way to protect herself against Altair, thinking who could have been responsible for the video, and who else knew what Altair and Layson had said. It was pointless to ask Layson, as she knew he would cover for Altair, Just as she started her seventh lap of her room; there was a light tap at the door.

"Who is it?" She asked.

"Janus, Your Highness, may I entre?" he replied.

"Certainly, come on in!" she replied as cheerfully as she could.

He entered the room and performed the perfect bow.

"I have been informed that the Princess has landed safely and has been prepared to meet The Elders. I would have appreciated being informed of her departure so I could make sure everything was perfect for her," he said, looking hurt.

"I'm sorry Janus, I would have informed you, but they demanded she leave immediately. I cannot go against their wishes as I'm sure you are aware," she replied with a smile.

Janus nodded. He knew Quintara couldn't refuse their orders. She was an Encelandent after all. Janus bid her farewell and headed back home to prepare for his college interview. The thought of the aqua-eyed woman burst into his mind. He realised he had never seen her before, this made him very suspicious.

When he arrived home, he told his Dad about the aqua-eyed woman.

"Her eyes were like nothing I've ever seen before. I don't recognise her Dad, that worries me," he said.

Altair listened as his son harped on about her. His gut told him it was Lyra but his head argued that she wouldn't dare step foot here again.

"Dad?" Janus said, staring at him.

"Sorry son. I was a million light years away there. You say you haven't seen her before. Maybe we should get someone to track her, leave it with me," Altair replied. "I just need to make a private call."

Altair retired to his room and pressed 7 on his phone.

"Status report," he barked.

"HA HA HA," came the reply. The line went dead.

Confused Altair tried again.

"THIS LINE IS CURRENTLY UNAVAILABLE. PLEASE TRY LATER."

Altair dialled 9 and waited for a reply.

'STATIC'

"What is going on?" he said aloud.

He dialled Layson, happy to finally hear a voice on the other end.

"Meet me at the fountain. Something urgent has come up. Five minutes." Altair said, hanging up just as Janus knocked on his door.

"I'm just heading out. I won't be long," Altair said as he threw open the door.

He stopped in his tracks when he saw Quintara standing before him, just behind Janus.

"In a hurry Altair, please don't let me keep you," she said, gesturing to the open front door.

"I'm sure it can wait for a moment Queen Quintara. How may I be of service?" Altair said, forcing a smile to cross his lips.

"I'm just checking on all those Elio placed in charge before his untimely passing. Is there anything you require? She asked, looking him deep in the eyes.

'You to die' he thought.

"Not as yet Your Majesty. If anything should arise, you will be the first to know," he replied. "I must be going. I will speak with you again soon." Altair said, bowing before he left.

"He's been acting strange ever since I told him about the woman with the aqua eyes," Janus said, staring after his Dad.

"Did you say aqua eyes?" Quintara asked.

"Yes Ma'am," he replied.

"How very strange. Try not to worry young Janus. I'm sure your father is just busy, that's all," she said, turning to leave.

A thought occurred to her, but she pushed it to the back of her mind. 'Altair said she died on the way to visit her parents, something about an assassin, he was very vague about the details back then but it didn't seem to faze him one bit. Lyra must have made some deadly enemies growing up.'

Chapter 6

ENCELADUS

"Welcome Princess Aquilia," Chylla said as she bowed her head. "Welcome to Enceladus."

Aquilia began to climb from the pod, unaware of where she was.

"Thank you?" Aquilia said. "Why am I here?"

Chylla smiled, the Infinity symbol tattooed on her forehead glowed pink. She was looking forward to showing Aquilia around. Quintara had told them so much about her.

"Let's get you settled then we will meet with the others and explain as best we can," she replied, still smiling.

Aquilia nodded and followed Chylla along the glittery walkway. Along the way, she was surprised that so many people were bowing and looking surprised to see her.

"Why are they doing that?" She asked.

"You are their Princess," Chylla replied.

"I thought I was Saturn's Princess?" Aquilia questioned a look of confusion crossing her face.

"You are, but you're also the Princess of Enceladus. Your mother is our Queen," Chylla replied, confused at why Aquilia didn't already know this, but then she was only five and probably hadn't been fully informed of her role within society yet.

Chylla led Aquilia to a grand Palace with doors made of crystal. There stood three other Encelandent Elders. Chylla introduced them as Sinclair, Zidan and Ammyn. They were each equally as excited to meet her as Chylla had been.

"Welcome Princess, it's so lovely to finally meet you," Sinclair said, his yellow star tattoo glowing as he spoke.

"We are so pleased to have you come to visit," Zidan smiled, his moon tattoo glowing silver and bright.

Ammyn just smiled at her, the blue eye on her forehead scaring Aquilia a little.

"Ammyn speaks very little My Princess," Chylla explained opening the doors wide.

The floor was made of emerald and sapphire, the chandelier draped in diamonds and the stairs were made of opal and onyx. The colours amazed Aquilia; her Palace back home was made of granite and marble with splashes of ruby and yellow topaz.

"Wow. This is so pretty!" Aquilia squealed. "Is this where I will be staying?"

"This is your Palace Princess. A sort of home from home if you will," Zidan said, gesturing to the whole Palace, his arms as wide as his smile. Aquilia liked him.

SATURN

Queen Quintara received another anonymous letter later that day.

I can see that the Princess is safe.

Please take care of yourself also.

Be prepared.

Altair is cunning and clever.

E.L

"Who could this E.L be?" She thought aloud.

"E.L?" Janus responded from the doorway.

"Oh sorry Janus, I didn't hear you come in," Quintara said.

"Maybe its Uncle Elio leaving notes for you to find," Janus said, having no clue what was in the letters she had received.

"Maybe young Janus, maybe. Now, what can I do for you?" She said with a smile.

Janus thought for a moment, unsure whether to ask his question or whether to ask his father, but he faced the situation and asked, "What happened to my Mum?"

The question floored Quintara. She didn't know how to answer. She only really knew as much as everyone else and that was what Altair had told them.

"I'm not sure how to answer that Janus. Have you asked your father?" She asked him before she said anything else.

"No. Every time I build up the courage, he darts off to somewhere, plus I wouldn't know where to start," Janus said, slumping down on a nearby chair. "Please tell me what you know."

"All anyone knows is that your mother died whilst on her way to visit her parents, your father said something about an assassin. Your mother must have made some serious enemies growing up Janus. That's all we know, but you should ask your father. Would you like me to accompany you?" Quintara said, reaching for her shawl.

"Would you?" Janus asked, a little croakier than he had hoped.

"Why of course. We will go now," she replied with a smile.

They walked across the town square together, discussing her ideas for a small water park for the Saturnite children. She wanted them to have something fun to do. Janus insisted on helping by drawing up the blueprints and searching for an ideal location, somewhere close by so the people didn't have to travel far.

"Layson," Altair whispered. "Where are you?"

"Here Altair. Why are you whispering?" Layson replied.

"Have you told ANYONE what we spoke about last night?" Altair said, ignoring Layson's question and getting straight to the matter at hand.

"Of course not! What do you take me for?" Layson replied, clearly hurt by the accusation. "I would never betray your trust."

"Someone must have overheard us. Quintara sent Aquilia to Enceladus this morning; it can only mean that she knows, but how?" Altair said, mumbling something inaudible, "aqua eyes."

"Did you say 'aqua eyes'?" Layson asked.

"Yes. Janus said he saw a woman with aqua eyes today," Altair replied.

"I saw one last night! Walked right past her to get to you. You don't think its...her?" Layson finished.

"It can't be," Altair said. "Could it? I couldn't reach any of my contacts on the outer wasteland edge this morning. You don't think she could have snuck back in do you?"

"Well, she isn't one for doing as she is told is she?" Layson replied. "Plus look how long she has had to perfect her gift."

"Dammit!" Altair said. "I have to find her and get rid of her before it's too late!"

Altair made his way back home, keeping a sharp eye out for any aqua-eyed women. He knew only a piece of what she was capable of, but she had had sixteen years to perfect her abilities. He knew nothing about her true powers.

Lyra watched him walk by, so close she could smell him. She took a deep breath, inhaling his scent. She had missed him and her son, missed watching her son grow up. She had been surprised to see him today. He had grown into such a handsome young man. Altair had done a good job. She only hoped Janus hadn't inherited Altair's hatred for Quintara.

Lyra had liked Quintara; she wasn't stuck up like Altair's mum had been. Quintara knew what it was like to be different. Not Lyra different, but similar. That's why she had informed Quintara of Altair's plan. She just hoped Janus wasn't involved too. It was then that she saw them. Quintara and Janus, walking her way. Quintara showing a lot of interest in what Janus talked about. She wasn't dressed the way a Queen would dress, which was another thing that Lyra liked about her; she wanted to be like everyone else. Lyra guessed that was why Altair didn't like her. She was trying to change too much. Well his plan will come undone and Lyra would prove her worth to their son.

"Janus, Queen Quintara, what brings you back so soon?" Altair asked as he entered the living room of his house.

"Janus has some question, which I'm sure your saw coming Altair. May I sit?" She said, gesturing to the couch.

"Certainly Your Majesty. Can I get you anything?" He replied, painting a smile across his face.

"Just your attention for now," she replied, motioning Janus to speak.

"Dad, what happened to my Mum? Why isn't she around?" Janus asked, his legs wobbling like a huge jelly.

Altair's smile faded. His look changed from fear to anger in the blink of an eye. Janus looked terrified. Quintara was ready for any form of argument Altair would throw out. It was actually a well thought out plan on her part. Get him angry; see if he says anything unintentional. She was ready. Little did the three of them know, so was Lyra.

Chapter 7

ENCELADUS

Aquilia looked around the room she had been given. Surprised by how much bigger it was compared to hers back home. She ran to the bed. A huge four-poster, draped with golden lace curtains and silk bedding. She climbed up and laid on top of the sheets. They felt so cool against her skin. A slight tap at the door made her jump off and stand straight.

"Come in," she said as loud as her voice would allow her to.

The door slowly opened and Ammyn came in, the blue glowing eye at the centre of her forehead catching Aquilia's attention again, still making her a little scared.

"Come. Meeting. Please." Ammyn tried to speak, but it only materialising into single words.

"I'll follow you," Aquilia said, pointing towards the door.

Ammyn nodded and began to lead the way.

"Why don't you talk much?" Aquilia asked.

"Accident. Voice box. Repair." Ammyn replied, pointing to the scar across her throat. "Learning. Slowly."

"Can I help you learn?" Aquilia asked. "I'd like to."

"I'd. Be. Grateful. Thank you. Princess." Ammyn managed, the eye glowing brighter.

Ammyn lead the way to a set of huge glass doors. Through them, Aquilia could see the others seated around a solid oak table, laid out with a selection of drinks and snacks. They looked up and beckoned her in. Ammyn gave Aquilia a smile, reassuring her that it was going to be alright. She was right. It was.

<u>SATURN</u>

"What have you told him?" Altair shouted at Quintara.

"Father! You can't speak to the Queen like that," Janus jumped up to defend Quintara.

"Hmm, either Janus doesn't think the same as Altair or he is a damn fine actor," Lyra whispered to herself and continued to listen.

"Only what we all know Altair, exactly what you told us happened. Unless you forgot something in the process. I think he's old enough now, don't you?" Quintara replied, not fazed in any way by Altair's outburst.

"DO NOT presume to tell ME what is best for MY son, especially considering YOU sent a FIVE YEAR OLD off to Enceladus ALONE!" Altair shouted again.

"She is going to her second Kingdom. She will be safe there. I have nothing to worry about," Quintara said softly.

"Dad, please," Janus begged. "I just want to know from you."

Altair watched his son's face. The longing to know. Altair wondered how long he could keep up the lie that Lyra was dead. Only Layson knew she still lived. He decided to keep it that way.

"She was assassinated on her way to visit her parents. You were all of six months old. I kept you with me that day; lucky I did otherwise you would have been killed too. Your mother made enemies easily son. On a more sombre note, you are safe. None of her enemies know you exist," Altair said. "I will say nothing more of it. You asked and you have discovered. It ends here!"

Janus nodded his agreement. Quintara was a little sceptical as to how dismissive Altair was of Lyra, like she had never existed, like he had never confessed his undying love for her in front of the whole Kingdom. Quintara kept these thoughts to herself. She said her goodbyes and left.

"The absolute liar! How could her have told everyone I was dead!" Lyra said in a hushed voice. She had seen Quintara leave but hadn't failed to see the look on her face. She didn't believe a word Altair had said. Lyra had to decide whether to come clean to Quintara or stay out of sight. It was a hard choice to make. She didn't know how Quintara would react to seeing someone who is supposedly dead. She decided to stay hidden for now. She would reveal herself when the time was right.

ENCELADUS

"So, let me understand. I'm here, because Uncle Altair is angry that I get to be Queen? Why would he be angry?" Aquilia asked after The Elders had explained, as best they could to a five year-old, why she was there.

"Your father changed all the rules just before he died, your uncle wasn't happy because it meant Janus couldn't be King," Sinclair said in a soft voice.

"Is Janus angry with me too?" Aquilia asked looking worried. "I like Janus."

"Janus doesn't know about his father's anger honey, don't worry yourself. We will keep you safe here," Zidan replied smiling at her.

"What about Mummy?" Aquilia said sounding terrified. "What if Uncle Altair hurts Mummy?"

"We have people protecting her sweetheart," Chylla replied. "There's no need to worry."

Aquilia thought for a moment. She looked at each person one by one. She settled on Ammyn. Ammyn smiled at her and said, "Trust. Us."

"OK. I trust you will keep us safe. Can I call Mummy now?" Aquilia asked, shoving a freshly baked cookie into her mouth and washing it down with some peach juice.

"Of course you can Princess. Come with me," Zidan said rising from his seat and leading her to a room with twelve small monitors hanging from the wall. He scanned his eye and the silver moon on his forehead and then there was a sudden shift in the air around her.

'ENCELADUS CALLING QUEEN QUNITARA'

"Quintara here how is she?" Quintara replied a few seconds before her face filled the monitors. All the monitors blending together to create a full picture, making it look like the monitors didn't exist.

"I'm here Mummy. Can you see me?" Aquilia said, jumping up and down.

"Oh I can my darling. Wow! That dress is amazing on you. How do you like it there?" Quintara asked, trying not to show how much she missed her.

"My room is gigantic! I have a huge bed! Miss Chylla says I am Enceladus' Princess too, is that right?" Aquilia questioned her.

"Indeed it is. For now, I need you to look after the Encelandents whilst I look after the Saturnites. Can you do that for me?" Quintara asked, surprised that Aquilia had found out so much already.

"Yes Mummy I can. They told me about Uncle Altair. He's a very bad man Mummy, be careful please. Bye Mummy. Mr Sinclair is calling me," Aquilia said, waving to her Mum before rushing out of the room.

"She is safe Quintara. She will be taught well, just as you were," Zidan said. "Any more thoughts?"

"I'm convinced that my initial idea was correct. If I am right, I will send word. Until then, look after her," Quintara replied and closed the connection.

Sinclair led Aquilia to a small room next to a huge window.

"This is going to be a huge step for you to take, but the people need to see who you are and who is going to lead them. Do you think you are ready?" He asked.

"I made a speech at Daddy's memorial. I think I can do this too," she replied, looking between The Elders and receiving reassuring smiles from them all.

"Ladies and Gentlemen of Enceladus. Let us introduce your leader. Princess Aquilia, daughter of Queen Quintara. Please show you appreciation," an announcement came from a distant speaker.

Applause erupted from behind a heavy draped red curtain covering the window. Aquilia stepped through and up onto a step built just for her. She looked out towards the crowd. Smaller than that of Astrodia but just as welcoming.

"Thank you all for coming out today. I am only five years-old so please let me know if I do anything wrong. I'm still learning." Aquilia said, as clear and as loud as she could.

Applause erupted again; she could hear chants of "Welcome Princess Aquilia." She smiled and waved at everyone.

"She's taken to this just as we expected. She is a true Encelandent," Chylla said to the others. They watched as she absorbed the environment. Tomorrow the work began.

Chapter 8

SATURN

After the exchange between Altair and Quintara, Janus took himself off for a walk. He couldn't get over the fact that his mother was, in fact, dead. Why didn't he feel that piece of him missing? Was it because he was so young when it happened that he didn't even remember her? He scolded himself for not asking sooner.

"Is everything alright young man?" An elderly woman asked him.

"I wish it were Ma'am. I've only just found out that my mother was killed when I was young and I feel guilty that I don't remember her at all," Janus replied.

"Oh you poor young man. I'm terribly sorry to hear that. I'm sure you will remember things later in life, or maybe something will trigger some buried deep memories," the old woman said as she smiled, waved, and walked away.

Janus thought to himself. Maybe she was right, most old people are. Why haven't I seen her around before? He brushed it off with a laugh. "I don't notice a lot of people so why am I questioning everyone?" He said to himself aloud.

"You're too trusting dear Janus," Lyra whispered to herself as she watched the interaction between her mother and her son. It was touching but worrying at the same time. Had Altair not taught him why strangers are bad? Maybe Lyra should teach Altair a lesson, one he wished he could forget.

ENCELADUS

"Absolutely correct Aquilia. Well done," Chylla praised. "Your understanding of Encelandent Monarchy is excellent."

"Can we tell Mummy?" Aquilia said jumping up ready to make another call.

"Maybe tomorrow darling, you know how busy Mummy is with Saturnites. It takes a lot of her time," Sinclair said softly.

Aquilia looked defeated and sad, but she agreed.

"Now!" Zidan said as he clapped him hands in one big swoop. "I think it's time for you to learn a few of the rules here in the Kingdom. Things you, as Princess and current Ruler, have to make sure are followed and punished if not," he finished.

Chylla and Sinclair made their exits and Zidan sat beside Aquilia with a book larger than she had ever seen before.

"Do I have to read it all now?" She asked her eyes now as big as Jupiter.

"Ha ha," Zidan laughed. "Absolutely not. This is yours to refer back to should you have any doubts. This is what you need to remember and it isn't very much at all.

'ALWAYS BE YOURSELF.

BE KIND TO OTHERS AND BE RESPECTFUL.'

Zidan said, slowly so she could take it in.

"Is that it?" Aquilia laughed. "I can remember that! Mummy always told me it, so that's how I remember."

"That's brilliant Aquilia, you are learning well especially considering how young you are," Zidan replied. "Now, I think we have time for one more thing. Come with me."

Aquilia jumped up and followed along behind him. She looked again at the portraits along the way.

"These are your Ancestors. They date back over three millennia. Here at the end, as you can see, is your mother, Queen Quintara," he explained.

"She was very pretty when she was young. She still is now," Aquilia said, admiring her mother's portrait.

"Indeed she was. Your picture will be there soon enough young Princess," Zidan said, placing his hand on her shoulder. He then guided her to a small room, draped in purple curtains with gold trim.

"What happens in this room?" She asked.

"Special. Things." Ammyn replied, emerging from the shadows carrying a rather sparkly gold dress.

"Eeee!" Aquilia squealed. "It's so pretty!"

"It. Was. Your. Mothers," she replied and placed it on the hanging rail.

"Time to change Princess," Chylla said, pushing Zidan out the door. "Your job is done now ZeZe."

Aquilia laughed when Chylla called him that. She was beginning to like being here. Ammyn was quick to whip off her current red dress and swiftly replaced it with the gold one and fastened the buttons on the back. She scooped Aquilia's scarlet hair into a bun and placed a gold necklace around her neck. A pair of diamond-encrusted shoes were placed at her feet, she stepped into them and they fit perfectly. Ammyn took her to the mirror. Aquilia's electric blue eyes sparkled in the light, her cyan skin shimmering against the gold of the dress. Ammyn took a quick picture and sent it to Quintara. 'A MINI QUEEN,' she added to the message.

"Everybody ready back there?" Sinclair shouted through the curtains.

"Yes, I'm ready!" Aquilia replied. "Ready for what?"

"PRESENTING HER ROYAL HIGHNESS, PRINCESS AQUILIA OF ENCELADUS AND SATURN," came a booming voice.

The sounds of trumpets and trombones followed. Aquilia could hear a crowd beyond the curtains. The sounds of whoops and cheers, of applause and the sound of her name being chanted repeatedly.

Aquilia took a deep breath and stepped through the curtains. The sight before her left her speechless. There were people stretching as far as her eyes could see. Streamers of gold and red hung around the room, a hue banquet table filled with food and drink. Chylla guided Aquilia to the front of a grand stage where a chair awaited her. What she thought was a simple chair was, in fact, her own custom made throne, adorned with sapphire coloured velvet and Mother of Pearl arms. Aquilia was amazed.

Chylla sat Aquilia down and raised a crown high above her head.

"We, The Elders of Enceladus, now pronounce you, Crown Princess Aquilia of Enceladus," Chylla boomed. The whole room fell silent. It was eerily quiet whilst Chylla lowered the Platinum crown encrusted with Ruby, Sapphire, and Emerald gemstones. In keeping with her throne, her crown was also engraved with her initial. A deep cut 'A' with 24-carat gold outline. The crown felt heavy on her head, a lot heavier than her tiaras had back home, but she held her head straight and balanced it on her head. She stood and smiled at the accepting crowd. She felt relaxed here but she missed home so much. She missed her Mum, missed Paxy and Plexys, she secretly missed Janus too. She let a single tear slide down her cyan cheek. She had a deep-rooted feeling that she wouldn't see them in person for a long time. She hated Altair for this, even at only five years of age; she inwardly promised he would get what was coming to him. She would make a deal with Karma should they ever meet.

Ammyn was videoing everything and relaying it to Queen Quintara, she watched with pride as her daughter took her place on Enceladus. She knew Aquilia was safe there, she just hoped that Altair kept his distance from her; she had a lot to think through.

SATURN

"Such a charming boy isn't he Lyra?" Benzyline commented.

"He is. A little too trusting of strangers though, Altair obviously forgot about my gift," Lyra responded. "It's time to teach him a lesson."

Her mother smiled. She had seen Lyra practise day and night, perfecting her gift, and learning when to best put it into practice. Her heart had filled with pride; something she had passed down was finally being used, as it should. Lyra's father was a waste of space, passed nothing down but those aqua eyes, although mesmerizing, they only helped lure the prey, they didn't help execute the plan.

"You alright Mum?" Lyra asking noticing how her Mum had zoned out a little.

"Of course, now, go do your magic," she said with a grin. "It will be fun to watch him squirm."

Lyra laughed as she switched from herself into a new look. She then tied her hair up, coloured her lips and took to the street.

"Good luck my child," Benzyline whispered, "You may need it."

Chapter 9

SATURN

Quintara spent most of her days overseeing the Kingdom's demands. She spoke with the people about their ideas, their fears, hopes, and dreams. This was one of the things she loved about being Queen. She loved to interact with the people.

Quintara noticed a woman sitting by the fountain alone, she made her way to her, just to make sure she was alright.

"Hello, how are you?" Quintara asked her.

"Oh! You gave me a little fright there dear. I'm fine, just waiting for my daughter. She told me to meet her here. May I ask, are you all right Your Majesty? I must admit, you do not look very well at all," the elderly replied looking closely at Quintara.

"Oh me, I'm just a little tired. I don't sleep well at the moment. It will pass, but thank you for asking. I hope your daughter doesn't leave you sitting here too long; it looks like a storm is brewing. You take care now!" Quintara replied waving as she made her way back to the Palace.

Quintara was right. There was a storm brewing but not in the way she was thinking. Altair had been watching her every move. He despised the way she interacted with everyone. A Queen is supposed to send others to interact with the people. This was the ideal opportunity to have her assassinated. He was sure he could find the right person to do it, for the right price, if not; he'd do it himself, for free. She would be an easy kill, just like Lyra's sister. She was unsuspecting too. Floated about as if she was immortal, until the arrow hit her head. She dropped like a rock from the sky. The laser arrows that had been designed to immobilise spacecraft had worked perfectly on her. Once targeted, it would lock on and chase the target for around five minutes. If it missed, which was very rare, it would self-destruct and scatter shrapnel in a ten-meter radius. Anything within that radius would be severely injured. It was a win/win weapon.

ENCELADUS

Ammyn and Aquilia spent a lot of time together. Aquilia, helping Ammyn how speak full sentences without pausing, and Ammyn supporting Aquilia as she tried to understand the running of the Kingdom. It wasn't easy but Ammyn was learning fast.

"I'd like to make a speech to the people. How would I let them know?" Aquilia asked.

"That's. Where. We come in," Ammyn said, managing to say the last three words without a pause.

"Great! Let's do it. Ten am tomorrow morning please Ammyn." She replied excitedly.

"Certainly. Princess Aquilia," Ammyn responded getting up to make the necessary arrangements.

Whilst Ammyn was walking to set up the gathering, she bumped into Sinclair.

"I thought you and Aquilia were spending the afternoon together. Has something happened?" He asked.

"Everything is. Fine. Princess Aquilia wants. To make a speech. Tomorrow morning. At ten am. I am. Sending. Out the. Message now," she replied remembering to take it slow, that way she could build longer sentences.

"You are doing so well with your speech Ammyn. Do you mind if I borrow the Princess for a while?" He asked.

"Of course. You can," Ammyn replied. "Please tell her. I will catch. Up with her. Later."

Sinclair nodded, smiled, and walked towards the Palace gardens. He had noticed how the Princess adored the flowers.

"Princess Aquilia," he said, bowing when she turned to face him. "We have some urgent matters we must discuss. Do you have some free time?"

"Yes I do, Ammyn is going to sort out something for me to make a speech tomorrow. That's OK isn't it?" Aquilia replied.

"Absolutely Princess. It is good to stay in contact with the people, they will respect you more for it," Sinclair replied.

"Great! Now, what did you need me for?" She asked, paying him her full attention.

Sinclair appreciated how she was always fully attentive to everything. She soaked up everything, just like the proverbial sponge. It made their jobs easier, especially when she asked many questions. That way, nothing went wrong!

"One question, please," she said before he could begin.

"Go ahead," Sinclair smiled.

"How did Ammyn damage her voice box?" She asked.

This was another thing Sinclair liked about Aquilia. She always asked direct questions. She didn't stray from what she wanted to say.

"That is for Ammyn to explain Princess. It's not my story to tell," he replied.

"OK, thank you for your honesty," she said. "Please continue."

"Thank you Your Highness. We have received word from Hyperion that an alien patrol is working its way around Saturn, What are your instructions?" He explained.

"Can you show me?" She asked

"Certainly, this way," he said, surprised by her answer.

He led her to a hidden room within the Palace. It housed all the security systems and communication systems. She was surprised by how advanced it was. There was a screen for every lunar body and a larger one for Saturn.

"Why are there so many screens?" She asked, looking from one to another.

"We are the main protectors of everything in the vicinity of Saturn." Sinclair explained.

"Can we contact them?" She asked, thinking of ways to diffuse the situation.

"I believe so, what are you thinking Princess?" He asked as one of the engineers programmed them in.

"Let me try?" She asked gently.

Sinclair gestured for her to continue but kept his radio close in case they needed to send in reinforcements. The engineer signalled that they were through.

"This is Princess Aquilia of Enceladus. Please explain your current presence?" She said in a commanding voice, one that shocked everyone in the room.

"We are passing through towards Mars. We mean no harm Your Highness," came the reply.

"Would you accept an escort? This would keep us both safe," she replied.

"We would be grateful; the rings are quite difficult to navigate. Thank you," the voice replied.

"Escorts will be with you momentarily. Safe journey to you," she said as she ended the call and watched the screen as the escorts arrived and led the patrol through the rings and on with their journey. "Keep an eye on them."

"That was fantastic! You handled that better than I expected. I'm proud of you," Sinclair said, a beaming smile joined with the glowing yellow star made it hard for her not to feel great about herself too. She couldn't wait to tell her Mum, when she finally got to speak to her again. It had been a whole week but she never pushed, she knew her Mum was a busy woman, but she had to know that she was safe.

"Can we look in on Mum?" She asked.

"Very briefly," Sinclair said as he keyed in a special code.

On the biggest screen came the feed from Quintara. She sat at her desk reading over what looked like official paperwork, she held a quill in one hand and was about to sign her name. Aquilia smiled; at least she was safe and alive.

"Thank you," she said and left the room.

At the dinner table that evening, Sinclair explained everything that had happened in the control room that afternoon.

"Princess Aquilia was amazing!" He gushed.

"It was nothing. I just wanted to know what they wanted," Aquilia replied, spooning heaps of pasta into her mouth.

"Oh please! I bet they had no idea they were talking to a five-year-old," Zidan said. "We are very proud of you."

"Your speech. Notification has been sent. Out. Princess," Ammyn said, quietly and slowly.

"Wow Ammyn! Aquilia has really helped you with you speech, it's amazing!" Chylla said with a shocked look on her face.

"She is helping. A lot," Ammyn replied. "I am grateful."

"What happened?" Aquilia asked. "To your voice box."

The room fell silent. Everyone unsure of whether a girl so young would understand. Ammyn studied Aquilia for a moment. She was able to string a full sentence together yet, but she hoped, if she took it slowly, Aquilia would remain interested enough for her to finish.

"It was in. Battle. I helped save. A child. Neptune waged. War with Saturn. I was. A warrior. Protector of Astrodia," she began. "I saved a young girl. Peasant girl. I was slashed. Across the. Throat. Angry soldier of. Neptune. Killed him. But voice box. Badly damaged. Repaired but. Still broken," she finished, showing off her scar.

Aquilia stood, walked around the table, and took Ammyn into her tiny arms. "Saturn thanks you Ammyn. I will continue to help you," she whispered as she hugged her close. "Now, you all need to rest. Please take the night off," she announced quickly wiping a tear from her eye. Ammyn's story had hurt her heart.

Aquilia went to bed that night determined to make her mother proud.

"I'll make you proud too Daddy," and with that she fell into a deep sleep.

Chapter 10

SATURN

"Excuse me young man," a small voice broke through Janus's thoughts. "Could you help me please?"

"Certainly. How would you like me to help?" He asked politely

"Just grab those bags and carry them into my house. I would grab them all but I only have small hands, see?" She replied, holding up a pair of hands no bigger than a child's.

Janus smiled, took a hold of all the bags and happily carried them into the house.

"Thank you so much. May I offer you a cold drink as thank you?" She offered with a smile.

"That would be wonderful, as long as it isn't any trouble," he replied.

"Certainly no trouble at all," she said as she poured the orange juice straight from the fridge and passed him the glass.

She led him to the living room and offered him seat, which he gratefully accepted. He began drinking from the glass before his vision became blurry.

"Oh, I think I'm coming down with something," he said, breaking out in a sweat.

"You do look an odd shade of pink young man, why don't you drink up and I'll send for a doctor. Put your feet up too," she said sounding concerned.

"Could you send for my father too, his number is in my phone, his name is Altair," Janus managed before passing out.

"Young man, can you hear me? Hello?" She said in his ear. There was no response. "Perfect."

Altair paced the living room. He hadn't seen Janus since he spoke about his mother. Altair hoped Janus was just walking off the shock, but he had a dark feeling it was more than that. He had no one to turn to. Layson didn't know how to handle Lyra. She had a gift. Something no one else had, passed through the bloodline on her mother's side. She could shape shift. He had seen her do it once when they first met. It was another thing that attracted him to her, but she hadn't perfected it then, she was still learning. She had now been gone for fifteen years, plenty of time to practice and learn more. This worried Altair greatly. If she has perfected it, she could easily make it past his spies without detection. This was worse than he thought. He couldn't tell anyone else she was still alive. It would make him look bad. Altair sat and thought hard about his options. There weren't many. He would give Janus a few more hours then report Janus missing; first he would check with Quintara. He may have gone there to calm down. He left his house to speak with her face to face.

Lyra watched him leave, and then began to follow him, staying exactly four steps behind him.

"You lied to him," she whispered.

Altair spun around to find emptiness behind him.

"Hahaha, do I look stupid?" she laughed.

He spun around again, again, nothing.

"I must be hearing things," he thought aloud.

Lyra stayed quiet. 'Let him think he's going crazy. He'll mess up soon. It will be fun to watch,' she thought to herself.

ENCELADUS

Princess Aquilia woke up early the next morning. She opened the walk in wardrobe using the iris scanner and selected an electric blue dress, which matched her eyes, a pair of silver shoes with gold bows and a simple necklace to accessorize her outfit. She selected a small tiara to wear for her speech and then made her way to the balcony room.

"Good morning Princess Aquilia," Chylla greeted her with a slight head bow.

"You can stop bowing now," Aquilia laughed. "There's no need."

Chylla looked at Aquilia and smiled. "You remind me so much of your mother. She used to say the same thing at your age. You have inherited so much from her."

"Thank you. I want to be just like her," Aquilia said, giving Chylla a kiss on the cheek. "I also want a cool tattoo on my head like you! Did my Mum want one too?"

"You only get this if you are chosen to have one, you have to do something extra special to be chosen," Chylla explained. "You can also get one for being a warrior. Sadly, your mother wasn't permitted to become a warrior. Royalty are not permitted to join up, but I'm sure she secretly wanted one too."

"That's a shame. I'd love to fight for my home. It's important to me. I'll speak with mother later," she said as Zidan and Ammyn arrive. "Where's Sinclair?"

"He is running late Princess, he sends his apologies. He will catch up soon," Zidan said.

"Are you. Ready?" Ammyn spoke slowly.

Aquilia nodded, and turned to face the red velvet curtain.

"INTRODUCING PRINCESS AQUILIA."

"I need to find that man!" Aquilia giggled.

She quickly composed herself and stepped through the curtain to the sound of applause and cheers.

"People of Enceladus. I come before you today to fully acquaint myself with you. As your Princess and daughter of Queen Quintara, I want to extend my hospitality to my people," she began.

Cheers rang out across the courtyard. Sinclair watched from the sidelines with Quintara on video call. He wouldn't have let her miss her daughter's big day. He watched like a proud uncle and shed a tear that her father couldn't bask in all the greatness that was his daughter.

"I will be speaking with the Queen later today, if there are any issues we should be aware of or any ideas you may have, there is a box at the front of the Palace in which you can place any and all things. I look forward to meeting you all personally. Please remember, my door is always open," Aquilia finished.

She waved to the many people below and stepped down from the podium feeling proud of herself. She stepped back through the curtain to find Ammyn with tears in her eyes. Aquilia rushed to her side.

"What is it Ammyn? Are you in pain?" She asked quietly.

"No. Just very. Proud and lucky. To know you," Ammyn said.

"As we all are," came a familiar voice from behind her.

"Mum!" Aquilia squealed and spun around to find Sinclair with his phone held out.

"I'm so proud of you. What did you want to talk about sweetheart?" Quintara asked.

"Well, I want to change one rule. Can I?" Aquilia asked.

"What rule?" Quintara questioned.

"I want to join the military but Chylla told me that Royalty aren't allowed to join up," Aquilia responded. "Please Mummy. It's important I look after my people."

" I will allow it on one condition. Where is Ammyn?" Quintara replied.

"Right here. Your Majesty," Ammyn replied.

"Oh Ammyn! Your speech! What happened?" Quintara asked with amazement.

"Princess Aquilia has. Been helping me. With speech. I'm very. Grateful. Very proud," Ammyn said with a hitch in her voice. "Very much. Like you."

"Oh Ammyn, I'm so glad! Now, my condition is that YOU train Aquilia. I know you are all very able to train her, but that is my only condition. Do we have a deal?" Quintara explained.

"Absolutely 100% Your Majesty," Zidan replied. "We will begin on her tenth birthday."

"Yay! Thank you!" Aquilia squealed.

Sinclair said his goodbyes to the Queen and prepared for the days jobs ahead.

"Aquilia, don't let your studies drop behind. They are important too," Zidan reminded her.

She hurried off to her waiting tutor. She knew he was right, they were just as important as training, and, her training didn't start for five years. She vowed to start early with gentle exercise daily, sit-ups, push-ups and casual weight lifting. It couldn't hurt, right?

Chylla's phone began buzzing, at the same time as everyone else's. They all exchanged glances and headed towards the control room. As soon as they entered they could see chaos across the screens. The patrol form yesterday had come under attack from the Jupitents; they were attacking the Enceladent escorts too.

"Send more. Backups. I'll get. Ready," Ammyn volunteered.

"No. I'll send backup but you stay here," Sinclair ordered in a voice everyone knew not to argue with.

Aquilia looked up from her science work just as the first five ships took off. She knew something was wrong. She ran to the control room. She was shocked by what she saw.

Chapter 11

SATURN

"Queen Quintara, please pardon the intrusion," Altair said politely through gritted teeth. He hated being nice to her. "I don't suppose Janus has been here in the past few hours has he?"

"Altair, lovely to see you. No, the last time I saw him was at your house. Has he not returned?" She replied, placing the emergency protocol paperwork back into the safe.

"No, I shouldn't be worried but it's not like him to be gone for hours without word," he replied as he began pacing the room.

"Why don't you go home Altair. I'll send some of my people out to search. Stay at home in case he returns," she told him.

Altair nodded. He said nothing else, just turned on his heel and headed home. Quintara ordered ten of her best men to search the Kingdom for Janus, granted them permission to search houses and garden. They were not to rest until he was found.

"Ah, door to door searches just for you my son," Lyra whispered peering through the silver blinds of her rented house. "Of course, they won't find you here. I've already prepared for that."

On saying that, she rested her hand on his head, closed her eyes and snapped her fingers.

He was gone!

A knock at the door grabbed her attention. She opened it wide.

"Can I help you?" She asked

"May we come in and search the property?" Came the reply.

"What exactly are you looking for?" She asked.

"The Queen's nephew is missing," the tallest of the three replied.

"Well, please do," she said as she stepped aside.

From the doorstep she spotted her mother looking worried, watching from across the street. She smiled, waved and closed the door.

After they searched high and low, they left.

"I hope you find him soon," Lyra called after them.

"Thank you Ma'am," they replied.

"Where is he?" Benzyline demanded as soon as she burst through the door.

"Right there on the couch," Lyra said pointing at Janus. Of course, no one could see him but them.

"You are a clever girl", her mum gushed.

Lyra smiled. She had longed for her mother's approval for years. She had done everything her mother had asked of her. After her sister was killed, her mother had spiralled into some dark areas, even dabbling in dark magic to try to work out who had killed her. No one had ever found out.

ENCELADUS

Aquilia surveyed the vast scenes before her. Working out for herself which screen showed the emergency and which were surveillance screens. She spotted the patrol from the day before.

"What happened? They were supposed to be escorted away by now," she demanded much to the surprise of everyone.

"One of the patrol ships suffered an electrical fault just on the outskirts of the Saturnese boundary.. Jupitents attacked thinking they were planning to attack them," Chylla replied. "We have sent more backups to help them."

"Can we contact Jupiter?" Aquilia asked looking at the technician.

"Working on it now Your Majesty," he replied.

They all watched as a light show of lasers shot from the Jupitents towards the alien patrols, the ships of Enceladus forming a protective shield around them. Aquilia could see that Enceladent technology outshone the Jupitents by light years.

"Ma'am, Jupiter's High Priestess on the line," the technician announced.

"This is Aquilia, Princess of Enceladus, daughter of Queen Quintara, call back your patrols," she announced.

"Princess Aquilia, this is High Priestess Katarina of Jupiter. We have reason to believe that the alien patrols you are currently protecting are set out to attack, we will stay in place until they have proven otherwise."

Aquilia put her head in her hands. How could she prove this?

"Do we record conversations?" She asked the technician.

"We do indeed Ma'am, what are you thinking?" He replied.

"High Priestess Katarina, we are sending over a transmission conversation from yesterday. I, personally, quizzed the alien patrol on their movements. They assure me they are travelling onwards to Mars and mean no harm," Aquilia replied.

"I will listen and judge for myself," Katarina replied with a hint of snobbery.

Chylla watched as Aquilia took charge of the situation at hand. Had she been on the other end of the radio, she would have no idea that this was a five-year-old child.

"I have listened and called off my patrols. We will, of course, follow them past Jupiter. You can call off your escorts," Katarina announced, then closed the communication line.

"How far can we see?" Aquilia asked, looking from screen to screen.

"As far as the boundaries of Earth, I believe. I upgraded the telescope myself," Zidan said proudly.

Aquilia turned to the technician and read his name badge, 'ZEEBRAKAAN'

"Zeebrakaan, you will be my personal security technician. You are to watch all patrols and report directly to me, are we clear?" Aquilia said.

"Y...Yes Ma'am, absolutely crystal clear," he replied a little shaken up.

Aquilia then left the room to return to her studies. She felt different after leaving the room, like something had changed inside her. She would call her Mum later. Maybe she could explain it.

"It's happening. Isn't it?" Ammyn said breaking the silence.

"It certainly is," Sinclair replied. "Faster than expected but yes it is. She has a thirst for it, just like her mother did."

"When do. We tell her?" Ammyn questioned.

"When the time is right, but not now. She's not ready for that much yet," Chylla replied. "Now, emergency over, back to work!"

SATURN

"No sign yet Your Majesty, but we will keep looking for him," the head of the search party announced.

"Thank you. I will send some others to relieve you shortly," Quintara replied.

She sat down and tried to think where he could be. She only knew him to visit the fountain but it would be too hard to hide there. She wasn't aware of any of his friends. He was always at the Palace or by his father's side.

"Another letter Ma'am," her butler announced.

"Thank you," she replied.

Looking at the envelope, she recognised the handwriting from the previous letter. Quintara still had no idea who had written them. This one had a small charm inside. The only person who possessed that charm was Janus.

'I have Janus. I won't harm him.

Remind Altair that he promised something many years ago.

When he has come to him senses, I will release Janus.

For now, farewell my Queen.

Send my love to little Aquilia.

E.L'

"Who could this person be?" Quintara thought aloud.

"Who could who be?" Altair replied from behind her.

She hadn't heard him arrive but then Altair was very sneaky.

"I received this letter. It says I am to remind you of a promise you made many years ago. This person has Janus. It says when you have come to your senses, they will release him," Quintara replied, showing him the letter, the other letter she would keep a secret for now.

"E.L? Who is E.L?" He spat. "This is probably someone's idea of a sick joke. They know how much Janus means to me."

"Hahaha if only he did," came a whisper.

"Did you hear that?" Altair asked.

"Hear what?" Quintara replied looking around for anyone else.

"Nothing. I think I must be tired and worried so much that I'm hearing things," he replied. "I think I'll head home, I'll call if Janus returns."

Quintara watched him leave. He seemed very surprised by the letter. Could he be right? Could someone really be joking about holding Janus prisoner? It seemed strange but all the while perfectly possible. A sudden ringing broke her thoughts.

"Aquilia, what is it darling?" Quintara spoke quickly.

"I think something is wrong with me Mummy," she said tears streaking down her face.

"What is it?" Quintara asked again.

"I come over all strange in the control room. Like I'm not me. I'm scared Mummy!" Aquilia wailed.

"Darling, go and speak with Chylla. She will know what it wrong. Janus is missing. I'm helping to search him. Do you think you could help from up there too?" Quintara said softly. She knew what was happening, but only Chylla could explain it.

"Yes Mummy, I can help," Aquilia sniffed.

"Fantastic. Run a check through all the surveillance of Astrodia. Find Janus. You're his last hope," Quintara replied. "Call me if you find anything."

"Yes Mummy. Goodbye," Aquilia said as she signed off.

Chapter 12

SATURN

Quintara paced her quarters wishing and hoping for some news on Janus. Surely, someone will have seen him somewhere. She crossed her fingers and called her lead searcher.

"Any news?" She asked dreading the answer.

"None as yet Your Majesty. A few citizens mentioned witnessing him helping a young woman with her shopping but no one knows who she is or where she lives, I'm sorry. We will continue to look for as long as it takes," he replied ending the call before she could say any more.

"Where are you Janus?" She thought aloud. "Where could you be?"

She continued to pace for a few more hours, before her feet became tired and refused to move anymore. Quintara secretly hoped Aquilia would find something, she held off calling again for another hour but the suspense was too much for her to bear any longer.

"Queen Quintara, how lovely to hear from you," Zeebrakaan answered cheerfully.

"Where is the Princess?" She asked.

"Right here Mummy. We haven't found where he went. He was last spotted near the old mill, he was alone. After that, it's like her just disappeared. That's very strange Mummy!" Aquilia answered from what sounded like a distance away.

Quintara could see her sitting in one of the large green chairs, eloquently using the security system as if she were a forty-year veteran. Quintara smiled to herself, certain she had made the right choice. Enceladus needed Aquilia, just as she needed it.

"Thank you sweetheart. Yes it is strange but we will find him. Now, go speak with Chylla. I will talk to you soon," Quintara replied, closing the connection.

ENCELADUS

After the call ended, Aquilia sat and thought for a moment. Did she really want to know what was happening or could she be fussing about nothing?

"Where can I find Chylla?" She asked Zeebrakaan.

"Probably in the combat room Your Highness, she likes to keep fit. Shall I inform her that you are on your way?" He replied.

"No, thank you," she said as she turned to leave. "Where is it?"

She had not been shown that room yet; she would have a chance to practise there soon.

"I'll show you," Zeebrakaan said, rising from his chair. "This way."

Aquilia hadn't noticed how small he really was compared to her, she was surprised.

"Are you five years old too?" She asked as they walked through the long brilliant white corridor.

"Ha-ha, no. I'm actually ninety-four tomorrow." He laughed.

"Funny joke," she laughed back. She stopped when she saw how serious he was looking at her. "How?"

"I was a warrior once, like the others. Unfortunately, a warlock attacked me. She cast a spell on me that prevented me from any growth and subsequently knocked my height back to the age of six." He explained. "I was unable to go back into combat after that so I learnt to become a technician and help protect from here."

"Oh wow. I'm sorry I laughed at you. You really do help protect everyone," she apologised.

"No need for you to say sorry. I'm happy! Ah, here we are," he exclaimed pointing at the large oak doors with engraved dragons across the front.

"Thank you. I'll come back and see you soon," she said waving and entering the room.

Zeebrakaan waved back and made his way back to the control room. He had been worried when Queen Quintara had informed them she was sending Aquilia so soon, he was worried she was too young and immature. How wrong had he been? Aquilia had taken her duties so seriously. He was sure, now, that it was the right time.

Aquilia entered the room to see Chylla performing some amazing feats of gymnastics carrying a spear with a rather bright red feather. She ran head on towards the wall only to run up it, flip three times and land on her feet. Aquilia was speechless. She had never seen someone perform such moves. She couldn't move whilst she watched Chylla almost float across the shiny, glittery grey floor. She imagined being able to glide like Chylla. Why hadn't her mother allowed Chylla to teach her to fight? Maybe she would ask later.

"Oh, Princess! I didn't hear you come in. Please come and have a seat," Chylla said, gesturing the seating area towards the right of the door.

"Why can't you teach me?" Aquilia asked as she sat down.

"Your mother designated Ammyn, she will teach you well," Chylla replied. "Ammyn is a fantastic warrior."

Aquilia wasn't sure. She hadn't seen Ammyn train, but Aquilia had other things to ask Chylla about. She was scared of the answers but her mother had advised she speak to Chylla about her worries, so here she was, about to, hopefully, get some answers.

SATURN

"Has there been any sign at all?" Altair boomed as soon as his foot was through the Palace door. "Surely he has been seen somewhere!"

"He has," Quintara stated. "He was seen helping a woman with her shopping. Where he went after is anyone's guess."

"Well why didn't you tell me?" He replied angrily.

Altair didn't scare Quintara as much as he once had. Now she had the upper hand, she knew what he had planned for Aquilia and herself, but she had saved Aquilia, she, now, had to protect herself. This wouldn't be as easy. Altair had contacts and some very devious friends. Those who would do anything for him. She would have to watch out for them too.

Lyra watched as Janus slowly woke up. She made sure she didn't change her appearance just yet. She wasn't ready to confess who she was at this moment in time.

"Morning sunshine!" She beamed at him.

"Ouch, what happened?" He asked holding his head.

"You don't remember? You were sitting there drinking your orange juice and talking about your father, Altair and then you passed out. Have you eaten boy?" She explained.

"I don't actually remember when I ate last. My Dad had just told me that my mother was killed when I was six months old. I stormed out; I don't even know how long I've been gone. How long was I out cold for?" He asked, sounding worried and angry at the same time.

"Only a few hours. I called a doctor; he said to leave you until you wake up. He checked your head for any wounds but, luckily, you landed exactly where you sit now," she said cheerfully. "Let me fix you some food, build your energy up for the trip home."

Janus watched her busy herself in the kitchen. She seemed indifferent as to who he was. As if she were unaffected by his relation to Royalty. Maybe he should leave before he started to develop feelings for this woman. Clearly stunned by his own thoughts, Janus stood up and suddenly felt dizzy again. He looked around and spotted her just before crashing down again.

"Poor thing, it hasn't worn off just yet sweetheart," Lyra whispered. "Mum, help me get him to the spare room."

Benzyline appeared from nowhere, she looked at Janus and smiled, "you'll be with us a while longer. I'll summon The Seeker. We have to check if he has inherited anything from your side," she demanded.

Lyra wasn't sure. She knew The Seeker had issues with Astrodia, especially since they were banished to the outer wastelands because of her foolishness. He was angry that they all were banished and not just Lyra.

"Isn't there another way Mum? You know he HATES this place. He threatened to lay a curse over the whole Kingdom if he ever came back. Can't we just send him some of Janus's blood or a lock of his beautiful white hair?" Lyra asked, stroking Janus's hair from his face.

"No!" Her mother boomed causing the floor to shake a little. "He has to been seen in the flesh!"

ENCELADUS

"So you see Princess, the same things that are happening to you, also happened to your mother a long time ago. I don't think she ever fully understood either," Chylla finished.

Aquilia sat there and blinked once, twice before responding.

"It's very confusing for a five year-old to understand under normal circumstances but, I think I get it!" She said confidently. "I age faster when I'm in the control room!"

"Oh dear, dear Aquilia," Chylla giggled. "That is one way of putting it, but only your mind ages, not you as a person."

Aquilia smiled, "I can handle that for now."

Ammyn could hear voices coming from the training room. She quietly slipped inside and listened in. She never really eavesdropped but she loved to watch the way Aquilia interacted with others. It gave her hop that, one day, she would be able to do the same. So, whilst they talked, Ammyn trained. With silent movements, she glided across the floor, spun in the air, and landed mere millimetres from the wall. She regained her position and sprang from the floor, twisted a complete 360 degrees, and landed on her hands in a handstand, all so silently, Aquilia didn't hear a thing.

"You still have the skills Ammyn," Chylla praised her.

Aquilia spun in her seat, surprised to see her.

"I didn't hear you come in!" She exclaimed.

"That is why she is best suited to train you, Princess," Chylla explained. "Ammyn is a trained assassin. That is why she was blessed with The All Seeing Eye."

As Chylla explained this, Ammyn tattoo glows blue. Aquilia squeals with excitement.

"I'm going to do my very best," she said, clapping her hands.

Chylla and Ammyn exchange glances. They are thinking the same thing. They believe she will be the greatest warrior yet.

Chapter 13

ENCELADUS

Aquilia lay awake for hours after everyone else had gone to bed. She still had so many questions to ask, but she was unsure whom to ask about them. She hadn't spoken to her mother again today. They were still trying to find Janus. Aquilia sat bolt upright after having a single thought. His Bilaphone! Why hadn't anyone thought to trace it? She sprang from her bed and made her way to the control room. Upon reaching the door, she was cautious to enter, recalling everything Chylla had told her earlier in the day. She took a deep breath and turned the doorknob. As she took one-step inside, she could feel the slight change as it drifted over her.

"Your Majesty? It's gone one am, is something wrong?" Zeebrakaan asked.

"Not as such. Can you trace Bilaphone signals from Saturn up here?" She asked taking the seat next to him.

He stared at her for a moment before pressing a few buttons on the terminal in front of him. He passed her the keypad, "key in the number, if you know it," he said.

She took the keypad, closed her eyes for the briefest of seconds, and ran her fingers over the numbers. The screen came alive with a rainbow of colours whilst it traced the signal.

"Is this to do with your missing cousin?" He asked her cautiously.

"Yes. It's not like Janus to go missing. He's too reliable for that. Something isn't' right about this. Not one bit!" She replied watching the colours change to a layout of Astrodia.

The signal zoomed into a house of the far side of the city. A side Aquilia hadn't seen before. It looked like the poorer side.

"Can we get satellite imagery?" She asked.

"Of course," he replied tapping a few more buttons on the console.

Aquilia looked at the screen; she noticed that her mother's search party were just a few houses up from the house. Confused as to why they hadn't found him, if they had already searched that house, Aquilia dialled her mother.

"What is it darling, it's late," Quintara said, clearly wide-awake.

"I've tracked Janus's Bilaphone. His signal is coming from a house just down from your search party, why didn't they find him?" Aquilia demanded.

"Which house?" Quintara asked abruptly.

"Two houses back. Its faint, maybe his battery is dying," Aquilia replied.

She watched on the screen as the search party backtracked and burst into the house. They were there a matter of seconds before Janus was carried out over the shoulder of another man and two women were brought out in lasercuffs. They didn't look like natural Astrondians.

"Thank you darling, now go to sleep," Quintara whispered then closed the connection.

"Maybe she is right Your Highness. It's awfully late," Zeebrakaan said as he turned to face her.

Aquilia was curled up on the chair, sound asleep having dropped off just as Janus was carried out of the house. Zeebrakaan covered her with his uniform jacket, switched the surveillance screens to dark mode and let her sleep.

SATURN

Quintara watched as the search party brought Janus to the Palace medical room. She had instructed that the women be held in cells until Janus had awoken. Quintara called Altair to inform him that Janus had been found and was now in the medical room at the Palace. She kept the information about the women to herself. It wouldn't do him any good to know that part yet. She would speak to them first.

Altair burst through the door within five minutes, demanding to see Janus. He was led to the medical room where he sat for hours until Janus finally stirred awake.

"Janus, take it easy. What happened to you? Altair asked watching as his son finally opened his eyes.

"A woman. I helped her with her shopping. I don't remember much else," he replied before dropping back off to sleep.

"He needs rest. Maybe you should focus your attention towards the two women in custody?" The doctor winked at him. He knew he wasn't supposed to tell Altair about them but it was the only way to get him to leave Janus alone long enough for him to rest.

Altair rushed out of the medical room and made his was towards the far wings of the Palace where he knew they held prisoners. He persuaded one guard to let him through and told another that The Queen had summoned him. Once alone with the women, he demanded they explain their actions.

"Well, if you hadn't have lied to him, I wouldn't have had to kidnap him," Lyra said finally revealing herself.

"YOU! I thought, no, I KNEW it! You've risked everything for what?" Altair demanded.

"For our son to know the truth!" Lyra hissed at him. "You have no idea how it has been for me without him."

"You didn't deserve him. You tired to poison the Kingdom. Why should I allow you any contact with him? No, it's better he thinks you're dead," Altair shouted back.

His eyes switched from Lyra to Benzyline. The hate grew more intense with every passing second in their company. After so long, she had broken her promise, SHE was trouble. He had to get rid of her. Of them both. He turned on his heels and left them in the darkness. He needed to plan how to get rid of them before Quintara started asking questions. He knew he didn't have long.

ENCELADUS

Aquilia woke slowly the next morning, a sudden pain shooting down her spine.

"Good morning Princess, would you like some breakfast?" Zeebrakaan asked softly.

"Ow, my back hurts," she said wincing every time she moved.

She slowly sat up realising she wasn't in her bed. She looked around at the screens, taking in the information they provided.

"Did Janus get out?" She asked, rubbing her neck,

"He did. Messages provided information that he had been drugged with something unknown to Saturnites." He replied.

"Thank you. Why don't you come for breakfast too?" She offered.

"I would love to," he replied with a smile.

It had been a while since he had eaten breakfast with company. After losing his beloved wife, Zyra, several years previous, he spent his time in the control room. He and his wife didn't produce any children. A curse placed on her family three decades before had prevented women from conceiving. It would lift later this decade, allowing females to produce again. Sadly, it was too late for them, but he enjoyed being a part of the Royal staff. He had watched Quintara grow into a Queen and he now got to watch Aquilia on her journey too.

"Princess Aquilia, good morning," Chylla greeted her.

"Good morning everyone! I invited Zeebrakaan to join us for breakfast. I hope you don't mind," she replied.

"Of Course not. Please come and. Sit with. Us," Ammyn said gesturing the seat beside her.

Zeebrakaan smiled and sat down. He looked at all the food on offer. It made him a little sad.

"Are you alright?" Sinclair asked sympathetically.

"Sorry, just all this reminds me of my wife, Zyra. She loved making breakfast," he replied.

Everyone gave him an apologetic smile.

"We didn't mean to make you sad," Aquilia said quietly.

"Just sad that she didn't get to meet you. She would have simple gushed over you," he replied. "Thank you for allowing me to reminisce in my memories Your Majesty."

Aquilia watched everyone as they made conversation. They spoke about Quintara when she was young, how technology had changed over the years and how angry the Jupitents had become. Once their easygoing neighbours, Jupiter had become hostile over the past ten years.

Zeebrakaan finished his breakfast, polished off his grapefruit juice and began to leave the table with his plate to wash up. Zidan stopped him.

"There's no need to clear away. We have a new system installed to do just that. Is everyone finished?" He asked.

Everyone nodded, wiped their mouths and sat back. Zidan pressed a glowing green button and the table instantly flipped over to reveal the underside. Aquilia crawled under the table in search of the plates but they were gone. She climbed back out looking surprised.

"Well, where did they go?" She asked.

Zidan laughed, "straight to the dishwasher. I've been busy inventing," he giggled some more, "now, off to Math with you."

Aquilia gathered her study books and made her way to the door, she stopped just before opening it. She turned back towards the room full of people and smiled to them all, "thank you for all being my friends," she said, opening the door and leaving them all stunned.

"Oh dear Aquilia, we're more than your friends. We are more like your family," Chylla replied with a tear in her eye.

"Don't get. Emotional. Chylla." Ammyn stuttered. "We all. Feel the same."

They all watched her leave. Promising, silently that they would watch over her all the time. They didn't anticipate what would happen next.

Chapter 14

SATURN

Quintara made her way to the cells, which held Lyra and Benzyline. She could finally find out why they had kidnapped Janus. Her guards had made sure no one had spoken to them before her.

"You called for me Your Majesty?" Came a voice from behind her.

Quintara spun round, her red cape trailing behind her.

"No, I didn't. Aren't you supposed to be guarding our prisoners?" She demanded.

"Altair said you requested my assistance," he replied.

Quintara's face changed from confusion to anger in the blink of an eye. She ran down the stairs, one flight, two, three, where she stopped dead in her tracks. One guard was down; the cell door was wide open and both women gone!

"Find them now!" She screamed.

The guards ran from the Palace, determined to find the escapees. Quintara was still confused as to how they escaped; she inspected the cell door only to notice it had been unlocked with the keys.

"Bring Altair to me," she demanded.

Her head guard dipped his head and went off to find Altair. He didn't have to travel far; Altair was emerging from the medical wing.

"Her Majesty requests your presence," he told Altair.

"For what reason?" Altair replied, trying not to show any guilt at having freed Lyra and Benzyline.

"She didn't give a reason," the guard replied. "Just that you are to be taken to her."

Altair followed the guard to Quintara's quarters, all the while thinking up an explanation. He wouldn't let on who they were. He had to keep that a secret, especially from Janus. He could never know his mother was still alive.

"You wanted me?" Altair said sounding bored.

"Why did you tell the guard that I requested his assistance?" She shouted clearly agitated.

"I heard it from someone else; I was just passing on the message. How was I to know it wasn't true?" Altair replied innocently.

Quintara glared at him, ready to insult him but, quickly decided to change her strategy. She didn't trust him, but she would never let him know that. The longer he was kept in the dark, the better. She had another plan.

"Was there anything else?" Altair questioned her.

"No, you may go, but go home Altair. Leave Janus here to rest, he will come to no harm," she ordered.

Altair turned away from her and rolled his eyes, like her would allow Janus to stay here alone; nobody knew if Lyra would attempt to kidnap him again.

At the boarder of the wastelands, Lyra stopped in her tracks.

"Why am I running again?" She thought aloud. "I know things"

She watched her mother continue to walk away, unaware that Lyra had stopped. She then spun round and began the journey back to Astrodia. She would show Altair who she had become and then reveal herself to Janus and watch Altair try to disprove her.

She sidestepped a trap she had set over a month ago; clearly it had done its job. Altair's spy lay old and decaying on the dried grass. Lyra laughed to herself; did Altair really think he could outwit her? Did he really think she had no idea he had people watching he? She had been watching them too, studying their moves, becoming them. It had been so easy to outsmart them, especially the leader. A flash of her aqua eyes and he had turned to mush, literally. She'd left his puddle right where he stood, not bothering to clean him up. The birds would have a field day with him. She laughed to herself again; Altair had no idea who she had become. It was about time he found out.

ENCELADUS

Aquilia had been studying so hard since arriving on Enceladus, Chylla thought she deserved some time off. Away from the Palace. She arranged a trip to visit Quintara as a surprise for them both.

"Aquilia, I've decided to take you on a trip. You have been so engrossed in your studies that you haven't had any time for fun," Chylla stated watching Aquilia's face change to a look of confusion.

"I thought I had to study hard to become a warrior like you?" She asked.

Chylla looked at the young Princess, eager to become a protector of her Kingdoms.

"Even warriors need a break now and then," Chylla laughed, "now, get ready?"

Aquilia squealed and ran off, passing Sinclair as he entered the room.

"Why is she so excited?" He asked clearly amused by Aquilia's squeals.

"I'm taking her on a trip. To Saturn," Chylla replied, knowing Sinclair wouldn't approve.

"She isn't safe there Chylla! You know that!" He boomed at her. "What will you do if something happens to her?"

Chylla rolled her eyes at him, "do you really think I would take her there if I didn't think it would be safe?" She said through gritted teeth. "The girl needs to see her mother."

Sinclair glared at her, unaware of who Chylla had suddenly become.

"And, even though she won't admit it, Quintara needs to see her daughter too!" Chylla added before turning on her heels and walking away to track down Aquilia.

Sinclair was worried, Chylla hadn't fully thought this through, he was sure of it. He went in search of the remaining Elders. He needed their advice.

"Are you ready yet Aquilia?" Chylla asked as she walked into Aquilia's room.

Chylla noticed how tidy it was. She looked at the bookcase, each book arrange in alphabetical order. Her reference books ordered by ascending size. Aquilia had arranged her dresses in colour batches. All the reds together, yellows, blues, greens. Everything was so neat and tidy, surprising for such a young girl.

"I've decided to wear pink today," Aquilia said from behind her. "I love this one; it looks just like one Mummy had when she was little."

Chylla spun round, her long gold and silver braids spinning with her. She took in the sight before her. Aquilia resembled her mother is so many ways. From her scarlet hair to the way she posed in front of the mirror, Aquilia was the carbon copy of Quintara, but with a mind all of her own. She would go as far as her mother, if not further, she was more determined to fight than her mother was. Once Quintara was told that Royalty didn't fight, she gave up on the idea, settling, instead, to becoming everyone's Princess. Chylla had seen how upset Quintara had been, giving up her dreams of becoming a warrior, but she succeeded in passing her dreams to the next generation. Aquilia wouldn't accept 'no' for an answer. She pushed to get her own way, and she got it.

"You look fabulous. Now, let's go, before it gets too late to leave," Chylla said, nearly pushing Aquilia out of the door.

"Why are you in such a hurry Chylla?" Aquilia asked sounding worried. "Where are we going?"

"To see your mother," she said with a smile. "You would like that, right?"

"But Mummy said it isn't safe for me there yet. Is it safe now?" Aquilia questioned a confused tone of voice surprising her.

"Not exactly, but safe enough for a visit, I'm sure of it," she replied constantly looking over her shoulder.

"I'm not sure. I'd love to see Mummy. Can I call her and ask if it's safe for a quick visit?" Aquilia asked heading for the comms room.

"It's supposed to be a surprise!" Chylla shouted. "If you want to see her, we have to go now!"

Aquilia was taken aback by Chylla's tone. "I don't think I want to go anywhere with you now!" She said as she turned and ran back to her room.

"I think enough has been said, don't you Chylla?" Zidan stated. "You're wanted in the comms room."

Chylla hung her head and walked away.

"Ammyn, check on Aquilia please. She could use a friend," Sinclair said, following Chylla down the corridor.

Ammyn made her way to Aquilia's room. She knew how Aquilia felt, not being able to see her Mum. She had lived through it but on a different level.

Chapter 15

SATURN

"WHAT DO YOU THINK YOUR WERE DOING?" Quintara's voice boomed through the overhead speakers.

Zeebrakaan winced at her voice. He didn't know what had happened in full, but he knew Chylla wasn't in Quintara's good books and he knew that wasn't a good thing at all.

Chylla rolled her eyes; luckily, the call was audio only otherwise she might have lost her Elder status.

"I just thought it would be nice for you both to see each other, it's been so long now. She needs to see her mother," Chylla replied.

"It's not safe Chylla! You of all people should know that," Quintara stated. "I trusted you all with the most precious thing in my world and you, alone, are making me regret my decision now!"

"I would love to apologise but I don't see why I should. A girl needs her mother!" Chylla bit back. "You should know how it feels to not have your mother around."

Chylla instantly regretted what she said as soon as it had left her mouth. Even Zeebrakaan felt remorse for Chylla. He was a technician back when Neptune attacked. Their army took Quintara's mother prisoner a little time after arriving. They held her for just over a week before killing her and sending her head back in a box to the Palace. Sadly, it was Quintara who opened the box to find her mother's face, frozen mid-scream, looking up at her. Quintara's screams and sobs have never left The Western Wing of the Palace. That wing had been barricaded up ever since, never to be reopened again.

"How dare you!" Quintara whispered, clearly hurt with the memories of her mother.

"I'm sorry. I don't..." Chylla began.

"DON'T! Don't you DARE!" Quintara screeched. "You have NO RIGHT to bring that up! You were the reason she was taken! You were supposed to protect her!" With that, Quintara hung up.

She paced her room trying to control her anger. 'How dare she even THINK of bringing my baby back here,' she thought. 'Altair could be planning anything!' Quintara realised just how alone she was with all this. She sat herself in Elio's old chair and cried. Silver tears streaked her face, they fell all too easily as she finally let out all the anger and grief she had been holding in for so long.

A swift knock of the door stunned her into silence.

"Who's there?" She managed without a croak.

"May I enter Your Majesty? I'd rather not announce myself through an oak door," came a wispy female voice.

"Enter at your own risk," she replied standing ready to protect herself. Despite to being trained, she had watched the warriors train long enough to know a few moves.

As Quintara watched, the door slowly opened, long rose-tone fingers curled around the edge, a wisp of magenta hair blew gently through the opening. Quintara gasped, 'could it really be?" She thought. As the door opened a little wider, Quintara caught the sight of a pair of aqua eyes. Quintara's own purple eyes widened in disbelief. The woman she had been led to believe had been assassinated was now standing in the Palace, as clear as winter on Pluto!

"Lyra," Quintara whispered. "Is it really you?"

"Yes, it is I," Lyra replied with a smile.

"But Altair told us you were killed, I don't understand," Quintara stated.

"There is so much to explain but we have no time now. I just wanted to be in contact with you. I see that my letters and hampers had the desired effect. Is Aquilia safe now?" She replied not moving from the doorway.

Quintara studied Lyra just as a scientist would study new species. She remained cautious of her and watched her closely.

"Yes. She is safe, thank you for bringing it to my attention, but what do you gain from this?" Quintara asked.

"Me? Nothing at all. I lost the chance to ever be Queen, but you were always so kind to me. Altair has always held grudge against you and Elio, but he is planning something atrocious. How could he even DREAM of hurting a child,"

Lyra replied, her eyes darting around at every sound. "I can't stay long, but I also wanted to apologise for kidnapping Janus. As a heads up, Altair knows it was me."

In the blink of an eye, she was gone. Quintara looked out of the window just as Lyra turned the corner and out of the Palace courtyard. She still couldn't believe what she had just witnessed.

Quintara and Lyra had been friends when she was with Altair. They weren't close, but Quintara liked Lyra, most people didn't. She couldn't risk Altair finding out Lyra had been there. She would have to play dumb. She gathered herself together and headed down to check on Janus. He had been through quite an ordeal.

ENCELADUS

Zidan watched as Chylla emerged from the comms room.

"You know how stupid that would have been, don't you?" He asked trying not to sound too harsh.

"Not you as well," Chylla said turning to walk away. "The girl needs her mother, and contrary to what she says, Quintara needs her daughter too!"

"It's not safe, you saw the video. Altair wouldn't hesitate to kill them both. He has always resented Quintara, especially when she rejected him for Elio," Zidan stated. "I thought YOU of all people would work that out!"

Chylla stood there staring at him. Her silver eyes wide with shock, her mouth wide open as if screaming a silent scream. She knew what he meant, but she hadn't expected him to bring it up.

Ammyn knocked lightly on Aquilia's door; she didn't want to scare her anymore than she had already been.

SNIFF

"Who is it?" Aquilia squeaked from behind the door.

"Ammyn. May I. Come in?" She replied as clearly as she could.

Aquilia opened the door just wide enough to see that Ammyn was alone. She opened it wider to allow her to step inside.

"Oh Princess. Look at you. Beautiful face. Let's get. You cleaned. Up," Ammyn said leading Aquilia to the en-suite just off of her bedroom.

Ammyn wet a cloth with warm water and dabbed at Aquilia's face, paying special attention to her eyes.

"You should. Not cry Princess," Ammyn said as she smoothed Aquilia's hair down.

"Why not?" Replied Aquilia.

"It's not. Good for. Your skin," Ammyn remarked with a smile. "I know how. Hard it. Is growing. Up without your. Mother."

"How?" Aquilia asked quietly.

"I grew up. Alone. I was taken. In by your. Mothers family," she replied looking Aquilia directly in the eyes. "My mother. Died when I . Was just two. Months old. It was written. That any orphan. Babies in the. Kingdom. Be brought. Up by a. Member of The. Royal. Family. That is. When your. Grandmother stepped. In."

Aquilia listened hard as Ammyn attempted to retell her story, pausing for breath every now and then. Ammyn told how she trained hard to protect the inhabitants of Enceladus.

"But I thought members of the Royal family weren't allowed to train, until now!" Aquilia asked sounding very proud of herself for changing one rule already.

"I wasn't Royal by. Blood. Only by. Upbringing. That made a. Difference," Ammyn replied gently touching Aquilia's arm. Ammyn was touched by how Aquilia had referred to her as a member of the Royal family.

Aquilia thought for a few moments. Maybe Chylla hadn't been trying to put her in danger, maybe she had seen Ammyn struggle growing up without her mother and didn't want her feeling the same.

"I shouldn't be angry at Chylla, should I?" Aquilia asked.

"Maybe. Not as. Angry. As you. Were. Chylla made. A mistake. I'm sure. Of it," Ammyn replied.

"I need to find her. Can you help me?" Aquilia asked again.

"Of course. Follow. Me," Ammyn replied.

Ammyn took Aquilia to the only place she knew to find Chylla. By the flowing blue river, next to the crystal waterfall. Chylla used this place to think.

"Chylla," Aquilia spoke softly. She didn't want to make Chylla any angrier.

"Princess Aquilia, I'm sorry about earlier. I must not have been thinking properly. I could have put you and your mother in serious danger," Chylla replied keeping her head bowed and avoiding eye contact.

"It's alright Chylla. Thanks to Ammyn, I think I understand why you did it," Aquilia replied pulling Chylla's head up to meet her eyes.

The Infinity symbol on Chylla's forehead wasn't glowing its normal bright pink, it was more of a dusty, baby pink. Chylla's silver eyes bore deep into Aquilia's electric blue eyes and something passed between them. A feeling of understanding.

After a brief moment, Aquilia's forehead began to burn.

"Ouch, make it stop!" She screeched.

And it did.

Aquilia now stood with a Golden Lightning Bolt adorned on her forehead.

Chapter 16

ENCELADUS

The events of the previous week were still the main talking point at the breakfast table. The lightning bolt sat proud on Aquilia's forehead. She had learnt why it had appeared the morning after.

Due to Aquilia's understanding of the situation she found herself in, she was gifted the lightning bolt from the Higher Elders. Aquilia had proven her worth to them.

Chylla had tested Aquilia. She never would have taken Aquilia back to Saturn. Had Aquilia not questioned Chylla about her safety, Chylla would have failed and Aquilia would never been given another chance. Luckily, for Chylla, Quintara knew all about it but couldn't risk letting on until she heard back from the Higher Elders. As expected, she was delighted and somewhat sad to see her daughter growing up so fast. The next five years would fly by before her training began. She trusted Ammyn to train Aquilia well. Quintara had watched Ammyn train as a young girl; she had power, speed and agility. Aquilia would learn a lot of defence and attack skills from her.

Sinclair watched as the inhabitants of Enceladus began their daily duties, from the baker selling the best homemade bread, to the draper selling the best silks and satins. They all busied themselves with their work, hoping to make better sales than the previous day or week.

"What are. You thinking?" Ammyn asked as she looked over his shoulder.

"Just how do they do it Ammyn? They sell the same things on a daily basis but don't make any more money than they did the previous day," he replied watching as a young boy sold the local newspaper to a passerby.

"It's their. Lives. They have. Never know any. Different," she replied clearly puzzled by his statement. "How could. We make it. Different?"

"I have some ideas, but I must clear them with Princess Aquilia first," he said before walking off in search of her.

SATURN

As Quintara approached the medical wing, she took a brief moment to look out of the Western facing window. There, she potted Altair making his way to the Palace; she contemplated questioning him more on Lyra, but then thought better of it. This sort of information would, likely, be a useful bargaining chip later, should anything happen. Instead, she continued towards Janus's room, he had never taken a step wrong in her eyes, she had always hoped, that if she and Elio were ever blessed with a son, that he would be just like Janus. She smiled at the thought of Elio, but how her heart broke at how much she missed him and craved his touch, even a smile from him would soothe her aching heart.

"It's nice to see you smiling again Your Highness," Janus remarked with a twinkle in his eye.

"Thank you Janus," she replied. "How are you feeling today? You look so much better!"

"I feel loads better. I just seem to be having some flashbacks. I can't seem to get a distinctive face out of my head," he stated looking very confused. "I remember a very pretty face with magenta hair and aqua eyes. My mind tells me I've seen her somewhere before but I just can't think where."

"Maybe form the knock to you head son!" Altair said as he barged through the door. "Maybe you have concussion and you're imagining things, just like the woman in the street the other day. Didn't you say she had aqua eyes too? It's ridiculous."

Quintara regarded him for a second. She knew who Janus had seen. Altair knew who Janus had seen, but, sadly, growing up, Janus had never seen a picture of his mother. Altair had burnt them all, but Quintara still had a few stashed away. She would show him when the time was right.

"Doctor, was there any signs of concussion?" She asked.

"None that concerned us Your Majesty, the tests only suggest a slight tranquilizer had been ingested. It wasn't toxic enough to leave any lasting damage. Would you like me to conduct any further tests?" He asked waiting for a reaction.

"No, thank you. I believe you have covered everything," she replied. "Janus, I believe you are discharged."

The doctor nodded in agreement.

"Let's get you home son. You look like you could so with a decent meal inside you," Altair announced.

"I'll send my caterers over, they will prepare everything," Quintara stated.

"No! Thank you, I'm quite capable to looking after my son," Altair replied trying to hide his bitterness. "Thank you for taking care of him."

Quintara bowed her head and watched as they left. She noticed how Altair shielded Janus from prying eyes as they left the confounds of the Palace. She didn't trust him, not an inch. Just as she turned from the door, she spotted Lyra again. She knew Lyra wouldn't accept Altair taking Janus back home and hiding him away. Quintara wouldn't get herself involved. Not yet anyway.

"Welcome home son. Finally back where you belong!" Altair announced as they entered the house left to him by his parents.

It wasn't a grand house; in fact, it looked more like a civilian house, one with a simple front garden decorated with a willow tree at its centre. It's weeping limbs brushing and tickling the surrounding grass at its base. The house stood detached from any others, but almost identical to every other house around. It had three windows at the front and a turquoise door with the number 46 engraved in the centre. It had been home for so long, a home Altair had shared with Lyra. The home which welcomed Janus when he was born, a home he had brought Janus up in and he had become a fine young man. Altair was proud of him.

"I'm fine Dad. I just need some space, that's all. Do you mind if I just have a shower and then get some more rest?" Janus asked looking at his father who was deep in thought.

"Of course I don't mind. It's your home after all," Altair replied.

He watched Janus make his way up the laminate covered stairs and breathed a sigh of relief that his son was finally home. Now he needed to plan how to get rid of Lyra and Quintara, and how to stop Aquilia ever coming home again.

<u>ENCELADUS</u>

After much consideration of Sinclair's ideas regarding the Encelandents, Princess Aquilia decided to give one idea a chance. It was common practice on Saturn for the Head of the Monarchy to distribute duties among the civilians, so Aquilia requested database of all available workers on

Enceladus. Along with Sinclair, she built up a range of jobs, which could easily be taken up, all with generous salaries. There were listings for extra military personnel, additional guards for the Palace, chefs and even a Royal leaf sweeper! There were so many positions available. Aquilia and Sinclair made their way through the database, selecting the most suitable person for each job, no one was left out.

Aquilia made a point of wanting to inform each individual personally. She felt a formal letter was wrong. She wanted to connect with her people, she wanted to be approachable. She would make time for people, to learn about their families, their dreams for the future and if there was any other help they needed. Even at such a young age, Aquilia had taken her responsibility seriously.

Ammyn and Chylla watched as Aquilia made her way between the houses.

"It makes me so proud to see how alike she is to Quintara," Chylla exclaimed a smile so wide it would rival a Cheshire Cat.

"She has. Come so far. Since she arrived." Ammyn said. "I'm proud. Of her."

Aquilia arrived at the final house on her list for the day. It was the home of a widow named Halana. Her husband, Reaver, had died in battle fighting for Enceladus when Neptune attacked all those years ago. He put his life on the line for this place and it only seemed right that his family be looked after.

Aquilia knocked on the door gently. She had been informed that loud noises startled Halana and caused a great deal of stress. A young girl answered.

"Oh, Princess Aquilia. Please, come in," she said, sidestepping to allow Aquilia to enter.

"Who is it Evadene?" Halana whispered as she entered the living space. "Oh Your Highness. Had I known you were coming I would have smartened up a little," she said, fluffing her short white hair. "Please, sit down."

"You are fine as you are Halana," Aquilia replied as she sat on the threadbare sofa.

Aquilia could tell she had chosen the right person for this job. Halana was a proud woman. She had brought Evadene onto this world and seen that she grow into a polite young woman. Evadene was just around the same age as Janus but she didn't act overbearing. She was kind and polite.

"How can I help you Your Majesty?" Halana said as she poured some ginger tea.

"I've come to offer you a position within the Palace," Aquilia replied just before she sipped her tea. "Oh, this is nice!"

Halana laughed, "it's what I drink to calm me down. Now what job is it exactly and can I bring Evadene?"

"Of course! I want you to be my head dressmaker! Evadene can be your apprentice! You would live in the Palace but still be able to keep this house." Aquilia replied excitedly.

"I won't be able to afford the lease on both properties," Halana remarked almost getting into a panic.

Evadene sat close to her mother and soothed her with a hushed song.

"You wouldn't have to lease any property. This house is yours. A gift, from my family to yours. The Palace dwelling doubles as a workshop. It is fitted with everything you could possibly need, you can always come back and stay here if you wanted to," Aquilia said softly.

She watched as Evadene gently rocked Halana. She had been her mother's rock when Reaver died. Aquilia's heart ached for her own mother.

"Please contact me when she's ready. This job is hers, I will not offer it to anyone else," Aquilia whispered as she rose to leave.

"Is everything you said true?" Evadene asked with a slight tremor in her voice. "IS this house really ours?"

"Absolutely," Aquilia replied.

She turned to leave but took one last glance at mother and daughter. It was how it was supposed to be. It was so natural. She wished that for her and her own mother, but she, secretly, knew it would never happen.

Chapter 17

ENCELADUS - FIVE YEARS LATER.

"AGAIN!" Ammyn demanded.

"I've done it twelve times already!" Aquilia complained rolling her eyes.

"If you continue. Like that you. Will do it. Twelve more!" She replied trying not to laugh.

Ammyn had grown close to Princess Aquilia over the five years she had lived on Enceladus. A soon as her tenth birthday had arrived; Ammyn began training her to become a warrior. She had taken to it so well, nailing every move within a few attempts, including the current one. It took sheer concentration to run halfway up the wall, somersault twice and land with both feet on the ground in the traditional battle stance. Aquilia had nailed it after only three attempts, but it was Ammyn's favourite move so she spent longer on it than others.

"Fine! Once more!" Aquilia gave up.

Ammyn watched as she poised herself ready to run, she became one with the wall. She ran, so eloquently, like a swan in flight, towards the wall. One step, two, three, four, lift on five, run up, one, two, three, twist, head back, flip once, twice, feet land, one, two and pose.

"PERFECT!" Ammyn cheered.

"I had it perfect ten attempts ago and you know it," Aquilia responded with a cheeky smile.

"I know but. You do it. So well!" Ammyn replied.

Chylla watched as Ammyn and Aquilia trained. She saw potential in Aquilia, much the same as she had hoped to see in Quintara. She hoped Aquilia never lost that hunger.

"How is she doing?" Zidan asked form behind her.

Chylla, slightly startled, replied, "She's hungry for it. Just like her mother had once been before being told no. I hope Aquilia doesn't lose that hunger. She's very keen to please."

Zidan closed his eye for a brief moment, he could imagine a young Princess Quintara begging her parents to train, and he could imagine her face dropping when they said no. It was obvious her hunger had left her from that point. He had heard how she then pushed to become the best Princess for the people. Something Aquilia already had tucked under her belt. When he reopened his eyes, he was alone. 'I must have dozed off for a while' he thought. He shrugged and left the room in search of Sinclair.

"Halana," Aquilia called out. "Evadene."

"Yes Princess? Oh heavens above girl, you don't give off nice smells!" Halana exclaimed. "Here, get those off and grab a bath. Evadene; set the Princess a bath of Lavender and Elder Flower. She smells worse than your father's boots did when he came home from work!"

Halana had taken six months to accept Aquilia's offer, but Aquilia kept her promise and held the job for Halana.

Evadene had joined her three weeks later after finishing school. She helped Halana with dressmaking and helped Aquilia with her studies, especially History. Evadene had a Major Degree in Saturnese History. Halana and Evadene spent most of their time at the Palace, but also took sometime out to spend at home. Mostly on anniversaries, birthdays and school holidays.

"Is the smell that bad?" Evadene questioned just before entering the room. "Eww, it really is!"

Aquilia giggled. It was like having an older sister but without the bossing around. Halana was like a second mother to Aquilia. She hadn't spoken to her own mother since her tenth birthday just over two months ago. Every time Aquilia called her, she was either too busy, out on business or doing something important. Aquilia had questioned as to what could more important than speaking to her own daughter, but her mother had no answer to her question. Aquilia decided to leave it, she would wait until her mother wanted to talk to her, then she would make out that she was too busy to talk, that would teach he a lesson or two.

SATURN - FIVE YEARS LATER.

"Your Majesty, there was another call form Aquilia just a few moments ago. I passed on the message that you were very busy. She doesn't seem very happy that you won't talk with her. Are you sure I can't call the doctor for you? You look awfully dark around the cheeks," commented Quintara's personal assistant, Arista.

"I'm sure she is perfectly fine, just throwing her weight around," Quintara coughed. "I'll be ok in a day or two. If I'm not then and only then, may you call the doctor, understood?"

Arista nodded and left the room. She had been Quintara's P.A for just over three years and she had never seen Quintara look so ill, but she would always abide by Quintara's rules.

"You really should see a doctor Quintara. You don't look at all like yourself," Lyra remarked as she emerged from her hiding place. "In fact, you haven't looked well since you had dinner at Altair's house three weeks ago."

Lyra had watched as Quintara had acted as normally as possible throughout the meal, trying not to draw attention to Lyra at the window. Despite Quintara being aware of Altair's knowledge of Lyra, she would not acknowledge that she also knew. Altair had been civil curing the meal, asking how Aquilia was coping being away from her mother for so long and also asking how it was affecting Quintara.

Now Quintara thought about it, he did seem very interested in how she felt, especially after the starter. 'What was it again?' She thought. Scallops with parsley sauce. Even remembering it made Quintara feel uneasy.

"Arista! Call the doctor, I suddenly feel a lot worse," Quintara shouted.

"I wish you well Your Majesty," Lyra commented and made a swift departure through the open window, down the wall and across the deserted courtyard, which hid beneath the shadow of Enceladus. She paused for a moment and looked up. "Stay safe Princess. I will try and protect your mother from here."

"Dad, why did we eat something different to Queen Quintara at dinner the other week?" Janus asked as he finished his military count.

"Sorry?" Altair responded looking up from his newspaper.

"When Quintara came for dinner, why did we eat something different from her? It's been on my mind for weeks!" He replied.

Lyra watched as Altair's face changed from calm to agitated and back again so fast that, if you were from another planet, you would have missed it. 'He's catching you out slowly Altair, it's only a matter of time,' she thought.

"She likes different foods to us son. I had to order things in especially for her," Altair lied, he was sure he had covered his back. He didn't turn to look at Janus as he spoke either, this made Lyra so angry that she created a lightning bolt so powerful it blew out all the electrics in Altair's house.

Altair glanced out of the window just as the second strike came down, it lit up Lyra's angry face at the window, Altair screeched.

"What is it Dad?" Janus asked running to his father's side in a split second.

"I thought I saw something, then I realised it was just my reflection. You're old Dad isn't what he used to be," Altair lied again.

Janus wasn't sure if his Dad was being truthful. He didn't want to cause any arguments so he left it at that. He went upstairs and recounted his soldiers, he was sure he was missing a few somewhere. Once Janus had closed his door, Lyra appeared in front of Altair.

"How dare you lie to him!" She hissed.

"What are you doing back here?" He replied in a hushed voice. "You were supposed to stay away, THAT was the deal."

Lyra looked at him and laughed. She laughed so hard and angrily that storm clouds began to swirl overhead, it grew so dark that Altair could barely see in front of him. He spun around in circles looking for her, his breathing becoming more and more laboured with each turn.

"It doesn't matter how many times you try to get rid of me. I will keep coming back until Janus knows the truth!" Lyra said from a distance.

As quickly as the clouds arrived, they disappeared, along with Lyra. Altair looked around for her but she was gone. He'd forgotten how quickly she could move when she needed to.

"Dad, we've got a huge problem," Janus said from behind him. "We're missing around two hundred soldiers. Their names are listed but they haven't been head counted."

"Are you one hundred percent sure Janus? This isn't something that can be estimated or unsure of," Altair replied sounding irritated.

"I'm certain Dad. I was kidnapped, not brain washed!" Janus replied as he span on his heels and left. "I'll double check with Quintara."

"Don't disturb her with this. She trusted us to sort out the military. Leave it with me, I'll take a look," Altair replied looking sheepishly out towards the horizon.

Chapter 18

SATURN

Quintara spent the next few weeks laid up in bed. The doctor suspected food poisoning but informed Arista to call again is Quintara's complexion changed translucent. Arista watched over her day and night, she wouldn't leave her bedside.

After a month of bed rest, Quintara began to feel well enough to walk to her balcony for some air. Arista became her walking aid. She managed to stay on her feet for a few hours, walking up and down her balcony and in and out of her room.

"You're feeling better I see," Altair's voice boomed from the doorway, frightening Quintara into a shriek.

"The doctor has specified NO VISITORS until Her Majesty is fully recovered, now if you wouldn't mind leaving," Arista demanded gesturing to the door he had just entered.

Altair laughed and looked down at her. Arista was all of four foot nothing and weighed about as much as a handful of sand, but she was strong-minded.

"I will visit when I please you mouse like woman, get out!" Altair blasted.

"No I will not! You will have to carry me out!" Arista replied standing her ground. Little did Altair know, Arista could lay down roots wherever and whenever she wanted to.

Altair let out an audible sign and rolled his eyes, 'this will be easy' he thought.

As soon as he began to try to move her, he realised it wasn't going to be easy at all. He looked down at her. She looked up at him.

"Want to try again?" She goaded. "Or are you too weak?"

Altair was furious. 'How dare she?' He thought as he grabbed her by the arms. He was determined to move her even if it was piece by piece. Still Arista remained rooted to the spot.

"Enough!" Altair shouted. He spun around to face Quintara, almost whipping Arista with his long cloak. He pointed at Arista, "I will be back when SHE isn't around!"

"You'll be waiting a while then, I'm not going anywhere," she replied sitting herself, comfortably, on the floor.

At nearly 84, Arista was surprisingly flexible. Quintara hoped to be like her when she reached that age, if she made it that far.

"Who does he think he is?" Arista questioned after he had left slamming the door behind him.

"Take no notice," Quintara replied. "He is obviously still shaken by what happened to Janus."

Arista regarded her for a second or two. In those brief seconds, she concluded that something was very wrong here, but she would continue to pretend she didn't see it.

"Maybe you're right Your Highness. It must have been hard not knowing where he was or what he was doing," Arista said.

Quintara thought for a moment. She hadn't realised how, having Aquilia away from her, would impact her so much. She missed Aquilia's giggle, missed how she would follow Quintara around mimicking her every move. She knew she had sent her away for her own safety, knew The Elders would keep her safe, nurture her and protect her, but Quintara missed her so much.

"I need to call Aquilia!" Quintara demanded.

"I thought you'd never crumble!" Arista said joyously.

Quintara threw her a deadly look. Arista knew she had overstepped.

"I apologise. I'll set up the call now," she said slinking away.

Quintara knew she meant well but she hadn't being proven wrong. She had wanted Aquilia to become her own person, but it was killing her being without her daughter. Literally.

ENCELADUS

"I see from your reports that your studies are improving!" Sinclair exclaimed over breakfast.

Aquilia had invited Halana and Evadene for breakfast, she loved having them around.

"I'm impressed. With your Maths work," Ammyn commented, her sentence structure improving week by week.

Aquilia had continued to aid Ammyn in retraining her vocal chords. She was indeed improving. She smiled across at The Elders, "thank you all. You have all taken me in and moulded me into who I am now," she said to them all, allowing a tear to roll down her cheek.

Zeebrakaan entered the room silently and waited for their conversation to end, he hated interrupting people.

"Your Majesty, Queen Quintara requests a video conference," he announced when it was a little quieter.

"Thank you Zeeb. I'll be there momentarily," she replied giving him a warm smile. She had become quite attached to him; he was like a Grandfather to her. "Please excuse me," she said standing up to leave.

She made her way to the Comms room, debating with herself over whether her mother deserved her attention but she overpowered the negative thoughts and realised she was still her mother.

"Hi darling!" Quintara gushed as Aquilia's form appeared on the screen. "Look how you've grown!"

"Mum, it's been, what, four months since we last spoke. I can't have changed that much!" Aquilia replied rolling her eyes. "Or have you been so busy that you forgot what I looked like?"

"I'm sorry sweetie. It's just after what happened to Janus.." Quintara started.

"So Janus was more important? Wow!" Aquilia interrupted hurt showing in her voice.

"No honey. It's just, I know you are safe up there and I have to protect everyone down here," she replied.

Aquilia refused to reply. She had already made up her own mind. Her mother obviously didn't want a daughter. She had wanted a son, just like Janus.

"Aquilia sweetheart," Quintara said.

"Goodbye Mother," Aquilia said and ended the call. She sat for a few seconds before bursting into tears. "Why doesn't my mother want me?"

Zeebrakaan didn't know what to do, he had never had to deal with a crying child before, because that is exactly what Aquilia was, a ten-year-old child. He slipped out of the comms room in search of someone slightly more qualified to handle the situation. Luckily, he happened across Evadene in the hall.

"Please come. Aquilia. Lots of tears," he shrugged making no sense at all, but Evadene followed him with a smile.

Aquilia's sobs were so sorrowful; Evadene's heart broke for her. She entered the comms room and Zeebrakaan locked them in for privacy. He hated seeing her cry.

"What happened Princess?" Evadene asked softly.

SNIFF

"She never wanted me! She wanted a son just like Janus. Why wasn't she worried about me up here all alone?" Aquilia sobbed.

Evadene questioned her next move but she did it anyway. She pulled Aquilia in close and hugged her hard.

"It's alright. I'm sure your mother absolutely wanted you. Who wouldn't? This mass of red hair and those beautiful blue eyes! She wanted you safe, why else would she send you here?" Evadene said as she stroked Aquilia's hair.

Aquilia pulled away from the embrace and focused on Evadene's face. "Maybe you're right. It still doesn't explain why she wouldn't talk to me for months after my birthday."

"I'm always right," Evadene laughed. "Except when I'm wrong. Why don't you call her back and find out?"

Aquilia nodded and reconnected the call. She discovered that the call hadn't shut off on Quintara's end.

"How can I tell my only daughter that I was so ill I couldn't even SPEAK let alone just sit there and smile," came Quintara's strained voice.

"You have to. You can't let her believe you only cared about Janus," came a voice Aquilia had never heard before.

"Oh please, tell me I didn't just hear that voice?" Came a voice from behind them

Aquilia and Evadene turned to see Zidan's face as white as the clouds.

"She's supposed to be dead! It was announced! She was assassinated!" Zidan rambled on, "Altair told everyone!"

"Who is she?" Aquilia asked clearly confused by the situation.

"That is Lyra, Janus's mother." He replied rapidly searching the Royal records for a picture of her. "Here, look!"

Aquilia and Evadene stared at the screen where a picture of Altair sat with a woman who had the most mesmerising aqua eyes and the brightest magenta hair ever. Aquilia gasped. She noticed how much this woman looked like Janus.

"What happened to her?" Aquilia asked getting closer to the screen; she stared as Zidan told them the story.

Chapter 19

ENCELADUS

"So that's what Altair told everyone," Zidan finished.

A gasp came from behind them all.

"Did you say she's still alive?" Chylla asked unsure of what she had just heard.

"I've just heard her voice Chylla, as clear as a summer afternoon on Mercury," he replied grabbing her by the shoulders. "Altair lied!"

Chylla shrugged him off and turned away from the screen. She couldn't look at the picture any longer. The woman he married should have been her. She declared her love for him just as Lyra had walked past flashing her aqua eyes at him, putting him in a trance. He had made his excuses and left, following her. Chylla's dream of a happy life had been destroyed. She had vowed never to let herself fall again, and she didn't, but she couldn't let anyone know how he had made her feel, they would pity her and she hated that.

"What is. It Chylla?" Ammyn attempted.

"It's nothing. It just makes me angry how easily he lied about her," she replied giving Ammyn a weak smile. "It makes me angry that Altair made everyone feel sorry for him, that poor boy didn't even get to see his mother."

"I know. How that. Feels," Ammyn said closing her eyes and searching for any memories of her parents but none would emerge.

Chylla watched Ammyn, a hurt and broken Ammyn, search for memories that simply weren't there. She knew Ammyn would never have to deal with finding out her parents weren't dead, Chylla had seen their bodies, but Janus would.

It would be hard on him. For the past five years, he was lead to believe his mother was dead. Chylla didn't understand why Altair would lie.

There was commotion coming from the, still open, phone line. Chylla switched to video mode and the subject of the conversation flickered across the screen. There stood Lyra, Quintara, and Arista, the latter looking paler than the surface of Pluto.

"But...you're...you're dead!" Arista struggled.

"Hmm...Do I look dead?" Lyra replied.

Arista promptly fainted.

"Mum!" Aquilia squeaked.

Quintara spun around, her scarlet hair swirling around her body, her purple eyes showing a look of shock and horror as she gazed at her daughter, Chylla, Zidan, Evadene and Ammyn on the video screen.

SATURN

Lyra stood, open-mouthed, at the sight of a ten year-old Aquilia. She was the perfect hybrid of her mother and father. Lyra's eyes then moved between Zidan, Ammyn, and Chylla. Her eyes then rested on the scar across Ammyn's neck.

"Didn't your mother ever teach you that it's rude to stare!" Aquilia snapped.

Lyra's eyes flicked between aqua, orange, and red as she looked Aquilia in the eyes.

"I apologise," Lyra replied bowing her head. "May I just ask, aren't you a little young for an Elder Mark? Can you even fight?"

Aquilia blinked once, twice. "Can you?" She replied, the lightning bolt on her forehead began to glow.

"She is wise beyond her years Lyra, much like Janus," Quintara remarked.

Aquilia rolled her eyes, 'another remark about Janus,' she thought.

Lyra turned to look at her. Her eyes filling with tears, "there's so much you all don't know. I don't know how to start, but you must all know why Altair lied," she started.

Quintara watched as Lyra helped Arista to the couch, which was so much more comfortable than the floor. She saw Lyra in a different light. She turned to see the reactions of the others on the screen. Chylla being the only one to look suspicious, there was an obvious, underlying reason there. Quintara knew Chylla had always been a suspicious person but she was showed an extra suspicious streak when it came to Lyra, she always had done.

"When you're ready," Quintara prompted, "we are all ears, but, if you begin, you can't stop." Quintara motioned towards the reading chair.

Lyra took the seat offered and took a deep breath. This would be the first time she had told anyone this story.

"I never knew what Altair had given up to marry me. I was an outsider, a commoner. I had no place with a Prince," she began staring off out of the window; this was going to be hard for everyone to hear. "To marry me, Altair had to give up his place in the Royal Line of Succession, hence the reason Elio became King after their parents' death and not Altair," she continued, looking over to Quintara.

"I had no idea," Quintara exclaimed, the shock showing on her face.

"I never blamed you or Elio. I was sure it was the Queen who hated me. She didn't want me to become Queen after her. I wasn't absolutely certain. When Altair's parents died, I was under the impression that Altair and I would ultimately take over. That was when Altair finally told me. I would never be Queen," Lyra continued her head dropping into her hands.

The next part would be embarrassing and would hurt everyone who was listening.

"What happened Lyra?" Chylla asked with more bitterness than she intended.

Lyra looked at her. She saw the hate.

"You loved him, didn't you? I saw you both talking before he came to me," Lyra said looking Chylla in the eyes.

"This isn't about me," Chylla replied through gritted teeth. "This is about you."

Lyra shrugged, "I'm sorry. When Altair told me that I would never be Queen, I ran to the fountain. I contemplated pouring a bottle of Cyanide into the water system."

Everyone gasped. Chylla shook her head. Lyra began to sob. Hard sobs that broke Quintara's heart.

"Why didn't. You do it?" Ammyn asked, breaking the silence.

"Before Altair caught up with me, and spotted the bottle, I had already decided not to. I wouldn't have done it. I was angry. I had been lied to," Lyra explained trying to plead her innocence.

"That's not the point!" Chylla screamed. "You could have wiped out the whole of Astrodia!"

"I won't lie. That was the point. If I couldn't be Queen then Astrodia would be no more," she admitted, "but when I was alone for the briefest of moments, the proverbial Angel on my shoulder talked me out of it, but I wasn't quick enough to hide the bottle."

"What did Uncle Altair do?" Aquilia squeaked.

Everyone turned to look at her, completely forgetting she was even there she had been so quiet. Quintara looked at her daughter closely on the screen and for the first time in almost two years, noticed how much she had grown up. Aquilia had been gone five years now and Quintara had hardly noticed any changes until now.

"Did he hurt you?" Aquilia questioned, pushing her way to the front.

Lyra looked at her, her heart-hurt thinking about how Altair could even THINK of hurting her. "No. He didn't hurt me physically, but he hurt me emotionally," Lyra looked at Quintara. "He banished me and my family to the outer wastelands of Saturn, we were never to return. Altair had a number of people watching over us, just to make sure we didn't venture back."

"What happened with Janus, other than the obvious?" Chylla questioned quietly.

Lyra let out a loud sigh. She had missed so much of Janus's life, it hurt when she thought of all the first's she had missed out on. His first words, first steps, first fights. "I had to leave him behind that much you all know, but I never thought for a single second that Altair would lie to him about me. To tell others that I was killed."

Zidan had been quiet up to this point. He had listened to everyone speak, argue and cry. "There are still so many unanswered questions," he said as his eyes darted to another screen, "but that is for another time. If you are still in hiding Lyra, I suggest you go. Altair is on his way to the Palace.

Everyone in the Enceladent comms room watched as Altair descended upon the Palace. Quintara quickly said her goodbyes as Lyra back flipped out of the window. Quintara placed her fingers to her lips as Arista stared in shock but then nodded her understanding. Arista knew to keep quiet, she made her way to her office, and there she stayed.

ENCELADUS

At breakfast the next morning, everyone was still reeling from the previous day's antics. Evadene sat closest to Aquilia at the table, constantly assuring her that she was safe here on Enceladus and that no one there would allow any harm to come to her. Aquilia's electric blue eyes were still wide with shock and disbelief when Sinclair entered the room.

"Wow! I've been to nosier prayer meetings. Who died?" He asked casually picking up a glass and filled it with Elderberry water.

"It's not who died," Chylla spat, "it's who wasn't dead to start with."

Sinclair looked as shocked as Aquilia did, "who isn't dead then?" He asked shoving a peppered egg into his mouth.

"Lyra!" Chylla grinded out. "Lyra isn't dead!"

Sinclair promptly choked on said peppered egg causing Halana to slap him on the back so hard he spat it out onto the floor. He nodded his thanks and gulped plenty of water.

"How do you know she isn't dead, have you seen her?" He asked quickly.

"We have. Seen and . Spoken to. Her," Ammyn replied taking a deep breath.

Aquilia smiled sweetly at Ammyn. She had come so far with her speech, 'I'm proud of you,' Aquilia mouthed to her. Ammyn smiled back, slightly embarrassed but proud of herself too. She hadn't even thought about trying so hard until Aquilia arrived. Ammyn believed Aquilia had a higher power, and she couldn't wait to see what else she could do.

Chapter 20

SATURN

Layson awoke with a sound ringing in his ears. He opened his eyes and checked the alarm clock next to him; it wasn't even two in the morning so the ringing confused him. He sat up in bed and reached for his phone. There in bright blue was the name 'ALTAIR.' Layson took a deep breath and answered.

"Hello?" He said trying not to sound irritated by being woken up.

"What took you so long?" Altair demanded.

"It's 1:43am Altair. I was sleeping, as most people are. What's up?" He replied.

"It's definitely her! I saw her with my own eyes! She was the one who kidnapped Janus, her and that wretched mother of hers," Altair hissed.

"Lyra? Are you sure?" Layson asked.

"Positive. I saw her as clear as crystal, only the water on Dione is clearer!" Altair declared.

Everyone who was anyone knew the water upon Dione was so clear and still it was as if it weren't there at all. There were no ripples, no waves, nothing to displace its smooth ice-like surface. The first time Altair had been there, he had ran straight into it, unknowing it was water. His parents had laughed so loud. It was a happy memory, but the happiness hadn't lasted long. They were demanded to return to so out urgent business. That was the last time they went away as a family. There was always work to do, a Kingdom to run, a family to look after. After Elio was born, it wasn't fun anymore. Altair's parents were getting older; they wanted to spend more time at home, watching the days drag on. They wanted their children to marry and have families.

When Altair had introduced Lyra to them, they didn't even try and hide their disgust and disappointment. Lyra wasn't Royalty by any means. She was an outsider, a servant. Elio had gone one better, again, and began dating Crown Princess Quintara of Enceladus. Their parents were thrilled; they welcomed her in with open arms. Altair had pleased his parents before by pretending to date Chylla. They were pleased because she fought for the Kingdom. According to his precious parents, she was worth one hundred of what Lyra was, but Altair didn't love Chylla, she was a great person, a true friend but he loved Lyra. That's when he was given a choice, one that he greatly accepted.

"So, what do we do?" Layson's voice broke through his thoughts.

"We need to plan their demise. Quintara, Lyra, Aquilia, and anyone else who stands in my way," Altair said. "I have already begun to assemble my army, scouting through those who have enlisted to find anyone willing to work for me for extra pay; I'm up to two hundred. Unfortunately, Janus has begun to notice discrepancies in the headcounts."

"How do we fix that?" Layson asked not wanting to hear the answer.

"Everything must run through me remember? Elio put me in charge of military. I'll make up the numbers somehow," Altair replied sounding pleased with himself. "Meet me just before nine by the clock." With that he was gone. The line was dead. Layson looked back at his clock, three am. Was he really on the phone that long? He couldn't even remember half of the call. He looked over at his wife, Bella. Luckily, she could sleep through a war so she wouldn't have heard anything. He went back to sleep for a few hours. He figured he'd need as much sleep as he could get. Once Altair had a plan, it could take days, weeks, months and sometimes years to perfect.

Arista awoke Queen Quintara at precisely 8:44:03am.

"Good morning Your Majesty. Can I get you some breakfast?" Arista asked whilst opening the heavy, crushed velvet curtains.

"Maybe something light Arista, thank you. How is it out there today?" Quintara replied gesturing the window. "I read that we are due a solar storm in the coming days."

"All seems calm at the moment. The skies look clear; I will keep an eye on the radar for you." Arista said. "I'll also call for frequent weather reports."

"Thank you Arista. What would I do without you?" Quintara replied with a smile.

"Not a lot judging by this place!" Arista joked.

The Palace really had become a mess since Aquilia had gone. Quintara just hadn't felt the need to call in the cleaner every day, but then, after a while, she just forgot to call them again.

Almost reading her mind, Arista said, "I'll call the cleaners today too. Maybe it will also make you feel better within yourself. You really haven't been yourself since you became ill."

Quintara smiled at Arista. She really would be lost without her. Arista bowed her head and left to make Quintara some breakfast. Quintara rose from her bed, took a brief glace out of the window where she spotted Layson and Altair deep in conversation, thinking nothing of it as they were old friends, she made her way to her wardrobe, flung open the doors and let out a bloodcurdling scream.

"PERFECT!" Altair said to Layson. "Just as planned!"

ENCELADUS

By the time everyone had made their way to the meeting room, Aquilia had already set everything up. The projector was clean and warmed up ready to go.

Every two weeks, they all meet up to discuss the events that have happened between meetings and what needed to be achieved before the next meeting.

'Today," Aquilia thought 'would be fun.'

Everyone was surprised to see Aquilia already seated.

"Good morning Princess," Chylla said cheerfully as she sat down, "I can't believe you got the room ready."

"Good morning everyone, I hope you don't mind, but I've put back everyone's duties this morning. They can continue this afternoon. I think we all need a deep conversation about the revelations of the past week," Aquilia stated in a rather adult tone. 'It's happening again,' she thought.

"Full understandable and I, wholeheartedly agree. Now, I need a drink, anyone else?" Sinclair agreed smiling at Aquilia.

Whilst everyone settled down with drinks, snacks and notepads, Aquilia asked Chylla why she had been having the same feelings as she did in the comms room.

"You have grown into your role. It may only be your mind that has grown at the moment, but it proves you are ready for this. Go with the flow and let the true you shine through," Chylla told her, "everyone understands. Even you mother."

"How would my mother know?" Aquilia questioned. "Did she go through this too?"

Chylla thought hard before answering, she didn't know how much Aquilia knew about her mother's childhood and being only ten, she concluded that it couldn't be much, "she went through something similar, that's all I can say for now, maybe ask her about it next time you talk. Now, let's get this meeting started, shall we?"

Aquilia nodded and took the seat next to Ammyn. She passed Aquilia a glass of Lavender tea and smiled. Ammyn had rapidly become a close confident for Aquilia, they had shared a troubled childhood, both growing up somewhat without their parents in their lives. It's true, Aquilia still had her mother, but she was absent from so much of her childhood. No thanks, in part, to her Uncle Altair. Aquilia had so many questions about him, but they would have to wait for now. Maybe soon, she would get her answers.

"Erm, I think we'll start at the most relevant subject. Lyra," Aquilia announced projecting a picture of Lyra onto the screen. "I don't know who she is, why Uncle Altair lied or what happens from now, but I would really like some answers."

Just as Aquilia finished her sentence, there was a tap at the door.

"Enter!" Sinclair announced.

"I do apologise for the interruption Your Highness, we have a major incident that requires your presence," Zeebrakaan said softly.

"Thank you Zee, I'll follow you now. Please everyone, stay put, we need to do this today," Aquilia requested.

"Certainly Princess," Zidan replied.

Zeebrakaan led Aquilia towards the comms room.

"What's happened Zee?" She asked as they turned the corner.

"It not for me to say Your Majesty. Your mother's assistant will explain more," he replied gesturing the door. "I will leave you in peace."

Aquilia entered the room and noticed a visibly shaken Arista on the screen.

"What's happened? Where's Mum?" Aquilia asked frantically.

"She's sedated Your Highness. She woke this morning ready to begin the day. She was looking forward to meeting with the Royal cleaner. When she went to dress, there was a horrendous scream," Arista paused to instruct a rather sickly looking patrol officer to the wardrobe. "I went to check on your mother," she continued, "and I found," she swallowed audibly, "a severed head in a box on the floor of the wardrobe."

Aquilia stood rooted to the spot, unaware of how to react. It was a full five minutes before Zeebrakaan re-entered the room to make sure everything was alright.

"Maybe you should get The Elders?" Arista prompted him.

"Certainly," he replied leaving Aquilia staring blankly at the screen.

Within minutes, The Elders had arrived and Arista recited the events again.

"Not again. She has seen that once before and her scream has never left the Western Wing. It hasn't been reopened since," Sinclair stated. "I will make arrangements, thank you Arista. Take care of Queen Quintara. Zeebrakaan, please lead the Princess to her room and ensure Evadene is present."

Zeebrakaan nodded sternly once and carefully took hold of Aquilia's hand.

"Send them in," Zidan demanded.

"We haven't sent them in for a long time, Zed. Are you sure?" Chylla asked carefully.

"I'm certain, if anyone can find out who did this, they can," Zidan said anger flowing over his face.

Chapter 21

ENCELADUS

Zidan and Sinclair took their places at the back of the hall and listened as Chylla gave instructions to Nymeria and her Stealth Raiders.

"You are to harm NO-ONE but the culprit!" Chylla warned them, "Any mishaps and you will be demoted. Is that understood?"

"Yes Ma'am!" Came a collective reply.

The Stealth Raiders were the Specialist Division of The Onyx Abyss Alpha Armada, the Enceladent army responsible for the protection of Saturn and its many inhabited moons. The Stealth Raiders would travel to Saturn, make faster and more precise enquiries than the Saturnese Patrol and eventually capture and interrogate the suspect. It would normally take them mere hours to find who had committed such horrendous crimes, but Nymeria had promised to make this her priority and had promised to be done within the hour.

"We start at the Palace and go from there, LEAVE!" Nymeria ordered. She turned and looked upwards. Aquilia stood on her crystal balcony looking down. Nymeria bowed her head and turned to Chylla, "she is a carbon copy of Queen Quintara."

"That she is, now go, find who did this," Chylla replied.

Nymeria saluted and left. Chylla watched as five ships left the atmosphere and shot to Saturn. With their hyper-jump technology, they would land at the remote landing strip within minutes.

"Why did. We send Stealth?" Ammyn asked as Chylla entered the room.

"We had to. Saturnese Patrol would take days, even weeks to find who did this. Anything could happen between now and then," Chylla explained, "we have to keep the Queen safe too."

Ammyn understood, but she also knew how The Stealth Raiders worked. She used to be part of them until the attack. She watched as Chylla postponed the meeting and set everyone about their day. Ammyn worried about many things, but today she worried about Chylla. She knew Chylla still felt guilty about what happened to Quintara's mother.

"You shouldn't. Feel guilty Chylla," Ammyn said softly. "It wasn't. Your fault."

Chylla looked at her and Ammyn felt her blood run cold, "you have no idea, do you?" She asked. "No idea at all. I was the Queen's protector!" She shouted.

"But you. Tried your best." Ammyn said still speaking in a soft tone.

"MY BEST" Chylla laughed. "I cowered in the corner whilst they took The Queen. She was reaching out for me, calling my name. I sat in the corner and cried!"

Chylla placed her hands over her ears. Ammyn took a step towards her but Chylla turned away.

"Please, do not ply me with sympathy. I don't deserve it. Just leave, please." Chylla said with her back turned.

SATURN

"So that was step one of your plan?" Layson asked when they sat down.

Altair and Layson had made their way to the nearby cafe just after hearing Queen Quintara let out an unnerving scream. It was so ear piercing, half of the Kingdom fell silent.

"Of course!" Altair said feeling proud of himself.

"Do you plan to scare her to death?" Layson asked. "That's pathetic even for you!"

"DO NOT QUESTION what I do," Altair hissed. "There's more to it than that alone," he gazed off into the distance, reaching for his phone, he blindly dialled Janus. "Who has entered our atmosphere?"

"No one that I'm aware of," Janus replied flicking through a multitude of screens, "I don't see anything."

Altair hung up. He knew where they had landed, he had used that remote landing strip himself a few times, and it was well out of the reach of cameras. He also knew that only one other selection of people knew it existed. Stealth Raiders.

"Why are you here?" Altair demanded.

"Not a concern of yours Altair, step aside and let us work," Nymeria said boldly.

"I am in charge of the military here on Saturn, you will answer to me!" He replied.

"Maybe for the army here, but we aren't your military to command. STEP ASIDE!" Nymeria replied with a sterner tone.

"You haven't heard the last of this!" He shouted as they walked past him

Nymeria rolled her eyes. She couldn't stand Altair, never had done. She pointed to the Palace and continued to look around. She had been trained alongside Ammyn and could spot an uncomfortable Saturnite at over half a mile. Someone stood out to her. She looked shiftily at Nymeria.

Nymeria pretended to have not noticed her and continued to work her way to the Palace, but when she was just out of sight, she made her way behind the girl.

"NAME?" She asked as she placed her hand on the girls shoulder.

"A..A..Anka," the girl replied visibly shaken by Nymeria's presence.

"What do you know of the recent events at the Palace?" Nymeria asked a little gentler this time.

"Erm..." the girls' eyes darted around. "I was sworn to secrecy. If I talk, he will kill my family. My brother is blind."

"Then you will accompany me to Enceladus, we will question you there," Nymeria stated. She then proceeded to instruct her forces to do a full sweep of the Palace and hyper-jump back to Enceladus in ten minutes.

Nymeria led Anka towards her ship, watching the girl's every move. She noticed the way she looked at Altair as they passed by. Once inside, Nymeria told Anka her family would be protected and that she was not to worry. Anka continued to look worried as they took off from Saturn.

"Where are they?" Altair questioned as he peered through Anka's parents windows. "They can't afford to go anywhere!"

"Maybe they are still sleeping?" Layson offered.

"Don't be so ridiculous Layson. Why would they allow a thirteen year old outside whilst they still slept, how stupid can you possibly get?" Altair laughed. "I'll come back later," he walked away leaving Layson to trail along behind him.

"Why didn't they know we were here?" Anka's father asked.

"I don't know. I was looking right at him," her mother replied, "how strange!"

ENCELADUS

"Please, be seated," Nymeria said gesturing to the chair.

Anka sat down, clearly nervous, "could I have some water please?" She asked.

Nymeria nodded once and left the room. Anka looked around, the room was pure white and windowless. Not a speck of dust could be seen anywhere. She sat for a while weighing up her options. What could she bargain for? She had nothing to offer, just information. She had almost started a full-scale argument with herself when Nymeria re-entered, followed by Princess Aquilia.

"I didn't realise it was 'bring your child to work' day," Anka laughed.

Aquilia took the seat opposite Anka. She looked deep into the girls brown eyes. An eye colour rarely found in the civilians of Saturn. "I am Princess Aquilia, daughter of Queen Quintara."

Anka's face paled, if it could get any paler.

"We thought you were dead Princess. We hadn't seen or heard from you since King Elio's memorial," she said bowing her head.

"As you can see, I'm very much alive. What do you know about the incident at the Palace?" Aquilia asked dismissing Anka's words.

"I was sworn to secrecy. He said he would kill my family, please. We don't have anything. My brother is blind," Anka pleaded.

"Your family are safe Anka. To keep them safe, you have to help us," Nymeria said as she took the seat next to Aquilia.

Aquilia kept her eyes forward and her mouth shut. The only way to get Anka to talk was to stay silent. They sat that way for a whole five minutes before Anka broke down in tears.

"Altair offered me money to place the head in The Queen's wardrobe. He said he would pay me when she screamed. She screamed and I went to collect my payment, but that was when those lot landed," Anka said pointing to Nymeria.

"Why?" Aquilia asked. Just one word.

"We needed the money for food, clothes," Anka replied letting her tears fall.

"Why did he want a head left there?" Aquilia asked again, this time raising her voice a little.

"I..I don't know," Anka said clearly not understanding the question.

"So he didn't explain why or you didn't ask?" Nymeria questioned.

Anka thought hard before answering, "I didn't ask. I didn't care. We needed the money."

Aquilia stood up. There wasn't much of a difference in her height compared to her sitting down. She walked around the table, sat next to Anka and took her hand, "why didn't you ask the Queen for help? She would have happily helped you."

"We wrote to her over three weeks ago with no reply. We guessed she didn't care enough," Anka replied, fresh tears pricking at her eyes.

"She was sick. That's why she didn't respond," Aquilia said softly. "I'll mention it to her next time we speak."

Nymeria whispered something into Aquilia's ear and she nodded. "Make sure her family remain safe. Take her home," she turned to Anka, "I will make sure you and your family are taken care of, financially and medically."

With that Aquilia left the room.

Chapter 22

SATURN

"I don't understand Dad. How could they just come and go as they please without going through the proper channels?" Janus said angrily.

"I don't know son, they just can!" Altair snapped. "It seems Uncle Elio allowed this before his death, or maybe it was before that! I didn't really know much about it when we were younger."

Janus watched his father stare off into the distance; he seemed focused on one house in particular. He had seen Layson and his father returning from that direction earlier today. It seemed odd as that's where the poorer civilians lived and his father never wanted anything to do with them.

"What is it Dad?" Janus asked.

"What's what?" Altair snapped, spinning around to notice his son was watching him.

"Why were you and Layson down those sides earlier today?" Janus questioned.

"I...We decided to take a different route back from the clock tower. We met up to discuss your upcoming graduation!" Altair lied.

"Graduation isn't for another six months Dad, and I may not even graduate," Janus replied, instantly sceptical of his father's answers. "I'm going to go over my headcounts again, see if I can work out what went wrong."

Altair continued to watch the distance. He saw a shift in the atmosphere, only a select few could notice it. He watched as the ship landed, then shot off again. He grabbed his phone and instructed Layson to meet him. He would find the girl and kill her and family, whether she had told them about him or not.

ENCELADUS

Zidan watched Aquilia as she spoke with Chylla. She had grown up so much in the five years she had been here. She resembled Quintara in so many ways. Aquilia looked up at him and smiled. She left Chylla's side and walked up the spiral staircase towards him.

"Mr Zidan, can we talk?" She asked politely.

"Of course Princess, what can I do for you?" He replied gesturing for her to take his arm as they walked. She smiled and hooked her arms through his.

"Were you here when my mother was little?" She began, "did you watch her and teach her like you do with me?"

"Oh I wish I been. I've heard so many stories it almost feels like I was here. Looking at the pictures of her as a young lady, I must admit you do look a lot like her," he replied.

"Can I ask how old you are?" Aquilia asked.

Zidan laughed, "even if I told you, you wouldn't believe me!"

Aquilia cocked her head to one side. One thing she had learnt was not to judge someone's appearance, "try me!" She said finally.

"I'm 108 next week," Zidan admitted. "Sinclair will be 115 on his next birthday, Chylla will be 102 and Ammyn is 95, she was the youngest until you gained your power."

Aquilia blinked more than five times before she spoke again, "will I live that long?"

"It's quite possible now you have that," he said pointing at her Golden Lightening bolt. "You have probationary Elder status. To keep it permanently, you have to prove your worth."

"You mean fight?" Aquilia asked.

"Sometimes it is not always fighting young Princess. Sometimes it is showing compassion to your fellow people, which you do already." He finished.

Aquilia regarded him for a second. She had instantly felt a connection to him when she arrived, but she had no idea why.

"One more question, if you have time," she asked.

"I always have time for you, go ahead," he replied with a smile.

"Why do I feel a strong connection with you that is stronger than with the others?" She questioned. "I can't figure it out myself and I don't want to bother mother with it."

"Maybe we should wait until The Queen is better," Zidan admitted, "now, what is next on your agenda for today?"

"I had so much planned, but all I can think about it mother, maybe I'll try and call her," Aquilia replied.

Zidan kissed her forehead and let her go on her way. She had grown up so fast in her years on Enceladus. He was so proud of her. He hoped she wouldn't be angry with him when she found out her connection to him.

"You didn't tell her, did you?" Chylla asked from behind him.

"No, but she will find out soon," he replied.

"Oh my head aches! What happened?" Quintara asked as she slowly rose from her sedation.

"I don't think we should go into that now Your Highness, I do have Princess Aquilia on the line should you wish to speak with her," Arista replied.

Quintara sat up straighter in her bed and beckoned the phone with her hands. "Hello darling, how are you?" She cooed.

"I'm fine mother, how are you?" Aquilia asked. "Are you OK to talk?"

"Absolutely sweetie, what is it?" Quintara asked getting worried.

"A girl called Anka wrote you a letter asking for some financial help. Do you think you could help her and her family?" Aquilia asked.

"Arista, find me a letter from someone called Anka, we must help them immediately," Quintara instructed, "are they poor dear?"

"Very mother, her brother is blind and has no education, but how will you help?" Aquilia asked.

"We will send money, an optometrist, and a teacher who specialises in braille," Quintara replied. "I'll get onto it straight away."

"Thanks Mum, I knew you wouldn't let me down," Aquilia praised. She thought about asking her mother about Zidan but decided against it until her mother was fully recovered, it may come as a shock question.

The call between mother and daughter only lasted a few minutes longer, Arista having called Quintara away urgently. They promised to speak again soon.

As Aquilia exited the comms room, she bumped into Evadene.

"Are you OK Princess?" She asked a look of worry crossing her face.

"Sometimes I wish I wasn't a Princess!" Aquilia said before running off.

Evadene watched her run; she would give her a few minutes before catching her up. Evadene thought for a moment, she had never seen the Princess ever wish to be anything but herself. This was serious. She contemplated asking The Elders for advice but refrained until she had spoken to Aquilia. It could be nothing. She is a young woman after all.

"Princess? Can I come in?" Evadene said as she knocked on her bedroom door. She could hear muffled sobs from inside and decided, just this once, to enter without invitation. "Oh Princess, didn't anyone tell you not to cry?"

SNIFF

"Yes, Ammyn. She *SNIFF* said it's not good for your skin," Aquilia replied in between sobs. "Was she right?"

"Absolutely! She forgot to mention that it makes you look ugly but I guess she didn't want to hurt your feelings," Evadene shrugged.

Aquilia jumped up and ran to wash her face, paying special attention to her eyes, just as Ammyn had done before.

"I'm not ugly am I?" She squeaked from the bathroom.

"In no way possible. You have the perfect blend of genes. I mean, look at Queen Quintara, she is magnificent!" Evadene remarked. "You look just like her."

Aquilia emerged from the bathroom dabbing her face with a crimson coloured towel. "Sometimes, I hate being a Princess."

"Why? I would love to have been born a Princess. Don't get me wrong, I love who I am, but sometimes I wish I had all this growing up, never worrying about what I would eat from day to day," Evadene replied, "you really should be grateful."

Aquilia slumped down on her bed and thought, "Eva, how can I help the poorer people more?"

"It takes more than money Princess. Some people may not have money to make them rich, some people feel rich just having friends. You could help financially with lots of people, little and often. Come, we'll go to the market!" Evadene squealed excitedly.

"Let's go!" Aquilia chimed in.

They grabbed a list of things that Halana needed for dressmaking and off they went.

Sinclair sat in his office working on a new concept for hyper-jumping when Chylla burst in.

"Where's the fire Chylla?" Sinclair joked.

"It's not a joke! Aquilia's gone!" Chylla shouted, "I've looked everywhere!"

Sinclair jumped up from his seat, "who saw her last?"

"She was last seen with Zidan, well I saw them together, I don't know where she went after that," Chylla hissed angrily.

"OK, stay calm. Who have you checked in with?" Sinclair asked, thinking rationally, being the eldest he was always the one who had to think of a plan.

"Well, no one!" Chylla replied.

Sinclair rolled his eyes behind her back, "let's find Zidan, and go from there."

Chylla nodded. Sinclair was starting to think that Chylla was losing her cool too quickly recently. He questioned whether having Aquilia here was good for Chylla. He would speak to Zidan later, alone.

"Zidan, where are you?" Sinclair called as he entered the security stock room.

"Right here," he called from behind a mountain of old screens. "What's up?"

"Where did Aquilia go after you both spoke?" Chylla demanded.

"Whoa, Chylla, I don't like your tone! She went to call her mother, after that, I have no idea. Now, if you don't mind," he said gesturing the pile of old screens ready for recycling.

"We're sorry Zidan. Chylla, go check with Halana and Evadene, I'll catch up," Sinclair instructed.

Chylla gave a brisk nod and left.

"We need to talk about Chylla. I'll catch up with you at nine pm, usual spot," Sinclair said when she was out of sight and ear shot. Zidan nodded and went back to logging the screens.

Sinclair caught up with Chylla just as Evadene and Aquilia crashed through the Palace doors laughing and giggling. Chylla stared at them both.

"What's wrong?" Aquilia asked suddenly stopping her giggling.

"WHERE HAVE YOU BEEN?" Chylla shouted.

"We went to the market. Princess Aquilia wanted to meet the people, it's nothing to worry about," Evadene replied shrugging her shoulders.

"HOW DARE YOU PUT HER IN DANGER!" Chylla retaliated.

"Chylla! That's enough!" Sinclair said slamming his hand on the banister. Everyone fell silent. "Go to my office!"

"I didn't mean to worry anyone, I thought I was safe here," Aquilia said, tears forming in her eyes.

"You are safe here. Just let us know next time," Sinclair said giving her a quick smile and a wink.

Sinclair walked to his office opened the door and then slammed it shut. He looked at Chylla, "explain yourself."

Chapter 23

ENCELADUS

Zidan waited by the magnesium fire pit for Sinclair, he was obviously running late. He couldn't figure out why Chylla had snapped at him. Aquilia was the leader of Enceladus, who were they to say where she could and couldn't go.

"Ah, you're here. Sorry I'm late," Sinclair whispered.

"What is so urgent and secret Sinclair, you've got me worried!" Zidan hissed back.

"I think something is wrong with Chylla. She practically snapped the Princess's head off earlier, not to mention how she was with you," Sinclair said.

"What don't we know that keeps making Chylla so worried?" Zidan replied staring up at the stars.

"Do you. Know what happened. To Quintara's mother?" Ammyn said from behind them. "Don't worry. No one saw. Me"

"Oh Ammyn, you gave me a fright! Zidan giggled. "I keep forgetting how quiet you can be."

Ammyn smiled quickly, but stopped when Sinclair spoke.

"Chylla told us. She fought with the kidnappers when they took The Queen, but they were too strong, is there something we don't know Ammyn?" He said quietly.

Ammyn looked around quickly, knowing it really wasn't her place to say, but she felt they should know the truth.

"She hid. In the corner and. Cried. She let. Them take. The Queen," Ammyn stuttered. "I know. She told me in. Secrecy but. It's wrong!" Ammyn became very emotional. "She. Blames herself. For the. Queens death."

Just then a high pitched scream filled the air. One they had all heard before. Someone had unbarricaded The Western Wing.

SATURN

"Sorry to disturb your reading time Your Majesty but we have a major incident on Enceladus that requires your attention," Arista explained.

"What is it?" Quintara asked placing her book down gently and pulling her dressing gown tightly around her waist as she stood up.

"It's Aquilia Your Highness. She has unbarricaded The Western Wing," Arista told her.

Quintara gasped, "oh no!"

"Enceladus here, who may I connect you with?" Zeebrakaan answered in a raised voice over the screaming.

"Get me Sinclair!" Quintara demanded. "Quickly!"

"Yes Your Majesty, connecting you now," he replied transferring the call.

"Queen Quintara, we don't know how she did it!" Sinclair shouted over the bloodcurdling screams.

"Where is she now?" She asked trying to shield her ears.

Sinclair panned the camera to show Aquilia standing in front of The Western Wing doors.

"She hasn't moved Your Highness. Anyone who tries to get near her gets jolted away. Zeebrakaan is currently nursing his arm." Zidan explained.

"Put me on loudspeaker," she instructed.

"You're on," Sinclair announced after pressing two more buttons.

"Aquilia sweetheart, step away from the doors, they will close and re-barricade themselves. Aquilia?" Quintara called out.

Aquilia turned to face the camera, but what Quintara saw was not the face of her beloved daughter. Aquilia's eyes were no longer electric blue but a ruby red. Her scarlet hair remained but its silver streaks were now blue ripples of flames.

"What happened to my daughter!" Quintara screamed.

In the blink of an eye, the screaming stopped. The doors closed and locked, and Aquilia fell to the floor. Ammyn rushed to her side followed closely by Evadene, they carried her off to the medical suite.

"I cannot risk her safety by travelling there; keep me informed no matter what time!" Quintara ordered and closed the connection.

"We need The Wraith Doctors, this wasn't a normal thing," Halana explained. "She has a higher power, something you will never control."

ENCELADUS

Aquilia lay in the medical suite bed with Evadene and Ammyn by her side.

"How is she?" Zidan whispered peeking around the door.

"A lot better than last night," Evadene replied beckoning him into the room.

Aquilia stirred in the bed, fluttering her eyes open.

"Oww, what…where am I?" She managed to croak out.

"Hey kiddo," Zidan said with a smile, "a little something happened last night, any recollections?"

"What? No, I don't remember much after Chylla shouted at Evadene," she admitted.

Zidan smiled at her and it made her feel safe.

A number of strange looking doctors came in to look over her.

"She seems back to her normal self," Zidan told them.

"She probably is, but we will run some more tests and, while she has bed rest, will work out what happened," the doctor smiled. She then glided away.

"Why wasn't she walking?" Aquilia asked after the doctor had gone.

"She's a Wraith. They don't walk silly!" Evadene laughed. "Have you never seen one?"

Aquilia shook her head.

"They are. Safe. They cause no. Harm," Ammyn informed her with a smile.

"Ha, at least not those ones anyway," Sinclair said from the doorway. "How are you doing little one?"

"I don't know what happened, why wont anyone tell me?" Aquilia said starting to cry.

"We don't really know ourselves Princess," Zidan replied. "We have to wait for some test results first then we will work it out from there."

"Pardon the disturbance," Zeebrakaan whispered from the doorway. "I have Queen Quintara on video call for the Princess."

"Come in Zee," Aquilia gestured with her hands.

Zeebrakaan edged closer, a little nervous at doing so. Aquilia noticed it.

"What's wrong Zee?" She asked.

"Is it...I mean...are you safe now?" He asked gently.

"Of course, why wouldn't I be?" She said looking between all their faces.

They each shared a look of nervousness. Neither knowing who would be the best person to tell her.

"Oh you're all cowards," came Quintara's voice from the call. "Honey, you zapped Zeebrakaan with a volt of electricity last night, show her!"

Zeebrakaan rolled up his sleeve to show a scar running up his arm that resembled a streak of lightning that would make Thor jealous.

"Oh Zee!" Aquilia squeaked pulling him in for a hug. "I'm so sorry. I don't remember anything from last night."

"It alright Princess, I've always wanted a tattoo!" He giggled through tears.

The door opened once more and The Wraith Doctors glided in.

"We have news Queen Quintara," they bowed. "Would you like this in private or is this to be open knowledge?"

"Please, there are no secrets between us, tell of your findings," she replied.

Ammyn jumped up onto the bed with Evadene doing the same, both providing a barrier and support for Aquilia. They had seen the looks and didn't trust what was about to be said. This would, no doubt, change Aquilia's life forever.

SATURN

Altair watched as Janus returned from another day at college. Watched him open and close the door and make his way up to his room. They had hardly spoken since the day the head was found in Quintara's wardrobe.

"How was your day?" Altair asked politely.

Janus didn't reply.

"I expect a reply when I speak! How was your day?" Altair raised his voice.

Janus still refused to answer him.

"Why are you so ignorant?" Altair asked grabbing him by the shoulder.

"I'm not being ignorant Dad! I'm hurting!" Janus shouted back shrugging out of his grip.

Altair took a step back and removed his hand, "hurting? Where? Should I call a doctor?"

"No Dad. We were informed by the college that a student was murdered less than a week ago. Decapitated. He was my friend Dad," Janus replied letting a single tear roll down his face.

"He...he must have made a terrible enemy," Altair said turning away from him. 'I told him to pick someone NO ONE KNEW!' he thought.

"Why don't you relax here, I'll get the headcounts and extra interviews done form the office," Altair offered.

"Thanks Dad," Janus smiled.

Altair grabbed all the paperwork and book and made his way to his office on the Southern border of Astrodia. Whilst on his way, he dialled Layson. "My office. Ten minutes."

Quintara sat in a state of shock for what felt like hours before Arista ventured into her room.

"Your Highness?" She asked waving in front of her eyes.

Quintara blinked a few time before answering, "It simply can't be! Not my baby girl!"

"Are you alright Your Majesty?" Arista questioned. "Can I call someone?"

"Lyra. Get me Lyra!" Quintara demanded. "Get her now!"

"I don't know how to..." Arista started.

"I don't care! Just find her!" Quintara barked.

Arista bowed and left the room. She knew she would have to be discreet, but she didn't know where to start.

Chapter 24

ENCELADUS

"So...what happens now?" Aquilia asked Zidan.

It had been two weeks since they established what happened at The Western Wing and they were all still processing it, especially Aquilia. Luckily no one was worried, which helped Aquilia a lot, but she had so much to learn.

"We carry on as normal I guess," Zidan said looking through a book on screen repairs.

"Zidan, where is Chylla?" Aquilia asked.

Zidan stopped reading and took a deep breath. He hadn't expected Aquilia to notice that Chylla was missing.

"She's gone for a break honey, things were getting too much for her, and she wasn't looking after herself properly, so we sent her on a holiday. She'll be back before you know it," he smiled.

"I hope she feels better soon," she said looking at the time, "oops, need to go. I'm late!"

He watched her bound away laughing when she slipped round the corner. He sobered quickly and called Quintara.

"Zidan, what is it? Is it Aquilia?" She asked quickly.

"Aquilia is fine, but we need to tell her, she has started to ask questions about why she feels so strongly connected to me," he explained quietly just in case anyone was listening.

"OK, tonight. Video call at eight pm. This is going to be hard for her to understand but you do realize you will then be compromised, you will have to tell everyone else soon," she replied after thinking hard.

"I know, let's see how she takes it first and go from there," he answered.

SATURN

Arista had searched for hours with no sign of Lyra anywhere. She turned the corner towards the Palace and spotted Altair with Layson. She watched, as he appeared to be shouting at Layson, she had always felt sorry for Layson. He had been Altair's friends for as long as she could remember but Altair had never treated him as an equal, always called him stupid, and always doubted his ideas.

She continued to walk every now and then glancing at the people she passed, hoping to bump into Lyra somewhere. She noticed Altair look up at her, she smiled at him and continued on her way, but she made a detour into the shop, almost knocking a lady over.

"I'm so sorry, I wasn't looking where I was going," Arista said bending down to pick up the woman's items.

"It perfectly fine Arista, don't worry," the woman whispered in her ear.

Arista looked at the woman and instantly recognized the eyes.

"Queen Quintara wishes you to visit; I've been looking for you for hours!" Arista hissed.

"I'm sorry. I don't normally venture around the town, but I've been following Altair everywhere. It was him, the head I mean," Lyra admitted.

"What!" Arista said stopping herself from shouting.

"Shh! Look, he got Layson to kill some kid, someone he HOPED no one would miss, turns out Janus is friends with the poor lad! Now, Altair feels guilty and he's laying into Layson for making a huge mistake," Lyra said dismissively.

Arista looked at them both in the distance, it really was true then, Lyra did have the hearing of a bat.

"I'll come tonight, tell Quintara to be ready, she will need to hear this from me," Lyra said before paying for her items and leaving like a shot.

Arista couldn't believe what Lyra had said. Why would Altair do that to the Queen? She quickly purchased a bottle of Lavender water and began her journey back to the Palace. She took a different route back, one that took her closest to the rings that surrounded their planet; she loved to watch as the rocks flew past with the flashes and glimmers of hidden gems. This is what she loved about being a Saturnite; she could watch the universe fly by just by looking up.

She took a deep breath and turned to face the Palace. Altair blocked her way.

"A bit far from home aren't we Arista?" He snarled.

Arista really didn't like him, but she wasn't afraid of him wither.

"Oh, I didn't realize I wasn't allowed out of the Palace grounds," she replied sarcastically rolling her eyes at him.

"Hmm, shouldn't you be keeping our Queen safe," he spat, "anything could happen to her, all alone up there," he looked towards the Palace.

"She's safe," Arista said before turning on her heels and walking off.

Altair watched her leave, 'you're next Arista' he thought.

Later that night, Lyra made her appearance through the open window as usual.

"No, Arista tonight?" She asked as she sat down.

"I gave her the evening off, she said you had something to tell me, but please let me speak first," Quintara pleaded.

Lyra gestured for her to speak.

"We had a major incident on Enceladus last week. Aquilia managed to unbarricaded The Western Wing of the Palace," Quintara began.

It was common knowledge that Quintara's scream was locked up there.

"How? I thought it could only..." Lyra trailed off. "No...no way."

"We found out the morning after it happened. The Wraith Doctors completed multiple tests and they all confirmed it." Quintara replied.

"Where in the bloodline did it come from?" Lyra asked.

"My great-great grandmother. She was the most notable one," Quintara replied. "I had hoped the gene had escaped our family as neither I nor my mother were one."

Lyra thought for a moment, 'if neither Quintara nor her mother had the gene that meant it was promised to the fifth generation.'

"What are you thinking Lyra, I can almost hear your brain clonking away in there," Quintara laughed trying not to cry.

Lyra breathed in so deep, Quintara was afraid she would be inhaled at any moment, "I think, and I could be so wrong here, but I think this runs into every fifth generation, you will have to go back through time to clarify."

"My great-great grandmother was the first known on Enceladus," Quintara answered quickly, "but she was a descendant of the Neptunites."

Lyra stopped breathing for only a matter of seconds, "that explains it!" She exclaimed. "They realized you mother wasn't one! That's why they killed her, had she been one, they would have taken her back to Neptune."

"So why didn't they kill me?" Quintara asked.

"They must have assumed you weren't one because your mother wasn't, so they left!" Lyra remarked.

"Do you think they will come for Aquilia?" Quintara began to panic.

"I highly doubt it. If they wanted to check they would have arrived by now, try not to worry," Lyra said.

"I'll try not to. Now, what did you want to tell me?" Quintara asked as she sat down.

"I'm glad you have sat down as this may or may not shock you," Lyra started, "I know who was responsible for the head in your wardrobe."

Quintara froze, "was it you?"

"Now WHY would I do that? Lyra asked visibly hurt by the accusation.

"I'm sorry, my mouth ran away before my brain could engage, please continue," Quintara apologized.

"I don't blame you. I would probably accuse myself too. It was Altair's idea. He talked Layson into killing and beheading a young boy, Layson thought he was a nobody but," Lyra stopped to regain her composure, "it was one of Janus's friends."

Quintara gasped, "Layson was in here? In my bedroom?"

"No, no, they paid a young girl to do it. Anka I think they called her," Lyra recalled.

"I've just made a sizeable donation to her family!" Quintara said angrily.

"She told The Stealth Raiders everything, she even spoke to Aquilia. She didn't know why she was doing it, she just wanted the money," Lyra defended.

Quintara began to calm a little, "what do we do about Altair? He is going to torture and torment me until I relinquish the throne, isn't he? Well I won't make it easy for him!"

ENCELADUS

Aquilia had arranged to meet with The Wraith Doctors about her recent discovery. It was daunting. They all watched her enter the room, walk around the table and sit down. There were four women and three men, none of whom were seated. They just hovered there.

"Can I control this? She asked them quietly.

"It will not dominate your life Princess. It has lain dormant for ten years; it could well be another ten years before it surfaces by itself again. We can keep a very close eye on you," one of the women doctors said with a wide reassuring smile.

This made Aquilia feel more comfortable.

Two of the men were whispering to each other. Aquilia could only pick out one word, 'Neptune.'

"Wait, why are you whispering about Neptune?" She asked feeling disrespected.

The third man cleared his shadowy throat, "they believe that this has been passed on by someone associated with Neptune. Does your bloodline run through Neptune?"

"I'm TEN, I have no idea. For the past five years I have lived here," she gestured to her surroundings. I know almost nothing about my life."

The last bit hadn't been explained to them before.

"We must investigate further. We will be in contact soon. Stay safe my Princess," one of the other women said. They then left.

Aquilia sat in the room alone and cried. Her electric blue eyes cried dirty orange tears. She sobbed and sobbed, all she wanted was her Mum, but she knew that she couldn't risk visiting. It was too dangerous.

Zidan walked past the room and looked through the window. He saw Aquilia crying and his heart broke. He called Quintara.

"What is it Zidan?" She answered.

"We have to tell her. Now. She can't cope with all this," he replied. "It's too much for her alone."

"Couldn't we wait a little longer?" She asked. "We said eight, it's barely five pm."

"No, either we do it together or I do it alone," he replied.

"OK, let's do it, I just need to prepare myself. Give me twenty minutes?" She asked.

"You have fifteen," he said and closed the connection.

Chapter 25

ENCELADUS

Aquilia had left the meeting room shortly after Zidan had passed by, she had watched him make a call to someone and walk away, his head down. She had met up with Evadene by the crystal fountain to discuss their upcoming Saturnese History lesson.

Zidan found them together and smiled as he watched Aquilia become engrossed in whatever Evadene was saying.

"Aquilia, could I borrow you for a few minutes?" He asked smiling at Evadene. "I'll try not to keep her long."

"Sure," Aquilia replied, "I'll catch up with you later; we can talk more Ancient Saturnese History!"

"You bet!" Evadene replied with a huge smile.

Evadene loved to talk about the history of Saturn. It was her favourite subject, followed closely by music. She particularly loved the Ancient Music of Dione. It was so hauntingly beautiful.

Zidan and Aquilia made their way to the comms room where Zeebrakaan was busy tidying up.

"Could we have a few moments of privacy Zeebrakaan, please?" Zidan asked.

"Absolutely. I'll head over to security. Shout me when you're finished," he replied giving them both a smile and sauntering off.

"What's this all about Mr Zidan?" Aquilia asked as she began to worry.

"Your mother and I need to talk to you urgently," he replied as he dialled.

"Zidan, finally, I've been going crazy wondering how to approach this, did you find her?" Quintara asked before the video link stabilized.

"Mum, is everything alright?" Aquilia questioned her looking from one to the other in quick succession.

"We need to tell you something. Something very important. It must NOT leave this room, do you understand?" Zidan said carefully.

Aquilia nodded slowly. She didn't know what to expect. Was her mother and Zidan an item? Were they related in some way? She sat in Zeebrakaans chair and waited. Zidan and Quintara each took a deep breath.

"I'm..." Zidan began. "I thought this would be easy!"

"It was never meant for anyone else to know, but we have started so we have to finish," Quintara said. "Zidan is your father sweetheart."

"He can't be. Daddy's dead! Plus Daddy was called Elio, not Zidan!" Aquilia said a worrying look crossing her face. "That's why there is such a strong connection between us?" She asked close to tears.

"Yes, I wished I could have told you sooner but after I was chosen to become an Elder, I had to promise to tell no one but your mother," Zidan explained.

"I don't understand. Why the name Zidan? Couldn't you have stayed being called Elio?" Aquilia asked.

"None of the Elders keep the names of their previous lives, in fact, not many of them remember their previous lives, only Ammyn and I were blessed with that," Zidan replied.

"Chylla was in fact Ravenna before she was chosen, mother to two boys who are not defenders of Saturn and part of The Stealth Raiders. Their father brought them up well." Quintara replied. "Sinclair was Reaver. Neither of them know this."

"Evadene's father?" Aquilia squeaked.

"Yes, He does not remember her or her mother but he was very happy with their position within the Palace. He claims that Evadene has taught you well," Zidan replied.

"She's great. I wish I didn't have to keep this a secret, but I understand why. Thank you for telling me," Aquilia said quietly. "May I be excused to eat?"

"Of course. We are both so very proud of you," Quintara said with a wide smile.

Aquilia smiled back and left the room.

"Do you think she will be OK?" Zidan asked looking at the now closed door. "I fear we may have caused more harm than good, but I couldn't lie to her anymore."

"I understand. She never would have had to find out if it hadn't been for that brother of yours," Quintara said.

Zidan's head fell into his hands, "I can't believe what he is doing! I want to just grab him."

"I know but that won't do any of us any good. Leave Altair to me. Lyra will help," Quintara said.

Zidan nodded. He wasn't happy about leaving his wife to take on Altair alone; he was known to be very cunning. "Alright, but let me know if there is anything I can do from here."

Quintara agreed and closed the connection. Zidan cleaned up after himself and radioed Zeebrakaan to return and resume his post. He then left and returned to his office.

<u>SATURN</u>

Janus spent the next few days mourning his lost friend. Westly had been a clever lad, had helped Janus when he hadn't a clue what he was doing. They had been friends since the third day of college.

"Janus, where are you lad?" Altair called as he walked through the door.

Janus got up and opened his bedroom door, "I'm here Dad. I haven't moved since the last time you asked."

"You need to stop moping around boy. I won't bring Westly back. Come on, we have work to do," Altair said dismissively.

"How could you say that? He was my friend," Janus shouted.

"He was a nobody, no one special; the only people who will miss him are his family. You will make new friends, better ones." Altair shouted back.

Janus stared at his father. He hadn't a clue who he had become recently. He turned his back on him and walked out. He didn't know where he would end up; he just let his feet walk. He walked past the fountain smiling as he watched the children playing and splashing in the turquoise water. As he turned the corner towards the clock tower, he looked back towards his house and noticed his father following him. He continued to walk, his feet taking him under the closest ring to Saturn's surface. Normally he would stop to admire the fast flowing rocks, but today he walked right past. He walked onwards towards the Palace, he had no idea why, but his feet continued to walk, through the courtyard and in the door. He looked back as he closed the door behind him and saw a disappointed look on his father's face. Janus thought 'he isn't my father anymore, that part of me is dead.'

"Janus, is everything alright?" Arista asked from behind him.

"Not really Arista. Is Queen Quintara available?" He replied with a sad look on his face.

"I'm sure she is, follow me," she replied gently touching his arms.

He smile at her and followed her up the winding staircase. 'Would Quintara let me live here?' He thought.

"Queen Quintara, Janus to see you," Arista announced as she opened the door to Quintara's room.

"Thank you Arista, would you get us some tea? Tea, Janus?" Quintara asked.

"Please. Thank you. I didn't want to disturb you, but my feet brought me here," he replied.

"Oh Janus, you know you are always welcome here. Now, what has you so upset?" Quintara asked gesturing for him to sit.

Janus sat on the sofa and took a deep breath. He didn't want to burden her with his problems but he couldn't talk to his mother about it. She was dead. "I found out my friend was killed. Decapitated actually. Father believes I should be over it and out making new friends. He says Westly was a nobody and that no one would miss him. I was so angry I walked out," Janus explained.

"Oh Janus, I'm so sorry to hear about Westly. Was he the one you were with when you helped Arista with the broken fence post?" She asked giving him a sad look.

"Yes, he was a very good friend," he replied.

Quintara stood to look out of the window. She spotted Altair at the entrance of the courtyard. He noticed her and suddenly turned and left. She looked across to the Eastern tower of the Palace and saw Lyra, disguised as a very odd-looking statue. Quintara knew it was her. She shook her head and the statue disappeared.

"Is everything alright Your Majesty? I saw you shaking your head. I fully understand if I can't stay," Janus asked.

"Oh don't be daft Janus, of course you can stay. I just can't believe what your father said to you. You can stay as long as you wish," Quintara replied. "Arista, make up the spare room for Janus, he will be staying with us for a while."

Janus smiled his thanks, not trusting his voice. Quintara, Elio and Aquilia had been the family he always wanted to be like, but his life had panned out differently. He had always hoped his mother was like Quintara, caring and nurturing.

There was a loud knock at the Palace door that shook him from his thoughts.

"Where is he?" Altair's voice boomed from the doorway.

Quintara opened her own door, stood on the landing and looked down on Altair. "He is staying with me for a while. How could you even THINK to dismiss the death of his friend? What kind of FATHER are you?" She demanded.

Janus had never seen this side of her and he was surprised, no one would ever think to speak to his father like that. He was appreciative of her defence of him. He felt like part of a true family.

"Come this way young man, your room is ready," Arista said breaking his train of thought once more.

"Thank you. You are very kind," he replied as he followed her.

"Speak for yourself. What kind of mother sends her five-year-old daughter away on her own?" Altair tried to counter argue.

"One who intends to protect her? One who promised, on the day she was born, that her life would mean more to me than my own," she replied. "Do your worst Altair. I'm ready."

He looked up at her stunned, 'what did she mean?' He thought. 'Did she know his plans?' Altair spun around, his long black and purple coat wrapping itself around his legs, and walked away. As he walked, he called Layson. It was time for part two of his plan, although it would have to be altered now Janus was staying here.

Chapter 26 – Five Years Later.

ENCELADUS

"Hold you positions!" Aquilia demanded. "What brings you within the boundary?"

"We mean no harm. I am Captain Smikes of Zen District Five. Reconnaissance Team from The Galaxy Albus," came the reply. "We are on a mission to The Galaxy Begove."

"I am sending some of my team to clarify your reports. Please stand by," Aquilia replied. She muted her mic and turned to Zeebrakaan. "Send Nymeria, she won't take any rubbish. She will find out exactly what they are up to."

Zeebrakaan radioed through to Nymeria, giving her direct co-ordinates and a full set of instructions.

"How do you think she is handling it all?" Sinclair asked Zidan as they watched her in action from the doorway.

"I think she is doing really well, she's had a lot of practice. There seems to be a passageway through our boundaries that we were unaware of, we will have to look into it," Zidan replied watching Aquilia bark orders to everyone who obeyed her.

Zidan had watched Aquilia's behaviour over the past five years since she found out he was her father, she hadn't faltered in how she acted. She hadn't spoken a word to anyone either, which he was proud of her for. It was a big thing to trust a ten year old with, but now, at fifteen, Aquilia understood so much more about why it was important to stay quiet.

Over the course of five years, The Elders and Aquilia had watched helplessly as Altair had continued to torment and endanger Queen Quintara. Sadly, for those on Enceladus, there was nothing they could do as Quintara had made them promise not to interfere; their job was to protect Aquilia at all costs. Aquilia had tried not to watch as Altair had arranged for her carriage to be knocked over a cliff. Unfortunately, for Altair, Quintara wasn't aboard that day. Thanks to Lyra, she had decided to stay at home instead of her usual weekly market tour. This had angered Altair.

His next step was to have her kidnapped. This, too, came out wrong for him. When the kidnappers arrived at the given location, it was discovered that they had kidnapped an elderly woman instead. Altair had questioned how they could mistake an old woman for the Queen, they had no answers.

Zidan had wanted to travel to Saturn to help, but Quintara forbade it. He was to guard Aquilia. Quintara revealed how Lyra had overheard Altair talking about sending a small army to Enceladus to 'deal with' Aquilia. What Altair didn't know, was that Aquilia was now a fully trained warrior. She could take out half on Altair's army alone.

"Nymeria here. All is above board Your Highness. Onyx Abyss Alpha will escort them through," Nymeria reported.

"Thank you Nymeria," Aquilia replied. "So if all is well, why are so many ships and fleets passing through our boundaries all of a sudden?"

"Working on that now Your Majesty," Zeebrakaan said. "We are unsure who has directed them this way, but we will establish a way to direct them elsewhere."

"Thank you Zee. I'd appreciate it," Aquilia replied.

<u>SATURN</u>

"How can every plan I make go wrong?" Altair demanded. "I've been working on this for over a decade. She should be dead by now! Her and that awful child."

"We can't access Princess Aquilia from here Altair, you would have to send someone to Enceladus and hope to catch her alone," Layson explained to him for the fifth time, although it felt like the one hundredth.

"Do you think I don't already know that!" Altair shouted. "Assemble a small team, we will send the men we can spare."

Layson nodded and went to gather a few men together. They would be told very little about their mission but would be greatly compensated for their time.

Lyra overheard everything. She had to warn Quintara but she couldn't just arrive anymore. She had to be very careful now that Janus was living there. He hadn't left Quintara's for five years. He had asked if he should move out to protect her but she insisted he could stay as long as he wanted. He was happy there and so he stayed. Altair had done little that would harm him but he still didn't trust his father. Lyra watched as Janus left for college and quickly dived in through the window.

"You have to warn Enceladus," she managed through breaths.

"Warn them of what exactly?" Quintara asked handing her a glass of water.

Lyra gulped as she looked out of the window, "of that!" she said pointing at the ship currently taking off. "They are after Aquilia. Altair believes if he can't get you his way, he will get to you through her!"

Quintara quickly dialled Enceladus. They took far too long to answer for her liking.

"Mum, what is it?" Aquilia answered.

"Altair is sending people there. You have to hide," she spat out quickly.

"How long until they arrive, Zee?" Aquilia looked at him.

"About ten minutes Your Highness," he replied. "Should we get you somewhere safe?"

"We'll be waiting. Let's see what Uncle Altair has to offer," Aquilia said closing the connection.

Lyra and Quintara exchanged looks.

"Shouldn't she go into hiding or something?" Lyra asked.

"She has been training for the past five years. She has been itching to put her skills into practice. I can't stop her," Quintara replied.

They both heard the door close behind them, this time it was too late for Lyra to hide.

"Mum?" Janus asked before hitting the floor.

ENCELADUS

Aquilia relayed her mother's message to the others.

"What is the plan?" Chylla asked. Having returned from her vacation three years prior, Chylla was well rested and back to her old self.

"We wait for their move. We don't acknowledge their arrival until they make first contact," Aquilia informed them all. "Go about your daily business, I will watch from here. Make sure your ear buds are in, radio silence from now."

Everyone proceeded to carry out their duties. Ammyn, who was now in charge of speech therapy at the local school, expressed a slight worry, "what about the children. In my class?"

"They are here for me. Your class is not in danger, I promise," Aquilia replied gently squeezing her arm.

Zidan and Sinclair went off to their respective offices, Zidan to the security office and Sinclair to the maintenance office. He had added extra protection to the Palace walls since she had arrived, little by little, the Palace had become a fortress.

Aquilia watched as the ship landed on the far side of the landing zone. It had made no radio contact and its occupants had disembarked quietly. Little did they know, Aquilia had access to every camera feed on Enceladus and Saturn. She watched them as they browsed the Market Place, as they made their way past the diamond waterfall with its flecks of emerald. Slowly they made their way towards the Palace, past Evadene who was painting in the courtyard. They made it to the Palace door. Aquilia's plan was working, just a few more steps.

"State your business? Chylla barked.

"Our ship is out of fuel, we were seeking assistance to continue our mission," one of the men pleaded.

Chylla looked between the five men, neither of them giving themselves away.

"Enter. I will request an audience with our Princess. Wait here!" she demanded.

The five men all gleefully smirked at each other. They had made it through the door. More than Altair had expected of them. They were mere seconds from grabbing the Princess.

"What can I do for you gentlemen?" Aquilia asked from above them.

They all looked up towards her; they had expected a scraggy teenager, not a Grand Looking Princess.

"Your Highness, a donation of fuel to aid our continuing mission to Venus," a second man answered.

"That will be all Chylla, I'll take it from here," Aquilia told her. "They mean no harm."

Chylla bowed her head and left with a smile on her face.

"I didn't think it would be this easy," whispered the first man.

Aquilia made her way down the granite staircase, "how much fuel do you need to continue?"

In the blink of an eye, a fourth man had grabbed her round the waist and lifted her off her feet, the fifth grabbed her arms to tie them up, but the third noticed something odd.

"Why isn't she screaming for help?" He said.

This pricked up everyone's attention.

"Why scream when I can do this?" She replied grabbing the fifth man with her feet and throwing him over her shoulder causing the fourth man to lose his grip on her waist.

She stood and watched them both in a heap on the floor. The other three hadn't moved, just were frozen to the spot.

"You go back to my Uncle and you tell him what you saw here. Tell him from me, I'm READY! Now, GET OUT!" She shouted.

The five men gathered themselves together and ran from the Palace. They didn't even bother to look back.

"Leaving so soon?" Evadene said as they ran past her.

"Very impressive Princess. Ammyn taught you well," Chylla remarked from behind her.

"I would have liked it if they had put up more of a fight, I was just warming up!" Aquilia giggled.

"We are proud of you Princess," Sinclair praised from the landing, "look, you didn't even make a mess!" He aimed the last comment at Chylla.

They all laughed about it. Chylla liked to leave marks on the person and the ground.

Chapter 27

SATURN

"What do you mean, 'you had her and then you didn't'?" Altair screamed at them.

When they had landed, Altair had been waiting expectantly, but when they disembarked empty handed he was angry.

"How hard can it be to grab a teenager? Do I have to go and do it myself?" He barked.

"I wouldn't advise it sir," one of the men answered, "she threw me with her feet!"

Altair shook his head, "imbeciles! All of you. Get out!"

Layson watched as they filed out hanging their heads. "You don't suppose they could be telling the truth? He asked.

"Don't be stupid all your life Layson. I know for certain that Enceladent Royals are allowed to train to fight," Altair said. "I think they hid the Princess and sent one of their warriors in her place."

Layson nodded as Altair began to think of another plan. His next hit would have to attack them both, but working out how, was going to take time, it had to be perfect.

Lyra looked down on Janus as he began to wake up, "are you alright?"

"Is it really you or am I dreaming?" He asked holding his head.

"Yes, it's really me. I'm sorry I didn't reveal myself to you sooner, there is so much to explain," Lyra replied. She looked up as Quintara returned.

"They left empty handed, Aquilia is fine," she stated. "How are you Janus?"

"I'm fine. What happened to Aquilia?" He asked.

"Nothing for you to worry about now Janus. She's absolutely fine," Quintara comforted him. "I think I'll leave you alone with your mother for a while, I'm sure she has lots to tell you."

Lyra smiled at her and mouthed her thanks. As Quintara left the room, she informed Arista that they were not to be disturbed.

ENCELADUS

As Aquilia continued her schooling, The Elders discussed her future.

"So what happens when Altair finally gives up?" Chylla asked, "Will she go back?"

"That would be her choice, but I have a feeling he won't give up without a fight. It would make all he has done so far, pointless," Sinclair replied. "What do you think Zidan?"

Zidan watched Aquilia put the finishing touches to her sculpture, "I think something bigger is yet to happen. I can feel it in my bones."

"I think that's just. Old age," Ammyn laughed.

She had come so far with her speech now that she could almost make full sentences. Aquilia had helped her so much. "I hope she doesn't go. Back. I would miss her."

"We know Ammyn. You have grown quite attached to her," Chylla replied with a smile.

"I think we all have in some way," Sinclair said.

They continued to watch her work for a while longer as she added extra details to her work. An outside invigilator would then grade this; this would determine if she passed her Art class.

Evadene wished she had longer to teach Aquilia. She had become the sister Evadene had never had.

"What's wrong Evadene dear?" Halana asked from behind the sewing machine, her hands full of sky blue material and purple threading.

"I just wish we had longer with Princess Aquilia, that's all Mama," she replied.

"Is she leaving?" Halana asked now looking over her wire-framed glasses.

"Well no, but she's growing up Mama and I don't know. I just don't want her to forget us," Evadene said slumping down on a chair next to her mother.

"Ah. Little Aquilia comes from a very respectful family of Royals who have never forgotten their helpers or community. She will never forget all you have done for her," Halana replied, "Even Quintara didn't forget about us when she married King Elio of Saturn."

"Mama, we hardly had any money after Papa died, how can you say that?" Evadene asked.

"How do you think we ate? Our cupboards were always stocked, money isn't everything my dear," she replied. "Now, hold this up there." She pointed toward the ceiling.

Evadene shook her head but helped her mother all the same. Seems she had a lot to catch up on and a lot to discover about life.

SATURN

"So all this time, Dad knew you were alive and didn't say anything? To anyone?" Janus questioned.

Lyra nodded. She had told him the whole truth of what happened including what she attempted to do to the water supply. She admitted she wasn't proud of her actions but she never thought Altair would tell people she was dead.

"I wish I could have been here for you as you were growing up. I've missed so much of your life and I'm so sorry," Lyra cried.

Janus regarded her for a second and then pulled her in close, "it's OK. You're here now. I forgive you. I always thought it strange that he never spoke of you. There were no pictures anywhere of you. It was Auntie Quintara who showed me what you looked like."

Lyra was glad her had had someone else to look out for him when she couldn't, and she couldn't have asked for someone better.

A light tap on the door caught their attention.

"Sorry to disturb you both. Oh my! How much alike you are! Sorry, Queen Quintara requests your presence at dinner," Arista announced.

"Thank you Arista, we will make our way there now, is the Palace protected well?" Lyra asked she couldn't risk Altair turning up and seeing her here.

Lyra had explained to Janus that Altair didn't know she had been feeding information to Quintara about the attacks. In fact, Altair didn't even know Lyra knew. It needed to stay that way for Quintara and Aquilia to survive.

"We have added extra provisions whilst you are here," Arista reassured her. "It's all in hand."

Janus held out his arm, "could I escort a lady to dinner?"

Lyra laughed and took his arm, "Of course you can."

They walked together to the dining room where Quintara had laid out a feast for them. Lyra hadn't seen so much food since her wedding reception with Altair. She caught herself before she began drooling. Janus held out chairs for both women and sat to the left of Lyra.

"Don't be shy," Quintara said reaching for the bowl of shrimp, "help yourself."

They all laughed as they each took a portion of the different foods on offer. Quintara told stories of Janus's childhood; how he was always so scared of Paxy and Plexys and how he was so close to Aquilia when she was a baby.

"It was sad when Paxy and Plexys passed. Have you told Aquilia yet? It's been, what, eight years now." Janus asked.

"Not yet, she hasn't even asked about them, but then she has other things on her mind. I'll tell her soon," Quintara replied.

"This is lovely food Your Majesty. My compliments to the chef," Lyra commented.

"I'll make sure Arista knows, this is all her work," Quintara laughed, "she said you looked like you could do with a good meal inside you!"

"It's nice of her to notice," Lyra laughed, "would she mind if I took some of this home?"

"There's no need, you will remain here at The Palace. Arista has a room set up for you across from Janus," Quintara replied smiling at Janus.

"Thank you Auntie Quintara! I have some much to discover about my Mum," Janus gave his mother a hug.

Quintara watched the exchange between mother and son and her heart ached to be with Aquilia but she knew she was safer on Enceladus. "I'll leave you both for now and speak to you in the morning."

Altair paced his living room. A view of the Palace from his window. He hated the fact Janus was choosing to live there with her instead of with him here! 'Where did I go wrong with you Janus?' He thought, 'you were supposed to be doing this with me.'

Altair shook his head; no dwelling was going to help him at all. He needed to plan the overthrow of Quintara. He needed an insider. Lyra! 'I could make it work,' he thought.

He pulled on his coat and made his way to the house he knew she was staying at. The bargain? Get him information in exchange for her life and MAYBE a chance to meet Janus, not as herself, obviously, but as a new love interest perhaps, they could be a family. Just as it was meant to be, just a little different.

Chapter 28

ENCELADUS

As Evadene and Aquilia walked around the market, they discussed Aquilia's upcoming sixteenth birthday.

"Do you have any plans set up?" Evadene asked excited to hear it all.

"Not really. It's just another birthday really isn't it?" Aquilia replied feeling how soft the turquoise silk material was. "I'll take six meters please."

The stallholder nodded and went to cut the material.

"Another birthday? What! It's your sixteenth. You should be having a grand ball, a huge banquet; everything should be shimmering in glitter!" Evadene said making grand gestures with her hands.

Aquilia laughed, "It's hardly a celebration if my parents can't be part of it. No, I think I'll just spend it in my room; I have some reading to catch up on. I'll probably get a call from Mum throughout the day, and then I'll just sleep the night away," she replied accepting the material and paying the lady.

Evadene watched Aquilia as she interacted with the Enceladents with ease. They loved her. They would send hampers and gifts for her all the time. Evadene had to admit it made her jealous from time to time but Aquilia would divide the hampers up, share them between staff, and return the more expensive items. She would include a letter of thanks but outlining why she couldn't accept such gifts. Instead, she would invite them for dinner, deliberately making too much and insisting they take some home. Yes, the Enceladent people loved their Princess.

Zeebrakaan watched the screens in the comms room with a puzzled look. He pressed the 'reset' button three times but nothing changed. 'Very strange' he thought.

He radioed for Zidan and unlocked the door to allow him to walk straight in. He heard the door open and close and then proceeded to explain his situation.

"I've done everything you told me before Zidan. I've even unplugged it and plugged it back in, nothings working," he explained.

When he didn't hear a reply, he assumed that Zidan was thinking so he gave him an extra minute. Zeebrakaan turned around, "Zidan, what do you...Oh, you're not Zidan!" He managed before he was strangled and dropped on the floor.

"Surprise! No, I'm not!"

SATURN

Lyra began to pack her bags ready to move to The Palace. She was grateful for the chance to be close to Janus. Quintara had been so kind in offering to let her stay there, especially since Aquilia was so far away. She folded jumpers and trousers, coats and t-shirts. She left some behind just in-case she needed to come back here.

A knock at the door made her freeze. No one knew she was here. She took a quick look through the window and spotted Altair.

'Why is he here and how did he find me?' she thought, but keeping her cool, she opened the door and let him in. She watched as he surveyed the house.

"Not your usual standard but then standards can slip right?" He smiled.

"Can I help you with anything?" She asked him making it obvious she was already bored of his presence.

"I have an offer that I think you would be interested in," he smirked.

She hated his smirk, but she decided to listen anyway, what harm could it do?

"I'm all ears," she said sitting on the sofa.

"Excellent," Altair replied taking the chair in front of her. "Now, I know you can shape shift and now, I know how good you are at it. I need you to spy on Quintara. Tell me her outing dates, times, and places. You understand?"

"What's in it for me?" She asked.

"You? Well, you could have what you always wanted. To be Queen. You wouldn't be Lyra, obviously, but we could pick up where we left off, and you could be Janus's mother again." He explained.

"Not be myself? How could I be Janus's mother if I'm not myself?" She asked.

"Well, we could marry again and you could adopt him! Once I've got rid of Quintara and that mistake of a child of hers, you could be Queen. Isn't that what you have always wanted?" He said looking at her reaction.

She hid her disgust well, she smiled. Her smile growing by the second. "I'm in. We can work out all the minor details later."

"Were you off somewhere?" He asked looking at her bags.

"Just getting rid of some old clothes. Now, how do you expect me to find out all this stuff, I can't just march up there and ask her can I?" Lyra asked changing the subject.

She got up, went to the kitchen and poured herself a glass of water, "drink?" She asked. Altair shook his head.

"You'll have to use that power of yours. Shift and apply for a job at The Palace, it's a no brainer. You'll have to work out the rest for yourself once you're in there. We will meet once a week at the clock tower to discuss the week's events," he used his bony fingers to count off each item.

Lyra felt sick to her stomach but she knew what she was doing.

They discussed how to avoid Arista; she could smell a rat within fifty feet. After another half an hour, Altair left. Their first meeting scheduled for seven days time. Lyra switched and followed him home just to be sure he didn't divert anywhere else. She then went home, collected her bags and made for The Palace. She had to warn them of Altair's plans.

ENCELADUS

"I got your message Zee, what's up?" Zidan shouted as he entered the comms room. "Zeebrakaan, where are you?"

Zidan walked around the room but couldn't see Zeebrakaan anywhere, 'that's strange, he never leaves the comms room unattended or unlocked' he thought. Zidan radioed Sinclair, "Zee called me down the comms and now he's not here."

"Maybe a toilet break?" Sinclair replied the sound of rustling paper crackling through the speaker. "He would never leave the door unlocked, even for the toilet," Zidan replied. "It's strange."

"I'll come down and look through the security feed. Give me a second," he replied.

Zidan paced back and forth outside the room. He thought so hard that he began to give himself a headache.

Evadene began setting up the study room for the last of Aquilia's Saturnese History lessons. After this, she would be sitting the exam. Evadene hoped Aquilia had listened to everything she had said.

"Hi Eva!" Aquilia said with a smile as she entered the room.

"Good afternoon Princess. I have a full lesson planned, and enough information to help you pass your exams." Evadene replied placing a book, face down, on the table where Aquilia now sat.

"Ooh, what's this?" Aquilia squeaked lifting on corner of the book to take a sneak peek.

Evadene slapped the book back down, "not so fast. That's for later!" She giggled.

Aquilia pretended to sulk but she burst into laughter instead.

"Now," Evadene began. "I want you to…"

There was a sharp knock at the door.

"I'm sorry to disturb. You Princess. We've an emergency that. Requires your attention," Ammyn announced with such seriousness.

Evadene and Aquilia glanced at each other. Both knowing, instantly, that this was bad.

"Accompany me Evadene?" Aquilia asked politely.

"As you wish Princess," she replied with a quick bow of her head.

Ammyn led them both to the comms room. Chylla, Zidan, and Sinclair all stood outside the room. The door was wide open but there was no sign of Zeebrakaan.

"Where is Zee?" Aquilia asked.

"That is the emergency," Sinclair replied. "He's not here."

"What do you mean? He NEVER leaves this door unlocked, never!" She replied her voice shaking slightly.

She pushed her way past them and looked around the room. She couldn't see him anywhere. Something nagged at her to check his locker. She walked, begrudgingly, towards it, her fingers beginning to become numb the closer she got. She took a deep breath and pulled open the door. Her cyan skin drained of all its colour and her eyes began to shed huge purple tears. She dropped to her knees and sobbed. Her heart hurt. Evadene, upon hearing her sobs, rushed to her side, trying to avert her eyes from an empty looking Zeebrakaan.

Chapter 29

SATURN

Lyra took a different route to the Palace, checking back every few seconds to confirm she wasn't being followed by anyone. She shifted a few times just to be certain. She knocked at the rear door of the Palace. Arista opened the door with a questioning look, peering over Lyra's shoulder to check it wasn't an ambush.

"I'm alone; I took a different route, just to be safe. You may want to listen in on my conversation with the Queen and Janus," Lyra explained.

Arista opened the door wider to allow her to enter. Arista checked one last time then closed and bolted the door.

Lyra made her way through the Palace, stopping every now and then to admire the paintings; they were full of detail and colour. As she walked a little further she could hear voices. A man's raised voice bellowed through the corridors.

"How could you have miscounted?" The man's voice shouted.

"I'm sorry, I must have been distracted by something," Janus replied sounding like a mouse being intimidated by a huge cat.

"It's not a problem Altair. We will just recount. Now, if you don't mind, it's getting late," Quintara said.

'Altair! What was he doing here?' Lyra thought.

"Quick, in here," Arista said opening a secret door.

Lyra ducked inside just as Altair appeared in the corridor. He stomped past their hiding place and out of the Palace doors, which were quickly locked behind him.

Arista opened the door, let Lyra out and led her to Quintara.

"Your Majesty, Lyra has something to tell us," she announced.

Quintara looked surprised to see her, especially considering Altair had just been there, "how long have you been here?" She asked.

"Long enough to hear him shouting at Janus. He came to where I was staying, offering me a deal," she replied taking a seat on the nearby sofa.

"What was his deal?" Janus asked sitting next to her.

"He wanted me to spy on you," she directed the reply to Quintara, "he wanted me to shift, apply for a job and give him all the details of any outings you have planned, times, places and days."

"Shift?" Janus asked looking confused.

"You still have a lot to learn about me son," Lyra said with a smile.

"And in return?" Quintara asked taking a seat in her reading chair.

"In return for helping him rid Astrodia of Aquilia and yourself, I would get to become Queen. We would remarry, myself under a different guise of course, I would then get to adopt Janus and become his mother again," she replied looking Quintara deep in the eyes.

They were all silent for the next few minutes, stealing glances at each other, unsure of what to make of this deal.

"I know exactly what we will do," Arista said breaking the uncomfortable silence. "We play him at his own game."

ENCELADUS

It had been just over a week since they had lost Zeebrakaan; Aquilia was still upset and had taken to spending time alone in the comms room.

"I'm worried about her Ma," Evadene said.

"She will need time to grieve my sweetheart. It is a huge loss for her. She was too young to understand the loss of her father," Halana explained. "Zee was like a father and grandfather for her. They had a bond."

Evadene remembered when she found out about her own father. It broke her heart.

"How can I help her?" She asked.

"There's no fixing a broken heart sweetie. But our poor Princess has a broken soul too," Halana replied. "Be there but say nothing."

Evadene hugged her Mum hard, "you're the best ever!"

Halana watched as her daughter ran off to be a rock for the only true friend she had ever had. She was proud of her.

"She's a lovely child Miss Halana," Sinclair said from behind her.

"She learnt a lot from her father, we miss him dearly," Halana replied cutting a deep purple strip of silk and began constructing a sash.

"She seems to have learnt compassion from her mother," he smiled, "you should take some credit too. You have done well."

Halana smiled at him, "thank you."

He bowed his head and turned to leave, just as he reached for the door, Evadene ran straight through and into him.

"Ah, Mr Sinclair. Aquilia has found something. She wants you to look, please come." She blurted out.

Lead the way child, not a second to lose," he replied.

Halana followed them to the comms room to find Aquilia watching a video on loop. Halana stifled a scream. There, on the screen, was a face she could never forget.

"It can't be," she whispered.

"Mum, who is it? I don't recognise him," Evadene asked watching the colour drain from her mother's face.

Halana dropped to her knees. Aquilia looked at her and joined her on the floor. "I know him. Who is he?" She asked in a soft tone.

"Oh Princess Aquilia, I'm so sorry. That's Layson. My brother," she replied sobbing.

"My uncle?" Evadene asked. "I didn't know I had an uncle."

Halana didn't trust her voice to speak.

"It's Uncle Altair's best friend. I remember him from some dinner party that my mother held after Dad died. His pink eyes scared me so I left early," Aquilia recalled.

Looking back at the video still looping, Evadene studied the man. Watched as he grabbed Zeebrakaan's neck, how he constricted his strength until Zee fell limp. She watched a man extinguish the life of another in the blink of an eye with no sign of remorse. Evadene let the tears fall, "how could someone do that and feel nothing?" She cried.

"Oh honey, Layson had an evil buried deep within," Halana began," he would capture animals and torture them. He was something different, something so very different. He was bullied in school until he met Altair, then they became friends but they were pure evil back then.

"It seems they still are," Aquilia said looking again at the face on the screen. "I don't hold this against you Halana. We will capture him. He can't hide long."

<u>SATURN</u>

"It's done," Layson confirmed over video call.

"And our precious Princess?" Altair smirked intertwining his long bony fingers.

"Beside herself. She won't put up much of a fight now," he replied.

"Excellent! I should have sent you to start with. This will all be over soon and you will be paid handsomely." Altair said, "keep me updated."

"Absolutely," Layson replied before closing the connection.

The idea to disturb the satellite frequency had been Layson's. He had created a device that would block all frequencies projected from any craft. He used it to fly to Enceladus undetected by either landing system. He had landed, found shelter, and spent time watching the Palace's movements. He had seen how close young Aquilia was with Zeebrakaan, had watched Evadene teaching her in the study room. He had decided on his target and made his move. He wasn't worried about the cameras, nobody knew who he was. Now, all he had to do was snatch Aquilia.

A knock on the window drew Altair's attention away from his paperwork. He drew up the blinds to see Lyra on his doorstep. He opened the door and gestured for her to enter.

"Did you have a think about my offer?" He asked.

"Like I said, I'm in. In fact, I already have a job there, secured it this morning," she replied smiling.

"Perfect, what are your duties? Please say it something worthy!" He asked rolling his eyes.

Lyra smirked at him, "of course it is. I'm second PA to the Queen."

"How did you manage that?" He exclaimed.

"A little gentle persuasion and a lot of begging," she said as she switched to her disguise, "I'm a single mother of three. My husband died in battle and I cannot afford to feed my children."

Now dressed in a navy skirt and cream blouse, splattered with food and black kitten heels, Lyra played on her act. Gone were her aqua eyes and magenta hair, replaced with jet black hair and blue eyes, Altair had to blink twice to check it was really her.

"That's quite the transformation!" He blurted out, "you definitely had me fooled."

"Then it works!" She smiled.

"So, what exactly do you do?" He asked gesturing for her to sit down.

"Simple. I check the diaries and arrange transport for her. Her head PA, Arista, tells me who to call for transport to and from events. I know every trip she has planned," she smiled as she sat down.

'This plan is going better than I expected,' he thought to himself, 'it's a shame Lyra won't benefit from her hard work.'

"So there's a trip planned for tomorrow. She is meeting with Major Enderberry at ten am, Lyra continued, breaking into his thoughts.

"Tomorrow is too soon! I won't have anything ready," he said breaking into a sweat.

"Her next trip will be a shopping trip three days later. Can you be ready then?" She questioned trying to contain her laughter.

"Yes absolutely. Send me the details," he replied.

Lyra agreed and got up. She looked around Altair's house briefly. "It's such a shame to give up such a nice house. Maybe we could live here after?" She asked.

"Maybe," He replied. 'You could always be buried in the garden,' he thought.

Chapter 30

SATURN

Lyra returned to the Palace with a smile that rivalled a Cheshire cat.

"He must have fallen for it if you're smiling," Arista said.

"Like a brick in water," Lyra laughed, "you should have seen his face when I shifted, and it was a picture!"

Arista had been sceptical of Lyra to begin with, especially with the story she told, but she had begun to warm to her. Arista had explained the whole plan the night before. They would feed Altair information about appointments and events that Quintara had in her diary, would allow Altair and his men to cross paths with her, but never allow her to be alone. They hoped it would be enough to put him off and that he would give up eventually.

"I've told him about the shopping trip in three days, he says he can have people ready by then," Lyra explained. A thought then crossed her mind. "Janus, do you still have the headcount figures that your father was shouting about?"

"Yes, upstairs, I'll get them," he said running up the stairs two at a time. "Here they are!" He said handing them to her.

Lyra scanned them quickly. She took a second and a third look. "He is scamming soldiers from your army to work for him," she told Quintara.

"How?" She asked. "I don't understand."

"Who conducted interviews?" Lyra asked.

"Me and, sometimes, Dad, why?" Janus replied.

"The people he interviewed, he must have offered them extra to go against the Queen, it's the only logical explanation as to how he has his own army," she replied placing the paperwork down on the table.

The room stayed silent for what felt like hours, and then a shrill tone grabbed their attention.

"It's Aquilia Your Majesty," Arista announced.

"Put her on speaker, we have no secrets," Quintara said.

Arista nodded and pressed a few buttons. Aquilia's face appeared on screen, her cyan skin paler than normal and the brightness of her electric blue eyes was missing.

"What is it darling? Is everything OK up there?" Quintara asked.

"No, not really. Just over a week ago, Zeebrakaan was murdered," she began.

"Why didn't you..." Quintara started.

"We know who it was," Aquilia said. "It was Layson."

"Are you sure Princess?" Janus asked.

"I'm fifteen, not five anymore, I know who I saw, and I have someone to back me up," she snapped.

"Who?" Quintara asked.

Aquilia made room for Halana on screen. "This is Halana, she is my head dressmaker and also Layson's sister," Aquilia announced.

Quintara was shocked, "I hadn't seen your brother on Enceladus. Obviously I know Layson from his friendship with Altair but I had no idea he had a sister."

"He was sent to Saturn at a young age due to his disruptive behaviour Your Highness," Halana replied. "No one really remembers who he was here. I guess that's why he thinks he can do something like this and get away with it."

"We are currently scouting him out, when we find him; do you want to deal with him there?" Aquilia asked.

"No, his crimes were committed on Enceladus; do with him what you will, but I do wish you would have told me about Zeebrakaan darling, how are you doing?" Quintara replied.

"I have Evadene. She is the bestest friend ever. Speak soon," Aquilia replied and then closed off the connection.

"How did Layson manage to get there without detection?" Janus asked himself aloud.

"A very good question Janus," Quintara agreed. "Very good indeed."

ENCELADUS

Aquilia sat in her room all evening trying to work out why Layson would do such a thing to Zeebrakaan. He hadn't harmed anyone. Only one thing kept entering her head, it must have been to get at her, but why go through him and not The Elders. It was a confusing question. Another was how he arrived here undetected. She set about hiring a new technician and some extra personnel for security. She made her way to Zidan's office.

"I need a list of all Enceladents with technological backgrounds, I need a new technician and added security," she announced.

"Are you sure? One of us could always step up for now," he replied.

"I'm positive. Layson is here for me, I've worked it all out. I won't let him take anyone else I love away," she said trying to hold back her tears. "It's not fair!"

Aquilia slumped on the nearby chair and sobbed. It hurt Zidan's soul to watch her cry; he put his hand on her shoulder. She slowed a little but the tears continued to escape her eyes. "It will be alright," he said.

Aquilia looked up at him. She saw no resemblance to her father but the connection was still strong, she couldn't deny it.

"Sometimes I wish I had never come here. I wish Uncle Altair hadn't been so horrible," she sniffed.

"I know, but he is and here you are. You need to be protected," he replied softly.

"So does Mum! No one is going to protect her. Janus won't stand up to him, I doubt Lyra will, Mum and Arista are the only ones who will argue with him," she screamed. "I will have to protect her myself."

"What do you mean?" Zidan asked although he had an idea of the answer.

"I have to go back," she replied.

"You can't do that Princess! Your mother forbade it," he replied as he started to panic.

Aquilia stamped her feet on the ground, "why couldn't I have been a normal child like Evadene? Why did I have to a Princess?" She ran off without waiting for an answer.

"The teenage years have begun I see," Chylla said coming into the room.

"Indeed they have. What can I do for you?" He replied watching Aquilia turn the corner towards the fountain.

"It seems there was an anomaly which jammed and scrambled our systems just before Zee was killed. We have checked with Saturn and the same happened there. We have to find him Zidan. He seems dangerous," she informed him.

"We will step up searches, but we can't make it too obvious, we need to catch him," Zidan replied.

"I'll have Nymeria and her team place themselves throughout the city, he is bound to show himself soon, and he doesn't exactly blend in," Chylla replied, she then turned and left.

Zidan sat back in his chair and let out a huge sigh, "oh Altair, why couldn't you just leave them alone," he said aloud.

Aquilia sat watching the crystal clear water swirl around at the bottom of the fountain. She envied how it had no problems in its life, how it just swirled around as entertainment for everyone who watched it.

"Are you OK Princess?" Ammyn whispered, not wanting to scare her.

Aquilia turned and tried to smile, "not really Ammyn. It seems with me being anywhere, I bring trouble."

"You are no. Trouble here, I. Promise," she replied slowly. "We love having. You here with. Us."

Ammyn had progressed well with her speech so well since Aquilia had been helping her.

"Thank you Ammyn," Aquilia finally smiled, "that means a lot to me."

"Have you been keeping up. On your training?" Ammyn asked.

"I've missed a few sessions since Zee passed, maybe I'll go now. Want to join me?" She asked.

"Why not!" Ammyn said jumping to her feel and pulling Aquilia with her. "Maybe you. Will feel better. After."

Aquilia loved spending time with Ammyn; she liked to watch how she moved so effortlessly.

Evadene walked silently through the Palace, still trying to get her head around the fact she had an uncle she knew nothing about. She blindly turned the corner and crashed into Sinclair.

"Are you OK child?" He asked, "You look somewhat troubled."

"I don't know Mr Sinclair sir. How could I not have known I had an uncle?" She began.

Sinclair led her to a nearby bench and sat her down, "some families have their secrets for valid reasons. I'm sure, if you ask Miss Halana, she will explain all."

"You're probably right, Ill head over there now, Thank you for taking the time to speak with me," she replied.

"I'm normally right, and I would take the time to talk to you always," Sinclair replied, watching her jog away.

<u>SATURN</u>

Altair had his men ready on Queen Quintara's shopping day. They followed her carriage, at a distance, into the town and then forced it down a dead end. There was no way out. The men covered their faces, grabbed the driver, and threw open the carriage doors.

"Come with us Your Majesty," they said as they opened the door, but to their surprise, the carriage was empty.

"Where is the Queen?" They asked the driver.
"Her Majesty was taken ill this morning," he replied. The men beat him and sent him on his way.

As the driver fled, the men contacted Altair.

"What do you mean the carriage was empty?" he shouted.

"Taken ill sir, that's what the driver said. We roughened him up a bit, so it didn't look too suspicious," they replied.

Altair growled on the other end of the phone, "Why wasn't I informed!" He closed the line of communication.

He scrolled to his messages and found one from Lyra sent at 7:35 that morning.

'Quintara ill. Shopping Cancelled.'

'Why didn't I see this?' He berated himself for not checking his phone in the morning. 'Hopefully they use a different driver next time,' he thought.

His phone beeped with a message from Layson.

'Princess spotted. Give the go ahead and I'll grab her.'

'Negative. Keep Recon,' Altair replied. 'Queen not captured.'

'Understood. Keeping Recon,' came the reply.

Altair sent a brief message to Lyra to meet him at the clock tower that evening.

'I'll be there,' she replied.

Chapter 31

ENCELADUS

"Princess, there is a sighting of Layson at The Brightside Cafe, your orders?" Chylla asked as Aquilia painted the sculpture she had finished of Zeebrakaan.

"Capture him quickly and quietly. Hold him in cell five," she replied painting Zee's shirt cream.

Aquilia had decided to turn her Art sculpture into a memorial for Zeebrakaan; she had been working on it for over three weeks. It was now at the painting stage and she didn't want to be disturbed.

Nymeria and her team had Layson in their sighted, waiting for orders from Chylla.

"Quickly and quietly," came Chylla's voice over the radio.

Nymeria gave the signal and two of her best agents stepped in.

"Excuse me everyone, would you all kindly follow us, we don't want to cause a commotion but we believe there may be an emergency situation, we need everyone to be safe, please remain calm and follow our instructions," they said softly.

Everyone gathered their belongings and slowly make their way out of the cafe, including Layson. Whilst the first two men kept the other occupants busy, Nymeria and her right hand woman, Celest, made their swoop on Layson.

"Except you," Nymeria said as she and Celest cuffed his hands. "You come with us."

Layson hung his head in shame. He had never been caught before, 'where did I go wrong?' he thought to himself as he was flung into a waiting humvee. A short ride later, he was walked into a cell. They took the keys to his ship and phone away from him and left him with a threadbare blanket.

"How long will I be held for?" He asked.

"As long as is needed, why, do you have to be somewhere?" Nymeria laughed as she locked the door behind him.

'Dammit, how will I let Altair know they caught me?' He thought, 'how would he react?'

Nymeria contacted Chylla via radio and informed her that Layson was in cell five as ordered.

"Very well executed," Chylla praised, "we wait until the Princess is ready."

"He is captured I presume?" Sinclair asked.

"Yes, quickly and quietly as ordered," Chylla replied.

Sinclair nodded once, now he could rest a little easier knowing the Princess was at least a little safer.

SATURN

Altair paced back and forth waiting for Lyra. She was already ten minutes late for their meeting. He hated tardiness. He continued to wait, getting angrier with every passing minute. He was about to call her when he heard the door to the tower open.

"Altair, are you here?" Lyra whispered.

"Yes I am, I've been here for the past half an hour, can't you tell the time?" He shouted.

"I'm sorry OK, I couldn't get away on time, Quintara is really very sick," she replied.

"How sick? Will she die?" Altair asked with a hint of excitement.

"I don't think it's THAT serious," Lyra replied.

His face dropped. He had been hoping she would just die and save him a job, but she was just as stubborn in sickness as she was in good health.

"Make sure you tell me when she is better and what her next movements are well in advance. I have to get her soon. Time is running out," he said.

"How is it?" Lyra asked.

"Layson is on Enceladus. He has Aquilia in his sights but I won't let him do anything until I have Quintara," he told her, unaware that he was being listened to by Janus and Arista.

"I don't know who my father is anymore," Janus said as he slinked into the shadows.

"Oh you poor boy," Arista whispered after him, "be glad you don't take after him."

It fell on deaf ears as Janus slithered off alone.

"Keep me updated, now, get out of here before someone sees you," Altair barked.

Lyra rolled her eyes and left. He took out his phone and dialled Layson, he needed an update. Layson hadn't been in contact for too long. This wasn't like him at all.

"Pick up you imbecile," he growled.

There was no answer, so he tried again. It rang and rang. Altair began to get worried. He typed a message and sent it off, 'tried to call. No answer. What's going on? I haven't heard from you. Contact me.'

He pocketed his phone and set off home. He wondered to himself if he should try and make peace with Janus but a high pitched ping made him stop in his tracks.

'Everything is fine. Was sleeping when you rang. Have been in recon for hours. Didn't want to give away my position. Layson out.'

'Finally,' he thought.

'Any developments?' He asked.

'None,' Layson replied.

Altair, once again, pocketed his phone and made his way home. He had begun to assemble a plan to lure Janus to his side. He just needed to implement it now.

ENCELADUS

Layson was dragged from his cell and thrown in to a chair at a very cold and uninviting table. He looked around the room. The stark white walls and ink black floor made him feel queasy. He felt as if he were on the edge of a hungry black hole, the deep abyss ready to claim him at any moment. His thoughts were disrupted when the door in front of him flew open. A woman entered, her long braids reaching her waist. Each time she blinked, the symbol on her forehead glowed.

He stared at her for too long, he couldn't seem to tear his eyes away.

"Oh do stop it. It's pathetic," Chylla reprimanded him.

"Sorry, who are you?" Layson asked.

"There'll be no questions from you," she replied sitting opposite him.

He watched as she flicked through a mass amount of paperwork. "Are we waiting for something?" He asked impatiently, tapping his fingers on the table and bobbing his leg up and down.

Chylla stared at him from across the table. She slammed her hand over his almost breaking his fingers in the process.

"Now, now Chylla. We haven't even drawn straws on who is the bad cop here," Aquilia said as she opened the door.

Layson pretended not to be shocked by how much she had grown up. He had watched her from a distance but had never got close enough to pick out her features. She did look a lot like Quintara, almost her double.

"So...Welcome to Enceladus. What brings you here?" Aquilia asked, her eyes staring into his soul.

"Work actually," he replied dismissively.

"Hmm, I don't remember offering vacancies to other worlders, and you're not an Enceladent. Where are you from?" She replied, not taking her eyes off him, not even to blink.

He tore his eyes from her stare and looked around, "here and there. I never stay in one place long. Just come to earn an honest few weeks or months pay. Is that a crime? Sorry, you didn't introduce yourself," he replied his face covered in sweat.

Aquilia regarded him for a moment, his green skin showing a hint of red. She had studied his species in Evadene's lessons, 'a red tint shows signs of guilt and fear.' She decided to see how red he could go. "We found your ship by the way, fantastic piece of equipment. It's made me an excellent bookcase and dining table," she said smiling, "other bits are still to be made but it was a great ship."

"The keys made it easier to bring to the warehouse, strip it down, and recycle the parts so, thanks," Chylla said throwing her head back and laughing.

"You can't have found it, it's well hidden," he replied attempting to make them think he didn't believe them.

"You didn't hide it well enough. The technology is, dare I say, out of this world," Aquilia countered looking back at him again.

Layson had turned a funny shade of red with only specks of green remaining. "How could you have found it?" He began to shout, his face turning completely red, "it was under the marshlands, and it was hidden from everyone!"

Aquilia raised her eyebrow, "quite the outburst, but your shouting doesn't scare me."

"You don't know who I am or what I am capable of," he snarled at her.

"You're nothing special, that's for sure," she replied.

At that instant he lunged across the table and grabbed her by the throat, "I could kill you right here and now if I wanted to," he said baring his teeth at her.

With a flash of red, she spun in his hands and held his face on the cold table with her feet, "but you won't because one, I'm too fast for you and two," she whispered, "Uncle Altair won't let you...yet!"

As quick as she had pinned him down, she had him cuffed to the wall. He looked at her again, the Golden bolt of lightning glowing brightly.

"Princess Aquilia?" He asked he hadn't been one hundred percent sure when she first entered the room, although she looked like Quintara, they could have been distant relatives; no one had seen Aquilia since she was very young.

There was a slow clapping from the doorway. Zidan, Sinclair, Chylla, and Ammyn stood watching.

"There are four Elders. Why do you have that?" He asked pointing at her head.

Aquilia refused to answer; she left the room with Ammyn. "Keep him there," she shouted back. "No chair!"

Chapter 32

SATURN

Quintara climbed aboard her carriage, bound for a lunch meeting with Lady Frision of Adorra. She was travelling from the neighbouring city to arrange a trade deal of silks and satins.

"Would you like some company Your Highness?" Janus asked politely.

"I would love some company. Are you alright?" Quintara asked as he climbed in beside her.

"No, I'm not Auntie Quintara, maybe we could talk along the way?" Janus replied.

Quintara nodded and ordered the driver to depart.

Altair's men watched as Quintara's carriage drove away. They followed at a safe distance and kept Altair informed of their position. He waited in place, just out of sight of the cafe Quintara was heading to. Lady Frision wouldn't be in attendance as Altair already had her tied up in his basement. He spotted the carriage as it rounded the final bend. It slowed to a stop. Quintara opened the door and stepped down. She looked around, surprised to see the square so deserted. Slowly, Altair's men began to closing in. Step by step they inched closer.

"Is everything OK Your Highness?" Janus asked climbing from the carriage also.

"BACKUP! JANUS IS ON SITE," Altair commanded.

"This place is normally so busy with people. Where is everyone?" She replied.

"I think we best leave Your Highness, this doesn't feel right at all," Janus remarked as he guided her back into the carriage. He commanded the driver to return to the Palace at speed and to stop for no one.

Upon arriving at The Palace, Janus updated everyone on what happened at the cafe.

"That's unlike Lady Frision to not make an appearance," Arista noted, "I will make contact with her right hand woman."

Quintara nodded, she signalled Lyra to check the room for any listening devices.

"All clear Your Majesty," Lyra told her.

"I hate that we have to play this game every time we go out, why can't we just confront him about it?" Janus said as he slumped onto the sofa with his head in his hands.

It was all becoming too much for Janus; he couldn't understand who his father had become. Altair, from Janus's memory, was a man with integrity, Royal by blood and loved the Kingdom of Astrodia as if he ruled it himself. Janus had tried to remember if Altair had shown any hatred towards Quintara or Aquilia, then it hit him. Ever since Aquilia's third birthday, Altair had made snide remarks about how Quintara and Elio were raising Aquilia. Twelve years. Altair had been harbouring these feelings for TWELVE YEARS.

"I'm going to head upstairs if that's OK?" He said, "I'm not feeling my best right now."

Quintara looked worried, "will you be alright Janus? I can't imagine how difficult this is for you."

"I'm sure I will be fine. I just need some time to rest, that's all," he smiled.

The women watched him leave, force himself to climb the stairs and walk out of sight.

"This is all too much for him," Quintara whispered.

"What do you mean?" Lyra asked looking worried, "you don't think he will tell Altair that we know, do you?"

"No, I don't think so, but we were talking in the carriage," Quintara began, sitting herself in Elio's favourite chair. "He doesn't know who is father is anymore, Janus believes he is a monster."

Lyra gasped but Arista looked bewildered.

"What is it Arista?" Lyra asked as she caught sight of her face.

"When we were listening in the night you met with Altair, he said the same thing. I feel for the young man," she replied. "He is having to watch his family wage war on each other and he just wants it to stop."

"Poor Janus," Quintara wept silently.

Lyra watched on, unsure of what to do. She had to make this stop, for Janus if nothing else.

ENCELADUS

"Did you find it?" Aquilia asked Nymeria.

"Absolutely, right where he said it would be," she shrugged with a smile, "it's in the holding bay."

"Excellent! Thank you," Aquilia replied. "Sinclair, Zidan, do you want to get your hands on the ship or Layson?"

They exchanged glances, "the ship," they said in unison.

"I guess we get Layson then," Aquilia said to Nymeria.

"I'm going to enjoy this. How are we playing it?" She replied.

"Go with the flow?" Aquilia said shrugging her shoulders.

Both of them giggled and made their way to the interview room.

Sinclair and Zidan were surprised at how average the ship looked; it barely looked big enough to hold a small child. They began by looking around the outside, checking for any off looking additions, but they found none, well, apart from a 'SATURN OR BUST' ship bumper sticker.

"It does seem rather odd, don't you think Zidan?" Sinclair questioned.

"Yes, very strange. Let's see what this button does," he said pressing a blue button on the key ring.

Zidan and Sinclair watched in amazement as the ship almost tripled in size and a set of steps appeared from nowhere.

"Let's step inside, shall we?" Zidan said taking the first step. He took another and then another. After the third, he was inside the ship. "Wow, it's like another world in here!" He called to Sinclair.

Sinclair had been a little apprehensive about entering the ship, but he made his way up the three steps and peered inside. It was a mass of flashing lights, screens of various sizes and a section you could live in that had been stocked up to last for weeks.

They both searched for various clues as to how he entered Enceladus undetected. A constant flashing button caught Sinclair's attention, he pressed it and a screen lit up with all the information regarding an advanced cloaking technology. Sinclair quickly read the screen.

"It says here that the cloaking technology Layson developed can bypass all satellite frequencies," Sinclair relayed.

"So he's a covert programmer? He'd still a danger to Aquilia," Zidan stated. "What else have you found out?"

"There's a message from Altair on here, should we listen to it?" Sinclair asked, his finger poised over a green button.

"Go ahead," Zidan replied with a flick of his hand.

Sinclair pressed the button and a video message appeared on the screen.

"Layson, when you finally check this, be warned. We still haven't managed to capture Queen Quintara as yet. I'm working on a new plan. I'll update you when I have more news."

"Thanks for the update Altair," Sinclair laughed.

They finished looking around and took pictures of the information for the cloaking technology. They locked up the ship and went back to Zidan's office to look over the information. They hoped they could use this technology for themselves.

Aquilia and Nymeria sat watching Layson squirm, still handcuffed to the wall.

"Is this how you treat all your guests?" Layson asked.

Aquilia tipped her head to the side and sighed, "For you to be a guest, you had to have been invited. Even I know that, but you weren't invited LAYSON."

"Who told you that was my name?" He laughed nervously.

"No one. I just guessed. Especially since you're the only other person I know with pink eyes. It was a pretty good guess don't you think Nymeria?" Aquilia replied.

"Oh definitely Your Highness, a really accurate guess," she replied.

"The only OTHER person?" He asked, still sounding nervous.

"Yes. You and my head dressmaker, come on in," Aquilia called.

Halana opened the door and walked in with Evadene at her side, "hello Layson."

SATURN

Altair finished his message to Layson and set about planning his next step. It seemed Quintara would never be travelling alone so he would have to think of something different. A knock at the door interrupted his planning.

"Who is it?" He called.

"Janus, may I come in?" Came the reply.

"Of course son, there was no need to knock, this is your home," Altair replied with a smile and open arms.

Janus stepped through the doorway and shook hands with his father,

"Why so formal?" Altair said sounding confused.

"This is my way of solidifying my decision. I am removing myself from being your son. I no longer want to be associated with you. This is goodbye," Janus replied.

Altair stared at his son, "I'm sorry, what? Why?"

"I know you had something to do with Westly's death, I heard all about it, it's everywhere. I can't be connected to someone who does that to others," he replied. He then turned and walked away from his father, He would never forgive him for everything he had done.

Chapter 33

SATURN

After Janus had parted ways with Altair, he made his way past the fountain, under the granite archway and sat on the edge of the cliffs above Astrodia. From here, he could see everything, Quintara's Palace, the clock tower, Altair's house, and the launch pad. He wondered what would happen with the military position he was given now he had parted ways with his father. With Altair head of the military, Janus worried for their safety.

As he watched Astrodia below, he noticed Altair leave his house and head in the direction of The Palace. He quickly sent a message to Arista, warning her of Altair's arrival. He then scrambled down and entered Altair's house, he looked through his office and found the list of men who had accepted bribes to fight against Quintara. Janus took some pictures and placed everything back where it had been. He left as quickly as he had arrived.

"He's done what?" Quintara asked, unsure of what Altair had just told her.

"Disowned me, that's what he has done. YOUR POISON has turned my own son against me," Altair shouted.

"I doubt that very much," Arista spat, "more likely, he has worked out what sort of man his so called father really is!"

Arista said her piece and left the room. She had no time for him.

"Who does she think she is?" He asked.

"She doesn't think she is anyone but herself, she just speaks more openly than others," Quintara replied dismissively, "now, was there anything else?"

Altair stared at her as she walked away. "How dare you just walk away from me," he shouted after her. "If you hadn't married my brother, you wouldn't be where you are today."

"While that may be true Altair, there isn't much you can do about it, is there?" She said as she closed the door to her personal quarters on him.

Altair spun round and began to leave when he came across Janus. He noticed how differently he carried himself. His head held high and his back as straight as a bridge strut.

"Janus, my boy. I fully understand your outburst earlier and I will forgive you, you're obviously very upset and angry," Altair said.

"You must have misheard me or just didn't listen. I will have NOTHING further to do with you Altair," he replied walking straight past him and up to his own quarters.

Altair stared after him, 'fine,' he thought, 'I'll so this without you.'

ENCELADUS

Aquilia sat in Zeebrakaans' chair in the comms room. After Halana and Layson's reunion, Aquilia had needed some time to herself. She couldn't believe half of the stuff Layson had come out with. How could he accuse Halana of making him behave badly?

"If you hadn't been so good I wouldn't have had to be bad," he had said.

"You didn't have to be bad," she had retaliated.

"Mum and Dad always loved you more than me, that's why I was shipped off to Saturn and you got to stay here," he had shouted.

"Now look at you, trying to kill our Princess, your niece's best friend. I'm ashamed of you," Halana had replied.

Layson had remained silent at the mention of a niece. He had let silent tears fall from his eyes. Halana had introduced Evadene to him. Evadene had looked at him with disgust and ran from the room.

"You will NEVER get any closer to her than that, over my dead body will you try to turn her like you did with me," Halana had said before running after Evadene.

When she had gone, Layson toughened up. "Did you think seeing Halana again would make me change my mind? I'm here for a purpose and I WILL complete my goal," he had said, squinting his eyes at her.

"Will she be alright?" Nymeria asked Chylla

"A little time by herself and she should be alright," Chylla replied, "our leader is more resilient hat we give her credit for."

Nymeria nodded and continued to watch Layson through the window, he knew they were watching. He had a habit of twitching his foot from side to side, flexing and unflexing his hands and arching his back, Nymeria began to get worried, "I think we need to be ready for something, I don't like what he is doing," she told Chylla. Chylla watched him too, she radioed to Sinclair, "Find Aquilia!"

Just as she said that, the window between the rooms smashed and a huge wolf like creature climbed through. He grabbed Chylla and threw her against the wall, knocking her unconscious. He set his sights on Nymeria who had armed herself with the largest shard of glass she could find. She swung it at the creature; it dodged it once, twice, three times. She managed to catch its arm on the fourth swing, a stream of neon green blood flowed towards the floor. It howled in pain and swung its tail, knocking her onto the spiked remains of the window, puncturing her lung in the process.

"Your Highness, I didn't want to disturb you, but Chylla..." Sinclair began.

The sound of breaking glass interrupting his speech, they both break into a sprint, they rounded a corner to the sounds of screams and howls.

"What's happening Sinclair?" Aquilia asked quickly.

Sinclair opened his phone and accessed the security feeds, "we have a breach. Nymeria is down, Chylla too."

"Get medics, he's mine!" She replied.

Aquilia took a breath, her form shifting to the magnificent being she had been trusted with; Layson stopped his rampage when he felt the air change. His wolf-like figure turning to face a new enemy. Aquilia pounced upon him, threw him with her claws against the wall. He fought back, snapping, with his razor sharp teeth, at her ankles, whipping her with his lethal tail and sending her flailing against the door. She regained her footing and aimed at his tail as it swung at her again. She bit down hard causing him to yelp like a puppy. She picked him up by his tail and swung him through the brick wall. He landed in the courtyard outside having shifted back to his natural form. He sat on the floor looking up at the gaping hole in the wall expecting the giant beast to jump through at anytime, instead all he saw was a fifteen year old Princess Aquilia looking down at him.

"Put him back in the cell," she demanded. "I'll deal with him later."

Aquilia moved away from the hole and collapsed.

"Call The Wraith Doctors immediately!" Zidan shouted.

SATURN

Janus hadn't moved from his room after his run in with Altair earlier that week, he had declined food and only drank water. He had been pouring over the photos he had taken, made lists of all the names that were on the papers and crosschecked them with the list he had in front of him. Over two thousand names had been missed. Altair had bribed them. In addition to the names, Janus had a list of bribe prices, some as little as a few hundred, and some as high as tens of thousands. 'Why would so many people be against Queen Quintara?' He thought, 'she's done nothing wrong.'

A commotion outside this door forced him to emerge from his room.

"What's going on?" He asked Arista as she ran along the corridor.

"It's the Princess. She's in the medical wing on Enceladus. It's not looking good," she replied as she hurried off. "Shut the Palace down! DO IT NOW!"

Janus looked worried. He ran along with her closing heavily draped curtains and glossy wooden blinds. He closed shutters and locked doors and windows. He silently prayed that the Princess would be all right. He followed Arista to Quintara's private quarters.

"Janus! So lovely to see you, please, sit with me," Quintara said patting the seat beside her.

"Go on son, she will need you," Lyra said from behind him.

Janus took the seat next to Quintara and she reached for his hand. "You and Aquilia were always so close. You were a gift for us, like a son," she said, "I hope I haven't overstepped the mark Lyra?"

Lyra was visibly moved by what Quintara had said, she just waved her hand, and she didn't trust trying to speak.

The video call interrupted their conversation.

"ENCELADUS TO SATURN," Zidan said.

"Saturn here. What's happened to her?" Quintara asked a solitary tear falling from her eye.

Zidan chose his next words carefully after surveying who was in attendance.

"How much does each person know?" He asked.

"The people in this room have kept me safe, they know enough," she replied.

Zidan aimed his next question at someone different, "Did you know Layson could shift Lyra?"

Everyone turned to look at her. She stared blankly back at the camera. She thought back to times she had been practising and caught him watching, she had asked her mother if someone could learn by sight but Benzyline had said no.

"No, he watched me a few times, why?" She asked.

Zidan described what had happened to Layson that afternoon. As she listened, Lyra zoned out of the conversation.

"...he can't be...could he?" She trailed off.

Chapter 34

SATURN

"Are you sure? I was told they were just a myth," Quintara asked after Lyra had explained what she meant.

"There hasn't been a sighting for over three million years, but I've seen books. I'm not saying I believe everything I read, well, not all of it, but that seemed too close to the description Zidan just gave for it to be false," Lyra replied.

"Would Altair know the truth?" Zidan asked, dreading the answer.

"I highly doubt it," Lyra replied. "Layson always acted dumb around him. No one could ever be better that Altair."

"How is Aquilia?" Janus interrupted. "I need to know that she is going to be OK?"

Zidan regarded Janus for a moment. How he had grown and how sad he looked, "it's not looking good but The Wraith Doctors are watching her"

Janus looked confused, "Why? What or who are The Wraith Doctors?"

"He doesn't know?" Zidan asked.

"I've not had a chance to update him yet. We found out it was Janus's friend who was killed and his head placed in my wardrobe. It didn't seem the right to add to his worries." Quintara admitted.

"I'll take him outside and explain," Lyra offered.

Quintara smiled her thanks and turned back to Zidan. "How bad is it this time?"

"The Wraith Doctors are unsure how long she will be down for, or even if she will wake up again, it's very tense here," he replied his eyes dropping. "Evadene and Ammyn haven't left her side."

Janus burst through the door with tears streaming down his face, "is it true? Is she really..?" He couldn't finish his sentence but they knew what he meant.

"Yes. I'm afraid it is and she is," Quintara replied.

"Prove it," he tested them. He wouldn't believe it until he saw it himself.

Quintara nodded and Zidan replayed footage from The Western Wing incident. Janus dropped to his knees. "Please don't take my cousin, not now. She has so much left to give," he cried out to anyone who would listen. Everyone sat silently, no one knowing how to comfort him. He cried and cried until he rose to his feet and said, "if anything happens to her, I will hold Altair responsible."

"You mean your father," Lyra corrected him.

"That MONSTER is NOT my father," he replied sternly.

<u>ENCELADUS</u>

"Any news? Is she progressing at least?" Chylla asked the doctors.

"Little by little Chylla, these things take time," one of them replied smiling at her.

"She's important to us," she said swiping at a tear that had escaped her eye.

"We understand," came the response.

Chylla sat for a while, as Evadene and Ammyn slept by Aquilia's side. The Wraith Doctors had placed a barrier around Aquilia. It would sense bad entities and repel them. There was a light tap on the doorframe which caught Chylla's attention but wasn't loud enough to wake the others.

"Sinclair has requested we meet him in his office immediately, he has some news," Zidan whispered. "How's our soldier?"

"No change. Let's see what he has, they will be safe here," Chylla replied laying her hand gently on Zidan's arm. "I know she means a lot to you."

Zidan nodded once and turned towards the door, he took on last glance back and walked away. 'You will pay for this Layson, just you wait and see,' he thought.

When they arrived at Sinclair's office, he couldn't be seen.

"Behind here," he called, waving his hand over a stack of paper and folders.

"Ah! So, what's new?" Zidan asked taking a seat on the chair closest to the window.

"Open the yellow folder on the table there and take a read," he said.

Chylla picked up the folder and opened it to the first page, "I think this is the wrong folder Sinclair," she said closing it quickly. "This seems more personal."

"Sorry?" He said popping his head up and looking at them both.

Chylla showed him the first page. His face turned a bright shade of red, "I'm so sorry, try the orange one."

Zidan opened the folder and read it aloud, "Test subject 004. Tested for mutant genes, namely shape shifter, 0 genes found," he was confused, "but we saw him shift."

"Keep going," Sinclair gestured.

"Genetics found to suggest test subject is a descendant of..." He stopped.

"What?" Chylla asked.

"It can't be, Lyra was right," Zidan replied.

"Right about what?" Chylla responded getting impatient.

Zidan passed her the folder and she read it for herself, "You have to be joking? There's been no trace of them for millions of years, how could it be?"

"We will have to speak to Halana. Only she will know," Sinclair said softly.

Chylla found Halana in the sewing room. She was putting the final additions to Aquilia's new training outfit; it had been changed more than ten times since her training started. She looked up as Chylla came through the door, "how is the little one?"

"There's no change I'm afraid. I came to see you about something else," Chylla replied.

"How can I help you?" Halana asked picking up the silk ribbon and sewing it down the hem of the bottoms. Chylla took the items from her hands and set them aside. "We need to talk about Layson."

Halana sighed aloud. "Ask your questions and then I'm done with him forever."

Chylla nodded. She understood why Halana felt this way. "Our Wraith Doctors ran some tests on him. They didn't find any mutant genes, but we know he shifted."

Halana's eyes grew wide, "what do you mean by shifted?"

"He changed his appearance to that of a wolf-like creature," Chylla explained.

"Oh no! They said it would happen if he stayed here. When he was on Saturn, it wouldn't rise," she replied staring off into the distance.

"Halana, what is Layson?" Chylla asked nervously. She was unsure if she even wanted the answer from Halana. She had hoped what she had read would have been false.

"Our great-great grandfather passed down the curse to Layson. He is a descendant of The Dark Wolf," Halana explained. "It only rises when he is in the atmosphere of Enceladus and is made angry. Mother knew what would happen if he stayed here so she sent him away. To protect him and everyone else."

SATURN

Altai paced his living room. It had been over three weeks since he had heard from Layson. He had called more than three times just today. He was staring out of the window when his phone pinged. He rushed to the table where he had left it. He was angry to see a text from Lyra.

'Still no joy with Janus. I will keep trying. Any news on Layson?'

'At least she is trying,' Altair thought.

'Still no communication from Layson. Starting to worry. I will give him one more day," he replied.

He went back to his pacing, planning his next move to kill Quintara. She had a trip planned the next day. He would intercept her then, she couldn't hide forever.

"He doesn't suspect anything," Lyra said as the others watched the exchange of messages.

"Janus are you sure about your decision?" Quintara asked. "I'm worried about you."

"Yes, I'm sure. He has become a monster. I don't want anything to do with him again." Janus answered. "I'm sorry, but I can't even admit who he is."

"We understand, don't we Lyra?" Quintara asked looking over at her.

"Of course, I don't think I could ever make a decision like that, but I am very proud of you," she replied.

Lyra looked at the people around her in the room. Her son, The Queen, and Arista, someone she now considered a friend. Her heart burst with love. She vowed never to betray them.

"So is there any news on Aquilia? It's been weeks" Janus asked breaking the silence that had fallen between them.

"The last time I checked, which was yesterday, there was no change. She was still out, let's try now, see if there is anything new," Quintara replied pulling her phone from her robe pocket.

Just as she did, it began to ring.

'ENCELADUS CALLING'

"Saturn here, please bring good news," she replied.

"Hi Mum," a groggy Aquilia said.

"Oh sweetheart! How are you feeling?" She replied with a smile.

"I'm sore. What happened? I only remember bits," Aquilia spoke softly. "WAIT! How is Nymeria?"

Chylla's voice came over the speaker, "she's fine, if you hadn't arrived and called the medics when you did, we would have lost her. Thank you."

"Oh my daughter the hero," Quintara squealed.

"May I speak with the Princess in private?" Janus asked.

"Absolutely, we will be back in ten minutes?" Quintara said.

Janus waited until everyone had left before he spoke. "Are you sure you're OK up there?"

"Cousin Janus, I'm fine. It took me a while to adapt but I like it here," Aquilia confessed. "Maybe I should ask you the same question, you look awful."

"Thanks! A lot has happened since you were sent away. How much do you know?" He asked.

"I know everything. I've known since I got here. Did you know what your father was planning?" She questioned him.

"No and he is no longer my father. I don't even was to be associated with him. He had a friend of mine killed just to get at the Queen," he replied.

"I'm sorry Janus, I didn't know that part. Did you know we have Layson as a prisoner here?" She replied.

"I heard yes. I also heard about you, how are you handling it?" He asked, watching how her eyes still held their sparkle even after everything she had been through.

"Let's just say it's going well. I control it, not the other way around. I wish I could come and visit but it's not safe," she replied.

"I know, look before you head off, you need to be warned. Altair has over two thousand soldiers skimmed from our army. Just so you know what he has in his arsenal," Janus said.

Aquilia smiled. She had always been close with Janus and she missed him, "thank you for telling me, have you told anyone else?"

"Not yet, I'm still getting used to having a mother. I can't believe my... Altair lied to everyone for so long," he replied.

"What did he say when you told him?" She asked keen to hear his excuses.

"He doesn't know. She is living here at the Palace now, just as I am. Look, I'll hand you back now, just stay safe OK. I want to see my cousin back here again," he said with a smile.

Quintara spoke with Aquilia for a while longer.

"We still have Layson locked up. Halana confirms The Wraith Doctors findings. Layson is The Dark Wolf," Aquilia explained.

"Why wasn't it spotted here on Saturn?" Quintara wondered out loud.

"Halana explained that it could only rise on Enceladus, that's why he was sent to Saturn," she replied.

Quintara put her head in her hands, "that's why he was always so quiet, he had a deep dark secret."

Look Mum, I have some ideas I want to work on, do I have your permission?" Aquilia asked.

"You're in charge up there, any decisions you make are on you Aquilia," Quintara replied, "do what you think is best."

Aquilia thanked her mother and closed off the call. Quintara sat and cried tears of joy and sadness. Her baby girl was growing up so fast and she couldn't be there for her. Janus sat with The Queen and held her whilst she wept.

Chapter 35

ENCELADUS

"She's been there every day for over two weeks now Zidan, what is she doing?" Chylla asked looking at Aquilia as she watched Layson's every move.

"She is studying his ways. After finding out he is The Dark Wolf, we have to be able to anticipate his moves. We can't be caught off guard again," he replied.

Aquilia sat opposite Layson and stared at him. He stared back but, clearly, felt uncomfortable. Her eyes flicked between blue and red, something she had taught herself to do.

"So...you're..." he began.

"Yes," she replied

"But Queen Quintara isn't..." he asked.

"No, she isn't," Aquilia answered.

"What happens now? With me, I mean. Can I go back to Saturn?" He asked.

"Do you really think I'd let you go after what you did to my friends? To Zee? You could have killed Nymeria," she shouted at him.

"I don't remember much about what happened to her, I've only ever shifted once before and I didn't know what happened then either. People said I killed someone but no one ever confirmed it," he sobbed.

Aquilia wouldn't break for his water works. She just watched him cry.

"You don't fool me Layson, you've spent too much time with Altair," she said rolling her eyes, "it's pathetic."

"What about my family? They will wonder where I am," he pleaded.

"You should have planned ahead. Altair really will be disappointed in you. You didn't fulfil your mission and you got caught! You're not very clever at all are you?" She goaded.

Aquilia, Chylla, and Zidan could all feel him getting angry. His eyes flickering from pink to green.

"Well, that's us done for the day. Enjoy your cell Layson. We'll pick up again tomorrow," she said standing to leave.

"IM NOT FINISHED!" He demanded.

Aquilia stopped and spun round, her scarlet hair wrapping itself around her. She let her eyes change to red and stared him down. She noticed his eyes now stayed an emerald green. She laughed. A wicked laugh, "you don't scare me Layson, not you, and not Uncle Altair. You see, since being shipped up here, I've learnt a lot more about myself," she walked back towards him.

Layson was backed into the corner, "what do you mean?" He asked, his voice shaking.

"Well, in case you hadn't noticed, I'm in charge here. I could have your body dumped into the Rings of Saturn, or towed off to Pluto for the Plutons to feast on, but instead, I kept you here. I think I'm being quite reasonable, don't you?" She said confidently.

"What do you want with me?" He began to sob, falling to his knees.

"We will talk more tomorrow. Get some rest," she said walking away.

"She has her Grandmothers ways," Zidan said with a hint of laughter.

"Zidan, could we have a private talk?" Chylla asked.

"Certainly, my office in twenty?" He replied.

Chylla nodded and went off to check on Nymeria. Although she had survived her attack, she still hadn't been cleared for active duty.

Nymeria tried to sit up when Chylla arrived but the pain was unbearable.

"Stay there you silly woman," Chylla laughed, "how are you doing?"

"I'll be better when I'm out of this bed. It's uncomfortable," she replied still trying to sit up.

"If you carry on like that, you'll be there longer," Chylla added.

"Did I really see what I think I saw?" Nymeria asked, hoping Chylla understood.

"Yes you did. We are indeed under the management of a Higher Power," Chylla replied. "She controls it."

Nymeria breathed a sigh of relief, "I'm glad I won't have to face her."

They both burst into laughter. They had been friends for such a long time. Chylla had a deep-set feeling that she had known Nymeria forever, even though it had only been around twenty years.

"I better be going. I have a meeting with Zidan," Chylla announced, "I'll swing by tomorrow if you're free?"

"It's not like I'm going anywhere anytime soon," Nymeria laughed.

Chylla left the medical wing and made her way to Zidan's office.

SATURN

Altair surveyed the area; everyone was in their place, ready to pounce. They had tracked the carriage from the Palace, and knew it would arrive at any minute. This time he didn't care if Janus was on board or not, he had waited too long. He had to get rid of her once and for all.

The carriage bounced around the corner. Altair's men began to surround it. They pulled on masks as disguises and threw open the doors. As they looked inside, they found Arista and Lyra. Lyra, cleverly disguised as the Queen's second P.A, cried out, "What do you think you're doing? Do you know who this carriage belongs to?"

Altair's radio crackled to life.

"Two females. No Queen. Instructions."

"Take them both. We will get the Queen later," he replied. Over the radio, he could hear cries for help, cries to get a message to the Palace, but their cries fell on deaf ears. Lyra and Arista were whisked away and placed in cold cells with damp walls and rats.

"This is disgusting," Arista cried as a rat sniffed her foot. "Get away you disgusting creature."

"It's a lot nicer than some places I've been. Mind you, it could so with a lick of paint," Lyra laughed.

Arista tried to laugh but the environment made it hard for her. Lyra felt sorry for her, she didn't have to come on this trip, Lyra was happy to do it alone, but Arista insisted she do her bit too. Only now, they had both been captured, that left Janus and Quintara sitting ducks for Altair.

"What do you think has held them up?" Janus asked looking out of the window for the sixth time in as many minutes, "They should be back by now."

"It does seem strange," Quintara added looking at the time. "We'll give them another ten minutes, and then we will inform Patrol."

Janus agreed and continued to look out for them. He still hadn't mentioned to the Queen or his mother about the amount of men Altair had recruited. He decided to hold for a while. He may still be able to claw some back without giving away too much, but he hoped it wasn't too late.

"Are you alright Janus? You seem very distracted by something," Quintara asked him, a look of worry crossing her face.

"It's just college things, nothing to serious. Try not to worry Your Majesty," he replied with a smile. "Look the carriage is returning."

Janus pointed towards the sloping hill. His face changing when he noticed the driver wasn't one of theirs. He ran down to the courtyard where the carriage had been dumped and threw the doors open. There he found a handwritten note:

> *I have your assistant and her associate.*
>
> *They may not survive the night where they are.*
>
> *Give up the throne and I will release them.*
>
> *You have three hours.*

"We should show The Patrol, they will find them," Janus said.

"No, this is Altair. He probably has Patrol on his payroll too," she replied.

"What do you mean?" Janus asked, clearly confused.

"I know he has been skimming soldiers from my army Janus, but Elio put him in charge of military and I can't change that. I knew it would happen as soon as Elio passed; it was only a matter of time. Not everyone likes me," she explained.

Janus looked shocked, "how could no one like you?"

"I am an Enceladent young Janus, not a Saturnite. They would have preferred one of their own," she replied sitting in Elio's favourite chair. "I closed myself off to the name calling but it seems Altair kept track of the people doing it and, I guess, they now see an opportunity to get rid of me for good."

Janus was horrified. He couldn't even find the words to comfort his Aunt. He had no idea of the emotional stress she had endured. He promised himself that he wouldn't let anyone endure that in their life.

"I wish I could change things Auntie Quintara, I feel so helpless. I want to fix things. How can I?" Janus asked sitting by her side.

Quintara sighed, "There isn't much you can do dear Janus, but never be the type of person they are. Accept all as equals," she smiled. "Now, let's work out where Arista and you mother are, we don't have long."

Janus ran to his room and gathered the copies of the headhunted names. He had also taken copies of some old blueprints he had found in Altair's office; maybe there would be a clue there. He laid it out quickly. He recognised parts of the blueprint as the basement of Altair's office, which was on the Southern border, "he could be holding them there," he pointed out.

"Maybe we could send someone to check it out, but we have to be quick. Time is running out," she replied.

Janus selected someone from their army who he knew he could trust and sent them on their way. He reminded them that time was not on their side.

Chapter 36

ENCELADUS

Aquilia had taken duties in the comms room. She couldn't trust anyone to look after the place like Zeebrakaan had. She left his chair there, untouched.

"There you are!" Evadene chirped making Aquilia jump. "I've been looking everywhere for you."

"I'm never anywhere else these days. I've done all I need to with Layson for now," she replied.

"Well Mum needs you. Your 16th birthday gown needs fitting, come on," Evadene said.

Aquilia didn't feel like having a big party if her mother couldn't attend, but the Kingdom expected a big banquet so she would oblige, but cry about it later. She followed Evadene to Halana's sewing room; her eyes grew wide with shock. Halana had made a gown from every colour imaginable. Some even had sparkles of ground up gemstones scattered across them.

"Wow! Halana, I'm...Oh I don't know what to say, they're beautiful," she squeaked.

"I wanted you to have a choice of colours," Halana replied.

Aquilia inspected each dress thoroughly. She made the decision to wear the midnight blue dress with the onyx-encrusted bustier. She tried it on and it fit perfectly. She twirled in the mirror and watched the light reflect off the onyx gems. A tear fell from her eye.

"What is it Princess?" Evadene asked.

"I just wish Mum could see it, that's all," Aquilia replied.

"It's a good job I can see it," Quintara's voice beamed through a nearby screen. "Oh you look beautiful."

"Don't you think Halana did a brilliant job Mum? All these colours and designs," she said.

"She has indeed. Aquilia, darling, open that drawer, the one with the eagle symbol," Quintara instructed. Aquilia found the drawer, pulled it open, and stood, speechless, in awe of the most beautiful tiara she had ever seen. Its band made of platinum and white gold, a centre stone of the brightest sapphire she had ever seen. It had surrounding stones of ruby and onyx.

"It's beautiful," she finally said.

"It's yours. It was made especially for you when you were born. It's been kept locked away for your 16th birthday, only two more days until you can wear it," Quintara explained.

"Can't I try it on now?" Aquilia asked, still inspecting the tiara through the glass case it was enclosed in.

"Definitely not, that's bad luck," she replied.

Aquilia promised not to touch it until her birthday. Halana locked it away again and pocketed the key.

"Is everything else OK mother?" Aquilia asked sensing something was wrong.

"Arista and Lyra have been kidnapped by Altair, don't worry yourself though. Janus thinks he knows where they are being held. He has sent someone to recon the area," Quintara explained.

"Do you need The Stealth Raiders? They are without Nymeria for the time being, thanks to Layson, but they are able," Aquilia stated.

"Be on standby please. I'm heading off now. Speak soon. I love you," Quintara replied.

"Love you too, bye," Aquilia said as she watched the screen go black. She stared at the screen for a while before changing out of the dress and handing it, carefully, back to Halana. She then left the room and headed back to the comms room. She arrived just as she received an email from Janus. This caught her attention, as he had never emailed her before.

SATURN

"Stealth Raiders have them both. They are en route now," Janus relayed to Quintara.

They had located and rescued Arista and Lyra in under an hour thanks to The Stealth Raiders. Janus's team had found the basement holding cells and The Stealth Raiders had busted them out.

"That's great news, I'll have clean clothes waiting for them both," she replied, "that was some excellent work young Janus."

He smiled at her and continued to watch for their arrival, but what he saw first stopped him dead. Altair was on his way to the Palace.

"Your Majesty, Altair approaches, I'll radio ahead to inform The Stealth Raiders," Janus told her.

"Good thinking. Now, don't act up. Be normal, be you," she replied.

Altair sauntered through the door as if he owned the place, running his fingers along the banisters and picture frames. Admittedly, the Palace wasn't as pristine as it once was but it was home.

"You really have let this place go haven't you Quintara?" Altair remarked, rubbing his thumb and finger together, "Mother would be turning in her grave, if she had one that is."

Quintara rolled her eyes at his childish remarks, "can we help you Altair?"

"No Arista today with her unhelpful comments?" He asked.

"No actually she hasn't returned from her shopping trip yet, which is strange because the carriage arrived back without her or her associate. I'm giving them ten more minutes before I call Patrol to search for them. Haven't seen them around town have you?" She purred.

"I can't say I have but then I don't mix with peasants," he replied.

"Speaking of...where is Layson these days? I haven't seen him around," she asked.

"He's on holiday. He needed a break. He and the family have gone to Dion for a few weeks," he replied, sweat beading on his head.

"Funny that," Janus said, "there's Bella now crossing the Square and heading for the Patrol office."

"What?" Altair screamed running to the window and then out the door.

"He's no good at being bad is he?" Lyra said from the doorway.

"Mum," Janus shouted as he ran to embrace her.

"I'm fine Janus. I feel for Arista though, that place was filthy," Lyra said.

Janus went over to Arista and helped her get comfortable. He brought her a Hot Mocha Chocolate. He smiled and she drank the hot liquid and the colour returned to her face.

"Thank you, I needed that," she told him.

"Arista, there are some clean clothes and a hot bath waiting for you, you too Lyra. I think you could both do with a bit of relaxation," Quintara said sending them both off.

Altair made his way to the cells below his office.

"Now, this will be quick, it's been over three hours and Mrs Queen is STILL THERE!" He blasted through gritted teeth.

He opened the cell door to find emptiness. He blinked a few times to check his vision. The cell was still empty.

"How?" He said aloud, "no one knows this place exists."

He ran from the basement and checked his security footage. There he saw The Stealth Raiders happily plucking his prisoners from their cells. He was shocked, 'how did she know where to find them?' He thought.

He quickly dialled Layson. He would check he hadn't told anyone about his mission. Layson's phone rang and rang. Altair got angrier by the second. He hung up and threw his phone across the room. He was done with everyone, he would do everything himself. He didn't need Janus, Lyra, or Layson. As soon as was possible he would take out Quintara and finish off Aquilia himself, how hard could it be?

ENCELADUS

Aquilia had taken some time away from Layson to formulate her plan. It had been nearly two months since she last saw him. She walked slowly towards the interrogation room, going over the conversation in her head. It seemed to make sense, so she decided to go with it; she had nothing to lose.

"Good morning Layson, have you been sleeping well?" She asked.

He grunted from the corner of the room.

"Not very talkative today are we?" She teased.

He growled at her, snapping his teeth towards her. She laughed at him and stayed just out of his reach. "Bit grouchy today?"

She sat down at the table and arranged all her Intel. Layson crept his way to the chair opposite her, drool pooling on the table.

"It appears you can't control your gift," she leered.

"It's not a gift, it's a curse," he growled.

"Hmm, either way. I have a deal to make with you," she replied, dismissing his comments.

"What's in it for me?" He asked.

"Well..." She began. "I'll have your family transported here to Enceladus; you'll be banned from Saturn obviously."

"I can't stay here! I'll be like this forever," he cried.

"Well, we can help you control it. We have specialists who can show you," she replied shrugging her shoulders.

"What do I have to do?" He asked narrowing his eyes at her.

"All you have to do is tell Altair I'm dead or that you've captured me, either one will do," she replied not taking her eyes off him.

"That's it? Then you will bring my family?" He questioned.

"Yes, but you have to make it convincing, not just a simple message. I'll get Ammyn to prepare a script. I'll also get our specialists to revert you back to normal just so you can record the video, how's that?" She explained.

"How long do I have to think about it?" He asked, licking his lips.

"Oh, not long. Your wife has already attempted to alert Patrol of you disappearance," she told him, "Altair stopped her obviously."

"Give me an hour. Then I will give you an answer," he growled before sulking in the corner again.

"You have forty five minutes, and then maybe you can eat," she threw back as she left the room.

The growl he let out made her giggle.

Chapter 37

SATURN

Altair sat at his workstation transferring funds to various soldiers on his payroll. He decided not to pay those who had failed, which included the five men he had sent to Enceladus to deal with Aquilia. They made themselves look ridiculous, pretending to get beaten up by a fifteen year-old girl! They were grown men!

Altair's email flicked with a notification. An email from Layson. It showed an attachment. Altair quickly opened it up and watched the video. There Layson stood in front of the camera, a girl behind him bound to a chair. A girl with scarlet hair and blue eyes. Altair's own eyes widened in shock. Layson had captured Aquilia. He turned the volume up and listened.

"Layson here. Apologies for the radio silence. As you can see, I've had my hands full," he gestured to Aquilia sitting behind him. "All plans are green; there will be no further distractions. I will re-contact again in due course."

Altair nearly fell off his chair. He couldn't believe Layson had Aquilia. He should have given him more credit.

"Now for my next step," he said to himself. He reached for his phone and sent Quintara a message.

'Dinner tonight? I wanted to apologise for my outburst.'

He sat back and waited for the reply, and he didn't have to wait long.

'I'd love to. Yours around 7?'

He smirked, 'this is too easy,' he thought.

'Looking forward to it.'

As he placed his phone back in his pocket, he laughed to himself, 'soon she'll be gone, and I can take over.'

Quintara updated Arista and Lyra on her dinner with Altair arranged for that evening.

"Do you think that is wise Your Highness? Arista asked.

"I want to see what he has to say, that's all. We know he will never back down," she replied.

"Keep your wits about you and don't eat anything he offers unless you see him cook it and eat it with you, I don't trust him," Arista said.

"Arista does have a valid point Your Highness," Lyra said, "he is very sneaky."

"That I know too well," Quintara replied, "it will be good to see him gloat, only for it to backfire."

"Alright, but I'll be nearby, just in case he tries anything," Lyra insisted.

Quintara was glad she had people looking out for her. She refrained from asking Arista to accompany her. Instead, she asked Janus in private.

"I'd be honoured Your Majesty," he replied.

"We are to arrive at seven, he doesn't know you are coming," she replied, "please keep things civil young Janus."

He nodded and prepared himself. 'This could be an interesting night,' he thought.

ENCELADUS

"It seems Altair bought your story, very well acted, I must say. I almost fell for it myself when I watched it back," Aquilia informed him as he sat chewing on a long discarded bone.

Layson's Dark Wolf state had returned mere minutes after recording the video. Aquilia had locked him back up before he could do anything disastrous. He growled at her in between bites.

"When does my family arrive? I did what you asked," he grumbled, slobbering over the floor.

Aquilia made a disgusted face at the mess he was making, "that's gross. I'm guessing Bella hasn't seen you in this state, good thing we can control it."

"WHEN?" He barked.

"I've sent my team to retrieve them, they should arrive within the hour," she replied waving as she left him there.

"Get me back to normal then, I can't greet her like this," he pleaded but it fell on deaf ears. Aquilia slammed the door behind her.

Layson slumped on the ground, threw the bone across the room, and then chased it.

'I'm such a dog,' he thought.

He heard a door open and watched, wide-eyed, as a group in white coats floated in. They shackled him and led him away. He was too shocked to attempt to fight them off. They led him to a dark room with only one dim light on the wall. In the centre of the room sat a leather bound chair complete with straps. They gestured to the chair and Layson sat voluntarily, he allowed his hands and ankles to be restrained. He felt relaxed. He watched as they prepared some form of injection, a concoction of liquids, and allowed them to inject his neck with this unknown solution. He observed, in the mirror opposite, how his appearance changed, how he became more like himself and less wolf-like.

He smiled at himself.

"You must have this injection every month, without fail," one of the white coated floaters told him.

He nodded. Anything to be with his family again.

Aquilia guided the Stealths in for a safe landing and met with Layson's family at the landing strip.

"Princess Aquilia, how lovely to see you, look how you've grown!" Layson's wife, Bella, remarked. "We always wondered where you had gone off to."

"Thank you. I was called up to take care of the Kingdom," Aquilia replied.

She guided Bella and Layson's son Zeke, to a dwelling that had been set up for them. "This is your new home," she announced and handed over the keys.

Bella looked surprised, "I thought I was just here to collect him after his ship broke down, that's what your team told me."

Aquilia thought hard about her next words. She didn't want to get Layson into trouble with Bella but, from what she had learnt from life on Enceladus, it was better to be honest. "I'm not sure how much of this you want Zeke to hear," Aquilia said.

"We have no secrets in our family," Bella replied.

"Then you should both sit down, this may come as a shock," Aquilia warned them.

SATURN

Quintara walked with Janus to her dinner arrangement with Altair.

"I appreciate you coming with me," she said as they walked. "I didn't want to ask Arista for fear she may let something slip."

"I understand Your Majesty, and mother?" He asked.

"She will be nearby, just in case," she replied, gesturing to the elderly woman in front of them.

Janus was shocked, "she can shape shift?"

"Indeed she can, maybe you have a spark of something inside you somewhere, look deeper and you may find it," Quintara replied as they approached Altair's house.

Quintara rang the bell, waited for a reply and then rang again. She checked the time to confirm she was on time then peered through the window to see if Altair just hadn't heard the door.

"There's no sign of him," she said, ringing the bell again.

"That's strange, I'll open the door, providing he hasn't changed the locks," Janus said pulling a set of keys from his pocket.

He slid the key in the lock and turned. It clicked open and the door widened allowing them to step inside. Janus checked upstairs while Quintara checked the kitchen. Altair was nowhere to be seen. Quintara sent a message to Lyra outside and asked her if she could track Altair. Lyra bounded off in search of him.

"We should head back, just to be safe," Janus said.

Quintara agreed. They made their way back a different way which took them past the closest Ring of Saturn. From there, they spotted Altair exiting Layson's house, clearly angry. Quintara's phone began to vibrate.

"Hello, Lyra, what's wrong?" She whispered.

"Layson's family are gone, Altair is angry. Where could they have gone?" Lyra replied. "I suggest you both go home."
"Already ahead of you. Meet you back at The Palace," Quintara said before closing the connection. "Let's go," she told Janus.

Altair arrived home and checked the time. It was 7:20pm. He rushed to the stairs and noticed a slip of paper he must have missed when he came in.

'Came at 7. No one home. Rearrange?'

'Dammit!" He shouted. "A missed opportunity."

He continued up the stairs and threw himself onto his bed. He needed to find Bella and Zeke quickly. If Layson returned and they were missing, he would go mad. Altair lay there for a while before sleep claimed him.

Whilst he slept, he dreamed of ways he could rid Astrodia of Quintara. Something nagged at him. Janus had, effectively, taken her side, even though he was Altair's son. It seemed he would have to be dealt with too. 'Could I kill my own son?'

The thought jolted him awake. He was drenched in sweat, his breath laboured at the thought of killing Janus. He rushed off to clean himself up; today he had a choice to make.

Chapter 38 – Two Years Later.

ENCELADUS

Sinclair sat in the security office monitoring the comings and goings of the Enceladent residents. He was content with living out his days sat there.

"How are things going?" Ammyn asked as she handed him a hot cup of lavender tea.

"Same as usual, thank you," he replied wrapping his hands around the cup, "it's getting quite cold."

"I wanted to ask you something?" Ammyn said sitting next to him.

"Ask away," Sinclair said, noting down a few names and times.

"Aquilia is coming up to eighteen. Do you think she will want to leave Enceladus?" Ammyn asked, showing off her impressive speech skills.

"That's a very good question. Maybe we should ask her at dinner?" Sinclair proposed.

Ammyn smiled, "yes I think we should."

After Aquilia had helped Ammyn with her speech, she had been speaking in full sentences with ease. She enjoyed having full-uninterrupted conversations with everyone. She had even become a speech therapist for children struggling to speak. Aquilia had helped her so much, for that, Ammyn was grateful.

Aquilia had been spending a lot of time with Evadene. She had been keeping a close eye on Layson since his family's arrival on Enceladus. He had kept up his end of the deal; he had no contact with Altair since the last video. Altair had attempted to land but Onyx Abyss Alpha had blocked every attempt made and there were many. Altair had managed to send a threat to Layson and his family but Aquilia promised them that they were safe here. Layson had continued his medication and, with Aquilia's help, had explained to his family everything that had happened. They were even building bridges with Halana and Evadene.

"It's strange having a cousin," Evadene said, mixing her paint together and creating a pink that shone brighter than neon.

"Makes me miss Janus even more now, I'm jealous," Aquilia laughed. "It's great though, I'm glad you have more family now."

It still wasn't common knowledge that Sinclair was, in fact, Evadene's father. That secret had been entrusted to her and she had promised not to say a word. Evadene and Aquilia continued to paint until dinner was ready. Aquilia had invited Layson and his family to join them. They talked throughout dinner, Layson was enjoying his new job at the market, and his son, Zeke, was now Aquilia's new comms operator. She watched him closely. She had found it hard after Zeebrakaan.

"May I ask a question You Highness?" Ammyn said.

"Of course Ammyn, go ahead," Aquilia replied giving Ammyn her full attention.

"Well, you're nearly eighteen. Do you want to leave Enceladus?" Ammyn managed in one go.

"Oh Ammyn, I don't think I could leave here even if I were forced," Aquilia began, tears forming in her blue eyes. "You are all my family. I do miss Mum but, I've grown up here, I feel like I belong here."

"I'm glad you won't be leaving," Chylla announced, "I'm sure everyone agrees, we love having you here, you're a breath of fresh air."

Everyone agreed.

"You're my best friend Princess Aquilia and I don't know what I would do if you left us," Evadene stated, one single tear escaping her eye.

"Good job I'm not going anywhere then," Aquilia hugged her hard.

The dining room door burst open and Zeke appeared.

"I'm sorry Your Majesty. It's important. Arista is on line three," he announced.

"It's not like Arista to call this late. Please excuse me," she said as she stood.

Zidan stopped her at the doorway, "this doesn't seem good, let me come with you."

Aquilia nodded and they went off. Aquilia couldn't pinpoint any reason for Arista to call until she entered the comms room. From the door, she could see a very pale Arista and an even worse looking Queen Quintara. Aquilia's pulse almost stopped.

SATURN

Queen Quintara wasn't feeling her best as of late. She hadn't ventured outside in months and she had not been eating well. Her normal pale complexion had taken on a menacing red colour.

Arista was so worried she called the Galactic Medics. They arrived within minutes and, while Lyra and Arista watched, examined The Queen.

"It doesn't look good," Lyra said.

"Can you hear what they are mumbling?" Arista asked.

"Sadly not, they speak another language," Lyra replied.

After what seemed like hours but was only minutes, the doctors conveyed their diagnosis, Quintara was suffering from Starlight Fever. It hadn't been treated on over three million years. The doctors needed expert advice but it would take a while to arrive. The experts were based in The Carbox Galaxy over three light-years away. They contacted them but, even with Hyper Jump technology, it could be months before they arrived. The doctors were advised to keep The Queen hydrated on water specifically from Mimas. A team had been sent there to retrieve the water.

The White Wings, as experts, advised anyone who had physical contact with the Queen over the past two weeks, to be tested too. Arista was the first, she had held Quintara's hair and she had been sick, she had tended her temperature with cooling cloths. The Galactic Medics found Arista to be positive too. Lyra had touched Quintara's hand whilst passing her a drink. Luckily, Lyra's test was negative. She was advised to leave the room.

"Call Aquilia," Quintara panted.

"Certainly," Arista replied, pressing a series of buttons.

The call was answered immediately.

"Fetch the Princess," Arista demanded.

Zeke, Layson's son, now overlooked Enceladus comms. He departed to get Aquilia instantly.

Upon his return, Arista could see the panic and fear on Aquilia's face. This would be hard to explain but she had to try.

"Arista, what's wrong? " She said a worrying look crossing her face.

"Princess, your mother, and I have, somehow, contracted Starlight Fever. We have experts on their way. Your mother wanted to speak with you," Arista explained.

"Mum," Aquilia pleaded, "Mum?"

"Ah sweetheart, there you are," Quintara spoke softly. "Don't be scared, you will be fine. Remember I love you. I'm so proud of you."

"Let me come to you, please?" Aquilia cried.

"It's still not safe my darling," she replied, stopping to take a sip of her water. "Altair is still out there."

"He hasn't tried anything in weeks, months even, Mum, please. I need to be with you," Aquilia begged.

"No my dear. You must stay where you are. You are...in... charge," Quintara finished before closing her eyes.

"Mum!" Aquilia screamed through the phone.

The Galactic Medics checked Quintara's pulse and shook their heads.

"I'm sorry Princess. You mother has departed," one of them relayed.

Arista let her tears fall silently as the doctors covered Quintara's body in a golden shroud.

"Arista, arrange National Mourning. It will last four weeks," Zidan instructed from behind a sobbing Aquilia.

Arista nodded and began the arrangements closing off the connection as she went.

ENCELADUS

A window-shattering scream could be heard throughout the Palace. Evadene was the first one up and out of the dining room. She sprinted up the corridor and fell around the corner. Up righting herself, she ran to the comms room, finding Aquilia sobbing in Zidan's arms. She cautiously approached and wrapped her arms around The Princess. Zidan allowed Evadene to take over. He took everyone aside and out of Aquilia's earshot to explain what had happened.

"Starlight Fever hasn't graced our world for, well, forever," Chylla said looking confused.

"Something is very wrong with this," Layson whispered, his back hitting the wall and him sliding to the floor.

"What do you mean?" Ammyn asked as she waved Evadene towards Aquilia's room, "take care of her please."

Layson looked between his wife, Bella, and Halana. "Halana please, explain. I feel too guilty."

"Explain what?" Sinclair boomed, "what is it?"

Halana gave her brother a sympathetic look, "this wasn't you," she said. "The curse which haunts my brother comes with Dark powers. His blood carries the genetic make up for Starlight Fever. To become infected, you have to ingest his blood."

Everyone looked confused. Layson had been here for years. There was no way Quintara could have let alone wanted to.

Layson let out a sigh, "when I signed up for the Army, they took some blood in case I needed a transfusion due to wounds, it was never needed." Tears had begun to fall from his pink eyes. "Altair had a hold over me for so long. He knew what I was. He knew what my blood held."

"If, and that's a huge if, why would he have toyed with Quintara and Aquilia for so long? Why not just force them to drink it?" Chylla asked.

Layson shook his head, "I don't know. He said he wanted to scare her off the throne. I didn't think he would actually kill her. How gullible am I?"

"It's OK Layson. We'll get to the bottom of this, now, everyone, head off for some rest. I will announce the National mourning," Zidan instructed.

"Can I do it?" Aquilia asked softly. "Please."

"Princess, how long have you been standing there?" Sinclair asked.

"Long enough. This isn't on you Layson. This is on Altair," she said reaching out to embrace him.

"We will make him pay," Chylla promised a dark look in her eyes.

Sinclair sent word for a mass gathering to all the residents of Enceladus. They appeared in their numbers to hear Aquilia speak.

"Are you sure you want to do this?" Sinclair asked her.

Aquilia turned to him, her black gown flowing around her feet, "I have to. I have to step up now. Please, stand with me? All of you."

Everyone accompanied her to the Royal Balcony. She surveyed the crowd. There were men, women, and children of all ages and species.

"Thank you all for taking the time out of your evenings to join me here," she began, her lip quivering slightly. "It saddens me to have to inform you that Queen Quintara sadly departed our lives this evening."

Gasps and cried were heard from the crowd. Aquilia herself had tears flowing from her eyes. She was sad at the sudden loss of her Mum, but happy to see how much her mother was loved.

"We issue a state of National Mourning to last four weeks," Sinclair finished for her.

"ALL HAIL QUEEN QUINTARA. ARISE QUEEN AQUILIA!" the crowd roared.

"They have accepted you as their new Queen," Ammyn explained to a confused looking Aquilia.

Aquilia sobbed, "I wish you were here Mum."

A new star appeared in the sky, shining brighter than the rest.

"She's here Aquilia," Evadene said hugging her. "We all are."

Chapter 39

SATURN

As news of Quintara's death filtered through Astrodia, everyone questioned Princess Aquilia's whereabouts. She hadn't been seen since King Elio's memorial well over twelve years ago. Nobody had any answers. Everyone at The Palace was sworn to secrecy.

Altair slithered in the shadows, listening to everyone gossiping. He was surprised Aquilia had stayed away so long, but now, Layson had betrayed him, and he had performed the ultimate revenge. Everyone up there would find out what he was and then they would blame him for Quintara's death. Altair believed he would be in the clear. He continued to listen as questions arose over who would be their new ruler. This gave Altair a new idea. He had to get rid of Janus. Arista was on her death bed and Lyra had gone AWOL. The only person standing in his way was Janus. Altair went off to set his plan in motion.

Janus paced his room. His mother had disappeared again and Arista was rapidly deteriorating. He had tried to contact Aquilia but she had refused to speak to anyone.

Arista only had a daughter, but when she took up the role of Quintara's PA, her daughter went to live with her father. So Janus stuck around to keep her company. It was devastating watching her fade away, but it was peaceful when it became her time. He covered her in a shroud and allowed The Galactic Medics to take her away. From his hiding place, Altair watched them load Arista's body on their vehicle and fly away. Now was his time to act.

"You're looking a little lonely son," Altair said following him into The Palace.

"What do you want?" Janus sighed, "I'm sick of your games."

"I'm through playing games now son. Please, let me look after you?" Altair purred, placing his arm around Janus's neck.

"What the..." was all Janus managed before he hit the floor.

Altair had developed his own sedative. A quick pin prick and it worked instantly.

"Ah, I hope I haven't given you too much. Just enough to last whilst I take over here," he slurred to Janus's sleeping body. Altair then carried him to the cells and locked the doors.

"Sweet dreams son," he laughed.

ENCELADUS

It had been six months since Queen Quintara had passed. There had been no state funeral due to her body being held on suspicion of murder. Layson had called The Saturnese Patrol and informed them of Altair's possible involvement in her death. They promised to investigate but Layson told Zidan that Altair had patrol on payroll too.

"I'm sorry Princess, I really wanted to help," Layson said as he ended the call with Patrol.

Aquilia smiled, only the briefest of smiles. She walked away and found herself at the crystal fountain. She had received word that Arista had succumbed to Starlight Fever also. He had added that Lyra was AWOL, which worried Aquilia. She could have killed her mother to take over as Queen, just like Altair had planned. Aquilia refused to reply.

"Aquilia?" Halana's voice came from behind her.

Aquilia looked up at her, her blue eyes filling with new purple tears.

"Oh come now," Halana pulled her close, "it's alright to be upset. You should never hide your emotions, especially when you have so many of us who care."

"I'm sorry. I just can't believe she's gone," she cried.

"I know. Just let it all out," Halana replied.

Zidan and Sinclair had tightened security since Altair's last attempt to enter Enceladus.

"Do you think he's given up yet?" Sinclair asked as they checked the footage from the night before.

"He won't give up until he gets what he wants," Zidan replied.

"Then we have another thing to do," Sinclair said. "We have to make him think that Aquilia is dead. It will stop him chasing her."

Zidan looked shocked, "we can't do that! Aquilia has rights, that throne is rightfully hers."

"Oh Zidan, don't you see? Altair will continue to attack the whole time he knows she is alive, we have to protect everyone, including Aquilia," Sinclair explained.

"No," said Zidan, "I won't allow it."

"As you wish, but trust me, it will only get worse," Sinclair informed him.

"We'll deal with it when and if it happens," Zidan replied, closing the door as he left the room.

SATURN

Altair entered the Palace via the front door. He looked around and smiled to himself. He had visions of how he would change the place once he had fully taken over. He sent a memo out to all the residents of the Kingdom stating there would be an announcement of the new ruler at 4pm. He raided Elio's old clothes, trying to find something regal looking.

"Urgh, this is all pitiful," he spat.

He threw open the nearest cupboard and his eyes lit up. There sat every one of Elio's crowns.

"Now, this is more like it," he said as he picked up the largest one there and placed it on his head. He looked at himself in the floor to ceiling mirror, turning left and right, he decided this one was best.

He sat himself at Elio's old desk and made a start on his speech. He would be so much better as King. This Kingdom needed a ruthless leader, not a pushover.

Janus awoke into pure darkness. He opened his hands to feel around. His hands touched the cold, damp walls of the cell. He fumbled around for his phone, hoping his battery would hold out. He flicked his torched on and looked around. The cell walls were almost black with moss and cold to the touch. Janus instantly recognised where he was. He hoped his signal was strong enough to send out a message. He pulled up the app and began typing;

'Altair is preparing to take over. I'm locked in the cells under the Palace. Send help please.'

He hit send just as his phone gave out. He hoped the message would be delivered. Heading for the corner, he curled himself into a ball and fell to sleep, praying his message would be received.

Altair put the final additions to his speech just as his email pinged to life. There sat a message from an unknown sender complete with attachment. Altair decided to ignore it and set about preparing for his new role as King of Astrodia. He dressed the part and placed the crown on his head, unaware of what was about to occur.

ENCELADUS

Aquilia ran in search of Sinclair. She searched every room she could think of but he was no-where to be found. She sat and thought of any other places he could be. She felt a hand on her shoulder and looked up into the eyes of Layson.

"Are you OK Princess?" He asked kindly.

"Have you seen Sinclair?" She asked, ignoring his question.

"Last time I saw him he was with my sister at the fountain. I think he has a soft spot for her," he replied, little did he know they had created Evadene together.

"Thank you," she said and ran off in search of him.

"Give her time Uncle Layson, she's fragile," Evadene said from behind him. She had been calling him 'uncle' now and then, testing to see if he lived up to the name. She had also been spending time with her cousin, Zeke. He was funny but still quite shy around her. She hoped he would open up more soon.

Aquilia skidded to a stop in front of Sinclair and Halana, struggling to get her words out. Halana took some water from the fountain and gave it to her. Aquilia drank slowly, finally able to string a sentence together.

"Thank you. Janus has been imprisoned by Altair. He's preparing to take over Astrodia," she managed.

"He can't possibly so that without you being dead Your Highness," Halana replied with a confused look on her face.

Sinclair sighed, "He believes she is already dead."

Both women looked at him in shock.

"What do you mean Sinclair?" Aquilia asked, slowly backing away from him.

Sinclair stood, took a step towards her, his hands outstretched, "I enlisted the help of Chylla to create a fake video to be released only to a handful of people, particularly close adversaries to Altair that you had died of a broken heart after losing your mother."

"I didn't play any part in this, how would anyone know or even believe it?" Aquilia questioned.

"I helped," came Lyra's voice from behind her. "It was the only way to keep you safe."

Halana threw Sinclair a disgusted look and ran away. Aquilia turned to Lyra, "to protect me, you put your own SON in danger."

"What do you mean? Lyra asked.

Aquilia showed her the message, Lyra's face lost all it colour.

"What's your plan?" She asked visibly shaking.

"I'm taking what's mine," Aquilia replied.

Chapter 40

ENCELADUS

"Princess, what exactly are you doing?" Zidan asked as Aquilia began scouting the military files for their best fighters.

"Taking back what's rightfully mine," she replied, sending messages to everyone she deemed fit for purpose.

"What do you mean?" Zidan questioned, taking some of the papers from her.

"Sinclair didn't tell you either I take it," she replied flopping down onto the nearest unoccupied space.

"Tell me what?" Zidan sat with her, clearly as confused as she was.

She watched him for a moment, still trying to comprehend how this man could possibly be her father and not understand how she felt. She took a deep breath and explained everything Sinclair had told her. There was a sharp intake of breath from the shadows.

"Who's there?" Aquilia stood, bracing herself for a fight.

Ammyn emerged from the shadows, her hands in a defence position. "I'm sorry, I came in as you were talking and I didn't want to interrupt."

Aquilia relaxed a little, "next time, at least knock something over so I know you're there," she said with a smile.

Ammyn nodded, "is it true?"

"I'm afraid so. I told him not to do it, but he wouldn't listen," Zidan said, pacing his office.

"Wait. You KNEW he had these plans and you didn't think to at least WARN me?" Aquilia raised her voice.

"Having thought about it Princess, maybe he had a partial idea. Your people on Enceladus need you," Zidan replied turning to face her.

Aquilia's eyes flickered red, "my people are on Saturn too! They need me more than the Enceladus right now!" She shouted as her phone pinged with multiple replies to her commands. "I have Onyx Abyss Alpha on standby, along with Nymeria and The Stealth Raiders. I'm doing this with or without you," Aquilia stated, hot tears running down her cheeks.

"I will help," Ammyn offered. "I have you back."

Aquilia smiled at the first friend she had made when she arrived here over twelve years ago. "Thank you Ammyn."

Ammyn nodded briskly and went off to prepare.

Aquilia turned to her father, "do I have your blessing or do I break the chain of command?"

Zidan looked out onto the courtyard where over three thousand soldiers had assembled, waiting for further instructions, he grabbed her head and kissed the lightning bolt, "go. Take your seat upon the Throne of Saturn, you have earned it."

Tears flowed down her face as she threw her hair into a flowing French plait of scarlet and silver. She turned and left Zidan to watch her command her army, he watched as they departed the safe haven of Enceladus into battle with Altair. Aquilia climbed into her own pod and took off like a slingshot. Bound for Saturn.

SATURN

As Altair practised his speech in front of the mirror, he admired how he looked wearing the most expensive crown Elio had owned. Platinum encrusted with emeralds and sapphires. The centrepiece boasting the rarest ruby ever known, mined from Plateaux in the Kintel Andromeda over one trillion light years away. As he twisted this way and that, he noticed little flashes in the sky every now and then. He walked to the window just as his phone buzzed. He saw another message from the same address as before. He angrily opened the attachment. A video of an angry Princess Aquilia sprang to life. His face paled.

"I'm coming for my throne Uncle Altair. Nothing you can do will stop me," she said, her eyes flickered between blue and red, "fight me if you must but I WILL TAKE WHAT'S MINE!"

The video cut off. Altair stood motionless. Minutes passed, he still stared at the blank screen of his phone. He blinked once, twice then sent commands to his own army to prepare for battle. "I'm not going to let a CHILD ruin my only chance," he screamed as he threw the crown against the mirror, which then shattered into million pieces. He stormed out of the Palace and met with his army in the courtyard.

"I was wrongly informed of Aquilia's death," he began. "She is en-route prepared for battle. Some of her army are already arriving," he gestured towards the glistening streaks in the sky.

"What are your commands sir?" A greying man asked from his right side.

"Fight to kill," Altair said, his face and eyes never leaving the sky, "but the Princess is mine."

"Orders Princess?" Nymeria's voice interrupted Aquilia's thoughts.

"You and Celest track down Janus, make sure he is alright, and then join me up front," she replied.

The two pods either side of her swayed left and right. She knew where to head. The Palace had a secret landing area on the Northern side that nobody knew about. She swung her pod in that direction. She could see the battle had already begun below. The sight of so much bloodshed made her angry. 'Why couldn't we have been a normal family?' She thought as she allowed her pod to make a silent landing. The pod opened and she set foot back on Saturn for the first time in over twelve years. She scanned the area, expecting an ambush. There was no sign on anyone in the vicinity. Her radio crackled to life.

"Found him, he's fine. He wants to join," Celest informed her.

"Is he aware its fight to the death, I will take no prisoners," she replied.

"I understand Princess," Janus replied. "I stand wholly by your side."

"Very well. Join Nymeria and Celest, we are losing comrades, back them up," Aquilia replied and muted her radio. She ran up the sloping roof and surveyed the scene below before making her next move.

ENCELADUS

Zidan watched the scene unfold on the screen. Sinclair touched his shoulder briefly before Zidan shook him off.

"I can't believe you actually went through with it," Zidan said softly. "How could you?"

"I thought it would be for the best. She would eventually forget about Saturn and remain here with us," Sinclair admitted.

"How could she forget about Saturn? It was her home, she was born there, and it's in her blood!" Zidan reminded him. "No matter how long it took, she would have gone back, eventually."

Sinclair bowed his head and, reluctantly, left the room, knowing her had broken a close bond with Zidan and, possibly, with Halana. He decided to go in search of her to explain himself. As he turned the corner, he ran into Layson.

"Maybe leave her a while, she's not good," he said kindly. "I understand why you did it, but it doesn't make it right."

Sinclair began to plead his innocence when Chylla appeared.

"You told them?" She demanded.

"I had no choice. Janus had been captured and he managed to get word to Aquilia that Altair was taking over," Sinclair replied, his energy drained.

"Where is she? Let me explain," Chylla asked frantically.

"You're too late Chylla," Evadene replied looking up from her phone. "She's already gone."

Chylla ran to the security room just in time to witness Aquilia ascend the Palace roof and single out her victim. They all watched as she gracefully slid down the roof, landing directly in Altair's path.

"Hello Uncle," she purred, circling him.

"P...Princess, thank goodness, you're alive! I've been so worried!" Altair said faking a worried tone.

"Cut it out Uncle," Aquilia spat, "you don't fool me. I know it was you all along."

"Then you know how ruthless I can be," Altair smiled just as he attempted to plunge the syringe into her neck.

She caught his hand and twisted his wrist back. He dropped the syringe and then stepped on the glass shattering it and allowing its contents to spill on the ground. He glared at her with his deep brown eyes, trying to hypnotise her into making a mistake, but she wasn't so easily distracted. She swung her French braid around Altair's waist and held him in a chokehold, her arm becoming a vicious boa constrictor. Altair twisted, turned, and finally managed to free himself from her grip. He ran, fast, across the courtyard, turned left and ran away from The Palace. Aquilia smiled. She'd let him run, for now.

SATURN

Nymeria and Celest gave as good as they got. Soldiers were coming at them from all directions. They passed a few of their fallen comrades, covering them over as they passed.

"You good back there?" Nymeria asked Janus.

"I guess, I can't believe how well I know so many of these people, it's heartbreaking to think they would kill their own for money," Janus replied.

"Ha, you need to get out more," Celest laughed. "Money talks to all evil my boy. ALL EVIL."

Janus smiled, "I see what you mean," he pointed to a slain soldier, "his father was a fraud and a con artist."

Janus felt comfortable with this new level of freedom. Having finally come to terms with the monster his father was, he wanted a new life. He looked up just as Altair ran across in front of them, Janus picked up his pace. Nymeria stopped him, "Altair is for the Princess to deal with."

He nodded and fell back in step with them. They made their way through countless Saturnese corpses. Took notes of those friends they had lost. Only a handful but still a loss. As Nymeria turned to speak to Janus, she noticed he had gone.

Chapter 41

SATURN

"Not running away are you?" Janus asked Altair.

"Janus! Where have you been? Princess Aquilia and her Enceladent army are attacking Saturn. You must fight against them," Altair replied sounding distressed.

Janus shook his head and laughed, "you know, I used to admire you, look up to you even, but I always wondered why you were never King, now I know."

"What do you mean?" Altair asked clearly puzzled by Janus's statement.

Janus laughed again, harder this time, "You're a coward. It's plain to see. Why are you running from a girl?"

Altair glared at Janus, his deep brown eyes flickered black, "you have no idea who I am boy!" He said as his eyes remained black and, from his back, giant black-webbed wings spawned.

Janus jumped back, his green eyes wide with shock, from behind him; he could hear fast approaching footsteps. They got louder and then ceased.

"Why did you take off like that?" Nymeria asked, "and what is THAT?" She said pointing at Altair.

"That's Altair. Well it was, I have no idea what it is now," he replied unable to look away.

Celest radioed Zidan back on Enceladus.

"Little help required, what is that?" She asked pointing at the creature Altair had become. She knew they could see them. "I need an answer fast and also a way to get rid?"

Janus hadn't moved. He just watched as this creature grew before him. A dark shadow shielding them from what little sunlight they had. Nymeria, Celest, and Janus needed help and they needed it fast.

ENCELADUS

Zidan stared at the screen, 'what was that?' He thought. A shadow caught his eye.

"Evadene?" He called.

"Yes Mr Zidan," she replied, her head appearing in the doorway.

"You're good with Saturnese history right?" He asked pointing at the screen.

Evadene entered the room, her eyes fixated on the screen. She tilted her head to one side and then to the other. She gasped and opened the only book she carried everywhere with her. She flicked through the pages and came to a stop at a webbed winged creature.

"That's it," she said pointing to the book, "it's a web-winged Libat."

Zidan stared at her and then at the picture. It was a strange looking thing. He looked at the screen where Altair's new form had emerged. It was strikingly similar. A large orange mane had formed around Altair's neck, his once dark brown eyes now as black as the deepest reaches of a black hole. He, now, strutted around on four legs with large black wings spread behind him. Had he not been made of pure evil, he would have been a magnificent creature.

"Can it be killed?" Zidan asked slowly turning to face the young girl.

Evadene nodded, "it can, but it isn't easy."

"Explain to me young lady, what do we need to do?" He asked, taking a seat next to her.

Evadene gulped and proceeded to explain what the book outlined.

"There has to be a sacrifice..." She began.

"I thought he was different," Halana cried, "I haven't felt this close to anyone since Reaver."

"What happened?" Layson asked, he had so much to catch up on. Halana was slowly letting him into her life despite wanting nothing to do with him at first.

He died protecting Enceladus from Neptune, he was a good man," she replied, wiping her eyes.

Layson smiled, "he sounds like it."

They sat together for a while in silence. Neither knowing what to say to the other.

"Dad," Zeke called.

"Sorry son, what is it?" Layson replied.

"Mr Zidan would like to see you both. There's a meeting. Everyone is there," he informed them.

They exchanged glances and followed Zeke.

"I wonder what it's about," whispered Layson.

"I hope it's nothing bad," Halana replied.

<u>SATURN</u>

"Any way round that last bit?" Nymeria asked into her radio, her eyes rolling at the answer.

Celest watched Janus continue to stare at the, now, gigantic creature. She focused on how Janus studied the creatures' movements.

"OK, so we now know, this is a Libat," Nymeria began, "the rest is slightly less easy to explain."

"Try," Janus said, not taking his eyes off Altair.

Nymeria took a deep breath and said, "the only way to completely rid the planet of him is to sacrifice someone special."

"Like who?" Celest asked, "the only thing special to THAT thing is ITSELF!"

"The others are looking into it now, we have to be patient and keep it here."

"Erm, too late for that," Janus said pointing at the Libat as his strode away.

Nymeria growled her anger. It made Janus's heart flutter. She stomped past him, following the giant beast, shouting warnings as she went so others could flee from its giant paws. Celest and Janus followed along behind. It strode back towards Princess Aquilia who had her back to them. As Janus began to call out to her, the Libat kicked out sending Janus sprawling into the nearby wall. Aquilia turned just in time to see the gigantic paw about to swipe at her. She jumped out of the way just in time. The creature let out a soul-shattering roar.

"What is that?" Aquilia screeched, scrambling to regain her balance.

"Species or name?" Celest asked, helping her to her feet.

"Name?" Aquilia replied clearly puzzled.

"It's Altair," Janus replied, climbing to his feet, a large gash on his head had started to drip blood.

Aquilia shook her head as if trying to clear away fog.

"Altair?" She asked.

"Yes, he appears to hold a dark secret himself. He is a Libat," Nymeria replied, "and there's only one way to kill it."

"Which is?" Aquilia asked shrugging.

"The sacrifice of someone special to it," she replied.

Aquilia continued to shake her head, "I don't get it, who could be special to it?"

Everyone turned to look at Janus, 'could he be the one?' Aquilia thought.

Celest's radio crackled to life, "it's not Janus," she relayed, "according to Evadene, it's his mate."

"Lyra," Aquilia stated. "Great! We know where she is, but I can't see her going for this."

Celest wandered away for a second, everyone watched her movements. "Are you sure?" They heard her say. She hung her head and shook it hard, "that's ridiculous."

"What is it Celest?" Nymeria asked.

"Lyra isn't the one," she replied.

"Then who is?" Janus asked his face showing a look of confusion.

ENCELADUS

"What?" Zidan asked shocked.

They all looked at Evadene. She felt as if she were on display and it made her feel uneasy.

"She's right," Lyra said from the shadows. "I was never his true mate."

A collective gasp escaped their mouths. Layson walked over to Chylla, laid his hand on her shoulder, and smiled, "he always had a soft spot for you."

"According to Royal Records," Evadene announced, "Altair was supposed to marry you Chylla."

Chylla didn't say a word. All this information she already knew. Altair knew too. He also knew how much hatred she had for him since he had taken an interest in Lyra.

"There's a small issue though," Evadene added.

"Which is?" Zidan asked.

"I have to reciprocate his feelings for me," Chylla said, almost in a whisper, "and I don't."

"So what now?" Halana squeaked, "we can't let him kill our Princess."

"He won't, not yet anyway," Evadene said reading from her book, "Libat toy with their prey before killing it. She may well find another way to kill it, I hope."

Halana began to weep. Layson gently placed his arms around her, she hugged him close. He turned to see his wife smiling at him. She had kept her distance whilst he tried to fix things with Halana.

Amid all the commotion, Sinclair had slid away. Zeke caught up with him, "is everything OK sir?"

"Ah, young Zeke," Sinclair replied. "I feel I may have scuppered things with Miss Halana."

"Don't lose hope Mr Sinclair, I feel Miss Halana may have a lot on her mind right now, and what you may feel is loss, may just be her way of dealing with things. Maybe give her some time?" Zeke replied with a shy smile.

"You could be right young man. I won't give up just yet," Sinclair smiled back. He turned to watch as everyone worked together to figure out a solution to the recent dilemma. He decided to help. It was the least he could do considering it was he, who caused this.

Chapter 42

SATURN

Aquilia surveyed the battleground in front of her. The army of Onyx Abyss Alpha were making short work of Altair's army. What was once a peaceful, friendly city was now full of anger and bloodshed. Queen Quintara's army had arrived and had begun to fight against Altair's men. Aquilia began to question her actions.

"Mother wouldn't have wanted all this," she said pointing to the scene before her, "she hated this sort of stuff."

Janus stepped beside her, "Queen Quintara wanted you to have what was rightfully yours, even if it meant fighting for it."

Aquilia hugged Janus tight, "it's good to see you again cousin, and I thank you for what you are doing," she whispered.

A sudden whoosh caught their attention and Aquilia pushed Janus aside before being whipped off her feet. She landed back first against the side of the Palace. After getting back to her feet, she ordered the others to help Onyx Abyss Alpha to finish up; she would take care of Altair.

Aquilia watched the black-eyed creature prowl around her. It's orange mane like a heavily knitted scarf around its neck. Altair's Libat form was incredible. She remembered reading bits about it, but hadn't paid much attention due to them being extinct, or so she thought.

"Come on the Uncle Altair; give it your best shot!" She shouted at him.

His ears pricked up, a roar forming in his throat. He reared up on his back legs and pounced towards her. She rolled left, just missing his front paws. Back on her feet, she goaded him again. He spread his wings and swooped down on her, again she rolled away unscathed. He looked at her with confused eyes, "IMPOSSIBLE!" He roared.

Aquilia shook her head and laughed, "you have absolutely NO IDEA, do you Uncle?"

A roar escaped from deep within him that stunned the city to silence, but he didn't scare her.

She closed her eyes, took four slow deep breaths, and allowed her form to change.

The whole city fell still and gasped. Altair stared wide-eyed at Aquilia in her full Phoenix form.

ENCELADUS

While everyone crowded around the table, discussing ways Aquilia could possibly kill Altair. Zeke kept an eye on the screens. He watched as Altair attempted to attack Aquilia, he was impressed at how she dodged him every time. He was surprised when they both stopped and stared at each other.

"I think something happened," he announced, "they aren't moving."

Everyone gather around the screens. All eyes rested on Aquilia, they watched in amazement as she closed her eyes and her magnificent form emerged. Her hair, now a mass of red and orange flames, golden wings erupted from her back and she opened her blood red eyes. A collective gasp of awe escaped everyone's mouths.

"Wow," Lyra said, "I never imagined it would be so beautiful."

"What is she?" Zeke asked.

"She is a Phoenix! She has become her ancestors rising from the ashes," Lyra explained, "maybe Evadene here could help you learn some of your history."

Zeke smiled, "I'd like that."

They watched as Aquilia danced around Altair, taking swipes at him with her long beak. He would dodge before she hit, but only just. He whipped his tail at her; she caught it in her beak and bit down hard, causing him to roar in pain. He growled a deep ferocious growl; jumped high in the air, and proceeded to circle her from above.

"What's he doing?" Zeke asked.

"He's playing with her. He expects her to fly up there and fight him," Evadene explained, "he's more powerful up high, but only by a small amount. If the sun is shining on a clear day, she would have more power."

Lyra had an idea, "Sinclair, I need your help, and you too Layson, please."

Both men looked at each other and agreed to help. Lyra smiled at them.

"Layson, I need you to implement your cloaking technology onto the biggest ship we have left. Sinclair, I need you to guide us through the Hyper Jump. This has to be completed quickly in order to work," she explained.

Layson ran off to complete his end of the job, while Sinclair questioned her motives, "who are you trying to hide from?" He asked, "Altair or Aquilia?"

Lyra turned to him, "if I was trying to attack the Princess, I wouldn't ask for your help, would I?"

Sinclair gave one quick nod and went to ready the ship.

"I have people in the outer wastelands that can help Aquilia, let me bring them back to Astrodia?" She asked Zidan. She then lent in and whispered, "I know Elio. I know who you are, but it is your secret."

He looked at her with gratitude, "bring your people. I'm sure The Princess will be grateful."

She quickly ran off to meet with the others. Sinclair had the ship ready and Layson had covered the ship.

"Let me help?" Layson pleaded. "Please. I feel partly responsible."

"How long since your last injection?" She asked him.

"I'm due tomorrow. If it shows then it shows. I owe it to the Kingdom of Astrodia that I was supposed to protect," he admitted.

"Very well, climb aboard. I will make sure you return to your family in one piece," she replied.

"Thank you," he smiled.

They closed the doors and departed Enceladus. This was a big thing to ask of the outcasts, but Lyra would try her hardest. She owed it to Quintara.

SATURN

Aquilia, Nymeria, Celest, and Janus watched along with the entire Kingdom of Astrodia, as Altair circled above her. He swooped and dived, trying to catch her off guard but she had lightning fast reactions, every time he missed her, she laughed. It made him angry. He swooped higher into the sky, circled seven times then dived at a phenomenal speed, his teeth bared ready to snap her exposed neck. She watched him as he edged closer and closer, every movement that he made, she would change her position. When he was within striking distance, she leapt from her position and grabbed him with her sharp talons, flew a short distance and dropped him into the Palace courtyard. She ordered the gates to be locked and the overhead cover be closed.

Upon entering Saturn's atmosphere, Sinclair, Layson, and Lyra witnessed Aquilia's spectacular action.

"I hope we aren't too late," Lyra said, watching the courtyard cover close over them both. "We have to hurry."

Sinclair pushed the ship into Hyper Jump and aimed for the outer wastelands, "be quick," he said as he hovered above the lands.

Lyra stood at the doorway and whistled a high long tone. From the bushes came a flock of people with orange hair and yellow tattoos. "Princess Aquilia needs your help," Lyra explained.

A man stepped forward, his hair the brightest orange that had ever been seen, "why should we help? That family banished us here!"

"That wasn't on Aquilia's shoulders. Please. Altair will kill her without your help. I have it on good authority that we will be allowed to return if we show our willingness to help," Lyra explained, the need showing on her face.

"Please, give us a moment," he replied as he turned to face the crowd that had gathered behind him.

"Well?" Sinclair asked her from the front seat.

"Give them a moment, I hope it won't take long," she replied, looking back to him. She turned to face the crowd again. The man stepped forward.

"We will help on one condition," he said, "we must all be given free passage back into Astrodia."

"Absolutely," Sinclair replied, appearing beside her, "you are all welcome back into the Kingdom."

With a swift nod from the flame-haired man, everyone who was needed to aid Aquilia was bundled aboard. They sat together, chanting a rhythmic tune. Layson watched as each person began to glow, with each passing line, another and another shone brightly.

"Quickly Layson, open the reach hatch, Sinclair, order the cover to be opened!" Lyra shouted.

Both men sprang into action, the rear hatch of the ship lowered as the cover of the courtyard drew back to reveal a downed Aquilia. From the ship came a beam that hit Aquilia in the chest. It made her wings brighter and bigger than before, her talons sharper and longer and her feathers shone like the sun.

"It worked!" Lyra exclaimed, she turned to the group, "thank you!"

A woman with a sun tattoo on her back smiled, "we help when it allows us to."

Sinclair gave the order to close the cover again. They would only know the outcome when one of them reappeared.

Chapter 43

ENCELADUS

"What, what just happened?" Zeke asked as he watched the events unfold on the screen.

The beam of light had temporarily blinded them. From the stream on the ships rear hatch, they witnessed Aquilia become stronger and brighter. They had all gazed in awe at her beauty.

"Evadene, do we know the nature of these being?" Zidan asked.

"If you give me a second I can find out," she replied.

"Take your time young lady. You're doing so well," he said.

Evadene turned page after page trying to put a name to them. She finally stopped after looking through seventeen pages. "Here it is," she announced. "They are The Guardians of The Solar Flare."

Zidan smiled at her, "thank you. Any other information we should know?"

Evadene scanned the page, reading faster than ever before, "they harbour the Sun's Solar Flares and use them only for good. If they use them for evil, then they spontaneously combust," she relayed.

Zidan nodded and everyone continued to watch things unfold on Saturn. They watched as Layson, Lyra, and Sinclair landed and helped fight off the remaining few soldiers.

"Bring the injured home Nymeria," Chylla commanded.

"We can't leave Aquilia alone," Janus replied. "He could kill her."

"It's not likely now," Evadene replied. "She has the power of the Sun on her side. She can defeat him, I hope."

"Hope isn't good enough. I won't leave her," He replied.

"I'll stay back with him," Lyra said, "take everyone else back."

Lyra looked at Layson, who had just taken a sudden slash on his arm. His face was changing fast. His ears became more prominent, his snout extended from his face and he growled a deep gut rumbling growl. He turned on his four limbs and sniffed out the culprit. He ran full speed, bared his teeth, and snapped the man in half.

"Now, now, Layson, that's enough," Lyra cooed. Layson dropped the man's body and padded to her side.

Layson's wife and son looked on in shock. He hadn't intended them to see this.

SATURN

Nymeria loaded the injured onto two of the ships and sent them off. She set the empty ships to 'RETURN TO BASE' mode and watched as they departed.

"Will you both be OK?" She asked Janus and Lyra.

Lyra nodded, "thank you for looking out for him."

"It was my pleasure. It's an honour to know him," Nymeria replied.

"He's a good man, you should be proud," Celest added, smiling at Janus.

"Indeed I am," Lyra smiled back.

Nymeria ordered Layson to the waiting ship. She checked that everyone who needed to be aboard was and then set her ships destination. It took off and left Saturn's atmosphere, leaving Lyra and Janus alone at the Palace. Janus leapt into action, tending to the injured soldiers who had come to fight on Quintara's behalf. Lyra watched her son take pride in what he did. He had grown to love this Kingdom as much as Aquilia had. Lyra rushed to help him stabilize a man's leg and add a splint to keep it straight.

"So, Altair, how did you become a Libat? That's definitely NOT part of you DNA," Aquilia teased, circling him slowly.

He laughed, "I spent some time watching Lyra and her family practise their magic. I may have picked up a few things," he shrugged. "I thought The Phoenix was burned out of your bloodline? I researched it."

"Obviously didn't research deep enough. I must admit," she replied, admiring her glow, "I quite like it."

Altair bared his teeth and leapt at her, her attention having dropped for just a second. He flung her against the brick wall and laughed as she slid to the floor, trickled of blood falling from her nose. She lay there for a moment, completely stunned.

Altair paced back and forth, "not so clever now are you? You're nothing more than a pathetic spoilt brat who has been given too much power with no idea how to use it," he laughed. "When I kill you, and I will, I will take over this Kingdom and rid your pathetic family from its history."

Aquilia lay there, listening to his well-rehearsed speech, trying not to laugh at his attempt to boost his own ego. She pretended to be dazed as she shook her head and opened her eyes halfway. She managed a hic of laughter, which caught Altair's attention.

"What exactly is funny, other than the fact that you will be dead soon?" He demanded.

Aquilia stood up to her full height, just over a foot taller than Altair, "the fact you think you could kill me," she replied, shaking all her golden feathers free of dust and dirt, "you couldn't even kill my mother with your bare hands, you had to use Layson's blood to infect her. Now who is pathetic?" She thundered as she spread her wings and leapt from the floor. She circled overhead a few times, diving and taking nips at him here and there. She swept her wings back and landed on a rugged part of the wall, she watched as Altair opened his wings and leapt into the air.

"Anything you can do, my dear, I can also do. You're nothing special I'm afraid," he slurred, landing directly opposite her. He began to admire his appearance; he glanced behind at the black webbed wings, which seemed to span the entire wall.

Aquilia rolled her eyes at how distracted he had become. She quietly soared into the air, lined herself up and nose-dived towards Altair. The wind rushing through her wings caught his attention but just as he looked in her direction, she made direct contact with the side of his body causing him to fall to the ground, over seventy feet below. She watched as he landed, full force, on the ground below, yelping as he landed.

He turned to see her still in the air, slowly flapping her golden wings, her feathers shining twice as bright as the sun. Her eyes glowing the deepest red he had ever seen. He growled from deep inside and tried to fly up to her but his wings wouldn't carry his weight. He looked back to find one of his wings were broken. His right hind leg was also broken, the bone protruding through the skin.

"I can t believe you would do this to me. I'm your Uncle!" He growled.

"No, you gave up that title when you planned to kill me and my mother all those years ago. You're nothing to me. Nothing but a worthless piece of meat, which I'm sure Layson would love to feast on," she replied with a sneer.

Altair's face retorted in confusion, "what do you mean?"

Aquilia laughed, "don't play dumb with me. I mean it suits you but just don't. That's how you killed my mother. Starlight fever. From the blood of The Dark Wolf?"

The look of recognition passed over his face so quickly that, had she not been looking, she would have missed.

"Not so clever now, are you?" She laughed as she soared higher within the courtyard. She circled a few times before perching on a ledge and watching him squirm below, silently laughing as he continued to stand and try to fly.

ENCELADUS

Zeke guided all the returning ships safely to the landing zones, sending medical personnel to the injured and the engineers to the empty ships.

Nymeria, Celest, and Layson arrived on the next ship, which Zeke made sure The Wraith Doctors got to him fast. Sinclair came in next, landing perfectly next to Nymeria's ship.

"Great work everyone, debrief in thirty!" Nymeria announced.

Nymeria and Celest made their way to the security room. Neither said a word on the way there. Neither dared. They opened the door to see everyone still crowded around the screens.

"Any news?" Celest asked breaking the silence.

"Nothing yet," Evadene replied. "Where is Ammyn?"

Nymeria and Celest exchanged glances. "I thought she stayed here," Nymeria replied looking around worryingly.

"No, she left with the first batch," Zidan replied turning to face them. "Zeke, check medical. Chylla, track her from when she first landed."

Chylla and Zeke both went off to complete their respective tasks. Evadene continued to watch the screen, hoping to see Aquilia emerge from the courtyard gates. There was movement at the side of the gates. Evadene used the controls to zoom in. There, hidden partly by the bushes, lay Ammyn. Her arm almost completely severed.

"Janus, Janus can you hear me?" Evadene shouted.

"Here, use this," Zeke said as he passed her his radio. "There's no sign in medical."

"Thank you," she replied. "Janus, get to the gates at the courtyard. Ammyn needs you!" She shouted.

"I didn't know Ammyn was here!" Janus replied quickly running towards the courtyard, Lyra following along behind.

"Tell Chylla we have her," Zidan instructed Sinclair.

They watched the screen as Janus and Lyra found Ammyn. Everyone stared as Ammyn smiled at Janus, at Lyra, and then her smile faded. Evadene sobbed.

"Janus, status report," Celest took over.

"She lost too much blood," he replied, holding his voice in check.

"Has she?" Celest asked.

Janus nodded; he no longer trusted his voice to remain stable. He knew this girl had been a close friend to Aquilia and that her death would break her apart.

"What's happening?" Zeke asked pointing at the screen.

Before them, they saw Ammyn's body glow and seemingly evaporate, but the light didn't fade away into the air, instead it glided through the gates to the courtyard and towards Aquilia.

"There is so much more we need to learn about our beloved Aquilia," Zidan said, "so very much more."

Chapter 44

SATURN

Lyra and Janus moved Ammyn's body carefully away from the gates and covered her with a discarded sheet. They knew it was going to be hard telling Aquilia. They arranged to have Ammyn's body recovered and returned to Enceladus. No one had spoken a word about what had happened. No one knew what to say. Lyra gently placed her hand on Janus's shoulder, his shoulders shaking with his silent weeps, "it's not your fault son," she whispered.

"I know, but she has been such a great support to Aquilia. Aquilia helped her to speak fully again. I wish I could have done more for her, but I didn't even know she was here," he cried. "I have to be the one to tell her."

Lyra had no words for Janus. She didn't feel it was her place to try and comfort him. She kept her hand in place and allowed him to silently cry until he was ready to continue tending to the injured.

"What just happened?" Altair remarked when the bright light faded.

Aquilia shrugged, "no idea but it felt good," she smiled, flexing her golden wings fully. She leapt from the ledge and landed just out of his reach. "So, how do you plan to kill me?" She purred.

Altair clawed at her from where he lay, his hind leg pouring with blood, "you could always make it easy for me and come closer, I could just rip your throat out and have done with it, or you could just kill yourself and save me a job," he said, scratching his claws on the floor, trying to drag himself closer to her.

Aquilia laughed so loud the gates rattled, "even now you're trying to get someone to do your job for you. You're worthless."

As she finished the last syllable, Altair leapt off his left hind leg and bit down hard on her leg. Aquilia let out a gut-wrenching squawk, limping away from his blood dripping teeth.

"Pesky brat, you're not as smart as you think are you? That throne is mine by birthright?" He roared.

"Is it really? Then why, oh dear Uncle, were you removed from the line of succession?" She spat back, "you're obsessed with something that isn't even yours." She used the power of her wings to catapult her back to ledge. She looked down on her leg to see it had already begun healing. She smiled. She knew what she had to do now.

ENCELADUS

As the remaining Elders prepared to receive Ammyn's body, they lit several candles and scent sticks around the embalming room. Here, Ammyn's body would be preserved until The Higher Elders called for her spirit.

"How much longer?" Evadene whispered. "Can I help?"

"Only mere minutes sweet Eva, and I'm sure Ammyn would love that," Sinclair replied placing a calming hand on her shoulder.

They all stood, watching from the window as the ship carrying Ammyn made its final approach. All wearing white, they made their way to a secluded landing station, stood shoulder to shoulder, and bowed their heads, as Ammyn was unloaded from the ship.

Wheeling her body towards the embalming room, they uncovered her face. There she lay, looking as peaceful as if she were sleeping.

"Where is the eye?" Evadene asked.

"The Higher Elders will now choose someone worthy to hold that position that could take days, weeks, or months even. They must find the right person and sometimes it isn't easy," Zidan replied looking down at Ammyn, "for now, we must keep Ammyn preserved until it is time for her to depart once again."

Halana had handmade a special cloak for Ammyn to be draped in during her embalming. It was made of the finest lace embroidered with blue roses and red eyes.

"It looks beautiful Halana, it really does," Sinclair remarked as she brought it forward.

"She was a very special person, it's what she deserves," Halana sniffed. She draped the cloak over Ammyn and promptly broke down in tears. Sinclair quickly rushed to hold her. She clung to him so tight. "She didn't deserve to die."

Sinclair held her whilst she cried. He watched how gently Evadene held Ammyn as Chylla dressed her in a white satin dress, pulled her hair into a high bun, and fixed it with white and blue roses. Had they not been embalming her, she would have made a beautiful bride.

The Wraith Doctors came once Ammyn was dressed. They spaced out around her and began to whisper. Each line that was spoken added an extra spark in the air above her, the sparks danced around above her body, then, one by one, her body absorbed them.

"What's happening?" Halana asked mesmerised by the light.

"The sparks preserve her body until The Higher Elders call for her," Sinclair replied, "they encase her in a special tomb, transparent, as you can see, so others can bid their farewells."

"It's a lovely gesture, allowing others to say goodbye. May I?" Halana asked.

Sinclair signalled to The Wraith Doctors, who confirmed she could approach. Halana walked slowly towards Ammyn, tears falling silently.

"Oh dear sweet Ammyn, you put so much into your friendships with everyone. You truly were one of a kind, I wish you a safe journey to wherever it is you are heading," she whispered. "Aquilia will forever be protected and guarded in your honour."

Halana wiped her tears away and turned back to face the group. Everyone had heard what she had said, they were all crying.

"That was magical Mum," Evadene sniffed. "I love you."

Before Halana could reply, Zeke cried out over the radio, "the gates, quickly!"

<u>SATURN</u>

Aquilia surveyed the scene before her. Altair lay over eighty feet below her, clearly in pain but she wasn't going to take him out unfairly.

"I see we are both injured dear niece," he said still lying on his side.

"You may be injured; I am, however, healed," she laughed showing off her leg.

Altair's growl became so deep and loud, "how?"

"If I knew, and I don't, I wouldn't tell you anyway," she replied, gently flapping her wings and circling above him, "but if this is to be a fair fight, I guess we have to heal you too."

She landed just out of his reach again and tried breathing on his leg and wing; she then swooped up and landed on the ledge again, watching the magic work. Within seconds, the bone was fixed and the skin had re-grown, his wing was flapping again and he could now stand.

"What do you know, I'm magic," she shrugged.

"Hmm, so it seems. Well, that's the only time you will use it on anyone!" He said as he leapt into the air, claws and teeth bared. He came within an inch of her exposed neck just for her to swat him out of the air.

"Didn't think it would be that easy did you? You may be healed but I am no pushover," she said as she dived to the floor below. She stood in her Phoenix form, her giant golden wings filling the space behind her. She rolled her head from left to right and transformed back to her true self. "If we are going to do this, then we do it as us, nothing extra," she said arching her back,

Altair was surprised how easily she changed, but he smirked, "I think I'll stay as I am thank you. I have a better chance at beating you," he said.

Aquilia rolled her eyes for what felt like the one-millionth time since she landed here, "as you wish," she said as she took her position. She called upon everything Ammyn had taught her, took a deep breath and focused on Altair.

He padded from left to right, took one-step forward and then one back, her eyes never left his. He reared back onto his hind legs and lunged for her, catching her arm in his mouth, throwing her high in the air, and watching her fall to the ground with a loud thump. She didn't move for a second. Two seconds. Three.

"That was too easy," he said, turning his back on her, "and I didn't even have to try!"

Whilst his back was turned, she rose to her feet, blood dripping from her arm. She regained her position, took three steps forward and jumped, ran five steps up the wall, turned a complete somersault in the air, grabbing Altair's head at the same time.

"Not as easy as this. I'm sorry Uncle, you make me do this," she said as she closed her eyes, summoned every piece of her inner Phoenix strength, and pulled hard. She landed in front of him. His limp body collapsing behind her. She turned to see what was left of her uncle. She had hoped things could have been different but he was set in his ways.

What had been done had to be done. She pulled the bolt to one side and pushed open the gates. The light hit her eyes hard; she shielded herself against it and looked out upon the Kingdom. It needed fixing. It needed her.

Chapter 45

ENCELADUS

Zidan was the first to reach the screen followed by Sinclair Chylla and everyone else. Zeke pointed to the gates, as they swung open.

"Prepare Janus and Lyra. Just to be safe. We don't know who is exiting," Zidan commanded.

Zeke promptly relayed the message to Janus.

"I'll make my way there now, just to be sure," he replied.

Chylla, Sinclair, and Zidan all held hands hoping for the best outcome. Evadene held onto her mother, praying for Aquilia to be OK. Everyone's fingers were crossed. They watched as the golden feathers flew from the open gateway. Halana shed some tears. Blood trickled out on to the stone pathway; one black booted foot stepped forward, followed by another. A wisp of scarlet and silver flowed forward. Everyone cheered but quickly fell silent as Aquilia held Altair's Libat head above her own, his spine dangling in the air. Janus fell to his knees but no tears were shed. He bowed his head, "thank you," he said.

"Janus, you need to bring her home, quickly," Zidan said to him, "it's nearly time."

Sinclair helped Zeke ready the landing strip. Zidan talked Janus through how to use the Hyper Jump. It would have to be a fast trip; The Higher Elders had called for Ammyn. Zidan had requested a few extra hours but those were nearly over.

"Why is there such a rush? My Kingdom needs me to help it rebuild," Aquilia asked, watching Astrodia disappear below.

"There's been an accident Princess," Lyra replied. "You must return at once."

"I don't understand," she said.

"Tell her Janus," Zidan requested, "do it gently please."

Janus took a deep breath, placed his hand over hers, "Ammyn was hurt during the battle," he began.

"We can fix her, can't we? You did before Sinclair," Aquilia said, feeling her throat tighten.

"This time it's different Princess, you will have to see for yourself," Zidan replied.

Aquilia sat on by herself on the way back, tears flowing from her blue eyes. 'Please don't let her die,' she thought.

Janus watched her as they approached Enceladus, he knew this would be hard for his cousin, he also knew she had a large support network here, he didn't want to step on anyone's toes. As they landed, he could see how Aquilia's large group had descended upon the landing strip. The doors opened and a girl ran straight to Aquilia, he guessed this to be Evadene.

"You scared us to death!" She said as she squeezed Aquilia's neck.

"I'm sorry. Where's Ammyn?" Aquilia asked.

"Come Princess," Chylla gestured. "It's good to have you home."

Aquilia followed Chylla to a large white room, where, at the centre, lay Ammyn.

Aquilia walked over and looked down on her.

"Wake up Ammyn I won. I won Ammyn," Aquilia sobbed, "why isn't she awake?" Aquilia tried to touch her but her hands hit the transparent tomb, which held her.

"What's this?" She said, tears pricking at her eyes. "Zidan? Sinclair? Eva?"

"I'm sorry Princess. Ammyn, she lost so much blood before we could get her back," Chylla explained.

"She died right outside the gates. She passed her strength to you," Zidan added.

"She can't die, we planned to open another school, and we were going to train new warriors, we..." Aquilia sobbed so hard, "you can't die!"

Halana made her way to Aquilia's side, took her hands from the tomb and took her back a few steps, "we have to say goodbye for now, my Princess, but Ammyn will always be in your heart, just like your mother and father. She was so proud of you. We all are," Halana whispered.

Aquilia looked back at the tomb just as a flash of light exploded silently. The Higher Elders took Ammyn's body. Aquilia's sobs became softer and softer until she fell asleep in Halana's arms.

"It must have been quite an ordeal for her. Eva, take her to rest," Halana ordered.

Evadene nodded and guided Aquilia away.

"You must be Janus," Halana greeted him. "Welcome."

"Thank you. I'm so sorry for all the hurt that has been caused. I hope I can help fix things," he replied.

"For one, you can help an old woman up," she replied, extending her hand.

He smiled and gently helped her to her feet.

"Oh, I feel a little giddy," she said, holding tighter to him.

Everyone watched on as something happened to Halana. Within a few seconds of being upright, Halana's head was now in ownership of Ammyn's eye.

The Higher Elders had chosen their match.

Zidan, Chylla, and Sinclair nodded their approval, they couldn't think of anyone better to replace Ammyn.

"I think Aquilia would approve too," Zidan said, answering everyone's unspoken question.

A sudden flash caught Chylla's attention. "I think we're being summoned by The Higher Elders," she said.

Along with Zidan, Sinclair, and now, Halana, she made her way to the East Wing of The Palace.

"What's going to happen?" Halana asked softly.

"Sometimes The Higher Elders will need to discuss the goings on between Saturn and Enceladus with us, it's absolutely normal," Sinclair replied, gently squeezing her upper arm.

They entered a sapphire coloured room with a white table at its centre, each chair had a symbol engraved on it, a moon for Zidan, a star for Sinclair, the infinity symbol for Chylla and an eye, originally for Ammyn , but now for Halana and finally the last chair had a golden lightning bolt that was obviously for Aquilia. They each took their respective places and waited for what seemed like hours but had only been minutes.

"Thank you for your patience Chosen ones. We have been discussing, at great length, our next moves, and have agreed on one thing, even though one has already broken the promise that was made," a voice announced via a loudspeaker.

They each stole glances at one another, trying to work out the guilty party.

"No need to try and work things out, all will be revealed soon enough. Now, where is our most precious gift, where is Aquilia?" The voice asked.

"Resting. She's had quite an ordeal," Halana replied.

"Ah, Halana. Welcome to our embrace. I will explain why we chose you in due course. Please bear with me. Now, let me begin by explaining a few things. When you became an Elder, you became entrusted with a gift. Only you know what that gift entails. Halana, you will learn your gift in due course. What two of you don't know, or have little recollection of, is your life before you became an Elder. Obviously, Halana, you know yours and Zidan, you, of course, know yours, but Sinclair and Chylla, you both had lives before becoming who you are today.

Sinclair and Chylla looked confused. Halana looked at Zidan but couldn't work out who he could have been previously, 'his personality doesn't match anyone of the very few people I know,' she thought.

"I won't hold you in suspense any longer. This is going to be harder on two of you more than the others, but please, support each other. Zidan, please stand," a soft, female voice commanded.

Zidan stood with his hands behind his back. He knew what was about to be said. He stood with his back straight and awaited the voice to continue.

"Zidan, having been with us for fourteen long years, you broke the promise you made, but for all the right reasons, this is why you were not punished. She needed to know everything in order for her to become who she is today. Everyone, I give you, King Elio," the voice concluded.

As soon as she said his name, his image changed back to that of his former self, his emerald eyes and silver hair returning.

"Your Majesty," Halana said, bowing her head.

"Oh stop, it feels good to be back. Thank you," he laughed.

"Chylla, please stand," the voice ordered softly.

A stunned Chylla stood nervously. She looked at Halana, her hands shaking. Halana stood with her, holding her hands.

"Chylla, I know you remember parts of your previous life. It shows by how protective you are of our young Princess. You were once Raveena, one of Quintara's mother's personal bodyguards, just as you were Quintara's before she left for Saturn. After she married King Elio and moved to Saturn, you were chosen to become an Elder based on your bravery," the voice explained.

"How do I, what did I look like?" Chylla asked.

"No different than you do now, take a look," the voice replied.

Everyone turned to face the table as it became a monitor and displayed two girls practising their martial arts skills. The second girl looked very familiar to Chylla.

"That's Nymeria!" Chylla exclaimed.

"It is. She is the reason you stayed on Enceladus. She is, in fact, your sister. She knows who you are, we allowed her to know, and unfortunately, we had to keep it from your parents. After Quintara married, you were in a bad way with no one to protect. We chose you to protect everyone, hence the infinity symbol," the voice explained.

"Thank you, can I go and find her?" Chylla asked, eager to get away.

"If you could hold off for just a second, Halana may need a friend for this," the voice continued. "Sinclair, please stand."

Sinclair stood on shaky legs. He had no recollection of a previous life. He looked around at the faces of his friends, a single tear escaping his eye.

"Sinclair, you were chosen after defending Enceladus against Neptune's attack, for that sacrifice, we owed you a life," the voice began.

"No. No please, no," Halana whispered. She walked up to Sinclair and held his face in her hands. "Reaver?"

The table flickered at displayed was a video of Reaver, Halana and Evadene the last time they had held each other. A gentle sobbing could be heard in the shadows.

"Come forward," the voice commanded.

"Dad," Evadene whispered.

"Evadene. Aquilia's most trusted aid. Please step forward," the voice said, a little softer.

"Who are you?" Evadene asked, looking around for someone.

"I am one of the five Higher Elders. My name is Zyra," the voice continued.

"Zeebrakaan's wife?" Zidan asked.

"The very same, and he was correct. I would and do gush over Aquilia. She is THE perfect leader," Zyra replied.

"Halana, are you alright?" Sinclair asked, gently touching her arm.

She flinched a little and then threw her arms around his neck, "oh Reaver. I've missed you so much, you have no idea."

"I think I'm beginning to," he managed, his face turning blue.

"Oh, I'm sorry," she said letting go.

Sinclair looked between Halana and Evadene. "Look how much you have grown," he said, holding his arms open.

Evadene hesitated then launched herself at him, "I've missed you Dad," she cried into his shoulder.

"What you will all discover is that your memories will return, they may be disturbing from time to time, but we have support for that," Zyra soothed. "I do have one more surprise though, but for that I need everyone here. Could you round everyone up and be back here in an hour?"

They all agreed and went off to gather the troops.

Chylla blindly headed towards the medical wing where she knew Nymeria was visiting Layson. She watched through the small round window in the door as her sister and Celest fussed over Layson.

"You did good today, you should be proud of yourself." Celest said smiling.

"So, did she win?" Layson asked, screw up his face in pain.

"No word yet," Nymeria replied looking down at the floor.

"Don't give up yet babe," Celest said hugging Nymeria. "It will all come good in the end, you'll see."

Chylla watched the exchange between them; she hadn't noticed how close they were until now. She was happy for them both.

"She won," Chylla said as she opened the door. "She actually won!"

Layson tried to throw his arms up in joy but the wound froze his movements.

"Don't worry big fella, I got an extra arm to celebrate on your behalf," Celest teased.

Layson smiled, he had enjoyed being part of a team and feeling like he was actually needed.

"Can I have a word in private Nymeria?" Chylla requested.

"Sure," she replied.

They went into the corridor and Chylla turned to face her, "I know who I am, I know who you are and I think I can guess who Celest is."

Nymeria stood with her eyes and mouth wide open.

"Say something please!" Chylla said.

"I was sworn to secrecy. How or what or huh?" Nymeria shrugged. "I don't understand."

"I know I am your sister, I know I am Raveena, or was Raveena and I think you and Celest are an item?" Chylla asked.

Nymeria let all her tears flow at once, then her words came flooding out, "I've known since you were chosen, I had to act like you ran away, Mum and Dad didn't care, then I met Celest and we just clicked," she paused to take a breath, "then Mum and Dad started gossiping about the gay couple at the end of the street and how it was wrong, so I had to hide it from them, then when they died, I felt free, that sounds terrible doesn't it?" She finished.

Chylla placed her arms around her sister, "as long as you are happy and she makes you happy, that's all I care about."

"I am and she does," Nymeria replied.

"Am I too late to join the party?" Celest asked from the doorway.

Chylla gasped. She'd forgotten about the meeting. "Quick, get Layson in a wheelchair, we have to be somewhere in less than five minutes."

Celest found a wheelchair and helped Layson aboard, "hold tight buster, this could get rough!"

Layson laughed. They left the medical wing and bumped into Halana, Evadene, and Aquilia on the way.

"Princess, how are you?" Layson asked looking up at her.

"A little tired and hungry but I'm alive, thank you. How's the arm?" She replied pointing at his cast.

"Broken but hey, at least the cast is a cool colour huh?" He replied showing off his neon orange cast.

Halana smiled at him, "I'm glad you survived."

Layson stared at her, his eyes recognising the mark on her head. He smiled and looked away, he was sure she would explain about it soon.

Everyone arrived at the meeting with only two minutes to spare. They all found places to sit with The Elders, Aquilia and Halana taking their respective seats. Zidan had rounded up Bella and Zeke, Sinclair had assisted Halana and Evadene in waking Aquilia, and Chylla had brought Layson, Nymeria, and Celest. A range of drinks and snacks had been arranged on the table, which, just under an hour ago, showed Sinclair and Chylla who they really were. Aquilia grabbed herself a glass of grapefruit juice and took a sip, the liquid easing its way down her throat, soothing the tightness she still felt from finding out about Ammyn.

"Thank you all for coming. I can see you all have had some form of recovery time and I do apologise for dragging you all here at such short notice," Zyra said.

"I'm sorry, who are you exactly?" Aquilia asked.

"My name is Zyra. I am one of the Higher Elders, and yes, Zeebrakaan was right, I can tell by the look on your face that you recognise my name," Zyra explained to a stunned Aquilia. "We, as Higher Elders, are so very proud of everything you have done."

Aquilia's normal cyan skin turned a bright shade of pink.

"There's no need to blush Princess, you should be so proud of yourself too," Zyra said.

Everyone turned to smile at Aquilia; she looked around the room to find a family she never knew she needed when she had arrived. She had made Enceladus her home.

"I'm proud of every one of you for all standing by me and standing by my decisions. It's been tough but we did it. You all helped to keep me safe and for that I am forever grateful," Aquilia announced.

Everyone in the room gave her a round of applause.

"Now, the reason I asked you all here. There has been some developments which we must discuss and since it involves almost everyone in this room, it's easier to do it all at once," Zyra began.

She explained about Zidan, Sinclair and Chylla's lives before becoming Elders, how Nymeria was Chylla's sister, Sinclair was Evadenes father and Halana's husband and how Zidan was in fact, King Elio.

"Wait. Where are Janus and Lyra? They should be here too," Aquilia cried out, "please, let me find them."

She stood to leave but Halana held her arm, stopping her from going.

"Lyra and Janus returned to Saturn while you were sleeping. Janus said he needed to help the Astrodians, he felt he needed to try to make amends for what his father did to the city, for what he did to your family. Lyra felt she needed to show her gratitude to your mother for allowing her to stay at the Palace. They will be in contact soon," Halana explained.

Chapter 46

SATURN

"You should have said goodbye Janus," Lyra said, following him through the town.

Janus made his way past the fountain that he once loved, now an unfamiliar purple colour.

"We will need to run a water treatment chemical through the system to make the water safe again," he said, ignoring his mother.

"Janus, just STOP!" Lyra shouted, "why didn't you say goodbye to Aquilia?"

Janus stopped, hung his head, and let out a deep sigh, "I couldn't. I saw all the support and all the love she had up there and I was jealous. I've never had any of that, sure, Quintara and Elio showed me attention, but they weren't my parents. Aquilia had everything, the big parties, the expensive gifts, and the big house. What did I get? A conniving, deceptive father who lied about my mother being dead," he cried, "the best thing I can do is clean up his mess after what he did to Aquilia."

Lyra watched as Janus helped the Astrodian people rebuild their city, piece by piece. She was proud of him but also glad he had picked up the compassion from Elio. She continued to help him throughout the day, refraining from mentioning Aquilia's name again.

As night drew in, Janus returned to what was Altair's house and set about making dinner. He set the table and served up pasta and fresh fish, which he had purchased from the local fisherman. They sat in silence to eat, neither knowing what to say. Janus cleared away the plates and sat next to his mother.

"I didn't mean to sound ungrateful today. I just wished I could have had just a piece of what Aquilia had," he said, not risking looking at her.

"I understand Janus, but we are all brought up differently. We can't all have the same parents, the same gifts or the same lives, but we must be grateful for the people who are in our lives. They make us who we are. You have a big family who live on the outer wastelands. Sinclair said he would allow them to live back in Astrodia, mainly because I got a group of them to help Aquilia, but Quintara said she would allow them back," Lyra explained, "it won't be the same as Aquilia, but they have a lot of love to give. I'll contact Sinclair and ask when they can begin arriving."

Janus nodded, leaving the room to allow her some peace. He made his way up to Altair's old room and was surprised by what he discovered, had he known Altair was this obsessed, he would have taken him out himself. He shuffled through paperwork, found lists of Quintara's outings; he even bribed a doctor to release Quintara's medical records. Janus got angrier with every passing discovery. He wished he wasn't related to him. Janus's last discovery made his blood boil. He held the booklet to tight that it began to cut into his skin. 'How could he have done such a thing?' Janus thought to himself. 'How will anyone forgive me for what he did?'

ENCELADUS

Aquilia retook her seat at the table, still shocked from Halana's revelation. She couldn't believe Janus would just leave without saying goodbye.

"Princess, are you OK?" Zyra asked.

Aquilia nodded quickly, "yes. Please continue."

"Very well. Everyone, as you can see, we have chosen Halana to continue the work of Ammyn by entrusting her with Ammyn's eye. Halana, you are by no means replacing Ammyn, you are simply continuing what she began, I trust you understand," Zyra explained.

"Of course. No one could replace Ammyn. She holds a special place in everyone's hearts," Halana replied.

She gave Aquilia's hand a gentle squeeze and a soothing smile. Aquilia smiled back. There was a flickering of the lights before everything dimmed and the white walls became screens.

"Neat trick!" Zeke exclaimed.

"I'm glad you approve young man. My Zeebrakaan would have loved an eager learner like yourself," Zyra replied with a hint of laughter in her voice.

On the screens in front of them, a face came into view. A gentle looking face with gold skin and long flowing white hair and a symbol representing the sun on her forehead. Aquilia was amazed.

"You're beautiful, it's understandable why Zee loved you so much," Aquilia said.

"Oh stop, you'll make an old woman blush," Zyra laughed, "now. I have three others with me who I would like to introduce to you all."

The room went quiet and the screen went dark, the occupants of the room glanced at one another. The screens blinked back to life and there sat a man with aquamarine skin and hair the colour of wheat. Adorned on his head was the symbol of a globe.

Aquilia gasped, "Zee!"

"Ha ha, Oh Princess, look how you've grown! Oh my!" Zeebrakaan replied.

"Oh I've missed you! How did you become a Higher Elder?" Aquilia asked.

"For duties to Royalty," he replied, "now I can do everything I couldn't before."

"Like grow up?" Aquilia laughed.

"You remember so much young one, you have done us extremely proud. Never change your ways," he said before fading from the screen.

"Oh Zee, I love you," Aquilia whispered.

Zidan had watched their interaction and his heart hurt that Aquilia had never met her own grandparents, but he was happy she had chosen Zeebrakaan as a substitute.

"That was number one," Zyra began, "Aquilia may need some added support for the next one. It may come as a shock," she whispered.

Again, the room went dark but this time, the screen glistened as if covered in stardust, everyone seemed to surround Aquilia. Each smiling every time she looked at them. She was unsure what she was about to see and it scared her. A flickering of the screen caused them all to look. As the screen came to life slowly, everyone gasped. At first, they saw long flowing black hair with blue tips and a glimpse of teal skin.

"Ammyn!" Aquilia cried.

Then the screen tuned a little more to reveal a mass of scarlet hair and a pale face.

"Mum," Aquilia whispered.

Both women giggled on the screen.

"I told you it would be better to do it together," Ammyn said without any trouble at all.

"Ammyn, you're not having trouble with your speech anymore," Halana said with surprise.

"It was a gift from Zyra for passing my strength on to you Princess," she aimed her answer at Aquilia. "I'm so glad it helped."

"Oh Ammyn, you have always cared for others over yourself, that's why you were chosen," Zyra said, her face appearing on another section of the wall.

"Oh Quintara, it's so lovely to see your face again. I'm eternally sorry for what Altair did to your beloved family," Layson said bowing his head.

"Layson," Quintara said softly, "I do not hold you accountable in any way. You weren't to know what lengths Altair would go to, to take over, be at peace now."

"Mum, is it really you?" Aquilia squeaked walking closer to the screen.

"My darling Aquilia. You have no idea how much I've missed you, and look at you now, all grown up," Quintara cooed. "I knew you would be safe there and I knew deep down that you would become the ultimate warrior."

"I was so scared Mum, I don't know where all my strength came from. I mean obviously Ammyn shared hers with me, but why wasn't I scared when I was fighting?" Aquilia asked.

"You were blessed the moment you landed here Princess. The Higher Elders could see your potential, you were so determined and so aware of what would be expected of you," Ammyn replied, "you were what your mother had wanted to be all those years ago."

"And you, my darling, fulfilled my dream for me," Quintara added.

"My darling Queen. How much I have missed you," Zidan whispered.

"Oh Elio, you mushy King. I, too, have missed you. Things will be different now. You can all decide whether to keep your Elder names or revert back to your original names, the choice is yours, but you will forever retain your gifts," Quintara replied. "Take your time to think it over."

As Quintara finished, Sinclair's phone buzzed.

"Time for us to go," Quintara announced, "we will stay in touch."

"Bye Mum, I love you," Aquilia said with a smile.

"And I, you," she replied as the screens faded to black.

From the back of the room, they could hear Sinclair's voice rising.

"What is in it?" He said.

No one could hear the other end of the conversation, they all strained their ears.

"We are on our way right now," Sinclair finished. "Aquilia, get ready."

Chapter 47

SATURN

"Sinclair and the others are on their way," Lyra informed Janus.

Lyra had found him in the corner of Altair's room, turning page after page and getting angrier by the second. Janus wouldn't listen to her so her only other option was Aquilia and The Elders.

"Why Mum, why?" Janus cried, his sobs were heavy and deep. "Why did he have to do it?"

"Is this to do with the booklet Janus?" She asked.

Janus looked up at her, his eyes red from crying, and shook his head, "most of what's in this book, I already know, but some of it is horrific to read. The things he wanted to do."

Lyra hadn't really known what kind of monster Altair had become. It had taken her years to build up enough courage to come back and she hadn't liked what she saw then. She gently took the book away from Janus and began to read it for herself. Within the first few pages, she discovered how her sister had died. She'd no idea she had been shot with a laser arrow. Lyra remembered the day so well; her sister had been practising her levitating skills. She had gone so far up, she had performed some somersaults and dives, and then she just stopped, and fell. Lyra hadn't seen her again; they didn't even have a funeral. Lyra let her tears fall silently; she couldn't risk Janus seeing her acting weak.

"Lyra, Janus," Aquilia called as she entered the building Lyra had directed them to.

Lyra cleared her throat, "up here."

Janus had dropped off to sleep after his tears had dried up; he was still angry, it showed on his face.

"What have you found?" Aquilia asked, looking around the messed up room.

Lyra stood up and handed her the book, "this."

Aquilia turned the book over in her hands, it seemed familiar for some reason, but she couldn't figure out why. She opened the book from the back as Lyra had instructed, and she read. Page after page. With each line, each paragraph, her tears flooded out. "How could I have been related to such an immoral, corrupt being?" She cried.

"That was Janus's thoughts," Lyra explained, "that's why he disowned Altair."

Aquilia turned the book around and over, she opened the first page and almost passed out. This was her handwriting book from when she was three. She remembered showing Janus the day her father had died.

"Will she be OK Sinclair?" Lyra asked.

They had stepped outside to give Janus and Aquilia some time to talk. Janus had awoken and seen Aquilia crying.

"I'm sure she will, it's been quite an eventful time for our young Princess. She discovered so much today," Sinclair replied.

Lyra looked at him with surprise, "what has she found out?"

Sinclair brought Lyra up to date with the events on Enceladus, much to Lyra's surprise.

"Wow, Halana an Elder! She deserves it! She really is great with Aquilia," Lyra said.

"She is a fantastic woman," Sinclair agreed.

"You would say that, you were married to her at one point. Now, I see why you liked her in the first place," Lyra laughed.

Lyra and Sinclair talked for a while longer about the other revelations that had been announced. The biggest surprise for Lyra was that Nymeria was Chylla sister!

"I didn't see that one coming!" She said.

"And Zidan being King Elio?" Sinclair questioned.

"I have to admit, I knew, not because I was told but because I overheard him talking to himself about it, I couldn't bring myself to spill his secret," Lyra admitted.

"It's so much to take in isn't it?" Janus asked, "how could he be so deceitful, to his own brother!"

"It's hard to read Janus. To think he was willing to attempt any of those things is beyond me. I can't say I remember him very well, but it hurts me that you had to read this about him," Aquilia replied as she sat next to him on the floor, "what sickens me the most is that it's in my old handwriting book."

Janus took the book and opened it the correct way round, "how sinister do you have to be to write this kind of stuff at all, let alone in a child's book."

They both sat in silence for a few moments, trying to come to terms with what they had just read.

"I guess you'll be living up there now?" Janus asked.

"There's been some, revelations, shall we say, today," Aquilia replied. "I don't exactly know what to do."

"Do tell," he said turning to face her.

She began by explaining that Chylla was Nymeria's sister, which shocked Janus. Aquilia told him that Sinclair was, in fact, Evadene's father, which explained his fondness for Halana.

"There are one or maybe three other things that you should know," she said. She had hoped Janus would have been there to hear this for himself.

"What is it?" He asked.

"Zidan is really my father," she began. She waited for him to react.

"Uncle Elio?" He asked.

"Yes. My mother knew. I had an instant connection to him when I first arrived on Enceladus. I questioned him a few years back and he and Mum told me, but I couldn't tell anyone," she replied.

"That's good news though isn't it?" Janus asked.

"In one way yes, but I had gone so long without him that it's hard to adapt, do you understand?" She replied.

Janus nodded, "it's the same with Lyra, I mean, I call her Mum now and then but, it's hard. I thought she was dead for so long. What are the other things?"

Aquilia took a breath, "my mother is part of The Higher Elders, and so is Ammyn."

Janus smiled, "you have your parents back little cousin, why the frown?"

"It's not the same, not as it once was," she replied, "I can't hug my mother and even though Zidan is 'my Dad', it doesn't feel the same."

Aquilia hung her head a little, she didn't want to seem like a spoilt brat, but it wasn't the same as it was before. They weren't her parents as they once were.

"Will you come back with us? Just stay for a while?" Aquilia asked him.

"Yes Princess, but only for a while, the Saturnites need help rebuilding and I feel I should help considering it was Altair who caused so much destruction," he replied smiling.

Janus got to his feet and helped Aquilia to hers, "you know, I'm proud of you little cousin. You did your mother and Ammyn proud too."

"Thank you. I miss them. It's going to be hard without them, but I've got you right?" She replied, elbowing him n the ribs.

He pretended it hurt and then gathered her into a hug, "always."

After informing Sinclair that Lyra and Janus would be accompanying them back to Enceladus, they made a slight detour back to the Palace. It had been over twelve years since Aquilia had entered her former family home. As she walked the corridors, she noticed how nothing had changed. She stopped at the painting of herself and her parents when she was a baby, not more than six months old, her scarlet hair and blue eyes almost jumping out at her, "was my hair always that bright?" She asked.

"Absolutely, that's how we always found you hiding in the bushes." Janus shrugged. "The silver is more prominent now that you're older."

"If I may say so Princess, you really do look so much like your mother," Lyra said with a tear in her eye.

Aquilia walked to Lyra's side and drew her in with open arms, "even though you made some mistakes a long time ago. Don't let it hold you back from being the mother than Janus needed," she whispered.

Lyra held on tight, "thank you. I will try my best."

They continued on to Quintara's personal room. Aquilia browsed the bookshelf, selecting a few of the books she vaguely remembered her mother reading. She placed them on the table and went to her mother's bedside table. She opened the top drawer and found a box with her name on the top. She pulled it out and opened the lid,

Dearest Aquilia,

If you are now in possession of this box, it means

I didn't survive. I have written you a letter every week since I sent you away.

There are birthday cards here too.

You have made me so very proud. Never change who you are.

You are my number one.

Sending you all my love and strength.

Mum

p.s. Look after Janus. He will need you, even if he doesn't admit it.

Xx

"Oh Mum," Aquilia cried, rummaging through the box. She found finger knitted animals, cards and letters.
"Why don't you read those back home. We need to get back now," Sinclair said gently.

Chapter 48

ENCELADUS

"Incoming ship," Zeke called out, "looks like Sinclair returning."

"You're doing an excellent job Zeke, thank you," Zidan commended him.

Zeke smiled. He enjoyed keeping an eye on the skies above Enceladus. In fact, he enjoyed living here. It was less stressful than Saturn was. "May I be excused? I would like to catch up with my father," Zeke asked.

"Of course you may. I don't expect you to lock yourself away in here forever lad," Zidan laughed, "off you pop, I have things here."

"Thank you sir," Zeke replied, leaving his seat and the room.

Layson and his wife were helping Halana in the sewing room, it had become very unkempt, and this made Halana scold herself.

"Please don't be so hard on yourself," Bella said, "it's been a tough time."

"Oh I wish I could go easy on myself Bella, I really do, but I have so many ideas and only myself to create them!" Halana replied, wiping her hands down her skirt.

"How about I help?" Bella offered. "It's no bother. I've been meaning to look for work now I've decided to stay up here with Layson."

"You mean you actually thought of going back?" Halana said her eyes wide with shock.

"We talked about it, and Bella had her doubts about this place. I think it's grown on her," Layson replied.

"Does that mean we are staying?" Zeke cried from the doorway.

"Come on in lad, it's rude to stand in doorways," Halana gestured.

"Thank you, I'm sorry. So are we staying Mum?" He asked.

"We certainly are darling. You can get schooling up here. I heard the Evadene is an excellent teacher," Bella replied.

Zeke ran to his parents and hugged them both, "I was just going to ask Dad to persuade you to stay. I like it here."

From the other side of the room, Halana smiled, her family was complete again, even if Sinclair only remembered a small piece for now.

Upon landing on Enceladus, Aquilia gathered the books she had collected from The Palace along with the box of letters she had found.

Chylla approached the door of the ship as it opened, "welcome back Your Majesty. I have set up the spare rooms as requested. Will there be anything else you require?"

Aquilia thought for a moment, "unless it is urgent, can I not be disturbed for a while. I have something I need to pay full attention to," she replied.

"As you wish Your Highness," Chylla said, bowing her head. She led Janus and Lyra to their respective rooms.

"Will you be OK Aquilia?" Sinclair asked as he stepped beside her.

Aquilia nodded, held the box tighter, and walked towards her own room. Sinclair watched until she was just out of sight then he made his way to his office, the day's events were beginning to take their toll on him. He needed to rest.

"Dad, Dad, wake up!" Evadene cried, "Dad please wake up."

Evadene shook Sinclair harder and harder but he refused to move. She grabbed his hand and noticed how cold it was. She gasped and dropped his hand back to his desk. She ran from the room in search of anyone who could help.

"Help, please someone help me," she screamed as she ran through the halls, "can anyone hear me?"

Aquilia was dragged from her thoughts by Evadene's cries. She threw open her bedroom door and caught Evadene in her arms.

"What is it Eva?" Aquilia asked looking her friend in the eye.

"It's, it's my Dad," Evadene replied, "he's..."

"Sinclair? He's what Eva?" She questioned.

Evadene couldn't find the words to reply; she sunk to her knees and cried. Deep sobs that broke Aquilia's heart.

"Take me there," Aquilia told her, taking her arm and gently pulling her to her feet.

The two girls made their way to Sinclair's office, the door was wide open, Sinclair was at his desk, at first glance, he looked to be sleeping peacefully, but the closer Aquilia got, the faster she discovered that he had departed. Tears pricked at her eyes. She had not been Sinclair's biggest fan when she first arrived but she had come to love him as a grandfather, much the same as she had done Zeebrakaan. Aquilia used her comms radio to contact the others. She carefully asked them to meet her and Eva outside Sinclair's office.

"This is going to devastate Mum," Eva managed to croak; "she just got him back."

Aquilia threw her arms around Evadene, "I won't pretend to know how you feel, even though I have suffered the same, as we all feel things differently, but just know I am here for you, always."

Evadene didn't trust herself to speak so she just nodded. They could hear footsteps approaching, so prepared themselves to inform the others of Sinclair's untimely departure. Aquilia looked at each one of the gathered crowd, Layson, Bella, Zeke, and Halana flanked by Chylla, Zidan, Janus, and Lyra, this would be so hard on them. Aquilia then looked at Evadene, whose tears fell freely.

"He's gone, hasn't he?" Halana asked, a single tear falling from her eye.

Aquilia felt her pain as she nodded, "I'm so sorry Halana."

"Can I see him?" She asked.

"Of course, we will give you some privacy," Aquilia replied.

Halana tried to smile, but it did not reach her eyes. She hugged Aquilia before taking Evadene's hands and entering Sinclair's office. Once the door was closed behind them, the remaining crowd gathered in the meeting room to await instructions from The Higher Elders.

Halana and Evadene quietly sat with Sinclair's body. For the first few moments, neither knew what to say.

"I'm sorry I didn't come to you first Ma," Evadene squeaked,

"It's perfectly fine my darling. You were obviously shocked by what you found, I'm glad Princess Aquilia was by your side," she replied, hugging her daughter close.

"I can't believe we've lost him again. We just got him back," Evadene cried, hot tears falling from her eyes.

"It's sad my sweet, but as an Elder, he aged a lot faster than you, I will too, so you must prepare yourself for the unexpected. Promise me that?" Halana replied, "as Elders, we never know what our time is up, but we have to enjoy each moment as if it's our last. Your father had a lot to take in, but he did everything he would normally do."

"What happens now Ma?" Evadene asked.

"Now we must prepare him for the afterlife. The Higher Elders will call for him soon," Halana replied.

The Wraith Doctors arrived to escort Sinclair's body to the embalming room.

"Deepest condolences to you both, he was a gentle soul," one of them said.

Halana couldn't bring herself to speak so she just attempted to smile.

"Can we help prepare him, like we did with Ammyn?" Evadene asked.

"You can," they said in unison.

They followed The Wraith Doctors through the halls slowly. It seemed The Wraith Doctors only had one speed at times like this, and that was slow. After three long corridors, passing several people with their heads bowed, they finally reached the embalming room. When they entered the room, everyone was dressed in white again; it was as if Ammyn's embalming was a dress rehearsal. Everyone stayed silent whilst Halana, Evadene, Chylla, and Zidan prepared Sinclair for his final journey.

Aquilia swiped at a tear that had escaped her eye, hoping nobody had seen it. Lyra appeared by her side and gently squeezed her arm. There were no words spoken but a sign of understanding.

Everyone stood in silence, saying their own prayers in their heads. Aquilia prayed for him to have a safe journey to the other side. Zidan and Chylla prayed for Sinclair to be at peace, but Halana and Evadene prayed to be reunited with him. Deep down they knew it would never happen, but they could dream. As they were silently praying, Sinclair's body began to glow; his features reverted to those of Reaver. Halana and Evadene got the chance to finally say a proper goodbye to him. They hugged him hard before his soul left his body for the final time. The Higher Elders took his body and his chair glowed.

"I wonder who will inherit his star," Evadene whispered.

"Only time will tell my darling, only time will tell," Halana replied.

Chapter 49

ENCELADUS

It had been a little over two weeks since Sinclair had departed. Aquilia had spent a lot of time reading over the letters her mother had written. Some were so emotional that Aquilia had to take a few days away from reading them.

Janus and Lyra had returned to Saturn with the promise they would contact her should they require anything concerning the clean up down there.

As Aquilia sat at her bedroom window, there was a soft knock at the door.

"Come in," she called.

Evadene opened the door slowly, "sorry to disturb you Princess."

"Eva! Come in, are you OK?" Aquilia asked.

"Yes, I'm fine. Mother sent me to fetch you. The Higher Elders have called a meeting," she replied.

Aquilia took a deep breath and gathered herself together, "let's go."

They walked together to the meeting room, finding Chylla and Nymeria on the way.

"Anyone know what this meeting is about?" Chylla asked.

"No idea," Aquilia replied, "I just hope it's not another attack. I don't think we are up to full strength yet."

They entered the room to find everyone else already there, including Lyra and Janus. Aquilia thought it must be important if they had been summoned from Saturn too. Everyone sat down to await The Higher Elders arrival.

"Thank you all for coming," Zyra said, her face appearing on the walls, "as you are all aware, we have been taking the time to discuss who should be gifted Sinclair's star."

"It has been a hard choice but we believe this is the right decision," Ammyn added, her face appearing to the right of Zyra.

"This person has shown bravery and loyalty to The Royal Family and has been of great support to Princess Aquilia," Quintara commented, her smiling face appearing to the left of Zyra.

"Please step forward Evadene," Zyra said.

Evadene looked scared. She stood up on shaky legs and held the wall while she stepped forward. Aquilia rose to support her friend. She held Evadene up as she stood facing the women on the screens.

"Evadene, you have shown every aspect of what this star means. It is for that reason; we bestow the gift to you. Protect it well and use it wisely," Zyra began, "only you will understand its true power."

In a flash of light, Evadene's forehead was adorned with a yellow star. Aquilia hugged her friend, Halana had shed a few tears, and everyone else smiled.

"I don't think I could have chosen anyone more deserving," Zyra announced.

"Thank you. I will protect everything with all my being," Evadene replied.

There was chatter amongst the group about how proud they were of Evadene and how much she deserved the star.

"That's not all!" Zeebrakaan announced, appearing on the screen furthest from Zyra, "we have two more surprises up our sleeves."

Everyone laughed, they all missed Zeebrakaan and his surprise announcements.

"So, what's surprise number two?" Zidan asked.

"Ah well that would be..." he replied, pointing to his left.

The screen flickered a little, and then gradually, pixel by pixel, a face appeared.

"Reaver!" Halana exploded, tears streaming down her face.

"It is in his truest form that Reaver becomes a Higher Elder. He gave his life to protect his home and we welcome him with open arms," Zeebrakaan announced a wide smile across his face.

"I'm so glad you have chosen someone as loyal as Reaver, he really is a great man," Zidan said.

"So what's number three?" Aquilia asked.

"Aquilia darling, now that I am gone, you will be crowned High Priestess Queen Aquilia of Saturn and Enceladus. With that comes pressure and responsibility," Quintara said, "are you able to handle that?"

"Yes, I am ready to do what is required," she replied.

"You must first decide where you will reside," Zyra added, "Saturn or Enceladus."

Aquilia looked around the room at the people she called her family from both places. She had grown up here. She felt more connected here, "I choose to reside on Enceladus. If they will have me," she replied, "but I do make one request."

"Go on," Zyra said.

"I request that Janus is made Duke of Saturn and that he govern Astrodia and Saturn on my behalf, also Lyra is to become Countess of Astrodia," Aquilia announced.

"That's not necessary Princess, I assure you," Janus said.

"It is done," Quintara announced. "Arise, Duke and Countess of Astrodia."

"I feel that Aquilia felt pressured because of Altair's behaviour," Janus said, "I feel she only gave me a Dukedom due to the fact Altair tried to steal the throne and I didn't join in."

"Janus, Aquilia gifted you a Dukedom due to your loyalty. It has absolutely nothing to do with Altair, I promise you," Quintara replied.

Janus had requested a private conversation as everyone had left the room. Four of The Higher Elders had listened to his speech, which was in detail.

"How can you be so sure?" Janus questioned.

"Aquilia has mentioned how much a part of this family you are and how much you mean to her, it was hardly surprising that she request something like this," Quintara replied.

"She always spoke so fondly of you in her younger years Janus. If she believed this is your role, then your role it will be," Zeebrakaan said gently, "any qualms you have, should be taken up with her I'm afraid."

Janus hung his head, "I don't mean to sound ungrateful. All I've ever wanted was to belong somewhere; I just don't want Aquilia to feel like she owes me anything."

"She doesn't," Aquilia said from the shadows. "Please sit down Janus. Could we have a moment?"

The Higher Elders smiled and left, the screens returning to the white of the walls. Janus sat down at the table.

"I chose you to look after Astrodia because it is your home. You were born into the Royal Family, only your father lost his place in the line of succession, not you," Aquilia explained.

"What about Lyra?" Janus asked, "where does she fit in?"

"Your mother put herself in harms way to inform my mother about Altair's plans in the first place, for that I owe her my life," Aquilia replied.

"That explains the E.L on the letters," he said.

"What do you mean?" Aquilia questioned him, "what letters?"

"Your mother was receiving letters after she sent you here; they were always signed 'E.L'. I assumed Uncle Elio had left her some hidden lettered to find after he had gone," he explained.

"Then even more fitting that she becomes Countess of Astrodia. You are both to live in the Palace. The Higher Elders will inform us of the dates for our crowning ceremonies. Will you stay for dinner or must you leave?" She asked.

Janus pulled Aquilia in for a hug. "Dinner sounds great, so does breakfast. Do you think we could stay a few days?"

Aquilia laughed, "you can stay as long as you both want."

They left the meeting room to join the others in the dining room. As they entered, they noticed how easily Lyra slotted into place.

"It's our own dysfunctional family," laughed Janus.

Aquilia laughed, "it's a little out of shape, but I like it!"

They joined the others at the table, Janus taking the seat next to Evadene and Lyra sitting with Aquilia. There were platters of food all laid out on the table with an extra table for drinks, all ranges of juices and sparkles.

"Evadene and Janus seem to be rather close, don't you think?" Lyra said to Halana as she poured herself a glass of sparkling melon juice.

"Our young Evadene picks her acquaintances based on loyalty. I believe she has chosen well with who she associates herself with, your son being a prime example of loyalty, as are you Lyra," Halana began, "we were led wrong about you, I apologise."

"No one's fault but Altair's, let's leave him in the past where he belongs," Lyra replied clinking her glass against Halana's, "here's to a new start."

Halana smiled, "a new start indeed." She watched as Evadene and Janus ate and laughed together. She was happy to see her daughter smiling again.

Chapter 50

SATURN

Janus and Lyra had stayed on Enceladus for an extra two weeks whilst work was completed on The Palace. The roof had been completely reworked and the courtyard ripped up and re-laid, along with a new design worked into the brickwork.

"I think it looks perfect," Janus said looking down at the mosaic of King Elio, Queen Quintara, and Princess Aquilia that had been incorporated into the new stone floor.

"It's a fitting tribute to them," Lyra replied, "now, let's start getting our stuff inside, I think I'll keep the room Arista set up for me, I quite like it."

"Me too. I want to leave Aquilia's room as it is, just in case she comes to stay," he replied.

They moved all their belongings into their rooms and set about checking on the rest of Lyra's family. They had been gifted the whole abandoned south side of the city to make their own. Everyone had integrated back into society with ease after the rumours were cleared up. Altair had made Lyra and her family look like criminals. Thankfully, the residents of Astrodia were very forgiving and they welcomed them warmly.

ENCELADUS

Aquilia had given Layson a job as head of security. He had a uniform, radio, and his own office. Well, it was Sinclair's old office but Layson had made it his own. He had also hung a picture of Sinclair on the wall as a tribute to the late Elder.

Aquilia was grateful for his gesture. She had watched Layson work over the past week and had noticed how efficiently he worked.

"What job did you have back home?" She asked him.

"I didn't really have one, not as such. I did whatever Altair asked of me and he paid me," he replied.

"How did you eat?" Aquilia asked.

Bella worked at the hat shop, she earned the money in the house. I felt stupid," he said hanging his head in shame.

"There's nothing to be ashamed of Layson. Judging by my uncle's tactics, it's highly unlikely you would have kept a job, Altair would make you leave it to help him," she said, "now you have a stable job. You will be paid grandly every month."

"I'm grateful for this opportunity Your Highness. I will not let you down," he replied.

Aquilia smiled, gently squeezed his arm, and left the room. As she wandered down the corridor, she could hear singing coming from the fountain. She followed the voice, which led to Evadene.

"Why so happy?" Aquilia quizzed her,

Evadene instantly began to blush, "erm," she laughed, "just a certain someone."

"Would that someone begin with a J?" Aquilia asked with a smile.

"He is so sweet; he sent me a message, inviting me to The Palace. I've not replied yet, obviously I don't want to seem too keen, but I do really like him," Evadene replied.

Aquilia smiled, "he's a good man. I trust him with my life, and if you do end up marrying him," she smiled, "you'll be related to me!"

Both women laughed and hugged each other.

"You're like the sister I never had," Evadene said, "I'm so glad we became friends."

"Me too," Aquilia replied, "me too."

"Sorry to interrupt," Zeke cleared his throat. "We have a slight issue on the pathway from Uranus, they aren't responding to my calls,"

"Lead the way Zeke," Aquilia said following him. "Coming Eva?"

Evadene jumped up and linked arms with Aquilia. She loved to watch her work her magic.

At the comms room, Aquilia placed the head mic over her head and spoke;

"This is High Priestess Queen Aquilia of Saturn and Enceladus, state your business or risk being shot down," she said firmly.

There was no reply.

"Prepare Onyx Abyss Alpha," she instructed Zeke. "This is your last chance, reply now," she commanded.

"Apologies Your Highness, we were experiencing communication issues. We are en route to Palades Andromeda, we appear to have been thrown off course, any help you can offer will be greatly received," came the reply.

"Send Nymeria and her crew to escort them to the edge of The Milky Way," Aquilia commanded, "we will send an escort, please be patient."

"Thank you Your Highness, we will wait patiently," the radio squawked.

Aquilia removed the headset and instructed Zeke to watch them closely. She trusted no one. She called Layson and asked him to run a background check on the ship. Within minutes, Layson returned with news.

"All clear Your Majesty, no criminal activity listed. Seems it is a family ship," he relayed.

"Thank you Layson, that was excellent work," she replied.

"Your Highness, Nymeria's crew have arrived on scene. They await instructions," Zeke said.

Aquilia placed the headset back on her head, "Nymeria, please escort this family to the edge of The Milky Way. I hope you enjoy your trip," she said.

"Thank you," came the voices of two or more excited sounding children.

Aquilia told Zeke to watch over them whilst they were being escorted. He turned back to the monitors.

"That was great!" Evadene said, "I don't know how you stay so calm."

"It's hard, but it's no good screaming at them, they won't listen," she replied, "maybe you could try one day."

Evadene looked shocked, "really?" She asked.

"Absolutely, why not?" Aquilia replied.

They both walked away together, planning Evadene's trip to Saturn.

"You will love it Make sure he takes you close to the rings, it's beautiful there," Aquilia said.

SATURN

"So, you're serious about Evadene?" Lyra asked.

"I am. She's a very special woman. I at least want to give it a try," Janus replied.

He had sent messages to both Evadene and Halana, offering Evadene a trip to Saturn; he wanted to spend some time with her without being watched. Evadene had agreed to travel down and meet him. She promised to stay a few days, she

had never left Enceladus. Halana had also given her blessing, on orders he look after her and show her how amazing Saturn really was.

Janus and Lyra had rebuilt most of what Altair had destroyed in the battle. Luckily, the residents of Astrodia didn't hold Janus responsible for his father's actions. Those soldiers who fought for his father and survived were punished and then made to leave Astrodia and live in the outer wastelands, just as Lyra's family had been made to do.

Since returning to Astrodia, Lyra's extended family had opened several stalls on the market and was fully settled back into normal life. Lyra's mother started a school for the younger children of Astrodia, there, they learnt to paint and make all sorts of models from clay, they also learnt to read, which helped prepare them for their future years at school. She found a lot of them were very bright and eager to learn. They spent more time reading than painting.

"Do you have any plans for when Evadene arrives?" Lyra asked as she swept the last of the dust away from the library floor.

"I thought of taking her to the fountain, and maybe up the clock tower. There's an excellent view of Astrodia from up there," he replied arranging a shelf of books into alphabetical order.

Lyra giggled to herself, "what about dinner?" She asked, "or lunch?"

Janus stopped suddenly, "I hadn't thought if that, Can you help me Mum? I'm new to all this."

Lyra smile at him, she was glad she was here to help him, she dread to think how helpful Altair would have been, more like helpless.

"A picnic under the rings, it's the perfect place. I'll pack everything," she replied.

"Thanks Mum," he replied.

Between the pair of them, the library was dusted and re-ordered in no time. Janus knew how much Quintara loved the library, so he promised to keep it tidy and well stocked, but also well used. As he surveyed the work they had done, he received a message from Evadene. "She will be here tomorrow, I need to prepare," Janus said in a panic.

"Relax," Lyra said, "it's Evadene, and she isn't a stranger."

Janus took a deep breath, "it's her first time away from Enceladus Mum. I want it to be a time she won't forget," he replied.

Lyra felt proud of how perfect he wanted everything to be for Evadene. She was glad he hadn't inherited his father's ways. "You wait here. I'll prepare her room, in fact," she said pulling a piece of paper from her pocket, "go grab the shopping for me."

Janus smiled, he was happy to be treated as normally as possible, despite being a Duke. He hadn't been crowned yet but he wouldn't push Aquilia. She had been through too much recently. He followed the list and paid the storeowner, he even added some extra to their tip jar. As he returned to the Palace, he could instantly see how much trouble his mother had gone to, there were fresh flowers in every vase and Evadene's room had been aired and laid out perfectly. Janus's eyes welled up, "it's beautiful Mum, thank you," he said hugging her.

Lyra couldn't speak; she just nodded her head and rubbed his back.

Chapter 51

ENCELADUS

"Are you sure you have everything?" Halana asked as Evadene climbed into Aquilia's private pod.

Evadene laughed, "I'm going for two days Mum, not forever. I'm sure they have shops there too," she kissed her mother's cheek and gave her a big hug. "I'll be back before you have a chance to miss me."

"Are you ready?" Aquilia asked.

"As I'll ever be. Are you sure this thing is safe?" Evadene asked.

"It got me here all those years ago," Aquilia laughed, "but it has been maintained ever since. It's as safe as it ever was."

Evadene took a deep breath and sat down. Aquilia buckled her in, much like her own mother had done all those years ago. She set the dials and radioed Zeke.

"Ready when you are Zeke," Aquilia said.

"Stand clear. Lift off," came Zeke's reply over the radio.

The pod lifted effortlessly, raising swiftly and then disappearing into the sky. Halana swiped at her eyes. It was hard for her to watch her only child take a journey so far all alone.

"She's on the radio if you want to talk to her, I'll cut off everyone if you want some privacy," Aquilia whispered.

"Oh, I'm just worried, I'm a Mum, it's what we do, but could I have a short while with her?" Halana replied.

Aquilia smiled, switched to a clear channel, and passed Halana the radio, "it's all yours."

"You're too precious," she said, stoking Aquilia's hair.

Halana waited until she was alone before calling, "Eva, are you there?"

"Yes Mum, I'm here, is everything all right?" Evadene replied.

"Everything is fine sweetheart; I just wanted to check on you. How is it up there?" She asked.

"Oh Mum, you would love it, It's so beautiful and peaceful, come with me next time," Eva said, explaining how magnificent Enceladus looked from afar and how beautiful Saturn looked, "I can't believe how amazing it looks."

"I'm sure it's beautiful darling, maybe one day I'll travel too. I just wanted to say how proud I am of you, after everything, you still remain so humble, please don't change who you are, even if you do fall for a Duke," Halana said.

Evadene rolled her eyes, "oh Mum. Janus is just as humble as I am. I do really like him, but I won't rush into things. I want to get to know him first," she said.

"That's my girl, now have a safe flight and let me know when you land," Halana replied.

"I doubt I could tell you before Zeke does," Evadene laughed, "I love you Mum."

"Oh I love you too baby girl, go have fun," she replied, cutting the connection and leaving the landing strip.

<u>SATURN</u>

"Thanks Zeke," Janus said, placing his phone back in his pocket, "she's about ten minutes out Mum. I know her so why am I so nervous?"

"Oh darling, it's normal to feel nervous about spending time alone with someone you feel a connection with, don't worry, I'm sure she is just as nervous, just be yourself," Lyra told him. She remembered the first time she spent some time alone with Altair. He was a completely different person back then, she shook her head and realised how wrong she had been about him, and she couldn't help but feel partially responsible for his actions.

Janus took one more look around Evadene's room before making his way to the landing strip; he could just make out the pod breaking through Saturn's atmosphere. Lyra watched as Janus followed the pod with his eyes, watching for any difficulties and ready to spring into action. Evadene's pod landed perfectly. The door opened with ease and Evadene climbed out. She looked around at her new surroundings, taking in how different it looked from Enceladus. There were swirls of orange and white that lit up the sky, swirling together to create pattern up above, it fascinated her so much, she didn't notice Janus walking towards her.

"I'm glad you landed safely," he said.

"Oh Janus, you scared me," she replied placing her hand over her heart.

"I'm sorry. I...I didn't mean to," he stuttered, lowering his eyes.

"It's OK. I was too obsessed with the sky down here. It's beautiful," she said, gently touching his arm, "so different to Enceladus."

Her touch made his arm tingle; it was their first physical contact. He stood with her while she watched the sky for a few minutes more, the swirls moving across the sky.

"Shall I show you where you will be staying?" Janus asked softly.

"Sure, let's go. Wait, does the sky change?" She replied.

Janus laughed, "not by much. Just a splash of black late at night, that's how we tell the difference. Sometimes the sky turns green but only when we have a storm."

"Wow, can we stay out to watch the change, or do we have to be in by a certain time?" She asked, unsure if there were certain laws to abide by.

"We can come back just before it changes, in fact, I'll take you to the perfect spot. Let's take your bags to your room and then we will set off," he replied, grabbing her bags and leading the way.

On the short walk to The Palace, Evadene took many pictures and sent them back to Halana. They walked past the fountain with its crystal clear water, past the children splashing around and squealing with laughter. She smiled at them and they smiled and waved at her. They arrived at the Palace gates and Evadene looked up in amazement.

"It's so beautiful," she gasped.

Janus giggled, "it's nothing compared to the one on Enceladus."

Evadene looked at him seriously, "you don't know much about its history do you?"

"I studied Ancient Saturnese Arts, with a side study of History but nothing about this Palace in particular, no," he replied, feeling a little embarrassed about his admission.

"There's so much to teach you and we only have two days! Oh, it's going to be so much fun," she exclaimed clapping her hands.

They entered the same courtyard in which Aquilia killed Altair. Evadene stopped for a second to survey the area, "how did she do it in such a small space?" She whispered.

"I guess we will never know the answer to that unless she is willing to share the details," Janus answered.

"Doesn't it feel strange? Knowing this is where your father died," she asked.

"Not really. If I'm honest, I don't think I ever knew who my real father was. All I have ever known was a monster," he replied.

"I'm sorry Janus," she hugged him, "I wish you could have had a better father, one you could have looked up to, but, on

the other hand, if you had, then we may never have met," she said, kissing him on the cheek.

He smiled as she released him, "I'm glad we met," he whispered.

"Me too." She replied.

"So...are you both coming up or shall I move the beds down there?" Lyra called from an overhead window.

Janus and Evadene laughed and made their way up the stairs.

The long spiral staircase, which sat at the centre of the entranceway, grabbed Evadene's attention, "wow, they didn't change a thing!"

Lyra looked confused; she glanced at Janus, who hadn't taken his eyes off Evadene since she landed.

"Sorry, there's so much history linked to the Palace. It's amazing to see it in its full glory," she exclaimed.

"Don't apologise, enjoy it!" Lyra replied.

"Mum, I'm taking Evadene to watch the sky change," Janus said as he bent to retrieve her bags.

"Ah, I'll grab the picnic basket for you," Lyra replied and she headed off to the kitchen.

Janus opened the door to Evadene's room, the smell of fresh flowers hitting her nose instantly. The voile across the open window blew gently in the breeze. Janus set her bags beside the bed.

"I'll let you get freshened up," he said, turning to leave the room.

"I won't be long," she replied.

Closing the door behind him he let out a breath he didn't realise he was holding. His cheek still tingled from where she kissed him; he reached up to touch the area.

"Everything alright?" Lyra asked interrupting his thoughts, "she kissed you didn't she?"

Janus could do nothing but smile. Lyra's heart burst with pride. She handed him the basket, squeezed his shoulder, and walked away. Evadene opened the door and linked arms with him.

"Ready?" She asked.

Janus looked at her; she had applied a small amount of lip gloss, just to the centre of her bottom lip and a small covering of foundation. She had pulled her emerald green hair into a high bun, allowing a strand of hair either side of her head to flow freely. Her baby blue eyes sparkled in the light of the chandelier above.

"Absolutely, let's go," he said with a smile.

They left the Palace and made their way to the point closest to the Rings of Saturn. Evadene's eyes lit up. She could see the flecks of gems and glass mixed with rocks and ice.

"It's just as beautiful as Aquilia described," she squeaked.

"Let me get a picture of you with the rings as a backdrop, you can send it back home," he said.

Evadene posed against the backdrop of the rings as Janus snapped a few photos. If he were to believe his heart, he may be falling in love with her. Evadene sent the pictures back to Enceladus and shut her phone away in her bag. They sat together and devoured the food that Lyra had made for them.

"Quick, look," Janus said, pointing up, "it's starting."

Evadene sat closer to Janus, placing her head on his shoulder. The sky sparked red before fading back to the orange and white swirls, but this time with a hint of black.

"That was amazing. Thank you for showing me," Evadene said softly.

Janus was about to reply when he noticed how shallow her breaths had become. He carefully picked her up and carried her back to the Palace. He placed her on the bed and covered her with a blanket; he then kissed her forehead and left her to sleep.

Chapter 52

ENCELADUS

Aquilia sat on her bed with the box of letters she had found from her mother. Even though Quintara was now a Higher Elder, Aquilia didn't have much contact with her. There was the occasional meeting but other than that, Aquilia felt much the same as she did before. Alone.

She had been told to still act as if her mother were dead and gone forever. It was hard for Aquilia, especially know that neither her mother nor father were truly dead. She picked up an envelope, dark blue in colour. She turned it repeatedly but there was no name. She put it to one side and pulled out a sunflower yellow envelope next. She opened the envelope and read the contents of the card;

'Dearest Aquilia,

Today marks your 9th birthday.

I long for the day when I can see you again.

I wish you the happiest of days.

All my love

Mum x'

It was the same simple message that had been written in every card since she had arrived here. She threw it back into the box and closed the lid.

"Could have mixed it up a bit," she mumbled bitterly, "it's almost like you didn't care."

There was a soft knocking at her door. She slid the box aside and went to open it.

"Is everything OK my dear?" Halana asked, gazing over her shoulder, "I thought I heard you talking to someone."

Aquilia stepped aside and allowed her to entre, "there's no one here. I was talking out loud," she sighed, planting herself back on her bed.

Halana sat beside her, "what is it? What has got you in such a state?" She asked.

Aquilia pointed to the box, "every card since I arrived here has the same generic message. It's like she didn't care about me," she said, swiping at a tear that had escaped jet blue eyes. She threw herself, face down, on the pillow and sobbed.

Halana, softly, rubbed Aquilia's back, "I'm sure there is a perfectly reasonable explanation, try not to get too worked up. Rest now, I'll come back later," she said as Aquilia dropped off into a weepy sleep.

Halana left the room and made her way to the meeting room. She wasn't sure how to handle this but she was going to try anyway. She searched for a while before she found the intercom to call The Higher Elders. She pressed the button three times in quick succession. Zyra's face appeared on the screen.

"I wasn't aware we had a meeting scheduled for today. How can I help you Halana? She asked.

"I need to speak with Quintara, urgently and privately, please," Halana asked.

"I can see if she is free to speak with you," Zyra replied, sensing something was wrong.

Her face vanished from the screen. Halana began to pace the room; time seemed to drag whilst she waited. Suddenly, after what had felt like hours, Quintara's face materialized on the screen.

"Halana, what is it? Is it Aquilia?" She asked sounding panicked.

"Aquilia, well, she's not fine. Health wise she is fine, emotionally, she's not," Halana replied.

"Well out with it, what's wrong with her?" Quintara demanded.

Halana sat herself down in an attempt to curb her anger.

"Aquilia found the box of letters and cards you left behind for her," she began, wringing her hands together.

"I don't see the problem, they were left there for her to find," Quintara interrupted.

"It seems every card that was written for her, since her arrival here, is some form of generic message, there is no personalisation at all, it's upset her. A lot." Halana explained.

"I really don't see the issue. I wrote each card the night before each of her birthdays and placed them in the box. What more could I have done?" Quintara asked.

"I understand how much you wanted to keep her safe, but she was five years old when she came here. Unaware, fully, what was happening. You could have tried harder to reassure her. She may not have emerged victorious after her battle with Altair; she would have gone to her grave thinking you didn't care. We watched her soldier through when you were too busy to take her calls. What YOU didn't see was how broken she was inside!" Halana's voice rose.

Quintara was taken aback, "are you trying to say that what I did for her, sending her away to keep her safe was wrong?"

Halana let out a sigh, "no. What I'm saying is, you could have handled things better."

Having said that, Halana left the room. She couldn't decide if what she had just done was right or wrong, but how Aquilia felt right now, was wrong. No child should ever feel that their parents don't care. She made her way back to Aquilia's room; she should tell her what had been said before she heard it from someone else. She poked her head in the door to see Aquilia sitting up and reading a poetry book.

"Come in Halana. I wondered where you went," she said spotting her head at the door.

Halana entered the room, "I need to tell you something. I'm not sure if you will be angry with me, but I would rather you heard this from me that through the grapevine," Halana said as she stood next to Aquilia's bed.

Aquilia closed the book and set it aside, "sit down Halana," she said.

Halana perched on the side of Aquilia's bed, ready to make a swift exit if she was to be dismissed. She took a deep breath and explained everything she had just said to Quintara, "I'm sorry if I overstepped the mark and I understand if you are angry with me."

Aquilia's face softened, "I can't believe you spoke to her, on my behalf."

Halana let some tears escape her eyes, "I can't imagine how hard it was for her to send you away, but I can see how hurt you are by those simple messages in those cards. You deserved so much more. I didn't mean to interfere."

Aquilia crawled across the bed and threw her arms around Halana's neck, "I don't think you interfered at all, in fact, you probably made a better job of it than I would."

Halana broke down in tears, "I don't make a habit of crying about these things. You've been so strong throughout everything. I just wanted her to show you how proud she was of you," she sobbed.

"She will, in her own way. I've learned not to expect the norm from Mum, maybe that's how she was brought up, but I've survived a huge battle without her. I made it to seventeen with little input from her. It did hurt reading the same message in every card," Aquilia said, "but it hurt a little less than it would have done had she been on my life constantly."

There was a sharp knock at the door and Zidan popped his head in, "there has been an emergency meeting called," he said, "everything OK in here?"

"Yes, thank you, just a girly chat," Aquilia smiled.

"What about Evadene? She's on Saturn," Halana asked.

"She will join us via video link," Zidan replied with a smile.

Both Halana and Aquilia followed Zidan to the meeting room.

"I hope this isn't about earlier," Halana whispered.

Aquilia grabbed her hand, "I've got your back if it is," she smiled.

<u>SATURN</u>

"Evadene signing in," Evadene said as the screen faded in to focus, "what's happened?"

"Nothing to worry about Evadene," Zyra said, "we have made a decision though. How is your trip progressing?"

"Erm, its going really well. I didn't realise how beautiful this place really is, there is so much history here," Evadene replied.

"I'm so glad you got to experience it," Ammyn said, her face to the left of Zyra's.

Evadene smile, she was glad too.

"Now that everyone has assembled, we can continue," Zyra said. "We have decided that it is time for your coronation Aquilia. It will be one week from today."

"Wait, didn't anyone think to ask me?" Aquilia said slightly irritated.

"It is not up for discussion," Quintara replied, "from anyone!"

"No offence intended here but why did I need to be told this?" Evadene asked.

"As you are currently staying with Janus and Lyra, we would kindly ask you to relay the message. The first ceremony will be on Saturn, the second on Enceladus. They will need to attend both," Zyra said, "now you may go and enjoy the remainder of you trip."

Evadene shook her head as she signed off from the meeting; she sensed some tension within Quintara's voice. She would find out later, first she had to tell Janus and Lyra about the coronation.

"What do you think she would say?" Janus asked Lyra.

"Don't you think it's too soon? I mean, you have hardly spent any time together," she replied.

"I just know Mum; I really think she is the one. I'm going to ask her tonight, at the top of the clock tower," he said confidently, a smile plastering itself on his face.

Evadene came into the kitchen and stared at him, "what's with the grin?" she laughed.

"Nothing, just Janus being Janus," Lyra joked, "everything OK back home?"

Evadene shrugged and sat down, "you will all have your coronation next week, here on Saturn. There will also be one on Enceladus; you're both expected to attend that one too."

"You don't seem too thrilled with that," Lyra noticed.

"Something seemed off, like really tense," Evadene said.

"Janus, go prepare for your clock tower visit, make it perfect," Lyra whispered, "go!"

"Where is he off to?" Evadene asked as Janus shot out of the door.

"He has plans to make. Now talk to me, there has to be more to your unhappiness," Lyra replied.

"I'm scared I'll never be able to spend time with Janus again, not like now. He'll be busy with Duke duties," Evadene confessed.

"How do you feel about Janus Evadene?" Lyra asked, gently holding her hand.

"Where do I start?" Evadene said, staring off into the distance.

Chapter 53

SATURN

"This really is a lovely place Janus, thank you for showing it to me," Evadene said.

"I used to come here to think when I was young. I loved to watch the city go about its day," he replied.

Janus took Evadene's hand in his and gazed into her eyes.

"I know we haven't had a long time to get to know each other and I really wished we had longer," he began.

"I know, I understand what you're saying," she said, her eyes dropping.

"You do?" He asked, clearly confused.

"Of course. You won't have time for this after next week, you're just trying to be nice about it," she replied.

Janus shook his head, "no, you don't understand. I don't want this to end. Marry me?" He said, pulling a small velvet box from his pocket, "be my Duchess?"

Evadene was speechless, she stared at the small red velvet box, resisting the urge to reach out and touch it.

"Please say something," he pleaded.

"I... I don't know what to say. Can I touch it?" She replied.

Janus laughed, "of course, open it!" He thrust the box into her hands, "please."

Evadene opened the box to reveal a simple platinum ring with an amethyst set stone surrounded by smaller diamonds.

"It's perfect," she exclaimed. "It's beautiful."

"So...will you be my Duchess? I don't think I can do this without you by my side," he asked again.

She jumped into his arms, "yes! Oh yes!"

She placed the ring on her finger and snapped a photo. She would tell her mum before sending the photo. They lay together and watched the sky change one last time before she would set off home to Enceladus tomorrow. They, then, made their way back to the Palace. Janus wouldn't see Evadene again until the day of his coronation and he would definitely count down the days. They arrived back at the Palace in each other's arms; they hadn't separated since she said yes.

Lyra watched them arrive, it was clear things had gone well. They walked together into the lounge and stood together to break the news to Lyra.

"She said yes!" Janus exclaimed, unable to contain his excitement.

Lyra smiled, so wide and so hard that her cheeks began to ache, "I couldn't wish for a better person for my son. I wish you both every happiness."

"Thank you. Please don't say anything to my mother yet. I haven't said anything to her," Evadene asked.

Lyra pretended to lock her lips, "I'll get some dinner prepared. You need lots of rest for your trip back tomorrow."

Janus and Evadene sat at the table still holding hands, but Evadene looked distracted.

"Is everything OK?" Janus asked softly. "You seem a little lost."

Evadene smiled at him, "I'm fine, just disappointed at having to go home."

He brushed a wisp of hair from her eyes and tucked it behind her ear, "we won't be apart long. Plus, we have a wedding to plan," he said excitedly.

She placed her head on his shoulder and smiled, "it's going to be the best ever," she whispered.

ENCELADUS

"SET DOWN IN 5, 4, 3, 2, and 1. SUCCESSFUL LANDING," Zeke announced.

Evadene had left Saturn behind just over twenty-five minutes before, using Hyper Jump to make it back faster. With a blast of air, the pod opened and Evadene removed her helmet, shaking her hair loose.

"Eva!" Aquilia screeched, running up to her, "how was it? Did you see the rings?"

Evadene giggled, "it was beautiful, the rings are just as spectacular as you described. I have news, but first, where is my mum?"

"Right here darling," Halana replied embracing her daughter. "What is your news?"

Evadene prepared herself. She took a deep breath and said, "Janus asked me to marry him," she waited for their reactions.

"And?" They both gasped.

"I said yes," she squealed, showing off the ring.

"Oh Eva, it's beautiful! I'm so happy for you!" Aquilia cried.

Evadene turned to her mother, "Mum, say something, please?" She begged.

Halana smiled. A pure and genuine smile, "my heart. It bursts with so much pride! I must make your wedding dress!"

"Oh Mum! I was so scared to tell you," Eva said, hugging her mother harder.

They stood for a while talking before heading to the dining room for lunch. Evadene smiled as they talked about her time on Saturn and she filled Aquilia in on the progress Janus and Lyra had made.

As they entered the dining room, the smell of freshly baked salmon, freshly caught from the nearby lake, pan fired tomatoes, and boiled vegetables hit their noses.

"This smells amazing," Evadene said as she took a deep breath in.

"Thank you, I've been practising," Bella replied. "I hope you enjoyed your trip."

"I did and I have an announcement to make," she replied. "Janus and I are getting married."

The room erupted in cheers and applause. Evadene even shed a tear of happiness. She wished her father had been here to see it. Zeke entered the room and began to clap too before turning to Bella and asking, "why are we clapping?"

"Janus and Evadene are to marry. Isn't it wonderful?" Bella replied.

Zeke cheered some more, but then remembered why he had come, "that may explain the emergency meeting that has just been called," he said as everyone started to quieten down.

They all made their way to the meeting room where Zyra's face covered every screen, she didn't look impressed.

"Please, everyone, be seated," she said.

As everyone sat, Evadene began to feel unsettled. Zyra's eyes were set on her.

SATURN

"Stop pacing Janus, she's only been gone a few hours and you're already at a loss," Lyra joked. "She landed safely and everyone knows the news. Everyone is happy for you both."

"Then why the emergency meeting?" He asked.

Evadene had sent him a message as soon as she had told everyone. She also mentioned the meeting. It worried him a lot.

"I'm sure everything is fine. It's probably to arrange things for next week, that's all," Lyra said, hoping she was right. "Shall we talk colour schemes?"

Janus left the room without a word. He locked himself in his room and pleaded to anyone who would listen to allow him and Evadene to marry. He even offered to move to Enceladus just to be with her. He watched for any messages from Evadene for over an hour before reaching for the book she had let for him to read. As he opened the front cover, he saw an inscription. It read:

'My darling Evadene,

Now you can learn the Wonders of Saturn, just like I did.

I'm so proud of you.

Dad x'

Janus turned the pages gently, careful not to damage any. As he turned the pages, he found little notes Reaver had made for Evadene. Ways to help her learn, things she would enjoy and facts she should remember, he now understood how much this book meant to her and why she carried it everywhere. When she left it for him to read, it meant she would be coming back for it. He had read several pages before a sharp 'ping' caught his attention. He picked up his phone and read the message; he then dropped it in disbelief.

'We need to talk. I have a decision to make. Saturn or Enceladus.'

ENCELADUS

"How is that fair?" Evadene asked clearly frustrated.

"It's how it works. You want to marry a Saturnite, you have to decide where to reside, it's as simple as that," Zyra explained. "Quintara had to make the same choice when she married Elio."

"He was a Prince!" Evadene exclaimed, "Janus is a Duke, well, will be. It's different, isn't it?" She asked, turning to Aquilia.

Aquilia shook her head, "I thought there would be more time to explain," she said, aiming her comment at Zyra.

"You all knew about the engagement?" Evadene questioned.

"No, not that you were engaged, but we all had a feeling, deep down, that he would ask you. That's why I thought I would have had more time to explain things to you," Aquilia said. "Even after your announcement, I hope Zyra would have given us more time to explain what would be expected of you."

Evadene slouched over on the table, "so I have to choose? What if I can't?"

"Then the choice will be made for you, by us," Zyra replied.

"Can I at least talk to Janus about it?" Evadene asked.

"You have two hours and not a second more," Zyra said and cut the connection.

Chapter 54

ENCELADUS

"Are you sure that you are all right with this Mum?" Evadene asked Halana.

"Oh honey. All I want is for you to be happy, and he makes you happy. Besides, it's not like you're leaving the Galaxy!" Halana replied with a smile so wide it rivalled the widest Ring of Saturn.

Evadene had broken the news to her first. Evadene would be moving and living on Saturn. Janus had even offered to make up one of the many spare rooms for whenever Halana wanted to stay.

"Let's inform The Higher Elders," Halana said, linking arms with her daughter, "then we HAVE to talk colours and materials."

Evadene giggled, "I'm actually getting married!"

"Yes you are my darling. Let's make it as special as you are," she replied.

As they entered the meeting room, Zyra's face was already plastered across the screen.

"Have you reached a decision?" She asked.

At one time, Evadene had liked this woman, and at this precise moment, she hated her.

"Yes. I am leaving for Saturn," Evadene snorted.

Zyra's face gave an unimpressed look, "I'm not sure I like your tone of voice."

"I don't take too kindly to being told I have two hours to decide the rest of my life," Evadene countered.

"I understand that it's not a lot of time, but we need to prepare," Zyra explained.

"Prepare for what? She asked.

"An Elder's wedding must be spectacular, no details disregarded," Zyra explained, "now, we know Halana is making your dress. Your ceremony must be held here, there are no negotiations on that, I'm sorry," Zyra smiled.

"That's suitable. I guess the reception will be held here too?" Janus said from the doorway.

Evadene ran to him, hugging him tight.

"Why did you come?" She asked.

"Well, if things need to be sorted, then I should be here to help," he said, tucking a strand of her green hair behind her ear.

She smiled at him, so grateful for his support, "Mum wants to make my dress."

"Then off you go, ask if she could make my suit too, I'll pay of course," he said.

"You'll do nothing of the sort!" Halana said from the table, "it is my gift to you both. Welcome to the family," she said kissing his forehead.

"Evadene, you're in charge, everything you want, you will have," he said.

Evadene smiled at him, "you might regret that!"

"Never," he said, smiling back, watching her as she walked away with Halana.

"Janus, you made a wise choice with Evadene. She is a wonderful woman," Quintara told him.

"Indeed she is," Aquilia agreed.

They all sat down to make plans for the upcoming coronation and wedding.

Halana and Evadene made their way towards Halana's sewing room. As they went, they passed Layson's office. Evadene stopped for a second; she looked in to see her uncle hunched over a computer typing in codes. She sat in front of him.

"Uncle Layson?" She said quietly.

"Oh Eva! How was your trip?" He asked, looking up at her.

"It was eventful!" She laughed. "I have a question to ask, feel free to say no if you don't want to."

"I heard about Janus and yourself, many, many congratulations. Please, ask away," he said, placing his hands in front of him.

Evadene cleared her throat, she had made this decision on the fly, "will you walk me down the aisle?"

Layson's mouth fell open and a swift intake of breath came from behind her. She turned to see her mother in the doorway, "I don't ask to discredit my father, but you are the closest to him right now," she explained.

Halana crossed the room and hugged her close; Layson had tears running down his face.

"I would be honoured, if the Mother of the Bride will allow it?" He replied, finally able to find the words to speak.

"Oh Layson! It is such a wonderful thing! Let's get you measured up too!" Halana said, embracing him tightly.

Halana and Evadene spent a fair few hours deciding which colour scheme to go for. The choices between the different shades of red and pink were unimaginable. In the end, Evadene settled for a pale pink wedding dress with a pure white lace veil, embroidered with ruby red roses. Her bridesmaids would wear dusty pink gowns with red and white rose bouquets. She decided on navy blue suits for the men, accessorised with a red rose buttonhole.

"Wait!" Evadene shouted from behind a privacy screen.

"What is it dear?" Halana asked a pin in her mouth and a tape measure between Layson's legs.

"I haven't asked anyone to be my Matron of Honour yet!" She replied, emerging from behind the screen wrapped in only a third of a roll of fabric.

"Who did you have in mind?" Layson asked, refusing to move. Halana had pricked him several times already.

Evadene flopped onto a nearby stool. Her eyes lowering to her shaky hands, "I wanted to ask Aquilia, but then I feel I'm leaving you out Mum," she said.

Halana laughed, "oh Evadene-Dionne! I'm as happy as ever just making the attire!"

Halana hadn't used Evadene's full name since Reaver had passed away. Evadene stood up, kissed her mother on the head, and ran off down the corridor.

"Eva, be careful! You're not wearing anything under that!" Halana shouted after her.

"Don't worry Mum. What's the worst that can happen?" She laughed.

Halana shook her head, "ah silly girl, does she forget the floor is..."

Before she could finish her sentence, a loud "OUCH!" could be heard from the end of the corridor.

"Slippery," Halana finished. "Quick, Layson, grab that dressing gown, I have to get to her before anyone sees her."

Layson grabbed the dressing gown and ran to catch up with Halana. He averted his eyes before stopping to leave Evadene with some dignity.

"Always in a rush, you'll never arrive," Halana said as she covered Evadene over.

"I know, I'm sorry," Evadene tried to laugh, "my ankle hurts."

Halana shook her head again, "of course it does, these floor are made or quartz and marble. Layson, will you fetch Janus and Miss Aquilia please whilst I get this silly thing back to the sewing room."

Layson nodded and ran off.

"I've made a fool of myself, haven't I?" Evadene asked as her mother scooped her up.

"Don't be silly," Halana laughed, "you're overexcited, it's understandable. Plus, you're only a fool if anyone, other than your mother sees you."

Halana helped Evadene hobble back to the sewing room, sat her down, and bandaged up her ankle. Within minutes, Janus and Aquilia arrived with Layson.

"What happened?" Janus asked rushing to her side.

"Evadene was in a rush," Halana began to explain.

"Evadene didn't arrive," Evadene finished.

Aquilia giggled, "I'm sorry, I can just picture it now."

"It's alright, it was my fault. I wanted to ask you something. Aquilia, will you be my Matron of Honour?" Evadene said, lowering her eyes, once more, to her hands.

Aquilia was shocked, "oh Eva! I'd love to! Wait, what does one of them do?" She asked looking confused.

"Oh Princess, there isn't anything special you need to do, just be there for Evadene on the day, now, arms up!" Halana instructed.

Halana measured everyone up and began to work on the dresses. Evadene had selected a few of the schoolchildren from Ammyn's class as her bridesmaids. Aquilia's dress was to have red roses embroidered onto the skirt.

After being measured up, Aquilia quickly left the room, returning five minutes later with a medium sized, red velvet box.

"I want you to wear this on your wedding day Eva, and you can't say no," she said, handing Evadene the box.

Evadene opened the box and her eyes widened at the sight of the tiara. It was eighteen carat gold with rubies and diamonds all around.

"I couldn't. It wouldn't be allowed, would it?" Evadene asked her.

Aquilia took it out of the box, placed it on Evadene's head, and pulled her emerald green hair up behind it.

"You look beautiful," Aquilia whispered.

Halana let silent tears fall as she looked at her daughter. Janus knew, at the moment, that he had chosen he right woman. He smiled as she and Aquilia hugged, he was glad he had chosen the right side.

Chapter 55 – One Week Later

SATURN

Two coronation ceremonies would be held, one on Enceladus and one on Saturn. The first of which would be Saturn. The Saturnese people hadn't seen Aquilia since the day of Elio's memorial, none of them knew it was her who rid the city of Altair.

Upon arriving on Saturn for only the second time since that battle, Aquilia was amazed to see how much work Janus and Lyra had completed.

"It looks amazing! Almost as if nothing happened," she said looking out from the balcony, "and the mosaic is beautiful, thank you."

"Ah, thank Lyra's family for that, it was their work," Janus explained.

"I'll make a point of thanking them personally later," she replied.

They watched as things were prepared for the ceremony. Huge coats of arms hung, flags were flying, and huge curtains hung from the wooden beams, erected just for this occasion. The Royal Arms designer had made Janus his own Coat of Arms, it depicted a man knelt before a Palace with wings protruding from him back. Janus had no idea whose it was. He wouldn't know until the ceremony, when it would be revealed as he was crowned.

"Are you all ready?" Zyra asked from the radio they each carried with them.

Aquilia looked at Janus, Janus looked and Lyra, they all smiled, "we're ready."

"Ladies and Gentlemen of Astrodia. Thank you for your patience. It is with great please that I give to you all Duke Janus of Astrodia!"

Aquilia swore to herself many years ago that she would find out whom that voice belonged to but so far, she had been unsuccessful.

She nudged Janus forward through the heavy purple curtains. His appearance met with cheers and applause. He was directed to a chair that was to the left of the huge, red cushioned chair. He sat down, waving to the crowd.

"Please, Ladies and Gentlemen, remain upstanding, as I present to you Countess Lyra of Astrodia."

Lyra looked at Aquilia; she appeared nervous, unaware of how the people would react.

"Go, it will be fine. I promise," Aquilia told her.

Lyra took a deep breath, held her head high, and stepped through the curtain. The crowd, again, erupted into cheers and applause. She took the seat to the right of the centre chair.

"Princess Aquilia?" Came a voice from behind her.

Aquilia turned to see a smaller woman with blue hair, her face instantly familiar, "Arla?"

Arista's daughter had moved to the Palace after Arista's tragic death.

"When mother said you were still alive, I didn't believe her, but now, look at you! All grown up!" Arla commented. "Will you be coming back now?"

"I'm afraid not, I'm going to stay on Enceladus now, but Janus will be in charge, please show him the same respect your family showed mine?" Aquilia requested.

"Certainly Your Highness," she said as she bowed her head.

"Ladies and Gentlemen, a moment of silence please."

The crowd grew silent. The odd whisper could be heard through the crowd.

"People of Astrodia. It was with great sadness that I announced the death of our beloved Queen Quintara and our beloved King Elio. May they rest in eternal happiness together. It is now my greatest pleasure to announce to you all today, High Priestess Queen Aquilia of Saturn and Enceladus!"

Aquilia straightened her back, held her head high, and walked forward. The curtains parted and the Palace grounds erupted with cheers.

The crowds people could be heard shouting:

"Did you know she was still alive?"

"Where has she been?"

"I'm glad she is taking over."

Aquilia smiled as she took her place on the throne that was rightfully hers. She sat between Janus and Lyra, smiling at them both as she sat down.

"You ready?" She asked them.

They nodded.

Upon Janus's head, a crown of solid silver was placed, encrusted with emeralds. Janus struggled at first to balance it, but he managed it in the end. His Coat of Arms dropped as the crown was in place.

"Is that mine?" He asked.

"Indeed. You own. Evadene will work with the Arms designer after the wedding," Aquilia explained.

Janus was impressed. He let out a sign. He finally felt like he belonged somewhere.

Upon Lyra's head, another crown of solid silver was placed, this one encrusted with opals. Lyra kept her head straight, hoping it didn't fall off.

"Please stand Queen Aquilia."

Aquilia stood perfectly still, just as Quintara had taught her. Upon her head, a crown made of pure platinum was placed, encrusted with amethyst and ruby jewels. A giant onyx perfectly placed at the centre.

Each of them were handed a scroll on which a pre-prepared speech was written. They took a brief glance over the speeches and prepared to speak.

"Duke Janus, if you will."

Janus took a breath and stood up; he opened his scroll and began to speak, "People of Astrodia, I stand before you today as your Duke. I want you to be aware that the door to the Palace is always open, as it has always been. I'm sure, most of you, if not all of you, are aware of what my father did, and for that I am deeply sorry," he began, keeping eye contact with as many people as he could as he spoke, "I hope you can entrust me with your lives as much as you did my aunt and uncle."

The crowd roared back to life as his speech ended, he stood for a few moments taking in the scene before him.

As the crowd began to settle down, the voice behind the announcements spoke again, "Countess Lyra, please address the people."

Lyra was wobbly on her feet; she focused her attention to the back of the auditorium and began to speak.

"Ladies and Gentlemen. I stand before you today to express my gratitude for your forgiveness, I'm sure you have all heard the stories by now. I will endeavour to be here for you all, day or night," she said with a shaky voice, "I will protect you all whenever necessary, and pledge to do all in my power to make Astrodia the happiest of cities."

The crowd whooped and cheered as she let one lonely tear escape her eye. She watched as her own family integrated with the crowd. Aquilia watched with honour as Janus and Lyra made their speeches. She was happy that she chose them to be Duke and Countess. The crowd mellowed down to a light hum of excitement.

"Ladies and Gentlemen, I give you. Queen Aquilia."

Aquilia stood, made her way to the podium, and placed her hands either side to steady herself. She looked out over the people of Astrodia and felt warmth within her. These were now her people to protect and serve.

"Astrodia. People young and old. I stand before you today as your Queen. You all served my mother and father well and I hope you will do the same for me," she began, "there has been too much heartache over the years and for that, I apologise. As I will not be residing here on Saturn, I hope you will extend you respect to my cousin and my aunt, both have done so much to protect you already."

The crowd cheered loudly.

"In other news, you will also be receiving a new Duchess in the coming weeks by the name of Evadene. I hope you will also extend your kindness, warmth, and hospitality to her. I appreciate that I have been out of your sights for many years, I hope to rectify that all very soon." Aquilia finished, the crowd cheering even more.

She sat back down and smiled at the others, "once more on Enceladus!"

They all laughed and stood up to wave at the people of Astrodia.

ENCELADUS

Lyra watched as Halana helped dress and already nervous Aquilia, who was busy rehearsing her speech for the Enceladent people.

"Slow down girl, no one will ever understand you if you mumble and speed through it all," Halana cursed.

"I'm sorry. I'm nervous," Aquilia replied.

"Why are you so nervous? The Enceladent people love you," Lyra asked, "I thought you would have been more nervous on Saturn!"

Aquilia let out a sigh, "I was nervous on Saturn, I just couldn't show it. I had to put on a brave face, just like mother had to when father died, it's what is expected."

Halana snorted, "nonsense! The Enceladents want a true Queen, one who shows her emotions and you, sweetheart, are exactly what they want."

Lyra raised her eyebrows, "you seem very certain of that Halana."

Halana blushed, "I have my ways of knowing these things."

Both Lyra and Aquilia looked at her.

"All right! I overheard a group of women talking at the market, but I will say no more!" She confessed, going behind Aquilia to button up her red and gold flowing gown.

Aquilia giggled, just a little, and quickly cleared her throat as Zidan entered the room.

"May I have a few moments with Aquilia? He asked.

"Of course!" Lyra said, dragging Halana out with her.

He gestured for Aquilia to sit with him on the balcony.

"I'm very proud of you," he began. "I know your mother is too."

"Thank you," she replied.

"I won't begin to say I understand how you are feeling because I don't and I never will, but I can sense something isn't settled between you and your mother. Do you think you could clear things up before the ceremony?" He asked.

Aquilia thought for a moment, she would love to clear the air, but was afraid she would say something she would regret later.

"I don't know. What if I say something that upsets her?" She asked.

"Then so be it, but you should never take on a Kingdom when you can't say how you truly feel, let's give it a try at least, for me?" He pleaded.

"Alright, but you are to blame if things go wrong," Aquilia warned him.

"Great. She's waiting in the meeting room," he said getting to his feet.

"Wait. How did you know I would agree?" She asked also standing up.

Zidan held his arms out to the side and shrugged, "you're my daughter after all," he laughed as he led her down the corridor.

Chapter 56

ENCELADUS

"Where is she?" Evadene asked impatiently, looking in every direction for Aquilia.

"She'll be here, just give her time," Zidan said calmly, "there's plenty of time."

"This better not take long Zidan," Zyra whispered.

Zidan had hoped it would have been over quicker than this. He smiled at Zyra.

"You best go check what the holdup is and fast," Zyra said through clenched teeth.

Zidan took off towards the meeting room, hoping to find Aquilia along the way but she never materialised. He made it to the meeting room and he instantly regret getting himself involved. All he could hear was shouting.

"A generic message in every card, ever year! That's all you could do?" Aquilia shouted.

"What more did you want?" Quintara replied.

"For it to be personal Mum. I've been here since I was five. FIVE! I've grown up around people I don't even know and they made it more personal than you did," Aquilia cried, tears streaming down her face.

"Being up here made you soft, stop crying," Quintara scolded her, "the people want a strong Queen, not an emotional mess!"

"You don't understand do you? I've spent over twelve years away from you, how could you understand," Aquilia said as she stood up, "you will never understand me."

Aquilia opened the door just as Zidan reached for the handle.

"Are you..." he began.

"Save it, I don't want to talk about it. I'm late," she said as she stormed off.

Zidan watched her walk away; he looked in towards Quintara whose face was still on the screen.

"GO, watch her be crowned. I'll be fine. I'll watch from here," she said.

Zidan nodded once and left to catch up with Aquilia.

"Where have you been?" Evadene asked as Aquilia entered the waiting area.

"Can we discuss this later, the people are waiting," Zyra said from the portable screen in front of them.

"Of course, yes," Evadene replied.

Aquilia allowed Halana and Lyra to fix her hair and apply a thin layer of make-up.

"Is everything OK?" Halana whispered.

Aquilia nodded once and averted her eyes from Halana's; she knew if she made eye contact, she would certainly cry.

"Very well," Halana accepted.

"Ladies and Gentlemen of Enceladus. It is my greatest pleasure to present to you. High Priestess Queen Aquilia of Saturn and Enceladus!"

Aquilia took a deep breath, stole a look at Zidan, and stepped through the heavy red curtains. The crowd erupted with applause, confetti rained down from above, and flowers were thrown into the air. She stood looking over the Kingdom, in awe of everyone who had gathered there, these were now her people to protect and guide.

Nymeria and Chylla had been tasked with crowning Aquilia; between them, they lifted the Golden Crown and settled it on top of Aquilia's scarlet hair, which now sat high on her head with a few streaks of silver left to hang free. The Golden Crown, with its sapphires and emeralds, shimmered in the light. She smiled at the two women who bowed to her as they left.

Aquilia stood to take her place at the podium, a memory of her five-year-old self, standing in the exact same position over twelve years earlier. She decided to wing her speech as she went.

"People of Enceladus, just over twelve years ago, I stood in this exact position, presenting as your Princess. I never thought that I would now be presenting as your Queen," she started.

The crowd applauded, she held her hand up, the crowd quietened down.

"Everything I said then still stands. I have fought against my uncle to preserve my family's Royal succession. I will fight to protect the people of both Saturn and Enceladus. As your Queen, I now present to you, Duke Janus of Astrodia, Countess Lyra of Astrodia and, soon to be, Duchess Evadene of Astrodia," she finished.

The crown began to cheer as Janus, Lyra, and Evadene made their appearances.

"That wasn't the plan," Zyra said to Zidan.

"She has her own way, who are we to tell her otherwise," Zidan replied.

"I must say, it was very well executed, considering her age," Zyra said.

"She is wise beyond her years, she's had to grow up faster than anyone else her age," he replied, watching with pride at how she handled the crown.

Zyra switched the screen to Quintara; she had tears running down her face.

"She really has grown up, hasn't she?" Quintara said.

"She has indeed," Zidan said, "I'll be with you soon my darling."

With his parting words, the screen went blank; he turned his attention back to Aquilia, watching her smile and wave to her adoring audience. He took one last look at his daughter before turning to leave. It was his time, but he didn't want Aquilia to see it, he wanted her to remain smiling, he wanted to remember that.

As he turned away, Halana caught his arm.

"Please, just let me go. Don't let her see me go," he begged.

"Oh Zidan, you know she will be heartbroken if she doesn't get to say goodbye this time," Halana replied.

"I know, but I don't want her to stop smiling. I'm going to miss her, an awful lot," he said.

Halana finally agreed to let him leave on his own terms, but she told him she wouldn't stop Aquilia searching for him.

"You are a good woman Halana. Look after my girl for me," he said.

Halana nodded and smiled. Zidan walked towards the embalming room. He made it to the door before he heard it.

Dad," Aquilia's voice broke, "where are you going?"

"Oh Aquilia," Zidan said, his voice laboured. "I only had enough time to see you become Queen, it's time for me to go now."

"Go where?" She asked, tears pricking at her eyes.

"Don't cry my darling. I don't want to remember your tears, only your infectious smile," he replied.

Aquilia tried to smile but it hurt, "I can't leave you now. Let me stay, please?"

"As long as you don't cry," he agreed.

They entered the room together and Zidan placed himself upon the table. He lay there as they reminisced about her younger years, about Paxy and Plexys, and how they always protected her. They laughed as they remembered Aquilia's third birthday, how Elio had spun her around so much she fell over. After she finished laughing, she noticed how Zidan's face had settled into a smile. She knew he had gone.

"Goodbye Dad, I love you," she whispered as she kissed his forehead.

As Aquilia left the room, The Wraith Doctors arrived, along with Halana, Janus, and Evadene. The latter of the three, each with sympathetic looks on their faces.

"Dad didn't want me to cry, so I didn't. We laughed until the end," Aquilia said, her voice shaky with sadness.

Janus drew her into an embrace and she crumbled with sobs. Janus rubbed small circles over her back and she let out an ocean of tears.

"The only family I have left now is you," she sniffed.

Halana grabbed her shoulder and spun her around, "no, he isn't," she said her eyes filling with tears. "You have us. The first day I met you, you offered me a job and a place to live, as well as gifting me the house I brought my daughter up in. I have watched you grow and learn, I've seen you knocked down, and I've seen you pick yourself back up again. We are your family; we will always be here for you, Always."

Aquilia looked at Evadene and Halana, both of them had become so much more than just employees. Evadene had become her teacher and her friend. Halana had become more of a second mother to her, always there to cheer her up or on.

Aquilia wiped her tears away and straightened herself up a bit.

"Thank you. I didn't mean to sound ungrateful or ignorant," she said.

"We understand, we take no offence, you've been through so much in your short life, who would blame you for feeling alone," Evadene said, hugging Aquilia tight, "now you have all of us, we will help you though this difficult time."

They stayed in an embrace for a few minutes longer before Zeke interrupted them.

"Sorry Your Highness and deepest condolences, but we have a major problem," he said.

Chapter 57

ENCELADUS

"There's still no reply and their numbers just tripled," Chylla said as Aquilia and Zeke stepped into the comms room.

"Eva, come here," Aquilia called to her.

Evadene stepped in and was instantly amazed by how many screens and buttons there were. She hadn't noticed before, when she comforted Aquilia after Zeebrakaan's body was discovered. Aquilia gestured for her to sit in the chair next to Zeke.

"Try and get them to answer," Aquilia said.

Eva placed the headset over her head, fixed it in place, and cleared her throat. "This is Enceladus, state your business," she commanded, waiting a few minutes before speaking again, "this is your final warning."

"It's pure radio silence Your Majesty, orders?" Chylla asked.

"Prepare Onyx Abyss Alpha. Get Nymeria and her Stealth Raiders on standby," Aquilia said, she then took the headset from Zeke and announced her presence. "This is High Priestess Queen Aquilia, Onyx Abyss Alpha is en route to your location, state your intentions."

"Ah, Queen Aquilia, it's about time. This is High Priest Freefla from Neptune. We are led to believe that you are harbouring one of our own, you have no choice but to let us land and search," came the reply.

Aquilia held her head high, she knew they were there for her, "I can't assure you enough that we have no Neptunites here, but you are clear to land and search for yourself," she replied.

She ripped off her headset and searched for Lyra. She had to find a way to hide the Phoenix presence and she hoped Lyra could help her. She found Lyra in the dining room with Bella.

"Lyra, I need your help and fast," she said.

"Sure, what do you need?" Lyra questioned.

"Neptunites are coming, they want the Phoenix, and I need help to hide her. How do I do it?" Aquilia replied getting more and more nervous.

"Alright," Lyra said calmly, "this should be quite simple but I'm going to need some help, how long have we got until the land?"

Aquilia checked in with Zeke, "about an hour," she replied.

"Simple!" Lyra said excitedly. "I need my mother here."

"I'll send Nymeria, she can get there and back fast," Aquilia said, radioing through to Nymeria.

"Great. First you need to calm down, you're too nervous, they'll pick up on it," Lyra said grabbing Aquilia's hands.

"I think I can help with that," Bella said softly, "smell this," she said, holding out a small amount of lilac dust.

"What is it?" Lyra asked before allowing Aquilia to smell it.

"It's lavender, it's able to calm nerves. I wouldn't put the Queen in any danger," Bella said looking hurt.

"I'm sorry, I've just never seen it before, and where did you get it?" Lyra asked.

"Layson and I made a trip to Earth many, many years back and I purchased some seeds there, planted them here and this is what happened. I looked it up and that's what I found out," Bella replied.

"It's alright Bella. I trust you," Aquilia said, bending down to sniff the lilac dust. "Wow, it smells amazing! I feel more relaxed already."

Aquilia's radio crackled to life, "Nymeria has arrived back with Benzyline. I'll send them straight to you." Zeke said.

"Thanks Zeke. How long until the Neptunites land?" She asked.

"Still around thirty five minutes out Your Highness," he replied.

"Your mother is here, she's on her way up now," Aquilia told Lyra.

"What's all this about?" Benzyline said as she walked through the door, "oh Your Majesty!"

"Welcome," Aquilia said with a smile.

"The Queen needs our help. She needs to hide something that resides inside of her," Lyra explained.

"Are you Phoenix?" Benzyline asked.

"Erm," Aquilia began.

"Neptunites are en route Mum, we have to protect her," Lyra said quickly.

"No problems come with us. You," she said pointing at Bella, "guard the door girl; you are our eyes and ears."

Bella nodded once and stood guard at the door. Aquilia followed Lyra and her mother into the kitchen area.

"Now," began Benzyline, "how long have you known about The Phoenix?"

"A few years, why?" Aquilia replied.

"Just so I can work out how much magic I need to use dear," she smiled, "now, take a seat, and relax."

"Will this hurt?" Aquilia asked.

"You won't feel a thing, I promise. You have done so much for our family, I wouldn't risk anything," Benzyline replied.

Aquilia sat on nearby stool and watched as Lyra and her mother chanted some strange inaudible words. The air around her flitted between pink and purple, green and orange then finally settled into a baby blue colour. There was a smell of water and citrus. Aquilia closed her eyes as she breathed in the air.

A distant voice calling her name aroused Aquilia from some far off place.

"Your Majesty, five minutes until landing," Zeke called, "Your Majesty, can you hear me?"

Aquilia shook herself awake, "yes Zeke, sorry, five minutes, thank you." She looked at Lyra and Benzyline, "did it work?"

"Let's hope so my dear, you were out for a while, I'm positive it's buried deep enough now," Benzyline replied.

Aquilia smiled, "thank you, I owe you."

"Not at all, a small token of appreciation for allowing my family to come home," she replied.

Aquilia left the kitchen and re-entered the dining room. Bella was still standing guard.

"No one has been, I've not moved an inch," Bella said as the women came towards her.

"Thank you Bella," Aquilia replied, "it's time to face the music."

They walked together towards the landing area, Aquilia meeting up with Nymeria and Chylla along the way.

"Everyone else to the meeting room, we will report back," Aquilia ordered.

No one challenged her.

"Let's go," she told Chylla and Nymeria.

They both followed her lead. She confidently strode up to the head ship.

"Welcome to Enceladus," she said, opening her arms wide.

High Priest Freefla gave her a strange look, "I thought you would be older."

"I'm sorry to disappoint, now, exactly what is it you are looking for?" Aquilia replied.

Chylla had to fight the urge to laugh.

"We came once before," Freefla began, "made an almighty mess," he said seemingly pleased with himself.

"So I heard. You killed my Grandmother," she replied, still smiling.

"So we did! She wasn't what we were looking for so we had no use for her," he smiled back. "Where is that delightful mother of yours, Quintara, isn't it?"

"Dead, if you really must know, hence when I am Queen," she said rolling her eyes. "Search for whatever it is you came for and leave when you don't find it. As I have already informed you, there are no Neptunites here," she warned him.

He smiled, looked around, and directed his troops to search. She knew what he wanted but she worried what he would do when he didn't find it. She worried that they would kill her, just as they had done her Grandmother, but she didn't show her fear.

"What do you think is happening?" Evadene whispered.

"We will soon find out," Lyra replied, "try not to worry."

Everyone fell silent when they heard footstep outside the door. Luckily, for them, no one could enter this room without prior permission from The Higher Elders.

Benzyline stood up and made her way to the door.

"Open it up;" Zyra said over the radio, "we will remain quiet."

Benzyline did as she was ordered, and the soldiers filed in.

"Everyone on their feet," they shouted.

Everyone stood up, except Evadene.

"I said everyone on their feet," one soldier said as he stood over her.

"You didn't say please," she replied clearly not frightened by him.

He grabbed her by the arm and pulled her to her feet. Halana shot Janus a look that told him to remain calm, he backed off a little.

"Get off me," Evadene said, shaking her arm free of his grip, "you have no rights here."

The soldier backed away from her.

"So I thought," she said sitting herself back in her chair.

Everyone followed her lead.

Two of the soldiers produced scanning devices and made their way around the room, scanning each person as they went. When they came to Lyra and Benzyline, their scanner began to malfunction and shut down.

"That's odd," one of them said, whacking the side of the scanner with one hand.

"How long have you had them?" Benzyline asked, stepping forward.

"Probably around fifty or so years," the soldier replied.

"Ah, they've probably outlived their time, here, let me look," she replied holding out her hands.

"Are you sure?" He asked, "you don't look like you would know much about this sort of technology."

Benzyline laughed, "I know more than I show young man."

He handed her both machines and she began her work.

"Now, this bit here has burnt out, but if we attach this to that," she mumbled, looking over at Lyra for a distraction.

Lyra fainted on cue.

"Oh Ma'am, are you alright?" The soldiers rushed to her side.

Benzyline fiddled with the microchip inside and slammed the machines back together.

"All done!" She exclaimed, turning around, "oh dear, are you OK darling?"

"I'm fine Mum, I just haven't eaten today, that's all." Lyra replied.

Benzyline quickly ran over to her and sat her on a chair, "here, eat some melon, it's good for you."

Lyra smiled, "thank you."

The soldiers re-booted the scanners and were surprised how fast they were working.

"Thank you," they said as they radioed through to Freefla, "no anomalies here sir."

"Fine, come back here, I need you to scan these three. We had Intel that it was here," he replied.

"On our way sir," the solider said.

They thanked everyone for their cooperation, apologised to Evadene, and left.

Benzyline closed the door behind them and waited until the footsteps had faded.

"Despite putting a cloaking spell on Queen Aquilia, I was worried that the scanners would run deeper," she began to explain to the confused faces, which now stared at her; "I rewired them. They, now, only scan for mortal forms."

"How did you learn that?" Lyra asked.

"From your Uncle Otsan, of course!" Benzyline replied shrugging her shoulders.

'Of course,' Lyra thought as she shook her head, rolled her eyes, and sat back down.

The waiting began.

Chapter 58

ENCELADUS

"So that's it?" Chylla said angrily, "this was all for nothing?"

"We had Intel that a particular historical creature was residing here, we had to follow Intel," Freefla explained.

"What happens now?" Nymeria asked.

"Nothing, now they go away and never return," Aquilia replied.

Freefla laughed, "I know it will return soon. It's generational, and it only runs in the female bloodline. I only have males so far," he explained.

"Wait, that means..." Aquilia noticed.

"Yes. We are related. Very far distant, obviously, but your great-great-grandmother was, for a time, married to my great-great-grandfather, they had a child and I am the product of that child," he explained, "like I said, very distantly related and it's too hard to explain to someone so young."

"Well, you're boring me now. I bed you farewell," Aquilia turned to leave.

"I'll be back," Freefla replied.

"No you won't," Aquilia shot back.

He then rounded everyone up and left.

"We have to do something to stop him coming back," Chylla said as they watched his ship leave the atmosphere.

"There's nothing we can do to stop it," Nymeria said.

"There is, but it's a big decision to make," Aquilia whispered, "first, let's update the others."

Aquilia, Chylla, and Nymeria began the walk to the meeting room. As they walked, Aquilia's radio squawked to life.

"Aquilia stop there, we need to talk," Quintara's voice bled through.

"You two go on ahead, I'll be there shortly." She told them.

Once they were gone, she replied to Quintara. "What is it Mum?" She asked.

"You can't do it," Quintara replied, "you can't banish The Phoenix."

"I wasn't thinking that. I have other plans," Aquilia said.

"Whatever you think will work, won't," Quintara replied, "we've tried everything."

"Not this you haven't, obviously. I have to go," Aquilia said and end the transmission. 'I just hope it works,' she thought to herself.

Aquilia entered the meeting room and was met with silence. Everyone watched as she made her way to her seat and sat down.

"Benzyline, I owe you a lot. They couldn't trace The Phoenix and for that I am grateful," Aquilia began.

"So, how do we stop them returning?" Chylla asked sitting next to her.

Aquilia looked around at the faces that sat with her. She never even thought about how different her life would have been had it not been for Altair and his ridiculous vendetta against her mother.

"I have given this some serious thought, and nobody can change my mind," she began. "I have to stop my bloodline going forward."

Everyone gasped.

"That means never having a family, are you sure?" Evadene asked.

"Eva, I don't think, deep down, that I was ever meant to settle down and have a family. I believe I was born to become the protector of Saturn and Enceladus, why else would I have been given such a gift?" Aquilia replied, a single tear racing down her face, "besides, I'm sure you and Janus will have enough children to fill the gap I leave behind."

"What happens if you change your mind in the future? You are only a baby yourself," Halana asked,

Aquilia stood and moved to sit by her side, "you have always been so supportive of everything I have done and all the choices I have made," she started, "I understand your question and if anything substantial changes my mind, I'll deal with it then, hopefully, with you all by my side."

Halana hugged her hard, "you know we will always be here, no matter what you decide," she whispered.

Aquilia swiped at her tears. She had found a family she didn't know she would ever need until Altair started his war, but she wouldn't change them for anything.

"I bet you mother wasn't happy about your decision," Janus said from behind her.

Aquilia turned from away from the window, "she doesn't know. This is something I have to do to protect everyone."

"And yourself?" He asked.

Aquilia felt guilty, "yes, and myself."

"There's no shame in that," he said, gently squeezing her shoulder.

Aquilia smiled at him. She was so glad she still had a close bond with her cousin. "How is prep work going for the wedding?" She asked.

"Slowly. I don't even have anyone to be by my side. Maybe I could ask Layson," he replied.

"Ah, sadly, Evadene has already poached him to give her away," Aquilia informed him.

Janus let his head fall back, "I don't know any other men, how does this look!"

"You know, you don't have to have a man by your side, don't you?" Aquilia said, "how about your Mum?"

"BINGO! Thank you, I'm sure she would love that. I'll ask her now," he said, kissing her cheek. "You're amazing."

Aquilia laughed, "I know, I surprise myself sometimes," as he ran off to find Lyra. She turned back towards the window and looked at Saturn below. Its rings acting as a barrier to invaders. She would miss what little she remembered of it, but she knew her place was here on Enceladus.

A sudden scream caught her attention. As she turned, she saw that Evadene had fallen to the ground. She rushed to her friends' side.

"I don't know what's wrong," Evadene said, panic rising in her voice.

"Try not to worry, we'll get the doctors to check you over," Aquilia comforted her.

Halana looked down at her daughter and then knelt by her side, "there's no need to do that," she smiled, "I know what it is."

Evadene's normal orange skin had become a brilliant shade of violet. Evadene looked down at her hands, "why am I this colour Mum?" The panic was showing.

"Oh my darling, "she replied as she held Evadene close, "you're going to be a Mama! To twins! One boy and one girl!" She replied.
Evadene started crying with joy, Janus was speechless.

"I hope I am half the mother you are," Evadene said to Halana.

"You will be fantastic," Halana replied.

Aquilia took in the scene before her. She knew she would never have this moment with her own mother, so she withdrew and joined Lyra and Bella at the table.

"I'm going to have grandchildren!" Lyra said sounding shocked.

"It's so lovely," Bella replied.

Lyra smiled before joining the huddle around Evadene.

"Are you OK Your Highness?" Bella asked.

"Seeing this," she gestured, "reminds me of how much I have lost."

"I understand, but also, look at how much you have gained," Bella replied, "I'm always here if you need an extra person to talk to."

"Thank you Bella, I appreciate that," Aquilia replied.

They watched as Eva, Janus, Lyra, and Halana all huddled together. The smiles were infectious. The happiness oozed around the room. Aquilia finally found a reason to smile, she realised she would have two small children to spoil! She rose to her feet and settled herself next to Evadene.

"You better choose some good names!" Aquilia teased.

"I think I already have," Evadene replied.

"Oh?" Aquilia questioned.

"Ammyn and Sinclair," Evadene said.

"They are perfect," Janus replied.

As Evadene said the names, Aquilia shed new tears, "Ammyn and Sinclair will live on," she said, refusing to wipe the tears away.

"Those children will be spoilt," Zyra said to Quintara as they watched the scene before them.

"Indeed they will," Quintara replied sounding defeated.

"What is it?" Zyra asked.

"The decision Aquilia has made for herself, she will never get to experience the joy of having a child grown inside her," Quintara replied.

"It is a conscious decision. To protect her people and herself, but you heard her. If things change she will re-evaluate her choices," Zyra replied. "It's not all bad."

Quintara watched as Aquilia and Evadene laughed and cried together. She was glad her daughter had found some great people, but also jealous that she couldn't share all the milestones her daughter would achieve.

"She will be fine Quintara," Zyra reiterated, "we can watch her from here, but we cannot intervene in her choices."

"But it's so hard to let her go alone, she should have an advisor," Quintara said.

"She has. She has two, three and more, in fact, everyone in that room advises her daily, and she knows where to find us, should she need us," Zyra replied, "just enjoy the scene."

The two of them watched for a few minutes longer before leaving. Quintara still felt a little disheartened, but she understood Zyra's comments.

Chapter 59

ENCELADUS

Janus and Evadene's wedding had arrived faster than anyone had expected. Evadene, now just over a third through her pregnancy, sat in front of the mirror whilst Halana and Bella fiddled with her hair. Evadene was getting increasingly frustrated.

"Just throw it up, please," she sighed.

Aquilia walked through the door at the perfect moment.

"Oh Your Highness, please," Halana pleaded, gesturing Evadene's mass of hair.

Aquilia giggled as she placed the tiara on top of Evadene's head and pulled the emerald green hair up behind it, "how's that?"

"Perfect!" Evadene cried, "finally."

"I'm sorry darling," Halana said softly.

"No, I'm sorry Mum. I didn't realise how ratty I would get being pregnant," Evadene said.

Halana hugged her daughter and rubbed her enlarging abdomen, "it won't be long now."

Evadene smile, "I can't wait to meet them."

"All the girls are ready for inspection," Aquilia said with a smile.

"Oh, let me see," Evadene cooed.

Aquilia threw open the door to a sea of dusty pink. Each bridesmaid wore a flower crown of pink and white carnations.

"Oh they look beautiful! You all look amazing!" Evadene cried.

"Thank you," they chorused.

"Are you ready?" Aquilia asked her.

Evadene nodded.

"One last thing," Halana said, placing Evadene's veil over her head, fixing it in place and pulling the rest over her face. "Beautiful!" Halana whispered.

"Do you think everything is alright Mum?" Janus asked Lyra.

"I'm sure everything is running to plan," Lyra replied, "brides are allowed to run a little late, plus, she is pregnant son."

"I'm so nervous," Janus said, rubbing his hands together.

"That's normal. I'll go and see what I can find out," she replied.

Lyra jogged off towards the entranceway.

"Are you OK?" Zeke asked, adjusting his jacket sleeves for the hundredth time in that hour.

"I'm just nervous, that's all. I just don't want to mess this up," Janus replied.

Zeke had been given the job of guarding the wedding rings and he had taken this particular job very seriously indeed. The rings hadn't left his sight or his pocket since they had been given to him. Janus checked his watch for the sixth time. The ceremony was due to begin in a matter of minutes but Evadene still hadn't arrived. Janus began to sweat, he started going over things in his head, asking himself questions, if he had said anything to offend her, if he had hurt her in anyway. He looked up from the floor to see Lyra running towards him with the biggest smile ever.

"She's here and she looks beautiful," Lyra announced.

Janus looked towards the doorway, just as the music began, to see the train of bridesmaids begin to flow in, dropping white petals as they walked. From the youngest of around three, to the eldest of around twelve, a sea of pink descended upon the room. Halana and Bella followed shortly after the sea of pink, both looking like extras from a fashion magazine spread.

Janus smiled at Halana who bowed her head towards him. He was glad he got along well with his future family. He looked back towards the door to see an amazing sight. There, arms linked with Layson, stood Evadene. Her wedding gown a pale pink with embroidered roses, the veil, pure white lace with ruby red roses. What stood out the most was the tiara gifted to her by Aquilia. It sat on top of her head as if it were made for her. Janus let his tears fall silently, unashamed of showing his emotions. Evadene looked every bit as beautiful as Lyra had said.

Behind Layson and Evadene, Aquilia followed. She had decided against wearing her crown. She didn't want to draw attention away from Evadene. On top of her head, sat a white rose flower crown, her scarlet hair flowing down her back. She stayed two steps behind Evadene and Layson and almost cried at how amazing her friend looked. Janus scrubbed up well too.

A very stout looking man, with a long white beard, and short purple hair, conducted the ceremony. His kind, orange eyes made him quite a remarkable sight. Aquilia questioned if she had seen those eyes before. Pushing it to the back of her mind, she settled next to Zeke in the front row, the mass of bridesmaids seated on the white carpeted floor surrounding the, soon to be, married couple.

"Welcome one and all, to this momentous and joyous occasion. We are here today to celebrate the marriage of two very special people, Evadene-Dionne and Janus Valera. Please stand," he said softly.

Everyone stood. Layson placed Evadene's hand in Janus's and kissed the top of their joint hands. Halana spilt tears everywhere, and the ceremony had only just begun. Aquilia held Halana's hand tight and smiled at her. Halana's face softened a little and the tears slowed their flow.

"It's alright to be a little sad," Zeke whispered, "she will be OK though."

"I'm glad you are so certain," Halana giggled.

"I can sense it," Zeke replied, "let me show you?"

Zeke, carefully, moved past Aquilia and took Halana's hand, "close your eyes," he said.

As she did a world of colour and beauty erupted in her eyes, scenes of Evadene, Janus and a whole host of children played out to her. As the scene continued, she saw herself seated at a picnic table in the garden of a grand Palace, bouncing a little baby on her knee. Before the scene blurred away, a woman came to collect the baby, Halana didn't see the woman's face, only a flash of scarlet hair.

Zeke put his finger to his lips. Halana understood. What she saw was for her eyes only.

"Thank you Zeke, that is a very special gift you have," Halana said hugging him close.

"I don't use it much. Mum and Dad don't know I have it," he replied.

"Then it will be a secret until you are ready to reveal all," she told him.

"Evadene-Dionne, do you promise to love and honour Janus Valera for as long as mortally possible?" The chaplain asked.

"Absolutely," Eva replied.

"Janus Valera, do you promise to love and protect Evadene-Dionne for as long as mortally possible?" The chaplain asked again.

"With every piece of me," Janus replied looking deep into Eva's eyes.

The chaplain bound their hands together with a silk sash, embroidered with Janus's new Coat of Arms.

"I pronounce, The Duke and Duchess of Astrodia," the chaplain declared. "I wish you both every conceivable happiness."

Evadene and Janus shared their first kiss as a married couple and confetti was thrown from all corners of the room.

"That was beautiful, wasn't it Reaver?" Zyra asked.

"Indeed it was. Thank you for allowing me to witness such a wondrous occasion," he replied.

The Higher Elders had watched the ceremony unfold but had kept their presence a secret from everyone. Reaver had only shed a single tear, when Layson joined Janus and Evadene's hands. He had been so gentle. They observed Evadene and Janus lead their bridal party to the reception, laid on, again, by The Higher Elders. The room was decorated in white, red and pink, incorporating the navy blue within the tableware.

"It's beautiful," Evadene exclaimed.

Everyone found their respective seats and sat down, whilst the food was prepared.

"This is...wow," Aquilia said taking in how much attention to detail there was.

"Imagine what your wedding would be like," Eva laughed.

"I don't think I'd have the pink," she replied, "I'd probably have black and red."

Evadene grabbed Aquilia hands, "promise me, you've thought everything through?" She said.

"I promise. I can't watch the same thing happen every time a girl is born into my bloodline, it's not fair," Aquilia replied.

"Then we stand by you, but, promise me, you'll be here for these?" Evadene said, rubbing her belly.

Aquilia looked down, "I promise, plus, they will have everything they could possibly want."

There was a clinking of glasses, which captured everyone's attention, "Ladies and Gentlemen, your food is ready," the caterer announced.

Nobody rushed to eat; nearly everyone was enjoying the music and dancing. Every now and then, someone would select a few pieces of food that could easily be eaten whilst still dancing. As the night wore on, a few of the younger bridesmaids fell to sleep. Aquilia made it her job to deliver each child back home with a gift bag filled with goodies as a way of saying thank you.

"She has a way with children," Lyra said to Halana as they watched her carry one of the youngest away.

"She's gentle and caring," Halana replied, "she will change her mind soon."

Lyra looked Halana in the eyes, "what if I knew a way that could prevent Aquilia from passing on that particular gene?"

Chapter 60 – One Month Later

SATURN

"Is everything ready?" Evadene panted.

"Yes. Nursery painted. Cribs built, painted and personalised," Aquilia replied.

"Janus," Evadene cried.

"Right here," he replied.

"I think this is it," Evadene said.

"Isn't it too early?" Janus asked.

"Babies don't work to schedule son," Layson chimed in.

"OK, can we put the phone away now, give Mum some privacy?" The nurse said gently.

"Call when everything has happened, and Janus, don't leave her side," Halana warned him.

Janus disconnected the call and placed his phone away. He held Evadene's hands and prepared for the arrival of their two babies.

"I'm not sure I can do this," Eva admitted.

Janus held her head with his hands, looked into her eyes and said, "you are Evadene-Dionne, you are the strongest, fiercest woman I know. You can do anything."

"I like him. Where did you find him?" The nurse asked.

"He's rarer than snow on Saturn," Eva replied.

The nurse smiled, "are we ready?"

"Do I get a choice?" Evadene laughed.

"I'm afraid not," the nurse laughed holding a little baby boy in her arms, "here's one!"

The nurse passed him over to Evadene, who snuggled him close.

"He's perfect," she exclaimed.

"Room for one more Mum?" The nurse said, holding a baby girl.

"Absolutely!" Evadene cried. "Oh look at this Janus."

"Beautiful, just like their mother," he replied.

The nurse looked confused, "will you give me just a second," she said trying to smile, and then she left the room.

"What's happened?" Eva said, trying not to panic.

"Let's get some pictures for Granny Halana. I'm sure everything is fine," he replied. He took some photos and sent them to Halana.

"Janus, can you find out what's happening?" Eva asked.

"Of course," he replied, running towards the door.

Just as he reached for the handle, the nurse came back in with another doctor.

"Can you tell me what's happening?" Eva asked.

"Certainly," the nurse replied with a smile. "It seems you have another two babies hidden in there!"

"How?" Janus asked.

"Sometimes, twins can hide other babies on the scanning equipment, it's perfectly normal," the doctor replied. "Let's get the first two settled, and then we can deliver babies three and four!"

Janus and Evadene were shocked, where would they find two more cribs at such short notice, and names! What would they call them?

The doctor settled Ammyn and Sinclair into temporary cribs, and then brought in extra provisions.

"Are we ready?" He said.

"I guess so," Evadene replied.

Evadene closed her eyes and felt a slight pulling sensation.

"Here we have another baby girl!" The doctor said, passing Janus a little bundle of blankets.

"He's holding her perfectly," the nurse told Evadene.

"He better be!" Eva laughed.

"Alright Eva, I need you to slide down the bed just a little, this little one is slightly stuck," the doctor informed her.

Eva quickly slid down the bed and relaxed.

"Just a slight pull, and there she is!" The doctor announced, "three girls and a boy! Congratulations!"

Evadene held their fourth baby, a girl, in her arms. Evadene let tears of joy fall from her eyes. Her own perfect family.

The nurse helped Janus and Evadene position the babies for their first family photo. All four babies stayed calm throughout the process. The nurse took the photo and Janus sent them off along with the caption, 'mother, father, Ammyn, Sinclair, Zeryn, and Aurel say hello!'

ENCELADUS

A scream from the sewing room had everyone running from their respective areas of the Palace.

"Halana, what is it?" Bella called as she entered the room.

"FOUR! Four perfect babies!" She cried.

"I thought it was twins?" Aquila said, looking confused.

"Look!" Halana said, thrusting her phone into Aquilia's hand.

Aquilia gasped, "four perfect babies. Three girls and a boy!"

"Oh congratulations Halana!" Bella cooed, "they are beautiful!"

Halana couldn't reply due to the tears. Aquilia passed the phone back just as Janus called. Halana put him on speaker.

"Is everyone there?" He asked.

"Yes we're all here," Aquilia replied. "Halana is a little shocked. Congratulations!"

"Thank you. Eva is sleeping at the moment but I thought I'd call just to say everyone is perfect," he replied.

"Oh dear boy," Halana said, "you go and rest too. Call us tomorrow. I love you all!"

Janus agreed and disconnected the call. Everyone hung around for a while admiring the four new additions to the little dysfunctional family they had.

After everyone had gone back to their duties, Halana called Lyra.

"Hi Halana, have you seen the babies?" She said as she answered.

"I have. They are simply perfect, but I called about something else entirely. How could you prevent the passing on of genes?" Halana asked.

Lyra had secretly hoped Halana had forgotten about that conversation, "it's hard to explain but I'll try. Mother and I had a young girl approach us well over twenty years ago now. She carried the gene for The Serpent Killer. She wanted the gene to remain with her and not pass over. We performed a ritual on her and, as far as we know, to this day, it hasn't passed down," Lyra explained, "but this may not work for everyone. The Phoenix is strong."

Halana thought for a moment, "I will talk to Aquilia about it," she said.

"Be careful Halana. It is still her choice," Lyra replied.

"I know, but she has to know there could be a way," Halana said before disconnecting the call.

It would be a tough conversation but Halana felt the need to tell Aquilia it could happen, that it was possible. After what she had seen through Zeke's gift, she hoped Aquilia would at least try.

Aquilia was sat at the crystal fountain, reading one of the many poetry books she had salvaged from her mother's possessions before they went into storage. She had read so many of them, she knew most by heart.

"Your Majesty, I've been looking everywhere for you," Halana exclaimed.

"Well, here I am," Aquilia replied, "what's wrong?"

Halana stopped to choose her words carefully, "at Evadene's wedding, Lyra and I watched how you handled the little ones, with such care," she began.

"I'm not changing my mind! I had no choice but to care for them. I'm their Queen, not their mother," Aquilia replied slamming the book shut and preparing to leave.

"But, what if there was a possibility that the gene wouldn't pass on," Halana pleaded.

Aquilia let out a deep sigh, "I can't risk that. I have to protect the people of Enceladus at all costs, even if that includes my happiness," Aquilia told her, "I'm sorry."

"Lyra did it once, she could do it again. Won't you even think about it?" Halana asked.

"No, I'm sorry Halana. My people come before my happiness," Aquilia replied before walking away with her head down.

Aquilia had never really thought about her future, whether she would have a family or not, but since watching Evadene and Janus fall in love, she couldn't help but feel slightly jealous. She made it back to the Palace and sat on her bed She swiped through the pictures Janus had sent of the babies, a tear falling from her eye. She closed down the messages and pulled up her contact list. She stared at the number and name for a while before connecting.

"Aquilia, how can I help?" Came the answer.

"How does it work? Can you guarantee it?" She asked.

"Nothing is a promise, but it has worked before," Lyra explained about The Serpent Killer girl.

"Do not tell Halana, but maybe we can try," Aquilia replied.

Chapter 61

SATURN

"Why is Aquilia coming?" Janus asked Lyra.

"Isn't it obvious? She's coming to see the babies!" Lyra lied. She hated lying to him, but she had promised not to tell anyone the true reason for her visit.

Aquilia was due to arrive that afternoon; everything was ready for the ritual. Lyra had informed Aquilia that she would have to stay a few days, just so Benzyline could keep an eye on her; she also informed her that it could be reversed if anything felt wrong.

"I'll tell Eva the good news!" Janus said.

"No, let it be a surprise," Lyra said, "Eva will be ecstatic to see her."

As Aquilia landed on Saturn, some old memories resurfaced. In her head, she could hear her mother and father laughing.

She smiled at those memories. When she closed her eyes, she could see the destruction that Altair had left, she sighed aloud and reminded herself that he was dead and gone, and he could no longer destroy what wasn't his.

It seemed so long since she was here last. She took a few moments to take in the view.

"Your Majesty, your carriage," Came a voice from behind her.

Aquilia spun around, her scarlet braid wrapping itself around her waist, "Arla! It's so great to see you! Where's Janus?"

"Helping Miss Eva with the babies. She doesn't know you're here, in fact, it was a surprise for everyone," Arla replied.

"A good one I hope," Aquilia laughed.

Arla opened the carriage door for Aquilia and they both climbed aboard.

"How have things been at the Palace with Janus?" Aquilia asked as they rode through the streets of Astrodia.

"He reminds me of King Elio; well, more what my mother told me about King Elio. Very kind and considerate," Arla replied.

"I'm glad to hear it. How about Lyra?" She asked.

"Lyra is different. She likes to be alone. She is always reading something," Arla explained, "but, I like her. She is very kind."

"Sometimes, being different is a good thing," Aquilia told her.

From outside the carriage, they could hear a lot of excitement, the carriage stopped slowly.

"Is she in there?" A little voice asked.

Aquilia popped her head out of the window, "is who in where?" She smiled.

"Queen Aquilia!" The children gasped.

Aquilia climbed down from the carriage and sat with them on the wall close to the fountain.

"Aren't you supposed to be in school?" She asked them.

A little girl with raven coloured hair tied up with a blue ribbon hung her head as she stepped forward, "when King Elio and Queen Quintara died, Altair made our parents pay for schooling, we can't afford it anymore," she whispered.

"Would you like to go to school?" She asked them.

All the children nodded.

"Then let's fix it. Arla, we'll walk from here. Children, follow me," Aquilia commanded.

As a group, they made their way to the Palace. People came out of their houses to watch them walk by.

Aquilia could hear the whispers of the townspeople, "she takes after Queen Quintara, always putting the people first." Aquilia smiled and waved to them

"What's all the commotion outside?" Evadene asked as she lay Zeryn down to sleep.

She walked to the window with Ammyn in her arms just in time to see Aquilia enter the courtyard followed by nearly twenty children.

"What is it?" Janus asked, joining her at the window, "what the..?"

Evadene was already halfway to the door when Arla opened it from the outside.

"Oh Duchess, I'm sorry. I didn't realise you were there," Arla apologised.

"It's perfectly fine Arla," Evadene smiled, "why is everyone here?"

"Well," Aquilia said as she poached Ammyn from Evadene's arms, "I'm here to see these little beauties and they," she gestured to the children, "are here to ask Janus to make school free again."

"Please!" The children begged.

"Don't leave them outside then," Eva said, "come in, there's room for everyone."

Janus descended the stairs and watched the children file in.

"How can I help the children of Astrodia?" he asked.

"It seems Altair forced their parents to pay for schooling after my parents died. Can we change things back?" Aquilia asked.

Janus was shocked. He hadn't a clue what his father had done. He looked amongst the children who now stood in his hallway. All of them having missed out on so much already.

"Consider it done, and until everything is up and running, school will be held here for anyone who wishes to attend," Janus replied.

"I'll teach you Ancient Saturnese History, Maths, and Geography," Eva offered.

"I can teach science," Arla said, "I gained a Masters in Science."

"That's settled, now, who wants ice cream?" Janus shouted.

All the children cheered and followed him into the kitchen.

"I better go help him," Eva laughed, "would you mind putting Ammyn down for her nap?"

"Leave it to me, I'm on it, let's go Ammyn, time to rest," Aquilia cooed as she took the baby back to her crib.

"Welcome back," Lyra said as Aquilia crept out of the nursery.

"You scared me then," Aquilia laughed.

"How are you feeling about the ritual? Don't feel pressured, it has to be your choice," Lyra asked.

"I'm still on the fence. I don't want to have to fight any more than I would necessarily have to, and if I decide to have children then I will have to, but seeing Evadene have her babies, well, I got jealous," Aquilia explained.

"Why don't you talk to my mother? She isn't as involved with you like Halana and I are. She will be unbiased," Lyra said, passing her the address.

"Thank you for understanding," she said as she slipped the paper into her pocket, "I'll go now while they are busy."

Aquilia headed out of the Palace in search of Benzyline.

"Where did she go?" Evadene asked when she emerged from the kitchen.

"She just went for a walk, a few memories that she needs to let go of," Lyra smiled, "she will be back soon. Shall we arrange one of the library rooms into a classroom whilst the babies sleep?"

"Oh yes. Good idea," Eva agreed.

Aquilia found Benzyline's house with ease. A small-detached house with a blue painted door and white brickwork. She walked up to the door and prepared to knock, but the door opened by itself.

"Come in Your Majesty," Benzyline's voice came from somewhere deep inside the house, "drink?" She asked.

"I'm fine, thank you," Aquilia replied.

"Take a seat, I'll be right down," she called.

Aquilia looked around at the tidy living room. Its dusty blue carpet clashed hard with the sea green walls. There were pictures of landscapes and galaxies dotted over the walls. Aquilia sat on the cream sofa and waited for Benzyline to appear.

"Sorry to keep you dear, now, what can I do for you?" Benzyline asked.

"It's hard to explain. I'm still on the fence about the ritual. I just have so many opinions," Aquilia confessed.

"Then we talk, come," Benzyline gestured for her to follow to the dining room, she showed her to a chair and took the seat opposite. Benzyline clicked her fingers once and a tea set appeared on the table.

"Speak your troubles my child, the tea will explain," Benzyline said.

Aquilia took a breath and explained how she didn't want to fight the Neptunites every time they sniffed that a new child in their bloodline had been born, especially a girl, but also how jealous she was about Evadene having her babies.

"I've never really thought about my future before. All I was concerned about was continuing my family's legacy," she finished.

Benzyline nodded, "I understand your concerns, and you make some very valid points," she said as she tipped one of the teacups over.

"Wait, that's full!" Aquilia cried before noticing that not a single drop had been spilt.

"Listen to the tea, it will help you with your choice," Benzyline said.

Aquilia closed her eyes and listened closely. She stayed like that for what felt like hours but was merely two minutes.

"I know what I have to do. Thank you Benzyline, I'll see you soon," Aquilia said as she got up to leave.

"One more thing," Benzyline said as she grabbed Aquilia's hand, "take this and keep it close."

Into Aquilia's hand, she dropped a pendant in the shape of a hand.

"What's this?" Aquilia asked.

"Wear it always. You know what it is, deep down," Benzyline replied, "be safe my Queen. Protect yourselves."

Aquilia was slightly confused with what she had said but smiled and made her way back to the Palace. When she finally arrived back, Lyra noticed the pendant around Aquilia's neck. She smiled at Aquilia. It then made sense to Aquilia, just as she felt movement in her abdomen.

Chapter 62

ENCELADUS – One Month Later

Having spent time between Saturn and Enceladus, helping Evadene with the babies and delivering supplies for their schools, Aquilia had been feeling unusual within herself.

"I'm worried about you Your Majesty, please see the doctors," Halana begged, "you haven't been yourself since you returned from Saturn over a month ago."

"I'm fine, I promise. I just over exert myself sometimes, that's all," Aquilia laughed.

As she turned away from Halana, she took a deep breath, 'it's now or never' she told herself. She turned back to Halana, "can we talk, in private?"

"Certainly, come," Halana gestured to her sewing room.

Once inside, Aquilia settled herself gently onto one of the padded window seats. She peered out over the Kingdom.

"I went to see Benzyline," Aquilia said, still looking out of the window, "she told me about the ritual."

Halana stayed silent, she didn't want Aquilia to stray off the subject.

"Lyra explained about The Serpent Killer girl. I was intrigued so I went there," Aquilia finished finally looking at Halana.

"I hope you don't feel like I pressured you into anything. I could see the pain in your eyes when Eva was pregnant," Halana admitted.

"It wasn't pain. It was jealousy. I'd never thought about my future before and I had such burdens to carry. Nobody understood how much I would lose if a female child carried The Phoenix gene," Aquilia confessed, she pulled out the pendant that Benzyline had given her, "she gave me this and told me to, and I quote, 'protect yourselves.'

Halana inspected the hand shaped pendant. It was heavy with a ruby in the centre, "did you ask about it?"

"No. She did something with teacups and then I left," Aquilia shrugged, "I've felt strange here ever since," she said holding her abdomen.

"I'm going to call The Wraith Doctors, they'll be discrete, I promise," Halana said, in her mind, almost positive she knew the reason.

Halana had noticed Aquilia's skin change colour now and then, her cyan skin glowing a tinge of neon pink, just flickers, nothing too noticeable.

"OK, but insist on absolute secrecy," Aquilia agreed.

Halana nodded and left Aquilia alone on the room. She dialled Lyra on her way to The Wraith Doctors

"Halana, what is it?" Lyra asked.

"What happened to Aquilia down there?" She asked.

"The ritual was performed differently for Aquilia. She spoke with my mother about her concerns. Mum used her teacups spell. It didn't persuade Aquilia or give her false hope. It just explains everything cleared than we can. Aquilia said she knew what she had to do. The Pendant, that is the spell, she must keep it on," Lyra explained quickly.

"Lyra, I think she's pregnant!" Halana whispered. "I'm getting the doctors to check her over."

"Go slowly. I'll call mother," Lyra said shocked.

Halana hung up and diverted to the kitchen.

"Bella?" She called.

"Yes?" Bella replied, her head appearing from behind a door. She had flour on her nose.

"Would it be possible to have some tea delivered to Queen Aquilia's bedroom, she is due back from her errands soon," Halana asked.

"Certainly. I'll make a fresh pot now," Bella smiled.

"Thank you. Oh, you have a little something on your nose," Halana laughed.

Bella wiped her nose with a small cloth, "oops! I'm trying a new cake recipe, would you like some slices with the tea?" Bella giggled.

"That would be lovely," Halana smiled.

As she left the kitchen, her phone vibrated.

"Lyra, what did you find out?" Halana asked.

"She is pregnant, but she has been since birth. She is a very special being Halana. She will give birth on her eighteenth birthday. It was all planned for her," Lyra informed her, "Mum did a quick check on her."

"Her birthday is mere weeks away!" Halana nearly screamed. "How do I tell her?"

"Let The Wraith Doctors determine her pregnancy, I'll bring Mum up to explain the rest," Lyra said and disconnected.

Halana continued to The Wraith Doctors room.

It took Halana nearly an hour to arrive back with The Wraith Doctors. During that time, Aquilia had witnessed her own skin change colour multiple times.

As Halana opened the door, Aquilia ran to her, "help me," she said, "my skin."

"Your Majesty, please, sit," The Wraith Doctor said softly, "we need you to relax."

Aquilia sat back on the padded window seat and tied to control her breathing. The Wraith Doctors didn't touch her in any way, they crowded around her and joined hands. A blast of light emerging from her abdomen, within the light, the silhouette of a baby. Aquilia's eyes glistened with tears.

"How?" She gasped.

"There is much to learn my child," Benzyline said from the doorway.

The Wraith Doctors bowed and left quietly. Aquilia sat with her back against the window. Her skin now glowing neon pink.

"I looked into your history before you came to me, I peeked even before then. You, my Queen, are from a special species called Alphirs. You are born pregnant and are timed to give birth at eighteen," Benzyline started to explain.

"That's only three weeks away!" Aquilia panicked. "Wait! I went into battle carrying a baby?"

Benzyline sat next to her and held her hand tight, "your species are built to protect and honour. Your body becomes armour when your child is growing, the only sad thing about your species is that you will only ever have one child and that is the one you are born carrying," Benzyline said. Aquilia was quiet. She looked down at her hands as they changed from cyan to neon pink and back, then pink with a fleck of dark blue and back.

"What's that?" She said, a look of fear on her face.

Benzyline looked confused, "that's impossible," she whispered, "get The Wraith Doctors back."

Halana ran along the hall catching up with them just as they turned the corner.

"Benzyline needs your help," she told them.

They followed her back to the sewing room.

"How can we...well..." they trailed off.

As they looked at Aquilia, they were shocked. Her once cyan skin was now neon pink with sapphire blue patches.

"Well, we know, obviously, The Queen is with child, but we now believe she could be with CHILDREN," The Wraith Doctors chorused.

"That's impossible for her species," Benzyline replied.

"Sadly, in normal circumstances, yes, but Aquilia is somewhat a Queen in Alphir status too. It means she will carry both a boy and girl," the head Wraith Doctor explained.

Benzyline slumped to the floor, "we are in the presence of complete Royalty."

"I'm confused, can someone explain in simple terms," Aquilia asked.

"It means you are a true Queen and you have two babies, one boy and one girl," Halana said slowly.

"Oh," Aquilia said just before passing out.

As Aquilia woke up, she realised she was tucked up in her own bed. She could hear a familiar voice in the distance.

"Eva?" She called.

"Hey sleepy head! Welcome back!" Eva said sitting on the bed next to her.

"How do I look?" Aquilia asked, almost afraid of the answer.

"Well, you're definitely a picture! Why didn't you tell me! Who's daddy? I didn't think you were with anyone, you dark horse," Eva teased.

Aquilia looked at her friend in the eye, "there is no daddy."

Eva stopped smiling, "are you serious? But, how?"

Aquilia sat up and made herself more comfortable. She took a sip of the freshly made tea and told Eva the whole story.

As Aquilia was telling Eva the story, Bella had opened the door and brought some cake, her face softening to how Aquilia looked.

"Finally," she said as she closed the door.

"Finally what, Bella?" Aquilia said as she stopped the conversation with Eva abruptly.

"I've known for so long. I was sworn to secrecy. Welcome my Queen," Bella replied.

"Now I'm even more confused," Aquilia shouted.

Bella explained that she, too, was Alphir, she had been placed on Saturn just before Quintara fell pregnant with Aquilia, "I was tasked with updating our Leaders of any developments. Lyra wasn't the only person keeping your mother out of danger."

Bella told of how she had overheard all of Layson and Altair's phone calls and had reported to the Leader of the Alphirs who cast spells to shield Quintara from view.

"Everyone tried to protect her, and for that I'm grateful, thank you," Aquilia cried.

Eva looked at her friend, "you might be a different species, but you're still Auntie Aquilia!"

Everyone laughed. Aquilia was so glad to have a newfound family.

Chapter 63 – Six Months Later

SATURN

It was a beautiful day on Saturn. Evadene and Janus had opened the Palace garden to the people of Astrodia, their four children toddling around the grass, picking up all sorts of strange bugs.

"I'm glad you came Mum," Eva said passing Halana a glass of fresh spring water.

"Me too darling, it's beautiful here," Halana replied with a smile.

She watched as all the children played on the equipment laid out for them.

A little blue haired baby crawled to her ankles and she bent to pick her up.

"You little munchkin, what are you up to?" Halana laughed, bouncing the baby girl on her knee.

The little girl laughed and wound her little arms around Halana's neck, pulling her close in an embrace.

"Come on Scarlex, time for a nap," Aquilia said, bending down to collect her daughter, her scarlet hair falling around her shoulders. "Halana, could you bring Eliontara for his nap too?"

"Absolutely Your Highness," she replied.

As she began to stand, Zeke appeared at her side to lend a hand, "how does it feel?" He asked.

"Just perfect. Everything is just as you showed me, but can I ask, how long will I have to enjoy with them?" She asked.

Zeke kissed her cheek, "forever," he whispered.

Halana felt a sudden breeze, which lasted mere seconds and she felt full of life. She spotted Eliontara and swept him into the air, "time for a nap little fellow," she cooed in his ear.

Eliontara's bright red hair bounced with every step Halana took as he slowly drifted off to sleep in her arms. She quietly walked into Aquilia's old room, which had been redecorated to house her children when she stayed.

Scarlex's blue hair sparkled in the daylight, the flecks of silver shining through. Halana softly laid Eliontara next to her, his hair as red as Aquilia's.

She pulled Aquilia into an embrace. "I'm so proud of you," she cried.

"Thank you for always being by my side. Mum." Aquilia whispered.

Halana tried to hide her sobs but she shouldn't. She had been there for Aquilia for so long, she felt like her own.

"I'll always be here. Always," Halana replied.

THE END.

<u>EPILOGUE</u>

Twenty years later, Aquilia made her only trip to Alphitrax, the planet she had been sent from, with Bella. She addressed the Alphirs but declined their offer of residence. She, instead, passed it on to Bella's sister, Alaysia.

In the twenty years since her first interaction with The Neptunites, Freefla never returned. Aquilia heard nothing from that Planet ever again. It seemed Benzyline's spell worked after all.

Scarlex and Eliontara went on to train alongside Chylla, Nymeria, and Celest. They became part of Onyx Abyss Alpha and finally part of The Stealth Raiders.

Janus and Evadene went on to have seven more children, Avalynn, Keana, Codex, Kodyn, Jaxson, Elaena, and Xandr.

Halana went on to become dressmaker for the whole Kingdom; she even had orders sent from other Galaxies. She lived forever, just as Zeke had told her she would.

Zeke eventually told Layson and Bella about his gift, it took him nearly eighteen years to do it though. He didn't use it often, and never to check on his own life.

Aquilia never married. She lived her life on Enceladus, watching the people come and go. She eventually secured herself two Ligers, and named them Paxy and Plexys.

Peace was finally settled on Saturn and Enceladus.

Printed in Great Britain
by Amazon